When Things Get Bent

A novel by John Fewster

To Tracy for her love, loyalty and unwavering support without which this book would not exist.

To Shannon and Sarah for their invaluable comments during the writing of this book.

Table of Contents

1 Paint by Numbers

The booming grows louder like exploding artillery shells fired in volleys from a distant battery of howitzers: boom, boom, boom. The sound of the bursting shells closes in on Cam, who remains indifferent to the booming. A tide of Bayview Stingers fans swirls around him, threading their way through the parking lot to the MKM Colossus.

The Colossus is a galaxy-swallowing sports and entertainment complex capable of wolfing down more fans than the entire Bayview population of two million souls give or take a couple of thousand. Even after scarfing down all the people of Bayview, TV sports announcers proudly agree that the Colossus still has room to guzzle several thousand Olympic sized swimming pools, the current measure for all things man-made. The Colossus with its latte-colored facade squats contentedly on several city blocks in the heart of Bayview. The football stadium within the Colossus is home to the Stingers football team.

Boom, boom, boom.

Cam waits for his friend, Dunc, who has the tickets for today's football game. Today the Bayview Stingers take on their lethal enemy, the Wallaceville Warriors.

The booming starts slow and then grows louder and faster. The cadence picks up. The shells drop closer to Cam. The booming stops. It resumes hard and deep with a thud through Cam's back and into his chest. Boom, boom, boom goes on for about a minute immediately behind him. He ignores the salvo. Then a final blow: BOOM! Silence follows.

Cam casually turns around to look at the source of the bombardment.

"Hey Wiff," greets Cam. Cam's face is painted in Stingers colors with half his face green and half yellow, the current face-painting convention. He wears a Stingers T-shirt and sweat pants to eliminate any doubt as to his loyalty.

"Hey Squib," is the response from behind the big bass drum that looms large over Cam. The greeting is followed by another barrage of booms, which are followed by, "Oh yeah! Go Stingers go!" Then there is more booming while Cam's friend, Dunc, beats hard on the bass drum strapped to his chest. "Go Stingers go! Woohoo!" booms Dunc and then, "Woohoo!" again, followed by more booms, faster and faster, resembling a giant prairie chicken beating its wings hard and fast in a courtship ritual.

Nearby Stingers fans stop. They take up the chant. "Go Stingers go!" they yell. Dunc beats hard on the drum. The fans follow along, picking up the speed of their chant to match Dunc. They can't keep up. They fall to whooping. Dunc beats the drum, flailing away and spinning round and round for all to see. Suddenly he stops. Dunc grins at the football fans. He makes one last slow twirl. He gives out several sphincter-puckering war whoops in honor of the fans that have stopped to watch his show. Everyone claps and makes whoops and whistles of their own devising, as they get ready to beat the Wallaceville Warriors, the sworn enemy of all loyal Stingers fans.

Dunc smiles his gap-toothed grin at Cam. Dunc is in full regalia for today's football game between the Bayview Stingers and the rival Wallaceville Weenies, as Dunc often calls them. He wears a green and yellow football helmet in the shape of a beehive cone. The bulbous helmet, being too large, keeps slipping down over his eyes, obstructing his view. He is continually pushing it up. Occasionally he removes the helmet to scratch his head. The helmet is itchy. On it is a picture of a green and yellow bee, the mascot of the

Stingers. The bee's eyes glare with the hit-to-kill intensity of an anti-ballistic missile. The bee wears a determined grin, revealing its dingy white teeth. When Dunc first bought the helmet, the bee's teeth were a brilliant white. Over the years through wear and abuse of the helmet, the teeth have turned a dun white. The Stingers fans see the decay as a badge of honor. The teeth and other signs of wear are considered a mark of a seasoned Stingers veteran who has served in the trenches through many long campaigns. The bee has a faded six-pack of flexed abdominal muscle. A large black barbed stinger points downward from the bee's ass. The bee's wings are a blur, whirling at the speed of egg beaters in determined flight. All of the bee's energy is locked in on an imaginary enemy that is about to get badly stung for daring to take on the Stingers.

Dunc's face is painted green and yellow. He wears a green football jersey. On the back of the jersey is the number of an admired Stingers player, who played for many years on the Stingers team. The player was recently traded to another football team. Dunc wears his yellow football pants complete with padding. He wears two-toned, green and yellow running shoes that he painted himself. Dunc is proud to wear Stingers colors.

"We'll get those pecker heads today, eh Squib?" Dunc says, with pride and determination.

"Sure will," says Cam. He smiles cheerfully and nods in agreement to keep up his end of the bargain with recognized Stingers fan behavior.

"Wally's Wankers are in for a rough ride," says Dunc revealing the language of his early boyhood before his family moved to Bayview. Dunc lets fly a couple of gut-clenching whoops. Several nearby fans answer with their own whoops and derogatory chants about Wally's Wandering Wieners. Dunc beats hard on the big bass drum. He turns round and round so all can see and hear his message.

"Hey Squib. Check this out." Dunc removes the bass drum and sets it down. He pulls up the back of his football jersey. Tattooed on Dunc's back is the picture of a dragon. Its enormous head is centered in the middle of his back. With teeth bared, nostrils flared and hungry green eyes focused straight ahead on its next meal, the dragon's long, muscular body curls back and forth, rope-like across his back. The dragon coils from side to side and up and down, always remaining centered along Dunc's backbone. Large, sharp claws the size of steak knives emerge from its muscular upper arms. The dragon is ready to strike. The upper half of the tattoo is colored. The lower half remains an outline in blue ink. The colored half has green scales along the dragon's back and a yellow underbelly. Dunc chose the colors in honor of the Bayview Stingers. The dragon's two small wings are gold. Its massive head is red. A red tongue shoots out rapaciously from the dragon's gaping maw. Blue tendrils snake along its jaw. Dunc will need many more trips to the tattoo studio, or what was once called a tattoo parlor, before the dragon is complete.

Dunc twists his neck and shoulders. He cranes his head around as far as it will go, straining with all his might to see the dragon. He contorts his mouth in order to get every last inch of twist that he possibly can. His eyes are swivelled in their sockets, ready to pop out of his head at any moment. Dunc reminds Cam of a kid sitting red faced on the toilet and grunting for all he's worth. "That's freedom. Eh Squib?" Dunc grins with satisfaction. He untwists and lowers his jersey. He has given up trying to see the dragon that he knows he cannot see directly. Later, when he is home, he'll take off his jersey. With his back to the bathroom mirror, he'll hold up a small mirror to see the reflection of his dragon in the bathroom mirror. In this way, he'll be able to admire the work of art that the tattoo artist is creating on his back.

4

Over the years, Dunc has accumulated other tattoos on different parts of his body. On his left breast is an angel tinged in blue. She has large firm breasts with small nipples, a thin waist that is accentuated by wide hips and firm thighs. She is a very earthly angel. Her large folded wings look a little tattered around the edges, although the tattoo artist had not intended the wing edges to look tattered. The blue tinge makes her look dead or dying from asphyxiation. When Dunc first showed Cam the angel, Cam thought that it was a tattoo of a fallen angel because of the tattered wings and the dead or dying look of it. Cam kept this opinion to himself because Dunc went to church every Sunday, and was very proud of his angel. On one of Dunc's shoulders is the head of a golden eagle with red thunderbolts shooting from its eyes. On his right breast are two swords in the shape of a cross. Above this is the head of Jesus in full color, although no one really knows what Jesus looked like. Dunc's Jesus has long hair and a scraggly beard that gives him a 1960s rebel look. The Jesus look has changed over the years. In more recent images of Jesus, he has curly hair and beard. Both hair and beard are neatly trimmed in the current fashion of the day. Dunc's Jesus has his hands folded in prayer. Jesus looks upward. There's no way of knowing what he is praying about. Cam once suggested to Dunc that Jesus was asking for more help down here on earth because there were way too many crazy blind people down here and there was way more shit down here than one guy could handle.

"Or maybe Jesus is pissed off because no one seems to get it and he needs more patience from above because he's feeling tempted to whip up an end-of-days type of miracle that would make his regular miracles look like church socials," Cam had suggested. Dunc had scoffed at these ideas, saying that Jesus was doing just fine. He was praying for one of his regular every-day miracles, like raising Lazarus from the dead, or feeding the multitude; nothing fancy just the usual.

5

On Dunc's left calf muscle is the Japanese character for peace. When he first got the tattoo, people who saw it would ask what it meant. Dunc would grin and say that it's the Japanese character for peace. After a while when people asked and he was tired of telling them what it meant, Dunc would run out of patience and get browned off and say that it meant tiddlewack, which was an expression used where Dunc was from before moving to Bayview. Only a few people understood what tiddlewack meant and they would either laugh or walk away embarrassed and angry. Later still, Dunc would respond with 'better to reign in hell than serve in heaven'. Dunc didn't know that this was a quote from Milton's *Paradise Lost*. He had heard it somewhere and liked using it on occasion. Every now and then Dunc felt bad about saying this, but said it anyway. Eventually people stopped asking, except for his friends who would ask what it meant even though they knew what it meant because Dunc had told them many times. Regularly they would lob their own answers in response to the question. Turd was a common answer, which has a special significance for Dunc, who is a plumber by trade. Those who knew Dunc's lingo would answer with 'trigger' or 'pucker string' in answer to their own question. They knew Dunc would understand the answer as an inside joke.

Dunc's oldest tattoo is that of the Stingers mascot that he got the day he turned eighteen when the government considered him old enough to stand trial in adult court if he did something bad. Dunc had the tattoo artist put the tattoo on his abdomen because, like the bee, Dunc had a six-pack abdomen when he was eighteen and was proud of it. Now, thirty-five years later, his rippling abdomen of hard muscle is gone. In its place is a gut that grows bigger with each passing year. He can no longer see the Stingers mascot, which has migrated south in company with his bulging abdomen. It's just as well he can't see the bee because the image has become stretched over the years, in tandem with

Dunc's gut. Now faded because the ink has migrated deeper into his skin, the bee has ballooned into a grotesque caricature of the mascot. Its mouth has changed from a determined grin to a stretched and lopsided leer. The bee's six-pack abdomen now has the look of a wooden barrel with its stays about to burst. Applying the tattoo was painful, but Dunc had persevered for the sake of his freedom.

"That's freedom. Eh buddy?" Dunc repeats this in case Cam didn't hear him the first time. "The right to be whatever I jeezeley want to be and say whatever I f'ing want." He lowers his voice to a whisper for the f'ing word because there are many families with young kids in the parking lot. They are heading to the football stadium for the big game.

"Beauty, eh?" says Dunc again fishing for a compliment on his dragon tattoo.

"Looks good Wiff," Cam replies with indifference.

Dunc is happy to view Cam's answer as a compliment. He ignores the disinterest in Cam's voice.

The dragon tattoo actually reminds Cam of a paint-by-numbers kit that he got one Christmas when he was a grade-two school kid. The kit came in a cardboard box. On the top of the box was a picture of a horse standing in a field. The picture served as a reference to show you what the painting should look like when finished. The box contained a paintbrush, and several paints in small plastic containers with lids. Each container sat in a cardboard insert in the cardboard box. The containers were arrayed in an arc to give the impression of a painter's pallet. There were about a half dozen different colors, including an earthy yellow and a couple of shades of brown for the horse, a couple of shades of green for greenery, black for shadow, white and blue for the sky. A picture of a horse standing in a field was outlined in blue on a piece of eleven by fourteen inch white, pressed cardboard. Each segment in the outline had a number that matched one of the numbered containers. In this way, you

7

knew exactly which color to put in each segment. The idea
was to apply each color one at a time. When you finished
one color, you let the painting dry for a day and then
applied the next color. You simply washed the brush in
water and let it air dry. Then the brush was ready when you
wanted to apply the next color. The manufacturers of the
paint kit had it down to a science. The only thing you had to
remember when you filled in each segment was to be careful
to stay inside the lines. Cam had started the painting, but
had difficulty staying inside the lines. His horse began to
look a little droopy in places. An eye and some other parts
were disproportionately large while other parts, like the
horse's muzzle, were disproportionately small. The horse
developed a sway back. The painting became reminiscent of
a Salvador Dali painting. Cam never finished the painting.
He called it his unfinished opus.

"Is that a Van Gogh on your back?" asks Cam with a
grin. Cam and Dunc have had this conversation before.
"Why do they call them tattoo parlors?" he continues
without waiting for an answer. "A parlor is a room my
grandmother had in her house. It was a special room for
entertaining guests. It was a sign of respect to be invited into
her parlor. She kept the room special and used her best china
when entertaining in her parlor. She'd invite her friends over
for afternoon tea or an evening of bridge. It was an honor to
be entertained in her parlor. A *tattoo* parlor is nothing
special." Cam imagines a tattoo parlor as a dirty, poorly lit
room with a few tables, inks on shelves, an overhead light
for close work, and needle paraphernalia. The walls are
plastered with dozens of examples of the tattoos that you
can get.

"Your brain is as busy as a fart in a mitt looking for the
thumb," Dunc answers, looking astounded. "You sure can
shovel a jeezeley pile. You know they're not called tattoo
parlors anymore. They're tattoo *studios*. Join the twenty-first
century, eh. Your grandmother and my grandmother, God

rest their souls, were a couple of old hens that had nothin' better to do on an afternoon than to sit around and drink tea and gossip about whoever wasn't in the room."

Cam smiles puckishly. "Oh, right. It's called a tattoo studio." Cam puts special emphasis on studio. "Kind of like an artist's studio, that kind of studio," he suggests. "I guess that's why they call them tattoo artists. Maybe I should make an appointment with Rembrandt down at the local tat parlor. What do you think? When's the best time of day, maybe early morning when the north light is best?" Every so often Cam enjoys winding up Dunc to hear him talk. "Maybe I'll get a tattoo on my ass. What about, 'Crack of Doom'? What do you recommend left cheek or right, or both? Maybe 'Crack' on the left, 'of' in the middle and 'Doom' on the right. What about a font, Gothic or Arial, or something less well known, Arnprior maybe?" he muses. Cam knows about fonts. He's a script writer for Maple Key Media, better known as MKM, a large communications and entertainment conglomerate based in Bayview.

"You're a sack full of maybes, aren't you? Tats aren't about that high-brow stuff that no one understands except for the book-smart life-stupid bunch up at the university. Tats are about tellin' all those bull cooks with a big feelin' who want to tell me how to live my life that they can go and get stuffed! And that includes your boss too, what's his name, Ed."

Dunc looks at his watch. The crowd is beginning to thin out. Most are already in the stadium. "Hey, stop chewin' the rag," says Dunc. "I need to get this drum back in the van. We'll miss the pre-game show if we don't get movin'. Come on. Everyone's already in. Let's go."

Security doesn't allow Dunc to take his drum into the stadium anymore. He used to bang on it in the stadium to rally the troops during a football game. There had been a security incident three years ago involving a fan with a homemade bomb and gun. No one was hurt. Now no one is allowed into the stadium with drums or other noise makers that might conceal a bomb or other weapon. Security is especially tight this year after the riot that occurred late in the regular season last year when the Stingers lost against the Warriors in the deciding game for a post-season playoff spot. Many stores near the stadium were vandalized. Cars sporting Warriors stickers were overturned. The police arrested a few fans for various minor offenses: drunk in a public place, urinating in public, etc.

There had been an investigation after the riot. The police determined that it had all started with too much beer and a lot of decidedly unflattering name calling by Warriors and Stingers fans alike. Warriors fans derided the MKM Colossus. They called it the MKM Colon of the universe and demanded that Stingers fans bend over for a colonoscopy. Stingers fans had countered with questions about the sexuality of Warriors fans if they were so bent on dispensing colonoscopies. The battle was on. This year, the police are out in full force to prevent a repeat of last year's fiasco. As well, bars near the stadium will close early to limit post-game celebrations.

Cam and Dunc line up with the other fans. They present their tickets without incident to the ticket takers at the turnstiles. Security guards at the turnstiles are searching purses and backpacks for weapons, beer bottles, or anything that might be thrown and hurt someone. Cam and Dunc find their seats in time for the opening ceremonies. The crowd is excited and ready for an electrifying game. Both teams are very close in the standings with many games still to be played before the final playoffs. Loud speakers stationed around the stadium blare music with nationalistic themes and songs about proud, honest workers doing their job and being ready to do their patriotic duty when called upon. A current popular song is Mortgage Blues sung by the band Liberty Blues. The song is about making ends meet in difficult economic times, high unemployment and the sacrifices made by men and women pulling together to keep family and country together. The song concludes with the refrain 'God helps them that help themselves'.

Now the music stops. The stadium speakers crackle. The announcer begins, "Ladies and gentlemen, Maple Key Sports, a subsidiary of Maple Key Media, proudly presents today's game between the Wallaceville Warriors and the Bayview Stingers!" The announcer puts extra emphasis on Bayview Stingers. "And now, here is the starting line for today." The announcer introduces the starting players on both teams, first the Warriors and then the Stingers. When a player is called, the player runs onto the football field, turns and waves to acknowledge the fans. Then he runs to the sideline where he greets the players on his team who preceded him in the player introductions. The players greet each other with a series of body wiggles, waggles, woggles, jiggles, joggles, shivers, shudders, quakes, quivers, thumps and bumps, plus hand slaps, high fives, fist bumps, hook 'em horns, peace signs and other complicated hand gestures. Of course many of the fans cheer the Stingers players. A few boo the Warriors players, but most fans are good sports who admire the athleticism of the players on both sides.

At the north end of the stadium, two giant doors mounted on steel wheels that run on tracks are slowly winched open by powerful electric motors while the players are introduced. Each door is ten-stories high and seven-stories wide.

"And now ladies and gentlemen, I direct your attention to the north end of the stadium," the announcer crackles over the stadium speakers.

At the north end, a detachment of Stingers fans pull a parade float slowly onto the field. The fans are chosen at random for this honor prior to the start of the game. Maple Key Sports generously issues to each fan pulling the float a Stingers T-shirt and Stingers beehive football helmet, similar to the one that Dunc wears. The T-shirt is free. The helmet must be returned. On the float is a replica of the Stingers mascot. Standing eight-stories high, it towers above the fans. Hidden in the float are large electric fans powered by a diesel generator. The electric fans blow a constant stream of air to keep the mascot inflated. Attached to the front of the float are three thickly braided ropes. Each rope is pulled by twenty Stingers fans, chanting 'Sting-ers' as they pull the float.

Accompanying the fans is a phalanx of hired drum players, each with a big bass drum strapped to his chest. Emblazoned on both sides of each bass drum is the Stingers mascot. The drummers methodically beat their drums, providing the slow, two-beat cadence for the chant: 'Sting-ers! Sting-ers!' Many of the fans in the crowd pick up the chant. Although the float appears heavy, it is light and easily pulled by the fans holding the ropes. A float director standing on the sidelines directs with exaggerated body gestures when to pull and when to ease off in tempo with the drums. When the float reaches midfield, the float director raises both hands, compelling the fans pulling the float to stop. On cue, the drummers stop too. The director in a kind of dance and using inflated gestures directs the fans to drop their ropes, give a monstrous smile, and wave like crazy at the fans in the stadium. The fans dutifully drop their ropes, grin, boisterously whoop and wildly wave as they jump up and down without moving from their assigned spots in the array of bee pullers.

All of the action is captured on TV cameras stationed around the stadium. The images are broadcast to TVs around the country. Images of the fans both on and off the field are projected onto a stadium scoreboard so that none of the action, color and pageantry is missed. The scoreboard is ten-stories high and nine-stories wide. Local fans refer to it as the Cyclops.

The announcer introduces a military color guard. The guard marches in military precision from the north end of

12

the stadium to midfield. All of the members of the honor guard wear medals garnered in battle and all proudly carry flags, representing the country and the various branches of the armed forces.

Next, the announcer introduces today's dignitaries, "Please welcome Tommy Pample, the mayor of Bayview, TV talk-show host, Adin Huffman, and Filana Hearth, our own shining star in the movie industry and a star in the soon-to-be-released film, The Lost View from Here."

The scoreboard immediately displays a still shot from the film. The crowd recognizes the shot right away. It's the same picture announcing the movie that appears in TV ads, Internet ads, billboard ads and ads in movie theaters. In the picture, two characters, a man and a woman, face away from the viewer. They gaze downward from the top of a cliff into a lush and green valley surrounded by high, sheer cliffs on all sides. The man is shirtless, revealing the back of his well developed torso. Leather straps run in an X across his back, indicating that he has two bandoliers strapped across his chest. He holds a shotgun firmly in his hand. He is wearing tight-fitting dress pants and a dress shoes as though he was on his way to a formal event when something terrible and unexpected happened. Beside him stands a woman. This is Filana, the heroine. Her once formal evening dress is torn and her hair dishevelled. She has removed her high-heeled shoes and holds them in one hand. Her other hand cannot be seen. It is in front of her holding up what remains of her dress. The viewer is left to fantasize what might be revealed if the heroine was to turn around.

From the sidelines near midfield, Tommy, Adin and Filana give their best camera smiles and wave to the crowd as they make their way to center field. Occasionally, Filana blows a kiss to her fans in the stands.

While they make their way to center field, close ups of first Tommy, Adin and then Filana appear on the Cyclops. Their heads loom large on the scoreboard while technicians, working with computers, digitize and divide images of their heads into millions of green, blue and red diodes that are the core of the giant scoreboard. At times the system gets out of whack with heads that appear much too big and bodies that are much too small. Sometimes the image is reversed with small heads and big bodies. When this happens, a technician, sitting in a windowless room deep in the stadium basement, hunches over a computer screen and adjusts the output of the image to the scoreboard.

Today Tommy is dressed casually in Stingers colors. Adin wears a beige suit. Filana wears a light summer dress in Stingers green and yellow. Fans whistle, cheer, or boo each time the Cyclops spits out a digital image of one of the trio. The whistling is for Filana, the cheering for Adin, and the booing for Tommy.

In the stands, Dunc cups his hands and shouts in derision, "Attaboy Tommy!" Then Dunc turns to Cam. "I'd jump the fence for her. Hey, how's Anna? Are you still puttin' the moves on her?"

"Yeah, were still seeing each other. How's Emma?"

"Oh, the old woman's fine," Dunc replies dully.

From center field, Adin Huffman, the pre-game master of ceremonies for today's game, begins, "Good afternoon and welcome to the matchup between the Wallaceville Warriors and the Bayview Stingers. Today we have Tommy Pample and Filana Hearth with us to help get this game underway. Tommy, do you have a few words for the fans?"

"Thank you Adin. Friends, families and neighbors, I am honored to be here today and I want to thank all of you for coming out to cheer on the Stingers. What a great team!" The crowd breaks into wild cheers for the Stingers. Tommy merrily grins, puts up his arms to ask the fans for quiet and waits until the crowd stops. "Look at our men and women in uniform. Don't they look great? Look at them! Their sacrifices keep us safe and free," says Tommy. He smiles blissfully and gestures magnanimously with a beckoning

14

wave of his arm at the color guard. The crowd riotously cheers again. The members of the color guard remain rigidly at attention, seemingly oblivious to the events around them. Tommy smiles unreservedly. He waits for the noise to die down. Then Tommy's smile disappears to be replaced by his grave face, which he has practiced many times in front of a mirror for moments such as this. Tommy continues, "Look, these are tough times for all of us and in these difficult times we need to pull together as a community."

From the stands, one of the fans shouts, "What? What did you say? Can you repeat that? I didn't quite get that. Will this be on the exam?"

Tommy is a retired high-school math teacher who turned to politics after retiring from teaching. An expert in the field of repetition, he often repeated the teaching points several times during class and then repeated them again when he had nothing more to say on the subject. He would also repeat the same points again in later classes with the same students, always using the same words because he had been teaching a long time. In his early years Tommy was passionate about math and passing his knowledge onto the next generation. Over time, he had been ground down by the indifference of many of his students who had passed through his classroom. Few of his students shared his passion. Many of his former students are in attendance at today's game.

"If you see your neighbor struggling, stop and ask what you can do to lend a hand," says Tommy.

From the stands, another fan joins in, "Hey Tommy, I'm short a few bucks this week. Can you spare a couple of bucks for a neighbor?"

"Stand by your loved ones, your wife, husband, parents, sons and daughters," continues Tommy.

Again from the stands, "Hey Filana, can I stand by you?"

Filana smiles nervously.

Tommy ignores the comments and continues, "It is our pioneering spirit of sacrifice and independence that have kept us strong. Self-reliance and hard work will see us through. This is the formula for success."

"Hey Tommy, what's the formula for success when the rent is due and you're an out-of-work welder? Square the circle on that one, eh Tommy boy."

In class Tommy would complain to his captive students about how much more money welders made in the Bayview shipyard than he did as the head of the math department. Comments about welding and welders were intended to remind Tommy of his welder comments, especially since the shipyard had closed a few years ago, throwing many highly skilled workers out of work. The city had suffered too. The shipyard had been one of the cornerstones of the community.

"Hey Tommy, how's that welding class you're taking coming along? Why don't you weld this!" shouts a fan making a hand gesture. The gesture is not in the spirit of the gestures made by the football players, nor is it captured on Cyclops.

"Hey Tommy, when are you going to apply for a welding job in the shipyard? I'll put in a good word for you."

Then someone else adds, "You can use my name if you need a reference. The name's Harry Wiener."

Others shout out names too, such as Ben Dover, I. P. Nickels, and Harry Balzac. This is considered great fun and adds to the entertainment.

"We're with you Tommy," another fan shouts sarcastically.

Tommy ignores the comments and continues, "Listen, we will get through this. We have before and we will this time. So look, I'll tell you straight out. I need your support. Help me to continue my efforts to help you, your family and this great community." Tommy is referring to his program of

municipal spending cuts to keep taxes low, so that citizens
have more money in their pockets and can choose how they
spend their money. This is Tommy's and many others idea
of freedom: the freedom to buy stuff. Tommy pauses. Then
he says, quoting Graham Greene, "Our worst enemies here
are not the ignorant and the simple, however cruel; our
worst enemies are the intelligent and cruel." Except for a few
isolated boos and taunts, the crowd grows quiet for a
moment while they take in what Tommy has said. They are
not sure what to make of it. "Go Stingers go! Thank you!"
shouts Tommy. He smiles happily once again, and
generously waves from the Cyclops at the fans in a bid to
whip up enthusiasm.

Adin applauds unreservedly. Then he turns to Filana,
"Filana, I want to thank you for joining us today. Do you
have a few words for our fans?"

Twisting in his seat to look at Cam, Dunc grins
enthusiastically. "I have a few words for Filana."

"Thank you Adin," responds Filana. "I'd like to say
thank you to all my fans. I hope you enjoy my new film, The
Lost View from Here, which opens next month. Thank you
and if you love somebody, give them a big hug." The fans
cheer. Filana smiles amiably and waves eagerly.

Sitting in his seat, Cam raises his arms toward Dunc in
an exaggerated manner, pretending he is about to give Dunc
a big hug. Dunc sees it coming and pushes Cam's arms
away. Cam laughs. "What's wrong? Don't you want a hug?"

"Smart ass," says Dunc smiling grouchily. He shakes his
head in bewilderment "Get away. Keep your hands to
yourself."

"And now a word from Reverend Mortul," Adin
announces solemnly.

A camera turns to Reverend Mortul who stands on the
sidelines. A member of the clergy from one of the local
denominations is invited to say a few words before the
beginning of each game. The invited clergyman is expected

17

to stick to references of God, but to keep the speech non-denominational, so as not to offend other religious groups with different points of views regarding certain hotly disputed religious beliefs. Clergy from all denominations are invited to participate. The address can be no longer than two minutes. Before this policy limiting the length of the address was introduced, one member of the clergy had spoken for five whole minutes. The pre-game ceremony ran longer than it should have. The overrun cost MKM thousands of dollars in lost advertising revenue and the fans became bored and restless. Fewer fans turned out for the rest of the Stingers games that season. Maple Key Sports had to lower the price of tickets to entice fans to the stadium, which meant lower revenues. A good turnout at the games is important to MKM so the fans at home can see all the stadium fans having a good time. This builds fan loyalty because the fans at home can imagine the excitement and feel that they belong to something that is big and important. The higher fan base at home means that MKM can charge advertisers more for commercial spots during the broadcast of the game.

Today Reverend Mortul will address the crowd. Reverend Mortul has practiced the delivery of his speech all week to ensure that his delivery will run one minute and fifty-seven seconds, and not a second more. He has carefully crafted his lines to make absolutely sure that he won't offend anyone, no matter what his or her denomination. Reverend Mortul starts, "Lord, keep us, your faithful servants, safe in our hour of need. Grant us thy grace even as we seek to follow the true path."

At the same time that Reverend Mortul begins his address, the field director's arms begin to frantically whir about in big circular motions to signal the Reverend that he needs to speed things up. The pre-game show is running long. The Stingers bee pullers took longer than usual to pull the float to the middle of the field. The frenzied motion of the field director flusters the Reverend Mortul, who abruptly ends his address. "God blind us and deliver us to our enemies. Amen," blurts Reverend Mortul in his hurry to finish. Immediately he realizes his mistake. His gut churns as though he has swallowed a bag of ferrets. This is not what he had meant to say. He had meant to say, God blind our enemies and deliver us from our enemies. The Reverend had become muddled and his words jumbled under pressure. The field director's flailing has put the Reverend off his game.

Cam turns to Dunc and asks, "What did he say?"

Dunc shrugs, "Don't know. I wasn't listenin'. Somethin' about us being blind enemies. Blind and our own worst enemies?" Dunc shrugs again, not really caring. "That must be it."

"Ah shit!" blurts Reverend Mortul not realizing that his microphone is still live until he hears his expletive crackle over the stadium loudspeakers. "Oh crap!" he mutters in horror, realizing his second mistake and now adding to his mortification as his last invective crackles into the ether world. "I mean, God..." A sound technician cuts off the Reverend Mortul's microphone. The pre-game show continues.

Only a few people in the crowd seemed to have noticed his original mistake about God blinding people and handing them over to their enemies. By his own words, the Reverend has delivered himself into the hands of his enemies. You can be sure his peers, other members of the clergy, will give him a good ribbing at the first opportunity; although most of his peers will not do it out of malice because they have made similar mistakes of this kind in their ministries.

Dunc and Cam grin. Fans applaud the Reverend Mortul's gaffe, adding to his discomfort.

"Holy shit! Did you hear that?" Cam says quietly to Dunc. "I didn't think he had it in him."

"Get outta that!" says Dunc, looking with disbelief at the Reverend.

Paint by Numbers

The opinion of the fans would serve Reverend Mortul well in the coming months because they now see the Reverend as one of their own.

The stadium loudspeakers crackle. Adin continues, "Thank you Reverend Mortul. Ladies and gentleman, would you please stand for the playing of our national anthem."

Cam and Dunc along with everyone else stand in unison. Men remove their caps, beehive football helmets and other head accoutrements. Dunc scratches his head. The national anthem starts. Many in the crowd put their right hands over their hearts. When the anthem is almost at an end, four fighter jets flying in formation appear above the stadium. The planes in their pallid-gray colors are silent as they outpace the sound of their powerful gas turbine engines. At the midfield point in their flight, the wraith-like whisper of the engines reaches the crowd. Everyone looks up in the direction of the sound. In unison the four pilots push their engine throttles forward. Immediately the powerful engines howl with a titanic, end-of-days thunder that roars and crackles while a searing, hellhound flame shoots out from the afterburner of each engine. The jet fighters make a put-to-the-whip jump, shoot forward and are gone. A whiff of engine exhaust carries on the wind to the fans below where it lingers momentarily. The national anthem ends. The spectacle is awe inspiring. Dunc has a lump in his throat, as do many other fans.

Adin interjects with pride, "Ladies and gentlemen, let's have a big round of applause for the men and women in our armed forces who keep our country strong and free!" A roar of cheers, whoops, and whistles rises from the crowd as the fans settle into their seats.

Through the frenzied waving of arms, the float director instructs the bass drummers to beat at triple time to hurry the fans pulling the Stingers float off the field and out of the stadium. The large electric fans inflating the Stingers mascot on the float are turned off to save time later. Immediately the mascot begins to deflate. The bee's determined grin turns into a look of surprise. Tom, Adin and Filana wave at the crowd as they depart the playing field.

Next the football referees for today's game are introduced and take to the field. There is the ritual coin toss. Over the loudspeakers a referee announces that the Wallaceville Warriors have won the toss and have elected to receive the ball. The Stingers will kick off to start the game. The players take the field and the game begins.

Cam and Dunc have good front-row seats at midfield and can hear the quarterback calling out signals at the scrimmage line, "Hit. Yellow 42. Yellow 42. Go. Go." This is a secret code that all members of the team understand. The center lineman snaps the football into the waiting hands of the quarterback when the quarterback hollers the appropriate audible. The team members charge into action, executing the play. The other team bolts into action. They run around too trying to stop the team with the ball from advancing and ultimately scoring. Now and then the team with the ball is successful and from time to time the other team is successful.

All the plays are captured by the TV cameras and the action repeated on Cyclops while the teams set up for the next play. If a player makes a spectacular play and the action is caught by one of the cameras, the TV production team reruns the play in slow motion so that the fans can admire the athleticism of the player.

If the Wallaceville Warriors look like they might score, the Stingers fans sing, 'Green and yellow, green and yellow. Mother be quick. I'm going to be sick'. This is a sign to the Stingers players that the fans are unhappy about the way things are going and the Stingers better stop the Warriors. The fans repeat the chant until the Warriors either score a touchdown, or the Stingers win possession of the ball. If the Warriors score, the Stingers fans finish singing and then make barfing noises to show their disapproval.

A small contingency of fans have become very good at making realistic barfing sounds. Many of the other fans think that they are a little too good. If a fan is too convincing and another fan complains, a stadium attendant asks the fake-barfing fan to be a little less convincing. Last year the Stingers fans made a lot of barfing noises. This year there is less barfing because the Stingers are doing better. Everyone is having fun, cheering, laughing, admiring the skills of the players, and making fake barfing noises.

At half time the score is close. The Warriors lead by a single touchdown. The Stingers rally in the second half. They win by kicking a field goal on the last play of the game. The final gun sounds to end the game. Overhead, a dozen giant firecrackers explode in celebration of the win. The fans roar their approval and then head for the stadium exits. The game is over.

2 Me and Bobby McGee

Cam stands upside down on his living room floor. He
has kicked up into a headstand with his feet pointing toward
the ceiling. His body trembles, jerks, twitches and shakes
from side to side and back to front while he makes constant
corrections to maintain his inverted stand. His head presses
on the hard threadbare gray carpet. He faces the television
with his back to the living-room couch. His arms and hands
are extended at ninety degrees to his body, forming a tripod
for balance. With a spasmodic jolt of his right hand he
reaches to adjust his glasses. Instantly he jerks back his hand
to sustain his rickety tripod. His glasses remain skewed.

Cam is wearing a yellow T-shirt emblazoned with a
picture of the Stingers bee. The T-shirt has fallen down
around his arms, revealing his narrow, bare chest. Recently a
few strands of gray hair have begun to sprout around his
nipples. A small stomach paunch is slowly taking shape. He
approaches middle age. At present, he is neither too fat nor
too skinny. He is neither too tall nor too short, but falling
somewhere in between. The legs of his green sweat pants
have fallen down, bunching around his tree-knot knees. His
legs narrow to gangly ankles where feet sprout as though
jammed on as an afterthought. On his feet he wears a pair of
white, ankle-length, athletic socks that lost their elasticity
long ago. His socks hang off his feet, dangling loosely about
his ankles. On one foot he wears an open-backed, charcoal-
gray, fleece slipper with worn, black foam sole. The other

slipper fell off when he pushed up into a handstand. Usually he loses both slippers.

The slippers are a birthday present from a former girlfriend, Debbie, whom he met at work. Their relationship lasted two months and ended when Debbie discovered that Cam wore athletic socks to bed to keep his feet warm. She found this creepy and gross, although she never told him this. Officially she told Cam that they weren't compatible without getting into details, but that they could remain friends. Unofficially Cam was pleased with the breakup because Debbie's laugh sounded like the first three notes sung by the Queen of the Night in the Queen's aria from Mozart's opera, The Magic Flute. In his own mind, Cam began to imagine Debbie as the Queen of the Night. He didn't tell her this.

With the exception of the light from the TV, the room is bathed in darkness. He has drawn the heavy window curtains to block the noonday sun.

On the couch behind him sits Evea, his niece, who holds the TV remote in her hand. Evea hums to herself while she waits for Cam's next command. Evea is a soon-to-be grade-six kid when school resumes in the fall.

"Guide. Down. Down," barks Cam above the din of the television as a jumble of images churn across the screen. With each command Evea presses the appropriate button on the TV remote. She has been performing this function on Saturday morning even before she was a kindergarten kid. The television jumps to another channel or displays the television guide that lists the programs that are currently playing. On the television screen people are pitching solutions to your inadequacies, or reminding you about an old or new war, or making you afraid or angry or something else about the most current state of whatever.

Cam is waiting for a commercial that he knows is about to air. "42 unmute," he bawls although he doesn't have to shout because the sound is turned off at the moment. The tension of maintaining his upside-down posture contributes more to his master-sergeant bark than the din of the TV when the sound is on.

Immediately the television jumps to channel 42 and floods the room with sound. Cam wrestles to hold his upside-down stance. A commercial begins with the appearance of a man in his late sixties with thick, dark-rimmed glasses and bushy black hair. The man is conservatively dressed in a dark pinstriped suit and black tie. He smiles warmly and begins to speak. When he speaks, Cam mouths the words the man is speaking. The man speaks in a calm, friendly and self-assured voice.

"Hello," the man says in his soft and gentle voice. "You may know me. I'm Edward Channel, the CEO of Maple Key Media, or as we call it MKM. Welcome to our family. Through our subsidiary, Maple Key Films, we produce many of the wonderful films that you will see today on many of the Maple Key Network channels, which are available through the Maple Key Cable Network." While Edward continues, the background on the television screen splits into several segments, showing short film clips from many of the popular films produced by Maple Key Films. "As a family, we are proud of our work and proud of our many accomplishments that have made it possible to bring this programming into your home." The background changes while Edward continues to speak. Each segment in the background splits into many more segments. Each segment displays one at a time still pictures showing a smattering of MKM employees working at their jobs. The employees have big shiny smiles. Each picture lasts only three seconds before being replaced by a still picture of another employee. Edward continues to talk. The background becomes a single screen. The MKM logo, a cluster of golden maple keys with each key representing a division of the company, fades in behind Edward. The maple keys begin to slowly twirl downward as Edward concludes "Thank you for sharing your time with our family."

"Mute," shouts Cam over the sounds of the television when another commercial begins. Evea dutifully complies. The room is filled with silence again. He can't hold his headstand any longer. He's losing the battle. He falls with a thud onto the carpet, losing the remaining slipper. He lies prone on the floor.

"Why do you stand on your head?" Evea asks. She has heard the answer many times, but still she ponders the question. Predictably, Cam pauses while he gathers his thoughts before answering.

"Well, the theory is that more blood accumulates in the head, helping you to think better," he answers. He isn't sure where he first heard this, or even if the hypothesis is true. Once he had taken a basic Yoga course, but this was not a pose that he had learned in class. Is the theory an urban myth, a story? He isn't sure.

"Does it work?" Evea continues as if reading from a catechism.

Every time she has asked this question, Cam has had to think before answering. Did standing on his head make a difference? He couldn't think of a single instance when it had actually did make a difference. He kept hoping that one day it would make a difference. That he would find the answers to the questions that occupied his mind from buying new snow tires for his car, to what color to paint the kitchen. The questions went endlessly around in his head with few clear answers. Sooner or later most of his questions seemed to get answered. And each time a question was answered, or he simply forgot about the question, a new question would materialize to replace the old one. There were lots of questions to occupy his time.

"No," Cam answers firmly.

"Then why do you do it?" Evea asks immediately.

"Habit, I guess." Cam replies unconvincingly. There is a pause while Evea thinks about this.

"But how can you see the TV?" she asks continuing the well-worn path of question and answer. "Everything is upside down."

"I've trained myself to look at the TV upside down," he answers confidently and with pride. This is true; over the years he has learned to look at the TV upside down by flipping the TV picture in his head to match his wrong-way-up posture. Inverting the picture has become second nature to him. In fact now he can sit upright on his couch and flip the picture in his head even though there is no need to do so. Evea remains as confused as ever by Cam's TV viewing habits.

Evea turns off the TV with the TV remote. The silence is complete. A clock chimes noon. Cam sits up in front of the TV. Abruptly Evea stands on the couch, and pulls open the heavy curtains behind her. The light pours in revealing the living room. There are the usual bits of furniture with a worn looking couch and matching chair, TV, and a couple of end tables. The walls are painted a kind of white with undertones of tan. The living room is small and cramped.

On the wall opposite the TV hangs a framed lithograph depicting a farm in winter. The artist is Tom Roberts. Cam found the lithograph at a garage sale and bought it for three dollars. A farm lane arches up from the bottom and to the right, ending at a farmhouse. The sun lingers silently in the late afternoon. The shadows of nearby buildings and trees have started to stretch, growing longer in the graying silence. Very soon it will be evening and dark. Four children dressed in their winter coats and boots and carrying schoolbooks walk up the lane. They are nearing the farmhouse on their way home after a day at school. Two smaller children, who are too young for school, stand near the house. They are looking down the lane at the older children who are only a short distance from the younger children. Their meeting is a quiet sharing of the moment in the stillness of the late afternoon. Casually and naturally they will share stories of the day's adventures, renewing their bond while the older children tell of their adventures in the outer world. Cam has always liked the picture, although he's not sure why. The picture quietly tugs at the unsaid and unseen, a memory.

Cam squints and throws up an arm to shield his eyes from the sudden sea of light. The light blasts a pale image of Cam against the blank TV screen. With narrowed eyes he looks at Evea silhouetted against the light pouring in through the window. Around her particles of dust drift slowly and aimlessly, pushed by the unseen micro-currents of air that circulate through the house. The clock finishes striking the hour. Evea begins to hum again. Cam's stomach growls.

"Come on. Let's have lunch. I'm hungry." Cam replies in answer to his stomach. "I'll make you a sandwich. How about a cucumber sandwich?" he teases knowing that she dislikes cucumber. "It's your favorite," he adds to play out the game that they have played every Saturday since the first dawning of their Saturday mornings.

Evea grimaces to maintain her part in the ritual. She has played this game many times before. She is growing tired of the joke, but has not told Cam. She knows their Saturday mornings are coming to an end. "No, not that; you know I don't like that. You know I like broccoli." She smiles ambiguously, not wanting to hurt her Uncle's feelings. Cam smiles a little uncomfortably. He realizes the joke has grown stale. He knows he must find a new joke if he can. He knows that Evea is going where he will not be allowed to follow.

"Okay, peanut butter and honey it is," offers Cam, to which Evea concurs with a nod of her head. She smiles uneasily, thankful that the moment has passed.

Seated at the kitchen table, Evea eats the sandwich that Cam has made. Between bites, she hums the song that she was humming earlier.

"What's that song you're humming?"

"God sees the little sparrow fall. Do you want to hear it?"

"Yes."

"I learned it at Sunday school. It goes like this: God sees the little sparrow fall. It meets His tender view. If God so loves the little birds, I know He loves me, too." Evea stops. "Do you like it?"

"Yes, I do. Do you?"

"Yes, they said that next week they would teach us more of the song at Sunday school." Evea is fond of singing. "But if God sees the little sparrow fall, why doesn't He catch it so it doesn't fall?"

"I don't know." Cam pauses while he tries to think of an answer. "It makes me think of a song called *Me and Bobby McGee*. The song is about two people who don't have much money, but they're happy together and like singing songs. It goes like this." He sings the first verse and chorus to the best of his ability. "Later in the song the two go their separate ways because Bobby McGee is looking for a different home. The singer misses Bobby McGee very much. I don't know why the song reminds me of God Sees the Little Sparrow Fall, but it does. Maybe it's about the choices people make because of what they want."

There's a long silence while Cam and Evea ponder. Then Evea answers, "That's sad that they didn't stay together."

"Yes, I think so too," says Cam looking at his watch. "When you're finished we can hop in the car and head to the pool for a swim." The afternoon swim is part of their Saturday afternoon ritual, a trip to the local swimming pool.

After lunch as Cam starts his car parked in front of his house, he peers at the house to reassure himself that the house is securely locked. As a boy, there were many years of moving from house to house. Finally his parents bought the modest bungalow after one of the wars. Cam can't remember which war. When his parents died, Cam and his brothers inherited the house. Cam bought his brothers' interests in the house.

The house is a gabled bungalow with light-brown shingles and sand-colored brick. The ginger-colored front door offers a narrow window slit that you can peep out to see if anyone is standing on the porch or passing by on the sidewalk. The window is made of a bubble-textured stained glass that distorts the view of anyone trying to look out or in. Short lengths of simulated wrought iron fencing are screwed on to both sides of a one-person-sized cement slab that serves as the front porch. The porch is not big enough for much of anything. A weathered aluminum awning overhangs the porch. The awning provides little shade. There are the usual flower beds that Cam's mother, Olivia, planted and that Cam now maintains. A pinched looking window squints back suspiciously from between the shingles of the roof. Satisfied that all is as it should be, Cam pulls away from the curb.

Usually Cam gets lost once during the drive, although he has made the drive many times before. In fact, he often gets lost when driving his car. Cam has installed a GPS navigation system in his car. He still gets lost. The GPS system has a female voice that tells him when and where to turn. Cam calls her Gerty. This is a pun on hurdy-gurdy, a kind of mechanical violin. The manufacturer of the GPS system has tried to give the voice a human quality and tone, but has not quite mastered the illusion. The voice is choppy and unnatural. It pauses in the wrong places and lacks the emotional tones of a human voice.

"Well Gerty, what can you tell me today?" is usually how the trip to the pool begins. Cam grins as he always does at this moment. Evea smiles to humor him.

As they make their way to the pool, Gerty sounds like this: 'Turn.' This is followed by a pause while Gerty searches its word bank for 'right in' followed by another pause and then 'two hundred' pause 'yards'. When Cam reaches the intersection, Gerty adds 'Turn' followed by a pause and then 'right' another pause 'at this intersection'.

The GPS navigation system uses the radio speaker to announce turns and provide other information. This means that the radio has to be on and tuned to a radio station in order to hear the directions. Gerty interrupts with her garbled instructions whatever the radio station is broadcasting at the time:

Newscaster: 'Today Tommy Pample, the mayor of Bayview...'

Gerty: 'Your... next... turn... is in... one...mile.'

Newscaster: '...cuts to...'

Gerty: 'Your... next... turn... is in... five hundred... yards.'

Newscaster: '...wrong doing...'

And so on.

Evea has learned to watch carefully when her Uncle drives the car to the swimming pool. She knows the route well. She tries to help him with directions, but this doesn't work because Cam doesn't hear her over the other voices.

There aren't many swimmers when they finally arrive at the pool. Evea enjoys swimming and wading in the shallow end. Cam likes to wade too. If the pool is quiet as it is today, Cam swims out a little ways until the water is deep enough that he can't touch bottom. From here he can watch Evea, and tread water at the same time.

Cam enjoys these moments with his head just above the water, bobbing slightly. His arms and legs push gently against the water. The experience of treading water reminds him of the time that he went to the ocean on vacation with his parents. He was a grade-three kid then. He remembers standing on a gravel beach with the wide ocean stretching out before him. The waves have worn the gravel round and smooth over many millennia with ocean swells nearing the shore, rising into waves, breaking on the shore, and then retreating back to the ocean: rise, break and retreat; rise, break and retreat. He remembers the gravel clattering and tumbling in the waves as the waves advanced and receded. He liked the soothing sound of the waves and the quiet clatter of the gravel.

Off shore, about fifty yards, a seal bobbed in the ocean swell with its head barely above the water. Occasionally the seal would disappear and re-emerge in another spot. At first Cam didn't know what it was that he was looking at because he had only seen seals on TV. Films about seals were always taken by professional camera crews. They always made sure to get good close ups of the seals, so you knew exactly what you were looking at. Usually they filmed captive seals in a man-made pool. These seals were trained to do tricks, such as fetch a ball or whatever a trainer had taught them. Meanwhile the commentator of the film described how clever the seals were to have learned a trick or two.

On cue a seal would nudge the trainer into the pool. The trainer would swim to the surface, splash about for a few seconds, and then with a look of feigned anger wag an admonishing finger at the seal. Everyone watching knew that it was part of the act, but still it was funny and you felt there was a friendly bond between the trainer and the seal even if there wasn't.

Standing on the beach it was different. At fifty yards the seal's head was small and hard to make out. It took Cam a little while before he realized that he was looking at a seal. The seal seemed to be looking toward the shore. He wondered what it was looking at. Was it tired and wanting to come ashore and rest, but couldn't because there were people on the shore? Perhaps it was trying to figure out what people are. Maybe it had never seen people before. Are people dangerous and to be avoided, or are they only strange looking seals standing on two flippers?

Cam thinks about his seal encounter while he bobs gently in the swimming pool. He begins to relax and imagines himself bobbing in the ocean swell while looking at the people wading in the pool. He tries to imagine the people the way the seal might have seen them on the shore that day. Cam bobs for a long time wondering about the people wading in the pool. What are they? He wonders. Who are they? What do they want? Why are they here? Detached from the waders he bobs suspended in the stillness, not a part of anything. Then no thoughts come to him, no thoughts anywhere, no thoughts, no thoughts, bobbing and bobbing and silence and on and on, waiting, and listening, and watching on the wide and open silence.

The pool empties of swimmers as late afternoon arrives. Cam takes Evea home.

3 Your Baby is Ugly

Click click. Clickety-click tap. Click. Clickety-click click.
Cam sits in his assigned MKM cubicle typing on his
computer keyboard. He's working on the script for the next
commercial that his manager, Jordan, has asked him to
create for Edward, the CEO of MKM. The same clickety-click
sound is heard emanating from other cubicles where other
writers work on scripts for different projects.

There are many cubicles in each row and many rows of
cubicles. There are two writers in each cubicle. At one time
each writer had their own cubicle; however MKM did some
research, comparing itself to best-in-class companies. MKM
discovered that these best-in-class companies allotted less
room to their writers. To improve efficiencies and thereby
reduce costs, MKM made the writers' cubicles smaller and
assigned two writers to each cubicle. Men are paired with
men and women with women to avoid awkward situations.

When Cam wants to leave his cubicle, he must perform
a kind of herky-jerky dance with his partner, the other writer
in the cubicle, who must remain seated during the execution
of the dance movements. Cam has to push his chair slightly
away from his desk without bumping the chair of the other
writer in the cubicle, stand, pivot, and then in a crab-like
side-step shuffle, edge his way out between his chair and
desk until he can step into the aisle. Cam has to keep his
arms at his sides while doing this movement so as not to
accidentally nudge the other writer with a stray elbow or
other appendage. The entire dance goes like this: and with
partner seated, push, stand, pivot, and with arms at sides,

crab shuffle, crab shuffle, and step. The crab-shuffle
hoedown is repeated in the reverse order when Cam returns
to his desk: with partner seated, step, and with arms at sides,
crab shuffle, crab shuffle, pivot, sit and pull the chair close to
your desk.

"Sorry," says Cam to his cubicle mate, Wayne, if Cam
accidentally bumps Wayne's chair while performing this
maneuver. This is the correct cubicle etiquette. Now and
again Cam says, "sorry just stepping out to change my
mind," implying that the cubicle is even too small a space in
which to think. If a minor bump transpires, Cam says
nothing because he's tired of the whole thing. Occasionally
the other writer tries to squeeze his chair closer to his desk
because he has breached etiquette by allowing his chair to
stray too far into the postage-stamp-sized, common area
shared by the two writers in the cubicle. Often a writer's
chair strays into the common area because the writer is
trying to get comfortable.

The panels that make up the cubicle walls are made of
fabric that is Cosmic Latte in color. Two scientists, who have
surveyed over two-hundred thousand galaxies, have
determined that generally the universe is beige white in
color. One of the scientists, in trying to describe this color,
described it as Cosmic Latte. This color is in keeping with
the idea that Cam's cubicle is representative of the universe
and that his cubicle is as old as the universe. This is true in a
way because all the matter that would ever be in the
universe, including the matter that now makes up the panels
of the cubicle walls, and Cam too, for that matter, was there
at the beginning when the universe came into being.
'Fffffft,' said the universe with the fizzy sound of a broken
firecracker instead of a stupefying and humongous
KABOOM because the medium to carry the sound is
emerging at the same time as everything else. So although
the universe is said to be expanding, Cam's cubicle universe
is shrinking for reasons of best in class. Cam hopes that the

worker bees running the company never learn that toilet paper is two sided because then the race will be on to implement best in class.

There are one or two small holes in the fabric of the panel immediately in front of Cam. He enjoys thinking of these holes as black holes. The holes themselves exist because the cubicle panels have been around a long time and are hand-me-downs. The panels started out brand new in the executive office space at MKM. During one of the many re-designs of office space, the panels were deemed unacceptable for the executive space and cast off to another department. Eventually the walls were inherited by the writing group after many office-space re-designs when more writers and other workers too were squeezed into less and less space. Over the years holes appeared in the fabric of the panels when panels were accidentally damaged during yet another re-design of the office space. After a couple of decades, many panels have acquired their own unique and randomly distributed set of holes.

One time Cam poked his finger into one of the holes and felt around to see what he could discover. Cam learned that his black holes are benign, unlike the real ones that bend time and space and destroy anything that gets too close. He discovered that there is empty space in the panel wall and that there is more fabric at the back of the panel. Cam imagines the writer on the other side of the cubicle wall poking his finger into a different hole in the same panel. Cam wonders what his, Cam's, reaction would be were he to encounter another finger in the cubicle wall. What would you say to another finger? Hi. I'm here. How's it going? What's it like where you are? And what can you say with a finger? Would you develop an elaborate finger language resembling football-player hand gestures such as hook 'em horns?

In his musings, Cam thinks of the *Creation of Adam* created by Michelangelo. Adam is casually extending a limp finger to God, who in turn is reaching out to Adam. God seems to be doing all the work. Adam looks a little too laid back as though he's taking things for granted. Oh well, thinks Cam, we all know how that ended. Cam imagines what it might be like if you were talking to God with your finger, but didn't know it was God because God is using the name Sam, which could be short for Samuel or Samantha. What if you thought it was just another writer, like yourself, and God isn't letting on? Cam imagines how the exchange might go.

"What are you working on?" you ask in the quickly evolving finger language.

"Right now I'm working on this piece about a writer," replies Sam in finger language.

Then you ask, "How's it going? I mean the piece you're writing."

Sam replies, "Slowly, possibly there's a little progress. I'm not sure."

This seems an odd answer to you. Usually as a writer, you know when a script is going well or not, so you change the subject because you think Sam doesn't want to talk about the script and you don't want to find yourself in the position of commenting on Sam's work and maybe leave the impression that you think Sam's script stinks. That would be the professional equivalent of saying your baby is ugly, a real insult.

"Who do you think will win the football championship this year?" you ask to change the subject.

"Wallaceville Warriors," Sam answers with assurance.

"No way," you answer.

"I have a hunch," says Sam.

"Do you want to bet on that?"

"No" Sam answers without explanation.

You wonder if Sam is the religious type who doesn't believe in betting. You change the subject because religion is taboo in the workplace. So you talk about the latest movies or other stuff, using the finger language that you're inventing while you go along, and you're trying to figure out who this Sam is who knows a lot about everything that you talk about. In fact you suspect Sam knows a lot more than he's letting on, but doesn't want to show off by saying too much.

And then, WHAM!

"Are you sitting down?" Sam asks. "Yes, of course you are," continues Sam. "I have something to tell you. You won't believe this, but I'm God."

There's a long pause before you reply.

"Yeah, pull my finger," you retort in disbelief.

There's a gentle tug on your finger.

"If you're God prove it," you respond.

"How's the coffee this morning? Why don't you taste it?"

You taste your coffee. It tastes like wine.

Unbelievable as it seems, you believe that you are talking to God himself. But now what? What do you say, realizing that by sticking your finger in a black hole you've dialed up God and not any old writer, like John Milton? Now you have to be on your best behavior and the conversation gets awkward and formal and you're afraid to say anything with your finger.

Then you start thinking about all the things you've done. Some of them you're not proud of. There was the time you stole apples from the neighbor's apple tree next door when you were a grade-five kid, or you were mean to someone when you knew it was wrong, but you couldn't seem to help yourself. You want to say holy shit, but you can't because that would be bad, and you fumble for words, although you've been doing great up to this point using the finger language to say whatever comes to you, and you wonder what's the finger gesture for Ye, as in the Bible, oh ye of little faith, and you want to start using old Bible words like thee and thou. And definitely God has a big grin on his face, if you could see his face, because God sees the humor in the situation even though God only knows you're baffled beyond belief. You begin to sweat. You're afraid to say anything because it might be held against you and send you straight to hell and you don't want to sound stupid either.

"Don't worry," says God finally with his finger while trying not to laugh because He doesn't want to hurt your feelings. "You don't have to be afraid. We can talk again later when you want to talk more. There's no rush. Let me know when you're ready. I'll be around. You know where to find me."

The conversation is over. Astounded, you slowly withdraw your finger from the black hole. You don't get much done for the rest of the week because you're replaying the conversation in your head, thinking about what you said, what you should have said but didn't, and why you really thought it was a good idea to try and bet with God on a football game. What were you thinking? And you don't know how long the conversation lasted. It could have been a minute or it could have been an eternity and you're not sure.

And perhaps you cry and laugh and a bunch of other stuff and pray and say you're sorry if you said anything stupid or offensive and you thank Him for not turning your hair white, the way He did in the movies after talking to Moses on Mount Sinai, and you hope to God that God doesn't hold the conversation against you, but there's no answer only this big silence and you wish to God that God would answer and say something: 'fear not', 'don't sweat it', 'relax'.

But there's this big silence, or maybe you can't hear God. Maybe God's shouting at you and getting wound up and yelling, 'Yes, everything is okay. Don't worry. You need to relax. Everything will be fine. Get a life. Stop being so afraid, BOO!'

But it doesn't sound fine at all because you're thinking that you blew it, but you didn't really and it wasn't an exam or a test or anything resembling a pass or fail thing.

This too is Cam's universe. He is free to explore it to the extent that time and his imagination allow. At first glance his universe seems less exciting than say Cortez standing on a peak in Darien and seeing the Pacific Ocean for the first time, but Cam's world does provide its own realm of exploration and discovery and there are no bugs chewing at him and the weather isn't hot and sweaty humid either, the way it must have been for guys like Cortez.

"Can I see you for a minute?" asks Jordan in his coughing-up-dirt voice.

Jordan joined the company as a script writer about twenty years ago. He was young and ambitious when he joined. He rose to the rank of manager after seventeen years. Currently he is responsible for about a dozen writers, including Cam. The exact number of writers fluctuates depending on how well MKM is doing financially.

Cam twists half way around in his chair.

"Hi Jordan, how are you?" says Cam.

"Let's find an empty meeting room." As a rule this is not a good sign when Jordan wants to see you in private.

"Okay." Cam does the crab-shuffle hoedown and follows Jordan to a meeting room.

"Close the door," says Jordan. Cam closes the door and sits down. Closing the door is a bad sign because it means that what Jordan has to say he doesn't want anyone else to hear. Jordan is wearing his usual dishevelled, badger-gray hair and pencil moustache, and his rumpled digging-under-rocks shirt and pants look. He leans casually back in his chair. He appears relaxed. Cam has attended enough of these meetings to know that Jordan is not relaxed. Cam wonders what it would take to unwind the spring-loaded

Jordan. Cam's mind races while he tries to guess what is on Jordan's mind.

Cam remembers the time during a department meeting when he, Cam, made a comment to the Employee Opportunities (EO) representative, Jo, who was in attendance that day. Jo talked enthusiastically about the low absenteeism rate at MKM and how the absenteeism rate was lower than even best-in-class companies. Jo wanted to believe that the lower absenteeism was because employees enjoyed their jobs so much more than at any other company. This was not the case. Cam pointed out that the downside of lower absenteeism meant that people who were sick were coming to work when they should have stayed home and that they were making other employees sick. These Typhoid Mary types who came to work anyway often had perfect attendance many years in a row. Often they were rewarded with a token of appreciation from MKM to recognize their dedication. Usually it was a pen, or a gift certificate redeemable at the local donut shop. Cam did not specifically make reference to Typhoid Mary types. Cam only said that sick employees were coming to work when they should be home and that they were making other employees sick.

Mostly sick employees came to work because they perceived themselves essential to the project that they were assigned to at the time. Without their presence all work would immediately grind to a halt because their piece of the project was absolutely critical to the overall project. And they believed the project delivery date absolutely could not slip. None of this was true. Work went on and project dates often changed when priorities changed, or now and then, although not often, management realized the delivery date that they had insisted on for a project was absurdly ambitious and unrealistic. And finally, no employee was crucial to any project. The annual round of employee cuts confirmed that no one was indispensable.

After the departmental meeting with Jo, Jordan invited Cam to a private meeting. Jordan raged that Cam was not to make such comments again because it reflected badly on Jordan's department. Jordan was notorious for coming to work when he was sick. He often claimed that he didn't get sick with a cold or the flu. In reality, he got sick like everyone else, but he chose to deny it and eventually he came to believe the lie himself.

A few days after the departmental meeting, a memo from the EO director reminded employees that sick employees were to stay home. In her memo the director instructed that managers, including Jordan, were to repeat this message at their next departmental meeting, which they dutifully did. Cam felt that he had achieved a small victory, but had paid a price. Jordan didn't make the connection between the message from EO and Cam's comment about people coming to work sick.

Jordan begins. "How was your meeting with Ed last week?"

"Fine," Cam answers. "We talked about the script for the next TV ad. Ed had a few suggestions. I said I would do my best to work them into the script. I pointed out that a couple of the ideas didn't seem to fit very well with the current focus of the commercial. The ad might lose its direction if we try to include too many ideas. I said that we should maintain the existing focus, unless of course Ed wanted to take a new tack. Why do you ask?"

Jordan ignores Cam's question and digs deeper. "So you didn't say no to Ed's ideas?" The unwritten rule is that you don't say no to Ed, or to anyone for that matter, whatever the request. Instead you discuss the request in a kind of crab-shuffle hoedown. Without foaming at the mouth, you provide seemingly rational reasons as to why the request is utterly impossible. You allow the requester to discover for himself what a flight of fancy the request was in the first place.

"No, I didn't. I did send you an e-mail outlining Ed's new ideas and what happened in the meeting."

"Do you know how many e-mails I get in a day?" says Jordan raising his voice slightly. "I don't have time to read every e-mail I get. Come and see me when you have something important." Jordan pauses to allow this to sink in. Anything that made it clear that Jordan did not know all the facts irritated him. In the role of omniscient god-like manager being, he was expected to know everything. At times he would lash out to throw you off balance to regain control. Cam had seen this method used by other managers, although it seemed to be dying out as a management tool. Jordan on the other hand held firm to this method. It was Jordan's way of trying to control the situation to his advantage. It was your fault that he didn't know.

Cam wonders how many years Jordan has used this tactic and if Jordan is even aware that he is using it to control the situation. Cam concludes that the ploy is now so interwoven in Jordan's DNA that he uses it automatically when he feels cornered, threatened, or out of touch, which is most of the time if Jordan were to admit it. Probably he learned this gambit long ago when he was a kid. Now the maneuver is part of the orthodoxy of his management style: when in doubt, run about scream and shout.

Recovering himself slightly, Jordan continues, "Did Ed say anything else?"

"No, mostly we talked about the commercial. He seemed satisfied with the progress. He understood my concerns. He asked me to do the best I could. I said I would."

"What ideas does he want added?" asks Jordan.

"He talked about family, loyalty, belonging, in that vein."

"Was anyone else in the meeting?"

"No one, only Ed and myself."

"Was Yaz there?"

Ah! Now it begins to make sense thinks Cam to himself when he realizes the source of his discussion with Jordan. Cam wonders why Jordan doesn't come directly to the point instead of this zigzag approach that he habitually follows. Cam decides that Jordan's strategy is another warped convention that Jordan uses to manipulate.

"Yaz came in about half way through the meeting. He had a brief conversation with Ed about an urgent matter and then left."

"How long was your meeting with Ed?" Jordan asks.

"I'm not sure, about ten or fifteen minutes."

There is a pause while Jordan thinks about the import of this and then continues his interrogation. "You're not sure?"

"Fifteen minutes at the most, possibly less."

"How long was Yaz in the room?"

"A couple of minutes, not long," Cam replies.

"Yaz stopped me in the hallway today. He said that you refused to add Ed's ideas to the commercial. He said that in the meeting you didn't want to include Ed's ideas in the next commercial. Yaz thought I should know."

"No, that's not right," Cam replies firmly. "Yaz may have overheard part of our discussion when he entered the room. I told Ed that I would do my best to work his ideas into the commercial, although it wouldn't be easy for the reasons I've already stated. Yaz wasn't there long enough to know all the details of the discussion." There is a pause while Jordan takes this in. Cam adds, "You can ask Ed."

This last statement is Cam's trump card. He knows that Jordan will not ask Ed, although Cam has no objection if Jordan chooses to ask Ed. Whenever Jordan must send an e-mail to anyone higher in the organization, he agonizes over the e-mail for hours or even days while he crafts the e-mail to convey precisely the right message. He doesn't want to offend or appear ignorant of various aspect of a situation.

Jordan once shared a draft of one of these e-mails with Cam before Jordan was ready to send it to his boss. Cam suspected that Jordan's real motive was to show Cam how brilliant he, Jordan, was. Cam had had to read the e-mail several times to make any sense of it. The sentences seemed similar to the double helix of long complex strands of DNA formed through the intricate interaction of verbs, adverbs, nouns, adjectives and other grammatical parts of speech that acted in the same way as nucleotides. The e-mail never seemed to come to a point as far as Cam could tell. Cam doubted that Jordan's boss, who had little understanding of writers and their role, would understand Jordan's e-mail. Cam made a few polite comments to help improve the message, knowing that making too many critical comments would not be viewed favorably by Jordan and would probably result in a poor review for Cam at his annual performance review.

"Well, thanks for clarifying that. There's been a miscommunication." says Jordan, referring to his hallway conversation with Yaz.

Yaz is famous for his hallway conversations. He conveys only enough information from the tatters of overheard conversations to appear informed and concerned.

"How are the revisions coming along to the commercial?"

"Just fine, I've managed to work most of Ed's ideas into the commercial and still maintain the focus. There are a couple of ideas that I'm having trouble with. I have a meeting with Ed later this week. If I can't fit all of his ideas in, I'll raise it with him at the meeting and see what he thinks."

"Well, if you need help, let me know," says Jordan. "Remember; don't spend too much time on it." Jordan never wants Cam, or any writer for that matter, spending more time than is absolutely necessary on any project. Jordan is always anxious to start writers on the next project. "I don't want you polishing shit," adds Jordan with a thin-lipped smile. "Get the job done and move on. Okay?"

There is a pause and then Jordan continues in a new vein, "I've noticed that you've stopped participating in the department meetings. You used to participate and had a number of good insights to share. Is there a reason why you've stopped?"

Cam pauses while he thinks of an acceptable answer. Jordan is right. Cam has stopped participating. He's had too many private chats with Jordan. Cam wants to say, yes, of course I've stopped participating in the department meetings. What did you expect after all these little chats we've had about comments that I've made in your department meetings? Are you industrial strength stupid? Cam can feel his anger beginning to rise. However, Cam knows that this is not the right answer even if he were to couch it in more diplomatic language. 'I say old bean. Bit of a sticky wicket that. You have a nasty habit of giving me a good hiding in our little *chats* after I've made an innocuous comment in one of your interminable department meetings. Not quite cricket you know. Not playing the game, is it? Damn nuisance really. There's a good chap. You stop giving me a good hiding every time I say something constructive in one of your damnable meetings and I'll start participating again. Shall we have tea?'

Every so often in his thoughts Cam falls into this pseudo British voice as he imagines how two seasoned Victorian British diplomats might have spoken when discussing the latest crisis in India, or other distant colonial outpost. Cam pictures them at their club sitting in their high wing-backed Victorian chairs. In the room a clock, sitting on a mantel, ticks quietly away and then respectfully chimes the hour as though asking for permission to continue ticking. Cam visualizes the two diplomats simultaneously looking at their gold pocket watches to check that the clock is correct. They are satisfied to discover that yes indeed all is right with the world. Cam associates England with civility and diplomacy, but he wonders how many poor buggers in distant lands paid for the chiming of the clock; English civility and diplomacy being a mask for the pointy end of a stick that is empire building and then holding on to empire. It must be hard to let go even when you have so much and the other bugger has so little. And after all, why should you let go? You've done very well by this one-sided arrangement. What price was paid for the chiming of the clock and by whom?

Cam draws his wayward thoughts back to the task at hand. Where is Jordan going with this question? What's he really after here? Jordan's attempt to find the truth resembles a game of hide and seek in a room full of mirrors where everyone must hide in plain view. What trap is Jordan setting this time? This kind of question-and-answer conversation is a twisted Socratic Method that would have Socrates rolling over in his grave.

"Yes, you're right," says Cam knowing there's no point denying it. "I have been quiet. I haven't had much to say. I've been busy with my projects," Cam adds, bending the truth. His projects have kept him busy, but not too busy to contribute to Jordan's meetings if Cam thought his comments would not lead to more chats. "I'll make an effort to contribute at the next meeting," Cam forces a smile, knowing that he will make what he hopes are the most harmless of comments at the next department meeting. Jordan seems satisfied with this answer.

"Do you know about the sweater?" asks Jordan.

"The sweater?" Cam queries feigning ignorance.

"Yes, the sweater."

Cam knows about the coveted purple, button-down sweater. Jordan has told Cam this story many times before, as he has told many other writers in his department. After each telling Jordan forgets that he has told Cam the story. It is better to play along and let Jordan tell the story because he loves to tell it.

"The sweater," begins Jordan, "is awarded to an employee who is instrumental in making a significant contribution to the advancement of the corporation in an area of endeavor that spans one or more company divisions whether in the realm of film, sports, cable, or other MKM division. The sweater is the recognition of a sustained contribution by an employee over many years of service. Few are awarded this honor. In the thirty year history of MKM, only three employees have received this award. The sweater is a mark of respect that recognizes the contribution made by the employee. All of us have the potential to earn this sweater and the great honor that goes with it." Jordan's eyes have this glazed look as he imagines receiving the coveted sweater, which was once a coveted leather jacket until an MKM accountant discovered in a time of austerity that best-in-class companies offered only a not-so-coveted sweater. The bouts of austerity seemed to occur in predictable yearly cycles at MKM.

Cam knows where this conversation is heading. Once, to reward the employees, the head of Cam's division had arranged an afternoon of entertainment at a local theater for the entire division. The company had arranged bus transportation to the theater for everyone. A singer was waiting to entertain. Prior to the singer's performance, presentations were made to employees who had contributed to the success of the company in the previous year. There were awards for everything from perfect attendance, to saving the company lots of money, to going above and beyond what was required to make a difficult customer happy.

Usually in this last instance the customer was unhappy because MKM had made a bad business decision that meant the customer did not receive what was promised. The make-a-difficult-customer-happy award required long hours of hard work and great personal sacrifice on the part of the recipient. The award was never called the make-a-difficult-customer-happy award because the name might draw attention to the bumbling at MKM that led to the many hours of overtime and personal sacrifice in the first place. Instead the award might be called something like the most-improved-project award. Cam enjoyed thinking of the award as the pulled-another-one-out-of-the-fire award. Often it was the individual who had created the problem in the first place who won the award.

Awards ranged from small gift certificates to company-sponsored trips to exotic places around the world where the employee would represent the division. The employee was wined and dined and generally allowed to have a good time and get lots of recognition during ceremonies similar to the one organized for the division.

Finally on that awards day, there were two awards left for presentation. Both awards were special: one was awarded to an employee who had risen from the lowest rank in the division to become one of the senior employees in the division and had made many fine contributions along the way; the second award was to an employee who had made many significant contributions to the company over many years and was to be honored with a sweater. All of the employees agreed that the awarding of the sweater was far above any other award because the sweater represented the pinnacle of achievement within the corporation.

To honor the employee who had ascended high in the ranks of management from her early filing-clerk days when filing clerks still existed, it was arranged that the recipient's mother would speak about her child. The employee's proud mother spoke from her prepared notes for fifteen minutes about her child's determination, strength of will and character. During the speech, the audience became restless until finally the speech ended and the employee was awarded a large crystal bowl with Maple Key Media ornately engraved on the side. The proud employee then spoke for five minutes about what a great honor it was to receive the bowl. About six months later, the employee left the corporation for a more lucrative job with a rival company.

Then it was time to award the sweater. The winner, whom Jordan knew, was announced. The recipient donned the sweater, which fit well. Speeches were given that in total lasted less than five minutes.

Then the singer entertained the audience with a medley of songs including jazz, rock and roll, sacred songs, country and western, and modern classics. Cam found himself close to tears when the singer sang *Non, Je Ne Regrette Rien* in the style of Edith Piaf. Cam didn't know why this song always got to him. The song always managed to touch something inside him. And although he didn't know what it touched or why, he had his suspicions. When the singer was finished, everyone got back on the buses and returned to their cubicles at MKM headquarters.

"One day," says Jordan, "I expect to have one of those sweaters, but to get it I need your help and the help of everyone in the department for that matter. You know of course, I have much more experience than anyone else in the department. I've seen it all. I'm so far above everyone else in this department in terms of knowledge and experience that sharing what I know is difficult because others have difficulty understanding. So, here I am, Jordan Mere." There's a pause. "When the student is ready, the master appears."

Cam is sure that this last sentence about the master is from a book of Zen Buddhist sayings that Jordan has read and then twisted to interpret from his own mangled perspective. To get people thinking outside of the box, Jordan, as an exercise, would quote koans. "What is the sound of one hand clapping?" he would say to the hapless victim who hadn't had the good sense to escape before it was too late. Then Jordan would provide his own unique interpretation without waiting for an answer. He always insisted the sound of one hand clapping is the sound that your shirt sleeve makes while your hand flails through the air in a clapping motion. No amount of discussion could make him change his mind. Eventually, most of his staff learned not to get involved in such mind-twisting discussions with him. It became routine to warn new staff not to argue Jordan's interpretation of koans.

One new writer when presented with the one-hand-clapping koan by Jordan as a test to see if the new employee could think outside the box and to show the writer how clever Jordan was, had parried, "Does the tiger eat its young?" Intuitively the writer seemed to understand Jordan. Jordan didn't seem to understand at the time what was meant by the writer's response. Shortly after, the writer was fired during one of MKM's purges when things weren't going well for the corporation. Employees speculated that for once Jordan may have managed to properly interpret a koan and he didn't like the answer.

"So, here I am," Jordan continued. "What can I do to help you to perform better, so that one day MKM will award me a sweater?"

To Cam this question is not a koan, but it may as well be a koan. There is no correct answer in this case, unlike a koan. Here we go again, thinks Cam. Old one-hand flailing is at it again. "Well," begins Cam, testing the waters "I could use a second computer monitor. I can work faster if I can display two documents at the same time without having to switch back and forth the way I do now because I have only one monitor."

There is a pause. "You're not thinking big enough," Jordan replies with a touch of impatience in his voice. "At a department level, what can be done? Think bigger," he encourages. Jordan knows that to impress those higher in the organization he must do something that has visibility in all management levels in the division.

"Okay," replies Cam who feels that he is beginning to sink. "How about giving everyone in the department a second computer monitor, so that we can all work more efficiently?"

Jordan rolls his eyes. "You're not getting the idea," Jordan replies with a slight measure of annoyance. He begins to fidget in his chair having not got the answer he wants.

Cam envisions a special circle of hell reserved especially for managers in the screwed up mold of Jordan. "Why don't I think about it," Cam answers calmly while he desperately grasps for anything that will save him from sinking further. "I'll drop by your cubicle when I think of something," Cam volunteers in a moment of inspiration. He knows that Jordan will forget Cam's commitment to drop by later. Cam knows too that he will also never see a second monitor.

"No," answers Jordan testily. "E-mail me anything important. Write it down," he adds for emphasis. "That way I'm sure to get it. The idea won't get lost," says Jordan nodding his head confidently to add emphasis to this last demand. Jordan smiles a polished smile below his pencil mustache.

There is a pause in the conversation. Each tries to think of what to say next. The meeting seems to have reached an end. Then Jordan blurts out, "you're fired. Now get back to work." This is his attempt to end the meeting on a positive note. Jordan in his warped way is telling Cam that he is doing a good job. However, since MKM is notorious for its annual purging of employees, usually a month or so before Christmas, and given the difficult economic times, this is not what Cam or any employee wants to hear. Cam smiles politely and says nothing. "Oh you know I'm only joking" says Jordan rolling his eyes. "Where's your sense of humor? Don't be so serious," Jordan smiles warmly to cover his tracks when he realizes his joke has not gone over well. A few employees have objected to EO about his joke. Now he doesn't use it as often and never in the presence of more than one employee.

Cam returns to his cubicle to waste the day pondering the significance of the meeting.

Thtttttt-squeak, thtttttt-squeak. Thtttttt-squeak.

While Cam sits at his desk he can hear the sound of the door to the men's washroom when it opens and closes. His cubicle is separated from the washroom only by the width of the aisle way between the cubicle and the door. He hears thttttt-squeak each time someone pushes the washroom door open to enter or leave the washroom. The door rubs, thtttttt, and then squeaks against the door frame when the door opens. Cam has asked the maintenance department to fix the door. His requests are ignored.

Flsshhhh, nnnnnnn, flsshhhh, nnnnnnn, flsshhhh, nnnnnnn. Sometime after thttttt-squeak, fsshhhh announces that a co-worker has finished his business and flushed either a toilet or a urinal. Nnnnnnn tells Cam that somewhere in the washroom walls a valve has opened and more water is filling the depleted reservoir used by the toilets and urinals when a colleague flushes.

Tock. Tock tells Cam that an associate has finished washing his hands. Tock is the sound made when the associate pushes down the metal tap handle on a sink faucet, causing the handle to strike the top of the faucet assembly and stop the flow of water. Tock says the faucet with confidence.

Rrrrrrrchtt, rrrrrrrchtt, rrrrrrrchtt, snap, fffffffft informs Cam that an employee is dispensing paper towelling from the dispenser to dry his hands. The paper towelling sits in a smoke-colored, sound-amplifying, plastic housing mounted on the washroom wall. When the operator of the dispenser pushes down on a spring-loaded plastic lever on the front of the dispenser housing, the action causes metal cogs to rotate and rubber rollers on metal rods to turn the roll of paper towelling in the dispenser and the dispenser to regurgitate towelling. With each ratcheting of the lever, rrrrrrrchtt, the

53

dispenser spits out a measured amount of paper towel. On the final downward push, the operator releases the lever at the bottom of the lever's stroke, causing the lever to snap back to the top of its stroke, snap. Rrrrrrchtt, rrrrrrrchtt, rrrrrrrchtt, snap says the dispenser each time it dispenses paper towelling. The sound made by the dispenser resonates in the plastic housing. The sound is further amplified as it careens off the tiling on the washroom walls, making the sound carry as far as Cam's cubicle. Then the operator of the dispenser tears off the dispensed towelling from the roll, ffffffft.

Vibrating at a frequency that Cam cannot hear, occasionally an odor escapes from the washroom. The odor is silent, but deadly. The smell lingers and then dissipates, helped by the air vent in the ceiling above Cam's cubicle.

Sssssssssssssssssss, sssslurp, sssslurp, sssslurp, whrrrrrrrrrrrrRRRRR, thunk, thunk. There is a water fountain mounted on the wall in the aisle way, next to the washroom door. Cam hears sssssssssssssssssss when a co-worker dispenses water to fill a water bottle, or to drink sssslurp, sssslurp, sssslurp. This activity is followed by a short pause, and then whrrrrrrrrrrrrRRRRR that grows in intensity. A pump in the refrigeration unit of the fountain kicks in to keep the water cold in the fountain reservoir. When the required water temperature is achieved, the pump stops with a shudder, thunk, thunk, announcing that the pump has finished its job for the moment. By the end of the day, the pump sounds tired and begins to protest; the

whrrrrrrrrrrrRRRRR grows louder and the thunk, thunk more pronounced.

Wwwwhhhhhhhhhhhhhhhhhhhhhh. On the roof a ventilation motor automatically cuts in and drives a fan that pushes air through the ducting. Wwwhhhhhhhhhhhhhhhhhhhhhhh whispers the air as it is expelled from the vent in the ceiling above Cam's cubicle. The once white ceiling tiles intended to dampen noise have grown dingy and black from the air pushed from the vent. Wwwwhhhhhhhhhhhhhhhhhhhhh says the vent.

Because the washrooms and fountain are popular spots, often there are impromptu aisle-way conversations and meetings while employees share bits of information. "I need a couple more players to firm up the third line for our hockey team. Are you interested in playing?" asks an employee, who is hidden from Cam by the cubicle wall. Bless me Father Cam for I have sinned, imagines Cam as though hearing a confession. I'm short players for the third line.

"I'd like to play, but don't know if I can make it," replies the other unseen participant.

"I really need you there for the first game until I see how we're doing. It would help if you can make it."

"Okay, I'll try to make it."

Click click. Clickety-click tap tap.

Thtttttt-squeak, thtttttt-squeak.

Wwwwhhhhhhhhhhhhhhhhhhhhh.

Rrrrrrrchtt, rrrrrrrchtt, rrrrrrrchtt, snap, fffffffft.

Sssssssssssssssssss sssslurp, sssslurp, sssslurp.

Flsshhhh, nnnnnnn.

WhrrrrrrrrrrrRRRRR, thunk, thunk.

Sssssssssssssssssssss.

Tock.

4 Orky Don't Take No Shit

Murmur, murmur, murmur whisper the walls in an undercurrent of jazz to anyone who chooses to listen. Cam sits in the anteroom adjacent to Ed's office. The tunes are meant to create a relaxing atmosphere as employees kill time while waiting to see Ed. The walls whisper Duke Ellington's rendition of *Money Jungle*, which is not having the intended soothing effect. Cam doesn't recognize the tune. He wishes the walls would hum something he knows, *Take Five*, for example.

The anteroom is spacious and tastefully decorated in a modern motif. Ed's second wife redecorated the room when she learned that Ed's first wife had decorated it first. Ed is between wives right now. Several paintings hang on the walls. These are reproductions. In one picture a large maple tree sits in a field. A simple metal-pipe fence cuts between the tree and the viewer. Cam's eyes follow the fence to the tree.

A jumble of plants of various types and heights are scattered throughout the room. There is a forest of giant ferns in one corner of the room. In another corner an anaconda-sized vine spills from a washtub-sized pot, weaves its way down a plant stand to the floor and threads its way along the base of a wall. A third gargantuan plant has blue flowers the size of dinner plates. A small bonsai sits on Yaz's desk. Yaz is Ed's personal secretary. As far as Cam can tell, Yaz seems oblivious to the bonsai and the other vegetation.

There are many other plants to give the room color and the illusion of life.

When Cam saw these plants on his first visit to see Ed, he had thought the plants were real. It was only on his second visit to see Ed that Cam realized that the plants were artificial. He discovered this when a small butterfly with black and orange-tipped wings found its way into the office. It was flying around the room ignoring the plants. Yaz didn't notice the butterfly. When Cam looked more closely at the flowers, he realized that he had been fooled, unlike the butterfly. Ed's second wife had wanted to use real plants, but the cost to feed and prune was not in the budget. After a short marriage, Ed and his second wife parted company citing irreconcilable differences.

Yaz sits behind his desk, staring intently at his computer monitor. Occasionally, there is the click of the mouse and then the clickety-click of the keys on the computer keyboard as Yaz types.

"What's that tune?" asks Cam.

"Tune?" asks Yaz who stopped listening to the music long ago.

As part of Ed's second wife's redecorating effort, she had an audio system installed that included hidden wall speakers. No one is sure where the audio system resides. It is thought to be in a basement room of the building. No one has bothered to investigate exactly where the room might be. Most people simply tune out the music. A few who hear the music while waiting in the room enjoy it and comment to Yaz on the fantastic jazz selection. Yaz replicates a smile in response.

Sometimes Yaz is startled to hear the music. When this happens, he makes a mental note to himself to see if he can have the music turned off. Then he stops listening again and forgets that he has made a note to himself, so the music continues humming happily in the walls. The selection of tunes changes daily. No one is sure how this is done. The

57

daily changing of tunes is as mysterious as the source of the music.

Money Jungle ends. Another tune, *Jabberwocky*, begins. Cam doesn't recognize this tune either. "What about this one?" Cam jerks his head in the direction of a wall. "Do you know this one?"

"No" answers Yaz, shaking his head. "I don't. Do you know it?" asks Yaz his eyes darting with a quick glance in the direction of the wall while his head remains bolted, facing the computer monitor.

"No" shrugs Cam. "I thought you might know. Is there a playlist?"

"Nooo," whispers Yaz. He slowly shakes his head while maintaining his focus on the monitor. Yaz is perplexed. He scratches his goatee. He laces his fingers on top of his head and continues staring at the computer monitor, lost in the details on the screen. His wire-rim glasses reflect the light from the monitor.

"Are you familiar with ProSidios?" asks Yaz.

"Yes, I use it."

"Do you know how to create a new file?"

"Yes. Which version?"

"What? Where?"

"Click Help, About ProSidios, version."

"Where?"

"At the top."

"Kay."

"Which version?"

"2.1.178 Pro."

"Click Close. Click Open, Tools, Magic, More Magic, Super Magic," commands Cam.

"What?"

"Open, Tools, Magic, More Magic, Super Magic."

"Magic?"

"Yup, Magic, More Magic, then Super Magic."

"Kay."

"Click Insert, New."

"Where?"

"Top right."

"Oh."

"Type a file name, but don't press Return."

"Error 3498763," answers Yaz, his frustration starting to show.

"It's a bug. Click Super Magic, Save."

"Yup."

"Refresh."

"Refresh?"

"Refresh."

"How do I...?" The question trails off.

"Press F5, or View Refresh."

"F5? Where is...?"

"Top of the keyboard."

"Oh. Good. Thanks."

The walls stop humming. There's a short pause. The walls start humming an instrumental, jazz rendition of a tune.

"Oh, I know this one," says Cam, "*Mairzy doats.*" He smiles, happy that he has finally recognized a tune. Cam sings along to himself as best he can. He remembers only a smattering of the words.

Yaz stares at the screen.

"You can go in now."

"Pardon?"

"Edward."

"Yes?" asks Cam uncertain what they are talking about.

"He'll see you."

"Now?"

"Yup, now."

"Oh, okay thanks."

Cam does a quick shuffle step in time with the music as he walks to Ed's office. Yaz does not notice. His eyes are fixed on the computer monitor.

Cam knocks on the door and quietly enters Ed's office, leaving the music behind. Ed stands at the opposite side of the room with his back to Cam. Ed is wearing his usual black business suit. His head sits on top of the suit. With arms akimbo, Ed looks out the giant floor-to-ceiling windows that stretch the entire length of two walls in his corner office. The windows are tinted a light shade of sea green.

On one wall opposite one of the window walls is an array of flat-screen televisions that fill the entire wall. All of the televisions are on and each is set to a different channel. There is no sound coming from the TVs. Many of the shows Cam recognizes. On one channel, Larry Talbot, who isn't pure of heart even though he says his prayers at night, is busy changing into the wolf man when the wolf bane blooms and the autumn moon shines bright. Poor Larry thinks Cam. What chance does he have? He's doomed to transform into the wolf man every time someone runs the movie.

Then Cam realizes that the signal is also beaming into outer space where it will wander for all time. Cam wonders what aliens might think of the film if they happened to pick up the signal billions of years from now. Maybe they'd understand, or maybe not. Probably they'd simply scratch their collective heads or bums, or other part of their anatomy if they have anatomy. Will they understand? Will it matter to us if they understand? No doubt our civilization is long gone by the time the aliens see this film footage. By the time the aliens pick up the signal, our sun has run out of energy, expanded and consumed the earth.

Most likely there will be an alien university where aliens specialize in the study of earth mythology. Perhaps they'd think that Larry caught rabies or another dreaded disease, or Larry is in the wrong place at the wrong time if the aliens subscribe to such notions, or Larry being Larry can't help himself. An alien professor will write a paper about the earthling's dilemma and another alien professor will write a

paper with a different slant on the wolf-man thing and then
another professor will write whatever and then another
professor and another and the whole thing will become
muddled because they can't ask anyone from earth what
was going on because the earth is long gone and even if they
could ask, they'd get a thousand different answers. An alien
professor from the biology department might argue that
people turning into werewolves is the natural condition for
all earthlings.

On another channel, a team of upbeat and friendly talk-
show hosts take turns smiling, laughing and talking to
guests. One of the hosts, Zanya, is a rising star at MKM.
There are rumors that she will have her own show soon.

Another channel shows team members on a game show.
They are voting which member of the team to kick off the
team and out of the game. There is lots of money at stake
and so there is lots of strategizing by the team members who
seem willing to do almost anything to win. Winning is
everything.

Kicking a player off a team reminds Cam of choosing
sides for a game when he was a kid. There was always one
kid that no one wanted on their team. One of the teams
would have to pick the kid in the end. No one liked being
picked last. In Cam's kid days it was Ronald who had no
athletic ability and didn't have much going for him. Poor
Ronald thinks Cam. What chance did he have?

Elsewhere on several other channels, Dr. David
Bowman is falling into the mysterious black monolith. Well
at least he made it thinks Cam.

There are too many images for Cam to follow.

At the remaining wall in Ed's office is a buffet that looks
largely untouched. There is a wealth of dips, sauces, soups,
crackers, sandwiches, vegetables, and desserts. Ed has a
buffet laid on every day for senior-staff members who often
meet with Ed over the lunch hour. There is an unwritten rule
that the lunch is for senior employees only. Those of lower

rank are warned by their managers before meeting with Ed not to touch the buffet. Cam sees the buffet as a sorcerer's spell: eat from the buffet and something evil will happen. You'll fall into a deep sleep where your career languishes unless a brave manager stumbles across your plight and is willing to risk all to resurrect you. There are very few managers who are brave enough. They're too busy trying not to get kicked off the team. Within MKM, Ed's buffet is known as the poison-apple buffet. Rumor has it that the last Joe employee to trespass was kicked off the team in a subsequent purge during a downturn in the economy. You couldn't link his being kicked off the team to the buffet incident, but many Joe employees thought there was no sense in taking chances. Others thought eating from the buffet and getting fired was merely superstition, but even they would not eat from the buffet. Why take a chance? And so the myth of the poison-apple buffet persists.

"Have a seat Cam," sounds Ed's voice from across the room. Ed continues to look out the window.

Cam sits down in one of the chairs that faces Ed's desk. He sinks into the soft leather padding. The chair is a kind of art deco club chair. If Cam cranes his neck, he can nearly see the top of Ed's desk. Cam twists slightly in the chair to look in Ed's direction. His view of Ed is obstructed by a large aquarium between Cam and Ed. The aquarium has a sickly greenish hue, the color of the windows in Ed's office.

Ed breeds fancy goldfish. Cam watches the fish for a while, hoping to catch a glimpse of Ed between the fish and the curtain of rising bubbles that hang across the back of the tank. The goldfish wiggle their bodies to move lazily through the water. Their long flowing fins are delicate and too weak to propel them with any efficiency. Most of the goldfish are various shades of gold with the exception of one, a Black Moor, which is black with a metallic-gold belly. Cam learned its name on one of his visits with Ed, who takes pleasure in educating people about the world around them by offering them tiny flakes of information. Like the other fish, the Black Moor has large protruding eyes. It is constantly bumping into things. All the fish have poor eyesight in spite of their large eyes.

So, Cam, what do you think?" asks Ed's disembodied voice, "Can you make water flow uphill?" There is a pause. "No pumps or mechanical devices of any kind and no optical trickery of any kind; can you make water flow uphill?" Ed continues to look out the window with his back to Cam.

Another koan groans Cam to himself. What's the answer to this one? What's he looking for here? Why can't people simply speak straight? "No, I don't think so," Cam answers although an answer is not really required. He answers out of deference to Ed's authority and out of politeness to acknowledge that Ed has asked a question and that he, Cam, is listening.

Ed continues to look out the window, while seeming to ignore Cam's response.

"Do you know what I can see from here?" continues Ed who seems to have veered onto a new topic.

Cam cannot see what Ed is looking at. He knows that an answer is not expected. He could respond if he wanted to, but this is Ed's play so best to shut up and listen. Cam watches the fish bump around in the aquarium. The fish remind him of the little bumper cars that you can drive around in on the midway when the fall fair comes to town.

Cam imagines Larry Talbot as the wolf man driving around in a bumper car. Larry snarls, snaps and growls at anyone who bumps into his car. There is panic and confusion. The other drivers scream in fright, pee their pants and try to get away from Larry as fast as they can. Other cars bump into their cars in a chain reaction. This only makes the wolf man angrier. The whole thing is a big shemozzle with snarling, snapping, growling, screaming, and the smell of fear. Everyone is afraid that the wolf man is going to leap out of his bumper car and bite one of them and turn the casualty into a wolf man.

No one wants to be a wolf man because they've seen the movie. They know that eventually somebody with a silver bullet, or silver dagger or silver cane will shoot, stab, or beat to death the wolf man who at this point is simply trying to get away from all the craziness. The wolf man knows that somewhere out there, there's someone with a thingamajig made out of silver that has his name on it, and he can't get away. He's trapped too.

"You needn't get up to look. I'll tell you," says Ed. He pauses to reflect on what to say next. "I see people," he begins "lots of people going about their lives." There's another long pause and then, "Have you ever watched *Invasion of the Body Snatchers*? I mean the nineteen fifties version, not the imitations that came later; the ones that didn't know what they were doing. Do you know the original movie?"

Cam is relieved. He's seen this movie. "Yes, there are pod things from outer space. They're like vegetables. If you fall asleep near one, the pod takes on your shape and then the pod takes over. The victim dies or is consumed. I'm not sure which. Then the..."

"Yes, that's the one," Ed interjects. "The story is set in a middle-class suburb. The pod people look the same as real people, except they're dead inside. The pod people work together. They transform the humans into pod people one at a time. A human goes to sleep and never wakes up. Soon most of the people in the community are pod people. Then the pod people start to spread to other communities. But the hero of the film hasn't given in. He's still human. He desperately tries to warn other people that the pod people are coming. Stay on your guard he warns if you don't want to be turned into vegetables. Don't fall asleep. If you do fall asleep, wake up before you're overwhelmed. Don't acquiesce. Don't give in. You have to be vigilant at all times." Ed pauses, thinking about what to say next. Silence fills the room.

Cam waits patiently. He watches the curtain of bubbles in the fish tank. The bubbles have a relaxing effect. The heat from the wall of TVs has raised the room temperature to sleepy warm. Cam's eyelids begin to close. His head begins to droop.

"Mostly people think the film is about the threat of communism at the start of the cold war," Ed continues startling Cam. "And it is in a way, but there's more to it than solely communism. Do you know what the film is about?"

"I've never really thought about it," Cam responds shaking off his drowsiness.

"Well, I'll tell you," says Ed turning toward Cam. "Listen carefully. It's about..." Abruptly Ed's train of thought is interrupted when he glances at the bank of televisions on the wall. Ed walks immediately to his desk. He turns on the volume to one of the televisions where a talk show host is interviewing a guest. Ed stares intently through the thick lenses of his black-rimmed glasses. He listens carefully for a moment. Then he mutes the television. "Just a minute," says Ed without looking at Cam. "I have to make a phone call. This won't take long. Stay where you are. Are you hungry? Have some food," says Ed, smiling and gesturing toward the buffet. Cam smiles uneasily. He makes no attempt to visit the buffet.

Ed picks up the phone and dials a number. "Hello," says Ed. "This is Edward. Put Phil on." Cam recognizes the name. Phil is the director of the talk show that Ed is watching. "Hey Phil, what's going on down there? Why is Jim off message? Why isn't he sticking to the talking points?" Cam can't hear the answer. "You tell Jim to stick to the talking points or he'll be back where I found him doing the Orky show with his hand up Orky's ass!" snaps Ed. "I don't want to hear anymore about his claim to artistic license! He doesn't even rate a dog license! He has the

65

creativity of a turnip! You're the director! You tell him to stick to the script!" snarls Ed.

Ed is referring to a popular kid's television show, Orky the Orca. Orky is a hand puppet and the star of the show. All the little kids love him. Orky has many adventures and there is always a message to the adventure, in the same way that Aesop's fables have messages about how you should behave. Generally Orky's message is about telling the truth and telling kids not to do bad stuff, for example bullying other people, because there's a thingamajig made out of silver out there with your name on it and this thingamajig is going to hurt really badly when it comes knocking. Orky doesn't actually talk about thingamajigs. Orky talks about consequences.

In the early days when Ed had scarcely begun to build his entertainment empire, Ed would actually follow through on his threat to banish a host to the Orky the Orca show. Unfortunately Ed's banish-a-host punishment ended badly when one of the banished hosts in the voice of Orky threw a hissy fit during an Orky the Orca show. Shows in those days were broadcast live. The former host was distraught and angry at his demotion, so he decided to say what was on his mind through Orky. He told the kids that they were lost or soon would be and bad things would happen to them, and Orky was a crock of shit, and there was no hope for them even if they tried to save themselves.

The other puppet characters on the show, Clatterbelle Clam in particular, tried to get Orky to shut up. Clatterbelle Clam tried to shout down Orky by yelling as loud as only Clatterbelle Clam could to drown out Orky's equally loud rant. It was too late to stop the banished host.

Unofficially within MKM the incident became known as Orky Don't Take No Shit. No one was brave enough to use this phrase in Ed's presence. After all, Orky the Orca was the first television series that Ed ever launched at MKM. He was very proud of his baby.

At the time of the incident, Ed was surprised and then angry by the on-air betrayal of the former television host. Prior to this incident, Ed had exiled other hosts in the same way. When Ed later reinstated them as televisions hosts, they always seemed more humble, having learned their lesson. In reality, the reinstated hosts were not humbled at all. Instead, they practised deception to appear humble for the sake of their careers, their house mortgages, their annual vacations to the mountains, or whatever else they held dear in their hearts.

The kids who watched the episode where Orky went ballistic were confused and upset for about a week before they forgot about the incident. Lots of kids peed their pants while watching the episode. This embarrassed the kids' parents. Lots of parents worried that the Orky episode had set back the potty training of their kids. Many kids never watched the show again. Parents wrote angry letters to MKM in which they talked about law suits. The talk of law suits blew over when Ed brought the stage adaptation of Orky Goes to Hollywood to Bayview at considerable expense to MKM. Ed let the kids in for free. Parents had to pay for their own tickets. Ed made sure the parents paid a premium price.

There were lots of valuable lessons for kids and parents in the Orky the Orca episode. For example, the kids learned that peeing your pants could have its rewards. The parents learned that the price of freedom, as witnessed by the ticket prices for parents, was high, but worth it if the kids learned that standing up for your rights was important when you're made to pee your pants. The rebellious former television host learned that telling the truth was not always understood or appreciated. Ed fired him immediately at the end of the show's episode.

Ed learned too. He no longer banished television hosts to the Orky the Orca show. Instead he simply fired them if they misbehaved too often by not sticking to the script. As well, Ed made every employee take an oath every year not to do bad things during a show that would be expensive or embarrassing to MKM. The oath began like this: 'Whereas the party of the first part, herein after known as the employee, shall not do, say, think or imply either verbally or through physical gestures or by any means express opinions that might be construed in any way as injurious to the good name of Maple Key Media, MKM, the party of the second part.' The oath went on for several pages. Essentially each employee had to acknowledge in the oath that if he or she did something that MKM construed as bad, MKM had every right to fire the employee on the spot with no questions asked. If you didn't take the yearly oath, you were fired immediately. All the senior executives and middle management took the oath seriously. The Joe employees thought the oath was a crock of shit. Secretly Orky Don't Take No Shit became the rallying cry of the Joe employees even though they took the oath too because they had mortgages or rent to pay, or something to pay.

The Orky incident was soon forgotten by MKM executives because it was embarrassing to the executives involved, in the same way that the kids who peed their pants were embarrassing to their parents.

Ed hangs up the phone. He continues, "I've seen a lot from up here and do you know what people want?" There's a pause while Ed lets the question sink in. "Do you know? I'll tell what they want. They want to love and to be loved. That's it! That's all! They just want to love and be loved. And people will do anything, absolutely anything for love even when they don't know what love is. And they will go to any lengths, any possible lengths to invent what love is if they don't know. And most of them don't know. A few find love and some find what they think is love, but it isn't. They want to touch it, smell it, run their fingers through it, swim in it, breath it, buy it, sell it, die for it, kill for it, lie, cheat and steal for it. They will deceive themselves and deceive others for it.

Anything! Anything! They will do absolutely anything for it!
They will conquer countries and continents in their search
for love. They will join sports clubs and bridge clubs and any
other club that you can invent. They will join political
parties; conservative, liberal, fascist, communist, or any
other party or ism you can dream up, or that somebody can
devise. They will join religious groups and non-religious
groups. They'll join the army, navy, air force or any other
military group that they can think of, or that someone else
can imagine for them, so that they belong and are loved. All
of this they do so that they belong to something or someone,
anyone, and can love others and be loved. But few of them
ever really find love. And do you know why they never find
it? Because they're looking in the wrong places and no one
can show it to them. Not you, nor I, nor anyone can show
them. Not any amount of talking, pointing, or showing will
help. And even if we could show them, they wouldn't
believe it." Ed pauses. "But we have to try. We have to try as
hard as we can." Ed pauses bringing his hand down hard
with a thud on his desk. "We are in a war to win hearts and
minds because there are those out there who will manipulate
and deceive people for their own selfish twisted love. And
we have to win at all costs. We have to save people from
themselves and if we can't save them, then at least we have
to give them values that they can use. Values they
desperately need like honor, loyalty, duty, devotion,
faithfulness, fidelity, allegiance, so that they have hope,
something to hold on to. Do you know what I mean? I know
you're thinking about Orky the Orca, and the afternoon talk
shows and the other shows and the message they deliver.
But at least they're a start even if things occasionally go
wrong. Oh I know. I know about Orky Don't Take No Shit.
I've heard through the office grapevine even though there
are those out there who would like me to forget that
embarrassing episode. The occasional slip is unfortunate,

water under the bridge. But we have to keep trying. We have to keep moving forward." Ed pauses.

Cam sits quietly, listening. Cam wonders how many times Ed has delivered this speech.

"Now I've got it down to a science, in the same vein as E equals MC squared. And I have the formula for success. The formula is about how to deliver the message each and every time. And you know what? It works. Look around you," says Ed, gesturing around the room.

Cam looks around the room one more time trying to see what Ed sees, although Cam has seen the office many times before. The room looks the same as before.

"And that's where you come in," Ed continues. "I've watched you since you joined the corporation. You have a creative spark that many others don't have. I need you to help me deliver the message. Don't worry about the formula. I know how to look after that. What I need you to do is use your creative spark to help deliver the message. Use your imagination. Do you think you can do that? Can I count on you? I want you on my team. It will mean a raise and an office of your own. You can get away from that cubicle next to the washroom. You'd be the lead script writer for the show that I'm developing for Zanya." Ed smiles generously. "So are you in?" Without waiting for a reply, Ed continues, "You've got a couple of weeks to think about it. I've set up a meeting, an informal interview between you and Zanya. If you like what you see and she does too, then the job is yours. After that, we can work out the details. What do you think?"

There is a long silence while Cam takes in all that Ed has said. The goldfish swim around in their aquarium: bump, bump. Cam is astonished. He doesn't know what to say.

"What about Jordan?" Cam asks after a little thought.

"Don't worry about Jordan. Yaz has already told him that I would offer you the job. Yaz will let Jordan know about the interview with Zanya."

Then finally Cam says, "Okay. I'll talk to Zanya."

70

"Good." Ed smiles. He is pleased with the end result.

"But what about the script? Do you want to talk about the changes I've made to it?" asks Cam.

"The script will be fine," Ed answers without looking up from his desk, having turned his attention to his computer monitor. "Thanks for dropping by." He motions with a look in the general direction of the door. The interview is over. This is not what Cam had expected.

5 The Big Person in Town

Knock, knock, knock.

Cam raps gently on the open door to Zanya's new and spacious corner office. Zanya is directing her assistant who is adjusting the location of the newly arrived office furniture. Zanya has her back to Cam. She wears a tailored coffee-bean-black pant suit that accents and compliments. Cam is always surprised at how much shorter TV personalities appear in person than on camera. Zanya, who has not heard him knock, is staring at a waterfall curio about the size of a small floor-sized photocopier. The waterfall is driven by an electric pump hidden in the body of the piece. The pump drives the water up in a kind of reversing falls. Zanya has temporarily assigned the curio to an office corner. She is trying to decide where best to put the oddity.

Knock, knock, knocks Cam again with a firmer hand.

Zanya turns and smiles sociably. "Hi, you must be Cameron," she says with a slight hint of an eastern European accent that Cam can't quite place. Zanya emigrated with her parents when she was a grade-four kid. After graduating from university, she started her career at MKM as an intern for the Adin Huffman Show, an afternoon talk show that was the holy grail of afternoon talk shows. After almost two decades and several transitions that have included intern, production assistant, weather forecaster, news reader, afternoon talk-show co-host, and so on, Zanya has worked her way to her current position with her own soon-to-be-launched talk show. Zanya has arrived.

"Hi, yes. I mean no," responds Cam, sounding a little unsure of how best to respond. "My name is actually Camden. It means wandering valley. I looked up the meaning once," Cam offers with a helpful smile. Cam often uses this bit of seemingly inconsequential information about himself to put people at ease. It is his way of saying 'Look, see, I'm unarmed.' Had they been in the military, Cam would have followed military protocol by saluting to reveal that he wasn't carrying a weapon in his hand and was therefore not a threat to Zanya while at the same time acknowledging her superior rank. "Most people call me Cam."

Zanya looks a little disappointed. "Oh, I was hoping you were a Cameron," replies Zanya. "Do you mind if I call you Cameron? Of course you do. May I call you Camden? Cam seems too...," the sentence trails off while Zanya searches for the right word and then, "informal. Well, what do you think?" she asks, gesturing at the curio without waiting for a reply. "Do you like it?" She is unsure of her own opinion in matters of art.

"Very interesting," Cam comments noncommittally. He is unsure of the social context of the piece beyond any artistic statement the curio may be intended to convey. "Where did you get it?" he asks in hopes of garnering more information about how other elements intertwine with the piece.

"It was a gift from Ed, a kind of office warming present. Do you know anything about art?"

"Not really," answers Cam. He feels better now that he has an appreciation for the political significance of the piece. He wonders how long the curio will remain in Zanya's office before it migrates to her assistance's office, and then to an out-of-the-way MKM lobby where it will remain until being discarded when the pump fails or the piece begins to leak, and eventually finds its way to a second-hand store where the store owner will relegate the curio to an obscure corner of the store. "Who is the artist?"

"I don't know anything about art either," responds Zanya, ignoring Cam's question about the artist. "Ed gave me a budget to dress up the place with a couple of paintings. We don't actually buy the paintings. We lease them. It has to do with best in class. MKM has an agreement with one of the local art galleries." Zanya looks at her watch. "Three o'clock, the art gallery is around the corner. Let's go and see what we can find that would look good on the walls. Are you ready?" Zanya reaches for her coat without waiting for a reply. "Come on. Let's go," she continues with a caught-you-off-guard smile. "Vanessa," she says turning to her assistant, "I won't be back this afternoon. See if you can find a better place for that waterfall where it doesn't stick out so much. Remember, Ed needs to be able to see it if he drops by."

The art gallery is called, Behind the Corner. No one is sure what the name is intended to mean. The main floor of the gallery is large and open. Smaller rooms adjoin the main room. A few potential clients drift between rooms. The main room sounds like a library with only the occasional cough or sneeze to fill the void. There is also an upstairs with a similar layout to the main floor. Original works of art, many by local artists, are hung on the walls with lighting carefully placed to show the paintings to their best advantage. The center of the room is open with various benches where you can sit and look at paintings to see if one of them suits you. Large and small sculptures of all shapes and materials are strategically located in the room. Several of the sculptures are on pedestals and others sit on the floor, depending on their size. A number of the shapes Cam recognizes and others not.

"Have a look around and see if you can find anything that would look nice on my office walls," whispers Zanya.

"What do you like?" asks Cam.

"Oh, you know whatever. It has to be tasteful and look nice," Zanya responds vaguely, waving her hand around at the paintings on the walls. "Nothing too overwhelming or garish looking. When you walk into my office I want the art to say this is who I am, but not dominate the room." She smiles glossily. "You know the TV industry. Style is everything."

Cam begins to wander the art gallery. He's not sure what he is looking for. He finds several pieces that have promise. One is a picture of a couple of abandoned farm tractors by an old drive shed on the edge of scrubland. The vegetation is slowly making inroads as it begins to encircle the tractors and shed.

"What about the tractors?" Cam asks trying to get a better sense of Zanya's preferences in art.

Zanya grimaces. "Too industrial, too rustic." She's not sure which. "I can't hang that in my office. People will think I'm a bumpkin, farmer Bob. I hope that's not how you see me. I need to convey energy and sophistication," answers Zanya pleased with her self-analysis.

Cam keeps looking having gained a better sense of Zanya. He finds a picture of a bunch of people waiting on a train station platform in a mountain valley. The same artist who created the tractor painting painted this scene as well. The nearby mountains dwarf the people. Overhead storm clouds threaten.

"What about this?"

"Too dark and ominous, it has to be cheerful, brighter, but not too bright, not too overpowering," Zanya responds.

Cam continues poking around on the first floor. He finds nothing that might suit Zanya. He climbs the stairs to the second floor. In the middle of the floor is a huge painting of a gorilla wearing reading glasses. The gorilla is seated at a small writing table. Discarded writing paper is strewn on the table and floor. The gorilla cumbrously holds a quill pen in one of its enormous and powerful hands. Hunched over a sheet of writing paper, the gorilla concentrates while it writes. You can't quite make out what the gorilla has written. The paper and table are awash in spilt ink. On a wall opposite the gorilla is a window with heavy, thick bars. Dozens of monkeys are hanging off an overhead light fixture, the window bars and anything else that they can cling to. Other monkeys are crouched in the corners in groups. There are old and new world monkeys. Many of the monkeys are harassing the gorilla. They are attempting to steal the gorilla's writing supplies. There seems little else of value in the room worth stealing. A number of monkeys are intent on bullying other monkeys. Many of the monkeys have joined together into collectives for protection. There is an economy of sorts that revolves around monkey shit. Each monkey group has its own hoard of monkey shit. A few monkeys are busy defending the group's monkey shit while others raid other groups. The scene is chaotic. The gorilla ignores the anarchy. Cam notes a card next to the painting that gives the title, The Five-hundred Pound Gorilla. With a chuckle to himself, he realizes a hulking gorilla and monkey shit will not suit Zanya's tastes.

Next to the painting is a companion piece. In it the windows bars are twisted and bent, having been ripped from their wall fastenings. The window is open. The gorilla has disappeared. The monkeys remain, hoarding their shit along with all the writing supplies they have stolen from the table. They make no effort to escape. A few monkeys lick up the remnants of the spilt ink. Cam notes the painting's title, Monkeys in Conversation. He likes the paintings.

Cam continues his exploration of the second floor. He discovers the many side rooms. Tucked away in one corner, Cam finds a doorway that is obscured by a wall that extends outward a few feet into the second-floor main room. You can't see the doorway unless you are standing in the corner with your back to the main room. The door to the room is open. The doorway frames the blackness of the windowless room. At first Cam thinks the room must be a broom closet for janitorial supplies. Then he steps through into the room, which feels bigger than he thought. In the dark he gropes for the light switch that he knows must be nearby. He flicks on the light switch. He is startled by what he sees when the room jumps into the light.

In the middle of the room stands an enormous painting of a man or a woman. Cam is not sure which. The painting is at least nine-feet tall and six-feet wide. It tilts backward slightly, not quite perpendicular to the floor. The figure's face is covered with a mask. The arms are angled out from the torso at about forty-five degrees and the legs spread slightly apart. The figure reminds Cam of Leonardo da Vinci's *Vitruvian Man*. Yet the depiction is more in the style of Picasso's *Nude Woman with a Necklace*.

Numerous black PVC pipes protrude from the figure. The pipes are the same kind of household plumbing that you find under kitchen sinks. Normally the pipes are used to carry away waste water to larger collection pipes that eventually lead to a water treatment facility where the water is treated before release back into the environment.

Cam steps closer to explore more closely the unexpected. He notices that the painting is not on canvas as you might have anticipated. Instead it is done on a piece of drywall, the kind you find used today in modern housing construction. A business-sized card that sits on a large easel next to the work gives the title of the work, The Big Person in Town. Below the title is the instruction 'Look inside'. Besides the piping, there are small wooden drawers in the body of the figure. One drawer on the figure's breast has a small drawer handle in the shape of a nipple. Cam opens the drawer. In the drawer is a peacock feather. He closes the door and opens another. In it is a dried apple core. Cam is enjoying the game. He opens another drawer and discovers an old wooden top, the kind that kids used to spin. Written in crayon on a piece of paper in the drawer are the instructions 'Play with me'. Cam removes the top and gives it a good spin on the floor. The top spins while it scurries about the floor, then loses momentum, wobbles and comes to a stop. He spins it a couple of more times before putting it back and closing the drawer.

He continues to open drawers. Several drawers have kids' puzzles; some have riddles with an answer to the riddle included while other drawers have riddles without an answer. You have to make up your own answer for these. You're invited to write down an answer, using the pencil and paper provided in the drawer, and put your answer in the drawer so that others can find it. 'What is always present, but often unseen?' asks one riddle. Someone has written 'air' as a possible answer. Cam doesn't think this is a good answer. Someone else has written, 'your parents'. Cam thinks this is a better answer. A few drawers have small objects, for example a ring, or a condom sealed in a pouch, or a tiny book with pictures. If you flip the pages quickly the pictures move and tell a story. One drawer contains crayons, and bits of colored paper along with instructions to draw something. At first Cam isn't sure what to draw. Then he draws a stick figure with a big smiley face. He puts the drawing in the drawer for others to find and closes the drawer. Various drawers contain instructions, such as 'Imagine something in this drawer'. Other drawers are empty and without instructions. At first Cam isn't sure what to do with these, but then he simply makes stuff up. In one empty drawer he leaves a nickel for the next explorer to find.

Then Cam notices that there are little electrical switches scattered all over the body. The wiring from the switches runs along the figure, resembling veins or long strands of nerve fibers. He flicks one of the switches to see what will happen. Suspended midway between the ceiling and the top of the figure, a disk with kindergarten hand-painted stars, planets and galaxies begins to spin slowly while a hidden light shines on the disk. He turns the switch off and flicks another. Miniature multicolored lights embedded in the figure's forehead blink randomly. The lights blink slowly at first, then faster and faster, now in unison and then abruptly quit.

A toggle switch where a nipple should be has handwritten instructions on a card that is attached to the switch: 'Stand on the X and turn me on.' He looks for the X. After searching, he finds an X marked with masking tape on the floor. Cam stands on the X, leans forward and flips the switch. Immediately the room goes dark. He stands his ground on the X while he waits to see what will happen next. Meanwhile his eyes adjust to the dark. An intense beam of light emanating from one of the eyes of The Big Person in Town shines suddenly into Cam's eyes, blinding him. Automatically he raises a hand to shield his eyes. He gropes for the switch and flips it. Instantaneously the room lights come back on as the beam of light from the eye is extinguished.

Cam tries all the other switches one by one. Birds sing. Bells ring. A pan pipe plays. One switch causes gumballs to drop and roll in an elaborate gumball delivery system shaped like an intestinal tract. He tries the switches in combination. At one point he has all the switches on. A big grin spreads across his face.

He looks into the open end of a pipe protruding from the figure's abdomen. At first he isn't sure what he sees until he realizes that he's looking at the crotch of his own pants. Through mirrors in the piping, the light is bent, as through a periscope.

The artist has conveniently provided a small stepping stool to reach the switches and piping that are higher up. Cam uses the stool to look in the end of a pipe protruding from the forehead of the figure. From here he can see the disk of the universe rotating above his head. He investigates other piping. In one pipe there is nothing, only darkness. Another pipe looks back at the doorway behind him. In another pipe is a kaleidoscope. Cam discovers that by rotating the pipe he can see symmetrical patterns in different colors. A tiger turns into a lamb and back again in the last pipe he looks into.

The artist has pasted pictures on the figure using a brush and ample gobs of a thick heavy paste made from flour and water. The artist has liberally slathered on the paste. The pictures look lumpy from the haphazard application of paste. One picture is that of a black-and-white cutaway picture of a penis inserted into a vagina. Cam recognizes the picture as the kind found in old high-school textbooks that were used in health classes where you learned how to keep your body healthy. Health classes never seemed to progress much beyond get exercise, don't smoke and eat vegetables.

Cam remembers his formal introduction to sex as mandated by the high-school curriculum. He was a grade-eleven kid. His Phys Ed teacher, Mr. Underschist, was tasked with teaching the sex lesson. He delayed presenting the lesson for weeks. Then finally, "Turn to chapter six in your health books and begin reading," said Mr. Underschist who was late for class that day. He could no longer delay the lesson. "When you've finished the chapter, close the book so I know you're done. Are there any questions?" There were no questions. "Then begin reading."

There was silence in the room while the kids struggled with Latin sounding words, such as Fallopian, labium and vulva. Most of the kids had been introduced to men's magazines long ago when they were about grade-seven or -eight kids. So by grade eleven most of them knew what was what. They knew what things were supposed to look like and they knew that every woman craved wild, unrestrained sex. This was true of all women except your mother who somehow managed to stay above the fray of hot passionate sex.

The magazine articles included stories with words such as her mound of joy, and her mound of Venus. The kids were confident that they already knew the correct nomenclature even though 'mound of Venus' seemed a hackneyed phrase, a throwback to Roman times. Even the most primitive knuckle-draggers in Cam's class were well schooled in the conventions of the men's magazine genre and the sensibilities engendered by the art form.

The sex in the textbook didn't seem like sex at all. The cutaway images in the health book were no more help than the text. The clinical pictures looked nothing like the sex offered in men's magazines. You really had to use your imagination to figure out what was going on in the textbook. Any hint of real-world men's magazine sex had been scrubbed clean from the chapter. Chapter six didn't seem the kind of sex that grade-eleven hormones and rampant imaginations proclaimed to the boys. "Sex! Sex! Sex!" shouted hormones and imaginations above the antiseptic sex of the textbook. "Go on. Pull out your big-as-Douglas-Fir pecker! *Play* with it! I mean really *play* with it," commanded hormones and imagination, interlacing into a single insatiable being. "Whoa! You'll need both hands to hang onto that king salmon!" exclaimed the fiend that resided in every grade-eleven boy.

Likely most of the kids came away with the wrong ideas from the textbook, given the complicated explanations. But grade-eleven Cam knew that as long as he remained grounded in what he had learned from the men's magazines and from talking to his peers, things would probably turn out okay.

As Cam read, he wondered if Keats had had a similar interpretive problem when he first looked into Chapman's Homer. Cam's grade-eleven English teacher had recently introduced Cam and his classmates to Keats' sonnet, *On First Looking into Chapman's Homer*, which Cam had found awe-inspiring with its sense of discovery when a new world of wonder never before seen is revealed. Cam concluded that Keats had the easier task when compared to the task he and his classmates faced, interpreting the dead technical sex presented in the textbook.

While reading the chapter, Cam and his fellow initiates had to read at a pace that indicated to the other kids in the class that this was simple sex stuff that they already knew. If you took too long reading the chapter, it was an indication to others in the class, your peers, that you really were brain dead, which they had suspected all along. You were expected to know this stuff already. It would be humiliating to appear stupid in such matters, although reading the chapter must have been a struggle for even the brightest kid in the classroom to say nothing of the less academically gifted kids.

After about twenty minutes everyone in the class had closed their textbook to show everyone else that this was boring and nothing new. The boys grew a little twitchy sitting at their desks. There was always the chance that Mr. Underschist would call on a student to explain what the student had learned, which was absolutely nothing. The classroom was silent except for the occasional groan of a chair as a student shifted nervously, or coughed to relieve the tension. There was no escape for the boys, having made the choice to suppress the fight-or-flee mechanism common to all living things and instead decided to brazenly stick it out in the hope that Mr. Underschist would call on somebody else. And with twenty boys in the classroom, the odds favored this strategy with only a one-in-twenty chance that Mr. Underschist would call on you.

The minute hand on the classroom clock advanced with a jerk to the next minute on the dial. There was an almost imperceptible click as the minute hand advanced. Usually you couldn't hear the click of the minute hand above the ambient noise of the classroom. On this day, the click was reassuring because it meant that time had not stopped. Panic would have spread through the boys if they thought that time had stopped, trapping them forever in Mr. Underschist's sex lesson.

Mr. Underschist sat behind his desk at the front of the room trying to look busy while the boys fidgeted. Mr. Underschist rapidly swung his legs back and forth as he tried to relieve his unease. He was uncomfortable at having to deliver the sex lesson. The boys could not see his jumpy legs behind the desk.

Mr. Underschist shifted uneasily in his chair as he prepared to address the class of boys. "Are there any questions?" asked Mr. Underschist in his best physical-education leadership voice when he could postpone the question no longer. One of the more academically gifted kids asked a question. Mr. Underschist responded with an answer that no one understood, not even the kid who asked the question. There were no other questions because no one wanted to appear ignorant in matters of sex; no one could phrase a question using the foreign vocabulary; and no one would understand the answer that Mr. Underschist would provide. Everyone was glad that Mr. Underschist had decided not to call on a student to provide a synopsis of what he had learned. If only Mr. Underschist had sensed their fear he could have ruled the boys the way he ruled them on the gymnasium floor. Fortunately for the boys, Mr. Underschist had long ago forgotten his own grade-eleven experience.

Cam moves around to the back of The Big Person in Town where he finds wires and piping going in all directions. A note on back of the work reads: 'Feel free to change the wiring and plumbing as much as you choose. Have fun.' He notices that each wire has an electrical connector and all of the wires run into a black box. The electrical connectors make it easy to unplug a wire and reconnect it elsewhere into another socket in the black box. By disconnecting a connector and plugging it into another socket Cam can't be sure what the effect will be. The plumbing too can be easily rerouted by simply disconnecting the piping at one location and reconnecting it elsewhere. He makes several changes and then goes to the front of the work to see the affect of his changes. Pleased with the result, Cam returns to the back of the work and makes more changes. Grinning, he makes change after change and surveys the effect of the changes.

Cam becomes a whirlwind of activity as he clambers about the figure making changes and discovering the effects. Now he is up high reaching and exploring and now he is down low on his knees exploring one of the lower switches or pipes. On his knees, Cam, wanting to see the result of his latest change, peers into a short length of pipe coming from the crotch of the figure. He discovers that he's looking at a kaleidoscope. The lights on the figure's forehead dance. A bird sings. A bell rings joyously.

"Ahem. Are you enjoying yourself?" asks Zanya who has quietly entered the room. "I hope I'm not interrupting you," she adds with a wickedly rich smile. With a red face, Cam twists around to look at Zanya. Quickly he stands and turns around. "I wondered where you had disappeared to," she continues, enjoying Cam's embarrassment. "How long has it been since I last saw you, an hour? I thought you had left. Have you been here all this time?" Cam has lost all track of time. He doesn't know what to say, having been caught in an apparently compromising position. "Did you find something you like?" Zanya asks, smiling and glancing at the crotch of the figure. The lights have stopped dancing. The bird has stopped singing. The bell continues to ring blissfully for a little while longer before slowly stopping.

"Yes," answers Cam, regaining his composure. His face returns to its normal hue. "But you wouldn't like it, too big for your office," he says grinning and waving a hand in the direction of the work, happy to have had the chance to discover The Big Person in Town before the appearance of Zanya.

"Yes, you're right. It is too big for my liking," replies Zanya enjoying the joke. "Come on we can go now. I found a couple of pieces that will look good in my office. Are you hungry, or do you need more time with your new friend?" she asks looking again at the crotch and smiling. "Let's have dinner. I know a nearby restaurant. Say goodbye to your friend and don't forget to turn out the lights." Trailing behind Zanya, Cam turns out the lights as he leaves the room.

Cam and Zanya sit at the bar while they wait for a table at the One-eyed Merchant, a popular restaurant with the dinner crowd. Both Cam and Zanya are turned halfway round on their bar stools to look at one another. Cam sips his B52 cocktail while Zanya works on a Fuzzy Navel. In the background, *I Wanna be Loved* plays quietly.

"So what has Ed told you?" asks Zanya.

"Ed said you're getting a show of your own and that you need a lead writer for the new show," Cam explains.

"No, what did he tell you about me?"

"Nothing really, he talked a little bit about the new show. He said we should meet to see if we can work together. And here we are." Cam smiles optimistically and motions with a bob of his head at the room.

Zanya masks her disappointment. "Do you know what people are afraid of?" She asks after a moment's pause.

Cam is surprised by the question. He tries to change the channel. "Did you know that this drink, a B52, was first created by a Canadian bartender? The story goes that the bartender named it after a rock band, which took its name from the American bomber." Cam holds up his drink to show Zanya. "I suppose it'll hit you like an atom bomb. So why not call it Fat Man or Little Boy?" poses Cam, making a problematic leap in logic. "And why call what you're drinking a Fuzzy Navel? Navels aren't fuzzy unless you count the lint. But then who wants a drink called a Linty Navel?" asks Cam with a questioning smile. "Anyway, I think Fuzzy Navel is reference to a part of the female anatomy. And speaking of drinks and human anatomy, what's a Screwdriver?"

Zanya ignores Cam's attempt to change the subject. "Listen I'll tell you what people are afraid of." Zanya pauses for emphasis. "They're afraid of heights, open spaces, closed in spaces, having body odor, bad breath, being too fat, too thin, people who are different, losing their house, no money to pay the rent, the end of the world, being old, being old and alone. They're afraid of getting what they deserve, not getting what they deserve, gangs, wars, fear of fear. People are afraid of dying, living, not getting laid, getting laid, getting pregnant, not getting pregnant. People are afraid of everything. Everything," she repeats for emphasis. "The list is endless." Her speech seems well rehearsed.

"It sounds rather bleak and not much fun," quips Cam trying to lighten the atmosphere. He wonders if this is a speech that Zanya has memorized and how many times before she has delivered it.

Zanya continues, "And fear drives hate because they're afraid of whatever that *something* is and they can't get rid of that something. So they hate it. You know, in the same way that they hate the government. Big government is too much in their lives, so they fear it and they hate it because they've been told that they're free and they want to hang on to that idea. They don't like the government telling them what to do. They want to be free to choose even if they choose badly."

Cam attempts again to take the conversation in a different direction, "I wonder if there's a drink called an Old Man Johnson; it takes away your voice and makes you want to yell at kids," Cam laughs. He isn't entirely sure why he's thinking about old-man Johnson. He hadn't thought about him in a long time. He speculates that his drink or The Big Person in Town has brought up this dusty memory of when he was a kid, or possibly Zanya talking about fear has bent him in this new direction.

"What's an old-man Johnson?"

"He was this old guy on our street who had too much time on his hands. He hated kids. I mention it because you talked about fearing whatever and hating it because you can't get rid of it," says Cam thinking quickly to tie his thought to Zanya's diatribe. "We had old-man Johnson when we were kids. At least that's what we called him, old-man Johnson. We never said it to his face. We never said anything to him. We tried to stay out of his way. I think he hated kids because we made a lot of noise when we played. If a ball went into his garden, it was gone; you didn't dare try to get it back. He had a big vegetable garden next to our yard where we played. He talked like this when he wanted to yell at us: 'Wha a da yo do mak ay noy ga su bu ka do'. At least he sounded that way to us. His voice was shaky and garbled. We couldn't make out what he was saying even though he was speaking English. He didn't have a foreign accent as near as we kids could tell. One day, after old-man Johnson had yelled at us over a perceived transgression, one of the new kids, who didn't yet know about old-man Johnson, turned to the rest of the kids and said 'What did he say?' This really set off old-man Johnson and he launched into a tirade about us and shook his fist at us. We couldn't make out what he was saying. Then he stopped yelling and glared at us. We stared back blankly not knowing what to say or do. We knew that we were supposed to respect our elders because they were older and therefore wiser than kids. Then old-man Johnson turned and walked away. We went back to whatever we were playing, probably cowboys and Indians, or a game of war because this was only a few years after the war, so there was lots of talk and movies about the war and being brave and doing your duty."

"What happened after that?"

"Eventually we moved away from the neighborhood. I heard years later that old-man Johnson had died."

"Yes, no doubt he felt abandoned and lost when you left," quips Zanya. "And what did you think of old-man Johnson?"

"We were afraid of him, but we didn't hate him. He was merely old-man Johnson and we didn't know what he was saying anyway. Now that I look back on it, I kind of feel sorry for him. It must have been hard for him trying to talk and people not understanding him. And he didn't seem to have much going for him. He seemed to have forgotten what a kid is, or how to be a kid, or never had much of a chance to simply be a kid. Sad really isn't it?"

Zanya responds with a polite smile.

Cam asks, "What do you think?"

"You have an interesting way of connecting things that don't seem to have much in common. You enjoy tying things together even if they seem unrelated. I like that about you, the ability to think outside the box," says Zanya.

"I like to see it as thinking in a little bigger box with maybe a few holes poked in the box."

"Well okay, but don't get too metaphorical on me. You'll lose the audience and the guest too. You definitely have a creative side. You got a lot of pleasure out of that piece of art didn't you? What was it called?" asks Zanya wearing her host mask.

"The Big Person in Town," Cam replies with an almost boyish smile. It was fun."

"Why was it fun?"

"It invites you to play, explore things. We don't really do that much anymore. Remember when you were a kid and you rediscovered one of your old toys, an old friend that you had forgotten about because you hadn't played with it in a long time? And at the same time, the piece was telling me about who we are."

"Which, the art work at the gallery or the toy?" asks Zanya.

Cam thinks for a minute, "Both. They both tell us about who we are, who we were and who we have the potential to be."

Zanya smiles decisively. "That was an interesting answer. I thought you might have been referring solely to The Big Person in Town. You're too deep for me. I'll stick to my Linty Navel, or whatever you want to call it. You're a thinker. Good! And you enjoy telling stories to get across your point. And you have an interesting way of introducing a topic, the way you introduced the old guy, what's his name, without providing a context. It makes people curious. That can be useful when interviewing a guest. Guests have their own agenda. They have their own message that they're trying to make and it may not be the message that I want to communicate to the audience. On occasion you have to catch a guest off guard in order to take them someplace they don't want to go. Definitely you make them squirm a little bit. You make them a little bit afraid. It was interesting how you introduced the old guy by connecting him to the names of the drinks. You sparked my curiosity. That was clever and creative, bringing those two things together. That tactic can be a good way to maneuver guests on my new show."

Cam is flattered.

"You managed to steer me onto a different topic and I'm not easily diverted. I need someone who is creative and at the same time likes details. I'm a big-ideas person. Too many details can get in my way. This is where the lead writer comes in. You do the heavy lifting when it comes to the details and make me look good."

"Tell me, was there really this old guy, what's his name?" asks Zanya.

"Old-man Johnson, yes he really existed. What do you think of him?"

"Oh, I thought you had made him up. He sounds scary," Zanya replies. "Beyond that he's like most people. I wonder what he was afraid of. Listen, you can't trust people. I know it and you know it too. And anyone who thinks differently is naive."

"Perhaps he was afraid of kids," responds Cam. "Whatever his rules were, I guess he figured that kids should be seen and not heard. He wanted them to shut up and be invisible. I'm presuming that he had forgotten a long time ago what he was afraid of, but it was still a part of him, his skin. Something that he had worn for so long that he took it for granted and couldn't see it."

"The guests on my show are intended to be examples for the audience. They're lessons," Zanya continues. "Here's somebody who followed the rules and here's one who didn't. My job is to strip away the mask of the guest and reveal them for what they really are. What drives them? What motivates them? Why do some follow the rules and others not? Look, we all wear a mask and people are surprised when the mask comes off or slips and we see the person behind the mask, which isn't always a pretty sight. Why we're surprised about what lies behind the mask is beyond me."

"A kind of saints and sinners approach," says Cam. "Are people that simple?"

"Listen, people are practical. They want black and white, and that's what I plan to give them," answers Zanya with determination. "And once I've sold them on the idea that they have to stick to the rules, I can give them hope, not too much, just enough that they think that things might get better if they only play by the rules. But mostly they need a good helping of fear. They thrive on fear. They wouldn't know what to do without fear."

Cam sips his third B52. By now he's only half listening to what Zanya is saying. Zanya is on her third Fuzzy Navel.

"So now, your turn," invites Zanya changing the subject. "You must have questions for me: who I am, questions about the new show."

"Okay," responds Cam. "Tell me about the paintings you chose."

Their conversation is interrupted when a member of the wait staff directs Zanya and Cam to a table. In the background, *It's Only a Paper Moon* is playing.

"That's an unexpected question," responds Zanya after they have seated themselves. "Not where I thought you would start, but okay. The one drawing shows a sunset at the Bayview harbor. The sun is a deep red. The leading edge of the sun is touching the horizon. There are silhouettes of a few boats returning to harbor. The color of the sun matches the walls nicely and projects the sense of energy that I want to present. The other is a picture of cut flowers in a vase. I don't know what kind of flowers. They were red, yellow, orange and what have you. The flowers suggest a feminine side that I want to project. The paintings are large. They give a feeling of larger than life. Image is everything. Style is everything. The key is how you present yourself and how others perceive you. Remember that. Now if I could only figure out what to do with Ed's waterfall. His *gift* doesn't fit the decor of my office. But it's from Ed, so I need to keep the monstrosity in the office. If only I could make the thing invisible except when Ed is around." There's a pause while Zanya thinks about this before continuing. "Did Ed ever say anything to you about water flowing uphill? I don't know what to make of that one. How do you make water flow uphill without pumps and things? I'm not an engineer, but I know enough about water to know that you need pumps and pipes to make water flow. What's your next question?" she asks without waiting for an answer.

"What can you tell me about the new show? Ed was vague on the details."

"The format is a talk show with a half-hour format. I interview celebrities, politicians, other notables and interesting people of the day. There'll be one or two interviews per show. If the guest is a big name, I'll feature him or her for the entire show. If lesser known, then there will be two interviews per show. I'll work with the lead writer to set the general direction for handling each guest. The lead writer works with the writers to develop the story and script. The writers do the research. The writers need to find out who each guest really is, get under their skin. What skeletons are in the guest's closet? What motivates him or her? What are their strengths and weaknesses? My job is to strip away the masks of the guest and reveal the guest for what he or she really is."

"Are you going for the jugular every time?"

"A few will be soft interviews and others hard," Zanya answers. "It will depend on who the guest is. If you've found a cure for cancer or have a formula for world peace, it will be a soft interview. If someone has broken the rules, it will be a hard interview with me as the prosecuting attorney and the audience as the judge. I'll work out the details with the lead writer in advance of the interview. Bottom line, I have final say on the script. My voice has to come through, not the writers. They have to be invisible. This is my modus operandi. The writers have to convey the message that I want. I'm telling the story." Zanya pauses while Cam takes in Zanya's latest statement. Then Zanya continues, "Now be honest, what do you think?"

"What about Ed?" Cam asks. "He has very strong views about going off topic; thou shalt not."

"Ed isn't a problem. I can handle him. If the show goes off message, I'll be the one who takes the blame, not the writers. Ed and I agree that people need guidance. They need to be shown the way. They're lost and don't know what to do or how to behave. We give them the values that they need to get them through this life."

By now Cam is on his second glass of wine, having switched from B52s. The conversation is becoming a little hazy, a kind of garbled tirade from old-man Johnson. Cam isn't thinking straight. Is Zanya simply parroting Ed with a few touches of her own spin on things blended into the mix? And where did Ed get his ideas in the first place and what slant did he put on the message before passing it on to Zanya?

Cam's conversation with Zanya reminds him of the exercise in grade school when the teacher whispered a long and convoluted message to the first kid in a line of kids. The first kid passed the message to the next kid in the line and then that kid passed it on to the next kid and so on until the last kid in the line received the message, which was at this point badly distorted and nonsensical.

Cam begins to think that Zanya and old-man Johnson have a lot in common. What chance does the last guy in the row have to understand the original message? Jesus' message, 'love one another', becomes 'after me, you're first'. Ghandi's message of nonviolence transforms into 'kick him when he's down'. These guys must be rolling over in their graves thinks Cam. The image makes Cam want to laugh. A small, wrinkled smile aided by the alcohol breaks across his face.

"Are you listening?" emerges from the haze. "Why are you smiling? Did I say something?" Zanya quizzes with a look of uncertainty.

"No, I had this image of Jesus rolling over in his grave."

At first Zanya is puzzled by his remark. Then she picks up the thread. "Well, that's part of the message I want to get across; I mean about God. He's in the show too. He has a part to play. I have to get spiritual guests on the show too. Guests who will say the right things and get people thinking about God and that kind of thing. Hopefully some viewers will start behaving a little better towards other people, stop lying and stealing from their neighbors. You know, Moses

93

and God's Ten Commandments. They'll find God and start saying their prayers at night. Wasn't it Jesus who said if you want to eat, get a job? But we don't want to push the spiritual side too much. We're not a bunch of Bible-thumpers. It takes a delicate touch where spiritual matters are concerned." Zanya smiles contentedly, pleased with the idea of helping God.

With a dip of his head, Cam acquiesces in agreement, but is doubtful. He doesn't remember anything about Jesus telling people to get a job. He remembers the story about the fishers of men and feeding the multitude with a couple of baskets of bread and a handful of fish, but nothing about getting a job. It must have been tough on Moses and Jesus and Buddha and the other guys trying to get their message across when they were alive. They must have had a lot of really tough days saying 'look here', 'see this' 'listen' 'think of it this way' and a lot of pointing and arm waving, and demonstrating stuff and gesticulating while they tried to get their followers and the skeptics to see the message they were trying to get across. There must have been a lot of confused looks and frowns on the faces of their followers who were trying hard to understand, and smirks from the guffawing skeptics. The skeptics must have had a field day making comments to Buddha: Get a life Buddha! Or comments to Jesus: Hey Jesus, you need to work on the human anatomy. Water doesn't flow from the belly. It flows from somewhere else smart guy. How much harder it must be to get the message across centuries later.

"Let's face it, people need to be told what to do," Zanya continues doggedly. "The Ten Commandments are there for a reason. You give people half a chance and they'll do the wrong thing. You can't trust them to do the right thing because ten times out of ten they'll do the wrong thing. And when they step out of line, they need to be punished. They need to be reminded that there are rules and they better stick to them if they don't want bad things to happen to them and the people around them. People die. People get hurt. The rules are there for their own good. Rules are there to protect people. Otherwise there would be chaos. I believe in an eye for an eye and a tooth for a tooth," says Zanya with finality.

Cam decides not to make a comment about being blind and toothless. He wonders if a lot of people have gone along for the ride because they're afraid of the consequences if they don't: hell and damnation or the rough justice of an eye for an eye. You don't want to find yourself banished to the Orky the Orca show, so you decide to go along because the penalty for not going along is too steep. So you act humble and religious, but inside you don't really feel it and you simply don't get it. Cam decides that he has already said too much on the subject.

Dinner is drawing to a close. "Ed can pay for this," says Zanya. "We talked business. I'll pick up the tab. I'll put it on my expense account." Cam bobbles his head in concurrence and smiles a watery smile as he prepares to leave the restaurant while Zanya pays.

"So that's your story?" asks Zanya, wrapping up their conversation as they leave.

"Yup, that's my story and I'm sticking to it," answers Cam, nodding his head a little dopily with the wine now reaching full tide.

"Well good, I've enjoyed our conversation today. I'll be in touch Cameron." Zanya beams brightly. "I've enjoyed our interview."

Cam does not correct her.

Outside the restaurant, Zanya hails a cab and is gone after exchanging the usual pleasantries.

Cam walks for a while to clear his head.

6 Paradise Lost and Kid Lawyers

The paved road ends, turns to gravel and gently glides downhill over rounded ridges, cascading to the water's edge where the road makes a sharp right, spilling into the parking lot of the Bayview Park. The parking lot runs parallel to the sanctioned swimming area where lifeguards patrol during the summer. To the left of the gravel road is a six-foot chain-link fence that ends at the shoreline. The fence divides the park from an ancient stand of maples, oaks and pines that escaped the axe when Europeans first cleared the land. To the right of the road is the park itself. A fountain sits at the entrance to the park. Workers dispatched by the city regularly cut the lawns and clip the hedges to keep the park tidy. For the younger kids there is a wading pool with water, provided the city fathers have paid the insurance to protect the city from lawsuits should a kid get hurt while wading in the pool. This year there is water in the pool. Large cedar hedge rows run throughout the park. The grade-nothing kids have tunnelled into the hedges, creating paths that wind through the hedge rows. The paths are as ancient as the cedars themselves. Here kids run and hide in the quiet coolness of the cedars where they imagine worlds long forgotten by adults. The tunnels are too small for the adults to follow.

On the side of the park opposite the chain-link fence sits a cemetery that is a partial boundary to the park. Beyond the cemetery runs a river that spills into the bay. The river completes the boundary to the park. The river's origin lies about a hundred miles to the north and west in the highlands. The river was once a road used to drive logs harvested in the highlands to the saw mills that dotted the shore of the bay. Now trucks haul the logs to distant saw mills. Most of the saw mills around the bay have closed. The river is dammed to generate hydroelectricity for Bayview.

Where the road bends into the parking lot sits a cement wharf that juts into the bay. The wharf is no longer used for commercial purposes. It was used when Bayview was a major center for logging. Now the wharf is a diving platform used by the older and braver kids. There are signs posted, warning that diving is prohibited. For the most part the adults leave the wharf kids alone, although the kids are breaking the rules by diving from the wharf. Occasionally, one of the kids breaks an arm or a leg while diving and then for a while the adults are more vigilant with more patrols by the cops to warn the kids about diving from the wharf. Usually the cop only lectures about the dangers of diving from the wharf. If the kid is a repeat offender, there are warnings about a fine that the kid's parents will have to pay, or about taking the kid home to his parents for parental justice. Every now and then this backfires on the cop because the kid would enjoy nothing more than to bring a sack full of grief home to his parents to show them that he's adult enough to handle his own troubles.

To many of the older kids getting a lecture from the cops is a badge of honor that marks their defiance and toughness. Most of the hedge-row kids look up to the wharf kids who the cops have lectured. Many of the older hedge-row kids, who have made tentative sorties to the wharf world, are already planning what they will say to win their badge of honor when faced with their first cop lecture.

Clickety-click tap tap clickety-click click click clickety-click.

Under the shade of a giant oak, Anna sits at a wooden picnic table. She is typing on her laptop with an intermittent clickety-click of the keyboard. Cam sits opposite Anna. He is reading a book. The sound of Anna's typing is interrupted occasionally by the wind in the oak tree. The sun is strong and the shade is welcome while Anna and Cam enjoy the late-summer afternoon.

Anna and Cam first met about a year ago at a picnic arranged by the local chapter of a service club, the Loyal Order of the Caribou. The club raises funds to support the protection of caribou in northern Canada. The picnic took place in Bayview Park. The theme of the picnic was 1961, before the hippy movement of free love. You were requested to dress appropriately. Anna wore a simple white blouse, a pair of turquoise-colored Capri pants, and sandals. Cam was dressed in the southern California attire that was popular in the early 60s. Cam and Anna didn't know each other at the time. They attended the event as invited guests of other members of the Loyal Order of the Caribou. The club was always on the lookout for new members.

A club member made a home video during the event. The video clip was posted to a web page a few months later. You can view it now, or wait until later. In the video, participants are playing a game called 'Pass the String', or 'Thread the String'. The participants are arranged into teams of nine. Team members stand in a line in girl-boy fashion. Anna and Cam are on the same team and standing next to one another. The object of the game is to thread a piece of string from one team member to the next. The first team member threads the string down through the top of her blouse and then her pants. She hands the string to the next person on the team who threads the string in reverse order through his pants and then his shirt before handing the end of the string to the next team member. Which team will finish first? The race starts when a marshmallow dropped by the organizer of the race hits the ground. As you can see from the video if you're following along, everyone is having lots of fun playing the game. If you choose, you can skip to the end of the contest because Cam and Anna are standing together eighth and ninth in the same team line up. Usually the men watching the video choose to jump to the end to get to the important bit and to see which team wins. The women usually choose to watch the entire race from start to finish, seeing every nuance of the race and the all-important moment when Cam's hand first touches Anna's hand while passing the string to her. Now as you can see in the clip, there's Cam threading the string. Struggling a little, he threads the string through his pants and shirt. And now, here's the important hand off of the string from Cam to Anna when their hands touch for the very first time. If you like, you can pause the video clip at the exact moment when they touch. There, did you see that? Their hands touched. Isn't it wonderful? Well, there's nothing electric about it, but still it was a beginning.

Are there any questions about the clip? No, neither Anna nor Cam joined the Loyal Order of the Caribou. Both of them did make donations to the Order that day. No, their team didn't win. Yes you can rerun the video clip whenever you choose. There are a couple of other clips on the web page that were taken at the picnic. You can watch them at your leisure, but they're not as illuminating. Are there any more questions? No, good, then let's continue the story.

"What are you reading?" asks Anna.

"*Paradise Lost* by John Milton. Do you know it?" asks Cam.

"I read parts of it for a university course. What do you think of it?"

"I like it even though the poem is hard to follow in places."

"Where are you in the poem?" asks Anna while she continues typing.

"Well, it's like this. Satan has deceived Eve. He says that if she eats the fruit from the tree of knowledge, she will live as a god knowing both good and evil. Eve eats the forbidden fruit. Then she has to decide whether to share the fruit with Adam. If she doesn't share, she may render herself Adam's equal, or possibly Adam's superior. In the end, she decides to convince Adam to eat the fruit. Adam eats the fruit because he loves Eve. This is wilful disobedience to God. Adam and Eve cast randy eyes at one another and then have a romp in the flowers. After, they argue fruitlessly when they realize what a monumental blunder they've made; eating the apple I mean. They blame each other for what both have done. Adam is unwilling to accept responsibility for his action and so is Eve. Then God leaves his seat in heaven and shows up in Paradise to check on the kids, Adam and Eve. Earlier in the poem God has already foretold of their fall. So when he shows up, God already knows what's going on. Adam and Eve are full of guilt, and shame, and perturbation, and despair and anger and lots of other bad feelings. God asks if they've been eating the forbidden fruit. Adam right away confesses his guilt. God says that Adam should know better."

"Sounds good so far," says Anna while she continues typing. "Where are you stuck?"

"I'm not stuck so much. I'm getting this feeling of déjà vu from my childhood."

"Déjà vu, how so?"

"Remember when you were caught by your parents doing something that they had warned you not to do, but you did it anyway and it was obvious what you were doing? And even though it was obvious, one of your parents would ask what you were doing even though they already knew the answer. Usually you and a bunch of other kids were in the basement or upstairs doing whatever you knew you weren't supposed to be doing and your parents would catch wind of what was going on. Then one of them, usually Dad

100

because he was big on making kids behave, would stand in the stairway to the upstairs or downstairs, depending on where you were, and snarl. Then he would say, Tchhh! Hey!" growls Cam dropping his voice to mimic his Dad. "What are you kids doing down there? If I have to come down there, there's going to be a gooney!" Then Cam continues in his regular voice. "Dad always said *Tchhh* when he was angry, which was most of the time, especially when it came to us, his kids. There would be dead silence from the kids who knew they shouldn't be doing whatever it was they were doing. Then one of the kids would answer 'nothing', meaning we weren't doing anything wrong."

"What's a gooney?" asks Anna, smiling at the scene that Cam has painted.

"A gooney was a whack on the head. It was also called a 'wrapper' or a 'bongo' and it hurt. Dad was pretty liberal when it came to handing out gooneys. He was an Old Testament kind of guy; none of this love-one-another stuff that you find in the New Testament. You were automatically guilty whether you actually were or not. If he caught you red handed, he would ask the obvious question about what you were doing even though he already knew. Mostly his rule was to hit first and ask questions later. Asking questions after the fact was his way of justifying what he had done. His interrogation was an unwitting parody of Milton's purpose in *Paradise Lost*, justify the ways of God to men. Dad would hand out gooneys like Halloween candy. Whether you were involved in the incident or not, didn't matter much."

"What did you do after that?"

"We cried. Later we learned not to cry to show Dad that his punishment wasn't effective. And then Mom would say, don't hit the kids. It doesn't do any good," says Cam raising his voice a half octave. "Then this would get Dad even more worked up, who would say, Tchhh! You don't make them behave. You won't do it! You wait until I come home from work." says Cam again lowering his voice to his Dad voice. "Of course Mom was right. It didn't help, but Dad didn't know that. He didn't know any better. I called it Dad's school of kid training: make them mind. And Dad was right too. Mom would wait for Dad to come home if there was an infraction of the rules. And there were lots of infractions."

"What does this have to do with *Paradise Lost* beyond justifying the ways of Ralph to his kids?"

"Anyway," continues Cam resuming his earlier thread on *Paradise Lost*, "I can imagine God sitting on his throne in heaven, and getting all worked up about what Adam and Eve have done and then God throwing in a good thundering 'tchhh' and then stomping down the stairs from heaven to Paradise, ready to hand out a couple of gooneys." Anna laughs and stops typing. Cam is encouraged. He enjoys these moments when Anna laughs.

"And what does Adam do?" asks Cam with a look of incredulity. "He confesses his misdeed to God. Adam just blurts out his admission of guilt in a 'mea culpa' moment!"

"What's wrong with that?" asks Anna looking puzzled.

"No kid in his right mind would do that! Every kid knows that you deny all culpability. Deny, deny, deny; that was our creed. And it gets better too. If there were two or more kids involved, the best thing to do was to bend the truth, make it look like it was the other kid's fault and that you were merely an innocent bystander. If you could only create doubt that perhaps you weren't the guilty party, you might get away with whatever you had done. Let somebody else take the fall, none of this honesty junk the way Adam did. Often there was enough blame for all of the kids involved, which was the usual case. But now and again you could bend your way out of it by shifting the blame to some other idiot kid; someone that you didn't particularly like, or who had shifted the blame to you the last time there was trouble, which happened frequently. Shifting the blame usually required a little deception, but it was better than getting hit, knowing that next time you were liable to be the one to take the fall anyway. And at times you had to shift the blame to a completely innocent bystander kid, who had absolutely nothing to do with the misdeed. But this too could be rationalized for the same reasons that I've already stated: he got you into trouble last time when you were the innocent party, or you didn't like him at that moment. There was lots of rationalizing going on. We would do anything to avoid a gooney. We all had this desperate look in our eyes born out of fear when confronted with the threat of a gooney. And I'm sure Dad could see the fear in our eyes, or smell it. I'm not sure which."

"And how were you at shifting the blame?" asks Anna smiling.

"I got pretty good eventually. It took practice. You only had to say the right thing at the right time to imply that it was somebody else who was the guilty party. Now and then it worked and sometimes it didn't. You had to be a pretty sharp kid lawyer to avoid Dad's fists of furry. As a kid, the Adam in *Paradise Lost* was a rank amateur. Dad would have eaten him alive with lots of gooneys thrown in for good measure."

"No doubt Adam didn't have your wealth of experience," comments Anna with a teasing smile. "Adam might have learned in time. He learned quickly enough about the blame game with Eve, who played the game as well as Adam," suggests Anna.

"True enough," responds Cam, "but the rules were always changing for us as kids. Adam had only one simple rule to remember: don't eat the fruit from the tree of knowledge, a no-brainer. As kids we had to know all the rules and all the rules were unwritten. They kept changing too, and no one would tell you when a new rule was added or an old rule modified. You were expected to know. How many times when you were a kid did you hear, 'You should know better' or 'Use your head'? And of course you had no way of knowing that a rule had changed, or when a rule had changed, or even that a rule changed after the fact. There was no grandfather clause in those days to protect you. Parents made up rules on the spur of the moment and revised them almost as quickly. Even Moses' people had it easier. They only had to remember ten rules and even they had trouble with only ten. Imagine what we faced. Every time you turned around, there were ten or twenty new rules that you'd never heard of before. What chance did a kid have? Even the sharpest of the kid lawyers lost a lot of cases. Countless kid lawyers sought refuge in legalities, 'You didn't say I couldn't do that. You only said I couldn't do that *with Dan*', whatever *that* was and whomever Dan was."

"I'm beginning to think that God set up Adam and Eve," Cam continues. "Sure they had free will, but He let Satan find his way into the garden and even when he's caught by several of God's angels after whispering things in Eve's ear, Satan manages to conveniently escape. I think the fix was in on Adam and Eve. I think God wanted to test them to see if their love for Him was genuine, or if they were merely pretending to love God because Paradise was a nice place to live and they didn't want God to give them the boot. And God didn't want to make the same mistake he made with Satan and his followers. What chance did Adam and Eve have? What chance did we, as kids, have?"

"Wait! What mistake did God make with Satan?" queries Anna.

"Well things were good for Satan in heaven until Jesus came along. Then God promoted Jesus to second in command. As a result Satan's nose is out of joint because he was well up the ladder in the chain of command in God's organization. Satan sees the rise of Jesus in the ranks as a demotion for himself. Then Satan makes a choice. He gathers his followers and convinces them without too much difficulty that heaven should be egalitarian with no one above anyone. This includes God. At least this is the message Satan tells his followers. Then there's a big war in heaven. Satan gets the bum's rush straight to hell."

"But it seems to me that in the poem there was one angel who resisted Satan's persuasive if deceitful call," says Anna. "Abdiel, I think, refused to follow Satan. And didn't God send Raphael, an angel, to warn Adam to always keep his love for God first in his heart?"

"Then there are my parents," says Cam, "I suppose, not wanting us to make the same mistakes they made, but only making things worse. The more they tried to make us behave and not make the same mistakes that they made, the more things got warped. I wish I'd had a Raphael in my corner when I was a kid, but maybe the outcome would have been the same anyway. You're born in the middle of things and you don't know which way is up when you start out as a little kid. And your parents are as bamboozled as you are or more so. The whole thing reminds me of Philip Larkin's poem, *This Be The Verse*. Do you know what it's about?"

"Hey, no fair quizzing me," Anna responds, enjoying the exchange. "You were the English major at university. You tell me what the poem is about."

"Well, the poem is about your parents fucking you up worse than they are and how they were fucked up by their parents, so don't have any kids yourself and get out as fast as you can. The poem is funny. I have a copy of it at home if you want to read it. It's a short poem."

"Why don't you show me tonight? How's the novel coming along?" asks Anna, deciding that a change of subject is needed. Cam is writing a detective novel that he has been working on for a couple of years in his spare time. The story is a murder mystery set in the early 1950s immediately after a war.

"Why don't I read you something from the latest draft and you can tell me what you think." Cam opens a folder that he has brought with him in anticipation of Anna's question. In the folder is a printed copy of his latest draft of the novel. The pages are heavily edited with lots of handwritten notes that Cam has scrawled on the pages for the next revision. He searches through the pages, looking for one of the passages that he enjoys. After shuffling through several pages, he finds a passage and begins to read to Anna. "Dirk sits at the lunch counter," Cam begins. "Two eggs, sunny side up, stare back at Dirk. The eggs are framed with two slices of bacon and two thin slices of toasted white bread with butter scraped across each. A mug of weak, lunch-counter coffee sits beside his plate. Behind the lunch counter, Mabel has her back to Dirk as she picks up a customer's order. Dirk takes in her shapely caboose. He makes a note to himself to ask Mabel to the big Saturday-night dance at the local Legion hall. Dirk's left arm leans heavily on the lunch counter. With a fork clenched firmly in his right hand, he digs into the eggs. The yokes run onto the plate. He mops up the yoke with the toasted bread. A few drops of yolk narrowly miss his dime-store tie. He chows down on the bacon. Finished, Dirk straightens up, pushes his fedora back, and lights a cancer stick. He stifles the urge for a good belch, not wanting to appear uncouth. Relaxed, having fed his belly, he drinks his cup of Joe while admiring Mabel's shapely backside. Mabel, aware of Dirk's staring, turns and offers a tepid smile. She refills his mug. Dirk cheerfully smiles and drinks in Mabel's well-endowed chassis purring on all eight cylinders." Cam stops reading. He smiles confidently while waiting for Anna's reaction. "What do you think?"

"I like the idea of Dirk drinking in Mabel's figure while he drinks his coffee," Anna responds, "but caboose, backside, chassis? I don't think anyone talks that way anymore," comments Anna, trying to tread carefully.

"They don't, but they did in the 1950s," answers Cam eager to explain. "The scene is there to give a sense of realism by providing lots of detail for the reader. That's one of the conventions of a good detective novel. You have to follow the formula if you want to write a best seller. Readers want to know that the novel will follow the rules. They want to know that there's a beginning, middle and a no-loose-ends ending. They don't want a jumbled novel where events appear random and disjointed. They want a good guy who's a little flawed but has a good heart and a bad guy who's bad to the bone. A reader expects that things will go badly for the good guy at the beginning of the novel. By the end of the novel the good guy has triumphed, vanquishing the bad guy. Generally that's how stories are supposed to work. They follow a predetermined structure that the reader is expecting."

"How does the scene help advance the plot?" queries Anna.

"It doesn't really, but it helps round out Dirk's character. It makes him seem more real to the reader."

"And how do you know they talked like that in the fifties? You weren't there. It was before your time."

"I've watched enough movies from the fifties to get a sense of how they must have talked and behaved."

"But the movies are movies. They're often the film director's depiction of how they perceived the way things were in the fifties. Wouldn't it be better to set the novel in the present?" Anna asks.

"They didn't actually have to talk that way back in the fifties as long as the reader of the novel associates their talk in the novel with the movies of the fifties," says Cam, who is having difficulty explaining the concept. "I'm leveraging the mythology created by the movies of the fifties as to how people actually behaved in the fifties. There's a little artistic license there too on my part. You have to bend the truth to find the truth. The novel gives the impression of how people are thought to have behaved in the fifties."

Anna frowns. "But what if someone reading your book has never watched any movies from the fifties?" Cam hadn't thought of this. He had assumed that everyone had seen at least a couple of movies from the fifties and consequently would understand the shadings of his novel. Before Cam can answer, Anna continues, "Are we in paradise, but can't see it? Paradise is here. Are we too fucked up to see it?"

Cam shakes his head at this apparent leap in logic. "I like it when you talk dirty," quips Cam, reverting to old habits when at a loss for words.

"Hi Miss Ferguson, how are you?"

A worried look crosses Anna's face. Anna twists around to see who is speaking. The voice belongs to one of Anna's students from last year. "Hi Rachel, have you been standing there long?"

"No, not long," answers Rachel.

"How are you? Are you having a good summer?" Anna's worried frown disappears.

"Yes," replies Rachel. "Are you?"

"Yes, I am. Are you looking forward to grade seven?"

"Yes, but I'll miss you." Rachel replies wistfully. "Are you looking forward to going back to school too?"

"Yes I am. You can always come and see me if you want. Come and visit in a week or two after school starts. Have a good summer." says Anna smiling wholeheartedly.

"Okay, I'll see you," says Rachel, running off to play with her friends.

"That one has hungry eyes," says Anna turning around to face Cam. "I hope she didn't overhear our conversation. She doesn't miss a thing. She drinks in everything. She's bright and eager to learn. I hope she doesn't catch grade-eight disease the way her brother did."

"Grade-eight disease?" asks Cam.

"Yes, something happens either in the summer before grade eight, or during grade eight. All of a sudden they want to be grown up. School and teachers and everything associated with school are passé. They start to rebel. They want to be free. They're hungry to grow up and be free. A few get the disease worse than others. What does it mean to be free anyway?"

"Well, Rachel has another year to go before it becomes an issue," responds Cam.

"Occasionally you can help point them in the right direction and at other times not. And the outcome depends on the parents too. The apple doesn't fall far from the tree." Anna's frown has returned. "As teachers we try. What else can we do?"

"You would know better than I. You're the teacher."

"It's getting late," Cam observes as the day stretches into late afternoon. "We should go. Why don't we go to my place and have dinner?"

"Okay, let's do that."

Cam and Anna pack up their things and stand to leave.

"After you." Cam gallantly gestures in the direction of the car. "I want to admire your caboose," he kids while giving his voice an only-slightly-convincing hard edge that he imagines a street-wise detective from the fifties might have acquired. Anna laughs.

Later that night after dinner, a light breeze quietly pushes against the curtain in Cam's bedroom, tumbles into the room, flows across the room and over Cam and Anna who lie quietly on the bed, enjoying the cool breath of the night as it plays across them after the heat of the day. Anna nestles against Cam, following the curve of his back. Cam is slowly drifting into sleep. Anna lies awake, not ready for sleep. The chirping of crickets carries on the breeze.

"Tell me a story," asks Anna softly.

"Your turn I think," murmurs Cam.

"No," answers Anna quietly, "I told the last one. Don't you remember? And besides, you're the storyteller."

"We're all storytellers," whispers Cam. He is pleased that she likes his stories. "What do you want to hear? "What about a story about old-man Johnson, or the one about man-trap pliers?"

"Tell me a new story. Something I haven't heard before."

"How about a dream I had a few days ago? Will that do?"

"Yes, tell me your dream."

"I'm sitting in a seat in a theater where actors give live performances on stage," begins Cam eager to tell Anna his dream. "The theater has an odd layout. None of the seats face directly toward the stage. The seats are arranged in rows the way you would expect, but the seats themselves are at about a forty-five-degree angle to the stage." There's a pause while Cam decides what to say next. "From where I'm sitting, I can see the left side of the stage and into the wing off stage. In the wing are actors waiting for their cues. I can't see the right side of the stage. There's a play or a vaudevillian skit of some kind in progress. Anything that happens on the right side of the stage, I can hear, but not see. No one in the audience has a full view of the stage." Cam pauses to let Anna take in the scene. He continues, "The house in front of the stage has a big V shaped wall in the middle of the house. The wall extends about two thirds of the way down from the back of the house to the stage with the bottom of the V nearest the stage. I can see only a handful of people in the audience because of the wall. Those in the audience opposite me on the other side of the house can see the right side of the stage and wing. Audience members who are farther back in the theater may not be able to see any of the stage because of the angle of their seats. Their seats face mostly toward the V-shaped wall because the seats are set at a forty-five-degree angle. Only by twisting their heads as far as possible can they catch a glimpse of the stage. I realize sitting in my seat that I'm strapped into the seat with leather straps. I can't move with the exception of my head. A plastic tube is strapped to my face. The tube is short and open at both ends so that I can see. It limits my view, like blinkers on a horse. I have to swivel my head to see more than what is immediately in front of me." Cam hesitates, not sure how much he wants to reveal. "I begin to panic because I can't move. I try working against the straps to free myself. While I'm struggling, I hear a woman's voice at my side. She says 'It's okay. Don't be afraid. Everything will be alright.' When I turn my head in the direction of the voice, there's a woman kneeling beside my chair. Her voice is very calming. I have the impression that she's there to help." There's another pause while Cam tries to remember what happened next. "I stop struggling and begin to relax. She removes the tube from my face. Now I can see more. And that's all I remember."

"What was happening on stage?" asks Anna.

"I don't remember, not much. The characters on stage seemed more interested in the audience," answers Cam. "The dream was about what was happening in the audience. What do you think it means?"

"I think the woman in the dream had the right idea. Don't be afraid. Everything will be all right," murmurs Anna, who is slowly drifting into sleep. "We're not expected to see it all at once, whatever *it* is."

"I like that. Remind me to tell you about The Big Person in Town that I saw the other day," answers Cam. He drifts into sleep.

"Mmm," answers Anna sinking into sleep.

In the middle of the night, Cam is awakened by a thunderstorm. The wind has picked up and is blowing the window curtains. He shuts the window and watches, enjoying the storm. Flashes of lightning illuminate the street in a half light. The storm moves through his neighborhood as waves of thunder roll and boom. He can hear the rain beating hard on the roof and then becoming softer. The storm is moving off.

He finds thunderstorms reassuring, although he isn't sure why. There's something about the immensity of a thunderstorm and standing alone and watching it roll in, watching the wind shake the trees, the lightning shake the night sky, and listening to the thunder booming somewhere in the distance and becoming fainter as the storm moves away. Everything smells and looks washed clean.

The storm ends. The calm returns. Cam returns to Anna.

In the morning, Anna is gone by the time Cam is out of bed. On the kitchen table, Anna has left a message, 'I had a good time. You're a good storyteller. See you later. Love, Anna'.

Over coffee, and bacon and eggs, Cam wonders where he and Anna are going in their relationship. He is reminded of the final scene from the movie *The Third Man*. The story takes place shortly after the end of World War II in Vienna when Europe is in the very early stages of rebuilding. The male and female leads walk past one another going in opposite directions on a desolate street. They have been through a lot together. The theme music from the movie plays in the background. Neither one turns to look at the other. They simply keep walking. Cam shudders.

7 The Door Left Ajar

"Nnnnnnnnn." Jack's face grows red. "Phooooo," says Jack, a grade-four kid. Jack exhales. He relaxes a little. "Come on," he urges quietly. "Nnnnnnnnnn, Phoooo. Almost," he says, his face growing redder. "Nnnnnnnnnnnnnnnnnnnnnn." His face is maple-leaf red and ready to explode. This time he doesn't exhale. Then, plop. Jack relaxes slightly again. "Nnnnnnnnnnnnnnnnnnnnnnnnnnnnnnn." Then, plop. "Phooooooooooooooooooo." He exhales and relaxes. His face resumes its normal hue. Jack reaches for the toilet paper on the dispenser and tears off a few sheets.

Cam and the rest of the kids stand watching Jack, waiting for him to finish. Jack reaches round with a handful of toilet paper. Jack is one of the neighborhood kids. Cam is a grade-three kid. Cam's older brother, Paul, who is Jack's friend, is a grade-four kid. John, who is also Cam's brother, is there too. John is a grade-two kid and with him is his friend, Joe, who is also a grade-two kid. Then there is Mike, who is also Cam's brother, and a grade-one kid. Mike is the lowest ranking kid in the bathroom along with Eddie who is thought to be a kindergarten kid. No one is sure what grade Eddie is in and it doesn't matter too much anyway when you get below the rank of a grade-one kid because you're pretty much ignored unless you have really great toys to share as a way to bribe your way into the inner circle. Eddie has great toys.

Each kid in the bathroom is heavily armed. Most are carrying several weapons: six shooters of all kinds, shapes and descriptions; rifles, including single shot, and semi-automatic; and submachine guns also of various shapes and sizes. The guns are made of metal, or plastic, or a combination of both. A few guns make gun-like sounds. These guns require batteries, which are always in short supply. Everyone has invented his own sound for his gun. None of them have heard the actual sound of a gun except on TV or at the movies. One or two of the kids have knives that are made out of rubber. John wears a plastic, dull-green, World War II army helmet that he got one Christmas. The helmet once had string netting on it so that you could add leaves to camouflage the helmet. The netting was lost many wars ago.

"Are you done?" asks Paul.

"Almost," answers Jack. Jack stands up, pulls up his pants and flushes the toilet. "Okay, let's go."

"Mom," yells a member of the bathroom brigade, "we're going outside."

"Don't slam the door!" shouts Olivia from the kitchen.

There are unwritten but well-known rules about coming into the house and leaving. During the summer break from school, you're expected to play outside. You only come in for lunch, dinner, a drink of water, or if you or a friend needs to use the bathroom. You have to go outside the minute you're done. When you come into the house or leave, you have to tell Mom. Mom guards the door as though she's guarding the gates of hell. She doesn't want a bunch of demon kids in her house making a lot of noise and making a mess of the house that she has to clean up. Generally, the rule is if you're outside, stay outside; don't come in the house. Another rule is if you're outside you can make as much noise as you want. The noise is likely to draw the attention of old-man Johnson. You can usually expect at least one visit from him during the day.

A bunch of the kids who are playing today have waited outside. There is a rule of etiquette here. If you're not considered a good friend of one of the kids who lives in the house, then you stay outside until the kids who are inside the house come back out.

"Who's on whose side?" asks Paul now that everyone is outside again.

The kids form into the two teams that were chosen before the bathroom trip. A new kid, Bill who is a grade-one kid, has shown up to play. It doesn't go unnoticed by the grade-three and grade-four kids that there are a lot of inexperienced little kids in the ranks today. The game is war, or sometimes it's called cowboys and Indians, or just cowboys. You can play if you have a gun of any kind. Guns are common in the neighborhood. They're easy to come by. A lot of kids get killed each summer, but no one dies from a kid bullet. Usually the youngest kids get killed first.

"You can be on my team," Jack says to Bill.

"No fair," protests Cam, who is on Jack's team. "We've got too many little kids on our side." None of the little kids are offended by this remark. They have not yet learned that this is an insult even if true. Those that do recognize the insult, ignore it because they just want to play the game. Cam doesn't see his observation as an insult. To him, he's only stating the truth of the matter.

The two leaders, Jack and Paul, re-organize the two teams so that there is a better balance between the big kids and the little kids. No one is completely satisfied with the results, but it will have to do. No one wants to spend time picking sides again because you might be the last kid picked and re-picking sides wastes valuable time.

"Our turn to hide," says Jack turning to Paul. "Count to a hundred by ones and then come and find us."

This is another rule. You have to specify the counting unit. If you don't, the team that is counting could count by fifties to a hundred, leaving the hiding team no time to hide and then you have a massacre. Alternatively, you could say count to a thousand by fifties, but usually counting to one hundred by ones is preferred. Most of the kids can count by ones to a hundred, even the grade-one kids.

"You count," says Paul designating one of his team members in the role of the counter, who is allowed to use his fingers when counting. Delegating one kid as the counter has proven the most reliable means of preventing foul ups during counting. This way you can pick a kid that you're sure can count to one hundred. And picking a counter means you don't end up with two or more kids counting. Counting can get muddled if the counters get out of synch when there is more than one counter. If the count gets mixed-up, you have to start over. This means that the team hiding has more time to find good hiding spots. A good counter is crucial because counting well can mean the difference between winning and losing. And being on the hiding team is always favored. The hiding team has a distinct advantage, as witnessed by the lopsided number of wins by the hiding team if any kid were to keep track of such statistics, which they don't. One of the kids on Paul's team starts counting to one hundred by ones.

If you're on Paul's team, you're not allowed to look where the kids on Jack's team run to hide. Looking is considered unfair and a breach of the game's conventions, not cricket as they might say in England. There are no restrictions on where you can hide provided you hide outside. The one exception when hiding is to stay away from old-man Johnson's place. Most of the better hiding places are well known and even after you're hidden you can move around when the kids on the other team start looking for you. This is another kid rule.

Cam hides in the bush behind the shed at the back of the house.

"One hundred, ready or not here we come!" the counting kid hollers at the top of his lungs. This announcement is considered a courtesy. You are not required to announce that the counting is over. A few kids are sticklers for rules. They consider it an egregious transgression if the seeking team does not announce the end of the count. Usually the sticklers are overridden. No one wants to get bogged down with rules. In Cam's neighborhood, stealth is preferred over advertising your intention to seek out and kill the kids on the other team. Not announcing that you're coming to kill the members of the other team is considered part of the game, especially when playing with kids who have played the game together for many summers. They consider themselves battle-hardened veterans.

There is a strategy to choosing or not choosing to announce the end of the count. You announce the end of the count the first couple of times when it's your team's turn to count and then you don't announce the end of the count the third time. By the third time, the hiding team expects the end-of-the-count announcement. When the announcement isn't made, the counting team gains the element of surprise. This strategy keeps everyone on their toes.

After the counting is done and the announcement made, or not made, nothing happens for a little while. All is quiet. Cam and the other kids on Jack's team wait with eager anticipation for Paul's team to make their advance into the defended territory.

The best strategy for Paul's team is to break up into smaller groups, usually in pairs. That way, the hiding team can't take out everyone on Paul's team in one big bloodbath.

Paul's team moves into enemy territory, probing for the kids who are hiding. This is when the little kids on the seeking team get wiped out because they don't know enough to hang back in big-kid style. The little kids become cannon fodder. The wary big kids lag behind the little kids. The big kids watch to see where the hiding kids are when they shoot the little kids. The big kids have learned this tactic through experience because they were once little too. Over time the big kids have learned to let someone else take the bullet.

"A-A-A-A-A-A-A-A-A-A!" shouts Mike imitating the sound of a machine gun. "Gottcha!" he yells when the shooting begins and the backyard erupts into violence.

"No ya didn't!" yells Joe. "You only winged me. And besides, you have a six gun, not a machine gun, so bang! You're dead," shouts Joe.

Mike has been caught on this rule many times before. In the excitement of the battle, Mike makes the sound of a machine gun even though he only has a six gun. This is an infraction of the rules because the sound is not realistic. Mike is counted among the dead for his error. There is more firing and counter firing and more arguing about who shot who and whether it was a clean shot or only a flesh wound.

Occasionally, a kid, typically a big kid, is so well hidden that no one can identify his hiding space even after he has claimed to have shot someone, frequently a little kid. When this happens, the dead little kid will ask the shooter where he is. If the shooter is an experienced older kid, he will not answer because answering will compromise his hiding place, making him vulnerable to a kid, often a big kid, who is still alive and on the same team as the little dead kid. The still-alive kid wants to know where the hiding kid is, so that the alive kid can shoot the hiding kid.

Sometimes a kid claims a ricochet shot that gets one of the other kids. Normally ricochet shots are disallowed because such shots are too improbable even for kids. If you want to claim a ricochet shot you have to add the sound for a ricochet before claiming that the shot is good. The official sound for a ricochet is 'cooveeeonnng'. This is the sound that the neighborhood kids imagine the bullet makes when it hits a hard object, like a brick wall or something equally hard or harder, and then ricochets and hits a kid. You have to stretch the 'onnng' out, depending on how far the bullet has to travel after it skips off a hard surface. This makes the ricochet shot more convincing. So to claim a ricochet shot, you have to say 'bang' and then 'coooveeeonnnnnnnng' and then yell 'gotcha'. Salesmanship is essential when making such a shot if kids are to accept the shot's validity.

By way of historical note, the ricochet shot was imported one day into the neighborhood when a visiting kid from another neighborhood joined the kids in Cam's neighborhood for the day. The outsider kid employed the ricochet shot to shoot successfully one of the local kids. At the time the shot was hotly debated, but the shot was accepted, setting a new precedent.

Even after the precedent-setting ricochet shot, ricochet shots are hotly contested. The kid making the shot has to make a good case. Many a shot is disallowed when the kid claims his shot ricocheted off a soft object, usually a tree. On occasion a kid cracks in a moment of silly desperation and claims a hit after a double or triple ricochet. In these circumstances, the shooter can't stop laughing while making the claim that the shot is successful. The kids recognize how impossibly ridiculous the shot is even before the shooter claims the shot as having effectively found its mark. These types of absurd shots are always disallowed. For a while Mike was mockingly known as the 'Coooveeeonnng Kid' for his abuses of the laws of physics with his incredulous claims to impossible shots that defy even the simplest rules of physics and geometry.

Ricochet shots may be claimed in order to draw your opponent into the open. In the heat of the moment while arguing against the validity of the shot and forgetting himself, your enemy may step out from behind his cover while he argues the ridiculousness of the ricochet claim. By revealing himself, he needlessly exposes himself to a clear shot and then 'bang you're dead' to which there can be no argument. You soon learn to stay cool under fire.

Soon the round is over. This is followed by an excited discussion about an extremely good shot when three opponents were dispatched with a single well-aimed shot, or when there was amazing carnage as the result of a particularly good hiding spot.

After the excitement dies down, the next round starts with team roles reversed: the seeking team becomes the hiding team, and the hiding team becomes the seeking team.

Little kids who are on the hiding team will use an especially good hiding place that was discovered in the previous round. This is a fatal strategy for the little kids that use the hiding spot. The little kids get picked off quickly by the big kids who know that the little kids will use the hiding place. The big kids adopt tactics that negate the advantage of the little kids' hiding location. Eventually the little kids learn, but not before dying many little-kid deaths. The game continues until the kids get bored or dinner time, whichever one comes first.

Old-man Johnson doesn't show up this time, but you know that he is never too far away.

It is Sunday morning and almost time for Sunday school. War games are not permitted on Sunday because the Sabbath is a day of rest. Already the sun is bright and strong when Cam, who is a grade-two kid, and his brothers stand in the backyard. They are waiting for instructions. Cam has the impression that the day is going to be one of those hot, prickly summer days when you imagine you're caught in a glass jar with no escape from the sun and somebody has put the lid on the jar with a few holes poked in the lid for air, so you can keep breathing and nothing more. He senses that someone is watching and there's going to be an experiment and that you're part of it and you don't know what the experiment is, but your instincts tell you that today's experiment won't be good because someone will shake the jar to see what happens.

Cam and his brothers are dressed in their Sunday clothes. Cam wears a checkered brown clip-on bow tie, dark-

120

blue suit jacket with matching itchy wool-blend pants and polished black leather shoes that he was made to polish the night before. Polishing shoes is a Saturday-night ritual. His shirt is his Sunday best with shirt cuffs that you have to fold double and poke cuff-links through where the holes line up. The shirts, like the suit jackets, are passed down through the ranks from Paul, the eldest of the gang, to Mike, the youngest, with each in turn shedding his jacket when he outgrows it and passes it on to the next youngest in line. Every so often an item of clothing skips the next kid in line, depending who is growing fastest this season. The sleeves of the jackets and shirts never fit. They are always too long or too short. Cam is constantly tugging or pulling at the jacket sleeves or the shirt sleeves, or hunching his shoulders to pull in his arms, trying to make the shirt-sleeve cuffs line up more or less with the jacket sleeves. The sleeves never line up the way he wants.

Routinely, both the shirt and jacket sleeves are too short with Cam's gangly tree-limb hands and wrists shooting out well beyond the shirt and jacket sleeves. This reminds Cam of film clips of chimpanzees that he has seen on TV. The chimps are dressed in ill-fitting clothes. Usually the chimps are doing something a human adult would do, like smoking a cigarette, having a cup of coffee, or that kind of crap. In the film clip, an unseen narrator describes the impish behavior of the chimps. The chimps have been carefully trained for the film by an unseen trainer. Cam wants to scamper about making chimp faces and noises. He restrains himself. Chimp behavior is not tolerated during unholy picture-taking events when decorum in all its brilliance is at its zenith. Glory be to decorum!

"Stand over there in front of the peonies," Cam's Dad, Ralph, commands, pointing at the flowers with their white petals drooping in the morning sun. "Stand over there in a line in front of the flowers and face me," he says pointing again at the flowers. Cam and his brothers march over and stand in front of Ralph's prized peonies. The kids form a straight line of sorts. Cam knows the drill because Ralph has taken their picture many times before and always in the same way.

A cicada begins its song in the still morning air. Its wings vibrate, first low and then high and urgent, and then higher still and more urgent, until Cam wants to burst, but knows he can't. The cicada stops. The stillness descends again, like a woolen blanket, hot and prickly and smothering everything on a hot summer day.

There's an eternity in the time it takes Ralph to look through the viewfinder of the Brownie camera, a black, box camera that takes black-and-white pictures. It has a gray plastic handle on top for carrying. There's another gray plastic bit, the shutter release, near the top-right, front corner that you depress to snap the picture. There is a small viewfinder lens not much bigger than a postage stamp on the top of the camera and a corresponding viewfinder window at the front of the camera. You point the camera in the direction of whatever it is you want to capture. You squint at the viewfinder on top of the camera to see what you are about to capture on film. The light enters through the viewfinder window, bounces around in the viewfinder and emerges through the lens on top where you line up the subject matter until you have everything exactly the way you want it. When you press the shutter release, the shutter snaps open and then shut, trapping the light in the box of the camera. A camera lens behind the shutter inverts the light and then the light blasts the chemicals on the film, creating a negative. With most rolls of film you get about a dozen exposures. A small lens on the bottom of the camera shows you a number that indicates how many pictures you have taken. When you advance the film to take the next picture, the number advances because each picture in the film roll has a number on the back of it. When the roll is finished, you wind it to the end of the roll, open the camera box, remove the roll of film from the camera, being careful not to expose the film to more light, reseal the roll in the foil pouch provided, and then take it to the local drugstore that sends it for development. In a week or so you retrieve the developed pictures from the drugstore and see how the pictures turned out. The pictures are glossy black and white with a white border around each picture. Now and again people's heads are cut off, or parts of heads or other body bits of the subject are missing because the viewfinder doesn't give you a true picture of what the camera captures when you snap the picture.

When you're finished looking at the pictures, you put the pictures and the negatives in a shoebox or other handy container, or in the drawer in the kitchen table. Always there is the intention of labelling the pictures later, so you know who or what the picture is about and when it was taken. Of course documenting the pictures doesn't happen and eventually you find the pictures decades later and try to remember when it was taken and by whom and so on.

Ralph stands with his back to the sun. This is one of the rules: when taking a picture, always stand with your back to the sun to avoid overexposing the film. Then, with his feet slightly apart, he holds the camera about waist high while using both hands to form a sort of tripod that steadies the camera. You have to keep the camera steady or you'll ruin the picture. If you move while snapping the picture, it will come out blurry with the subject unrecognizable. This is the other rule of picture taking: when taking a picture, stand as rigidly as you can. With his head drooping forward peony fashion, Ralph looks into the viewfinder. The subject must also stand perfectly still to get a nice sharp picture without any blurring.

Cam stands still, waiting, while he faces into the bright sun. His face contorts as he squints hard to cut the glare of the sun. His tired smile droops into an unintended snarl. "Get closer together," Ralph orders without taking his eyes off the viewfinder. "You're too far apart." Everyone obediently shuffles closer together and then stands still again, waiting for the click that tells them that Ralph has taken the picture. Another eternity passes while Ralph again lines up the kids in the viewfinder. "Paul, fix Mike's tie. It isn't straight," he orders. Paul dutifully walks to the other end of the line where Mike stands, fixes Mike's tie and returns to his place at the head of the line. The kids are arranged according to age from oldest to youngest, grades one to four. "Move closer to me," he commands. It would not have occurred to Ralph that he could move closer to the kids. The kids shuffle one step closer. Their line grows a little ragged, but still acceptable. "Move to the left. You're not lined up with the peonies." The kids shuffle left a half step. "Stand still. Don't move," he orders. "Smile," he orders. "Smile! Cam you're not smiling. Smile. Oh! Come on! Tchhh! Smile! Can't you smile?" With all his might Cam tries to arrange a convincing, grin to feign happiness. He contorts his face even more into a snarling, rubbery, artificial smile while squinting as before. He is doing the best he can. His face is tired from smiling for so long while waiting for Ralph to snap the picture. Ralph does not understand spontaneity, although he must have been kid at one time, as difficult as that is for Cam to imagine.

Cam senses that Ralph is ready to take the picture. "Tchhh!" says Ralph. He has forgotten to advance the film. After you take a picture, you wind forward the film using the gray knob on the side of the camera. If the film isn't wound, you can't depress the shutter release to take the next picture. You must advance the film before you can take the next picture. This is a feature of the camera that prevents you from capturing two different images on the same piece of film. In a few years, Ralph will get a 35 mm camera with the same kind of feature to prevent double exposures. The picture-taking drill will be the same with more Tchhhing in the 35 mm world. Ralph turns the knob on the camera, advancing the film. Again he lines up the kids in the viewfinder. There are more orders about moving in one direction or other. "Don't move," he orders finally. The kids hear the click when the shutter snaps open and shut, capturing them on film for posterity.

"Don't move," Ralph orders. "I want to get another one in case the first one doesn't turn out," he explains. The kids know the drill. They've heard this explanation many times before. A second picture is standard procedure for reasons of best practice. Again, Ralph turns the knob on the side of the camera, advancing the role of film in the camera. Another eternity passes while Ralph methodically and with mathematical symmetry lines up the kids in the viewfinder. The shutter clicks.

The kids fly in all directions.

"Pick pick pick."

"Paaaaaaaack," yells Cam and a couple of dozen boy scouts as they rush to the center of the church gymnasium. They form a parade circle around Scouter Leif, the Assistant Scout Master. The yell is a little muted this evening because Scouter Leif with his thick accent has mispronounced the call. The call should be 'Pack pack pack' with the words spoken in short, sharp succession.

Usually Scouter Weylin, the Scoutmaster, calls the troop to order. He is a wise leader and a role model. He has learned much through his many years of scouting experience, first as a cub-scout leader and then later as a scout leader. As the leader of a cub pack, he was known as Akela. Cub-scout leaders derive their names from animal characters in Rudyard Kipling's *The Jungle Book*. In the book, Akela is the wise alpha wolf and leader of the wolf pack.

Scouter Weylin has earned the right to lead the troop and pass along his wisdom to the inexperienced scouts that he leads. He hopes to teach the kids discipline, provide good values, and prepare them for the adult world, so that they are ready no matter what they encounter. Scouts are expected to be respectful to the Scoutmaster and all scout leaders for that matter. All scout leaders are older and therefore thought wiser than the scouts they lead.

While a Cub Scout, Cam learned the Wolf Cub Law: 'The Cub gives in to the Old Wolf. The Cub does not give in to himself.' Cam carried this knowledge with him when he advanced from Cub Scouts to Scouts. Cam is a grade-six kid now.

The opening ceremonies begin. Scouter Leif nods to Paul, who is a grade-seven kid and the senior patrol leader in the troop. Paul leads the troop through the opening ceremonies, including the breaking of the flag, the singing of the national anthem, recital of the scout promise, and the Lord's Prayer. Opening ceremonies completed, the scouts break into their patrols and wait for the start of the evening's activities.

As they wait, Cam sees that Paul is curling his lip into a snarl, which is aimed at a tenderfoot in his patrol. The junior member has broken one of the unspoken rules. His low standing in the unwritten hierarchy as a needy scout requiring constant attention and supervision has earned him the ire of Paul. Other ranks in the unwritten hierarchy are the hangers-on to which Cam belongs, and the natural leaders of which Paul is one. The hangers-on typically defer to the natural leaders to avoid ostracism. At times the natural leaders are not the leaders recognized by the scout leaders.

There are many games and activities led by the scout leaders that are intended to teach the scouts valuable lessons and skills. Toward the end of the meeting, there is always a segment when the boys are taught a new skill. The teaching is done with purpose. This time Scouter Weylin does the teaching.

"Pack pack pack," he calls. Immediately the boys stop what they are doing and form a circle around him. He carries a sack and a small brown paper bag. He directs the boys to sit.

"As you know," he begins with serious intent, "it will soon be time for the annual scouting jamboree. This is a time when scouts from all over the world come together to camp and share scouting experiences. A number of you have camped at many jamborees and for several of you this will be your first camp at a jamboree. Whether you are an old camper or new camper, you need to be prepared for the unexpected." The Scoutmaster hunkers down so that all of the scouts can see what is about to transpire. "As a camper, one of your responsibilities will be to help prepare meals for the other members in the camp." He stops. The circle is quiet while the scouts listen carefully to him. "What happens when it's your turn to peel potatoes, but there isn't a potato peeler?" Scouter Weylin pauses to let the scouts dwell on the question. "What do you do?" he asks, pulling a potato from the sack. He holds it up so that everyone can see. "The other scouts will be hungry. They won't want to wait while you run miles to the nearest store to buy a potato peeler."

Cam smiles quietly to himself. He imagines a poor, starving, half-dead scout running countless miles to the nearest grocery store and then running back to camp while waving high a potato peeler, a Promethean torch snatched from the hand of Zeus himself on Mount Olympus. Meanwhile, the starving camp-bound scouts languish, too weak to move, while they wait for the return of the carrier of the potato peeler, the implement that will save them from starvation and certain death.

"You must be prepared for the unexpected," Scouter Weylin continues. He pulls a kitchen implement from the paper bag and holds it up for all to see. "Do you know what this is?" One of the scouts raises his hand. "Yes, Murray," says Scouter Weylin, nodding at Murray.

"It's a knife," answers Murray.

"Yes, a knife. Does anyone know what kind of knife it is?"

"A paring knife," one of the scouts pipes up.

"Yes, a paring knife," says Scouter Weylin repeating the answer to reinforce the idea. "There is probably one in your kitchen at home. You use it to prepare vegetables for dinner. Do you know what else it can be used for?" There is no response from the scouts. "A paring knife can also be used to peel potatoes," he says in answer to his own question.

"Remember, knives are sharp. Hold it this way so that you don't cut yourself." He demonstrates the correct way to hold the knife. "Be careful not to cut too deeply. Make sure you remove only the outer skin," he advises as he carefully begins peeling the potato. A short thin strand of potato peel dangles from the potato. "You don't want to waste food by removing more than just the skin," he adds for emphasis. The peel grows longer. By way of preparation for tonight's demonstration, Scouter Weylin practiced peeling several potatoes at home the night before.

When he has finished peeling the potato, he holds up the potato for all to see. The peeled potato is only slightly smaller than a hardball. Next he holds up the potato peel to show the scouts what the peel should look like when finished. The peel is almost as thin as a sheet of paper.

"Are there any questions?" he asks. There are no questions. "Then if there are no questions, you will each have a turn peeling a potato," he says, glancing at his watch. His demonstration has taken longer than expected. Tonight's meeting is running late. "Listen carefully. Are you listening? When I tell you, I want you to quickly form into rows in your patrols. Then here's what I want you to do. In front of each patrol there will be a paring knife and enough potatoes for everyone in your patrol. When I give the word, the first member in the patrol will run forward, take a potato and peel it as fast as they can using the paring knife. When you're done, put down the potato and paring knife and run

128

to the back of your row. Then the next one in your patrol will run up and peel a potato as fast as he can. The first patrol to finish, wins. Are there any questions?" There are no questions. "Scouts, form into your patrols," orders Scouter Weylin. The scouts leap to their feet and form into their patrols while the scout leaders put potatoes and a paring knife in front of each patrol. All of the potatoes are roughly the same hardball size to ensure that the race is fair.

"Is everyone ready?" he asks.

There is silence. The scouts are intent on the race. Each scout, including Cam, is eager to take his turn. Cam is the last one in his row.

"Go!" commands Scouter Weylin.

The first scout in each row flies forward, grabs a potato and paring knife and begins madly peeling. The other scouts in the patrol shout encouragement. When finished peeling, the scout drops the potato and paring knife and races to the end of his row. The next scout runs forward and begins furiously peeling. There is more shouting of encouragement as each scout takes a turn. The neediest scout in each patrol is singled out for special attention by the other members of the team who goad him on to greater potato-peeling heights. Any goading must be done carefully. For example there must be no name calling, such as pecker head, which would contravene Scout Law: a scout is courteous to all, even to the neediest of scouts. Each scout burns with a passion to win. The race is very close.

Now it's Cam's turn. He flies forward, grabs the last unpeeled potato for his patrol and begins peeling. Another patrol is also on its last potato. Cam peels furiously as though endowed with the lightning-fast potato-peeling hands of Hermes, had Hermes ever been tasked with potato peeling in addition to his messenger duties. Cam must cut corners if his patrol is to win. He is on fire. He finishes, amazed at his swiftness. Quicker than thought, he kicks in his afterburners and jets effortlessly to the back of his row.

All of the scouts in his patrol sit down immediately to show that they are done. They have finished first! There's a lot of celebratory cheering, giggling and laughing while they wait for the other patrols. One by one the remaining patrols finish.

Scouter Weylin inspects the results. He scowls at what he sees. The scouts can tell that something is wrong. Scouter Weylin is disappointed with his findings. He picks up a potato. Cam recognizes it. It is the one that he peeled moments ago. He knows that it is his potato because of its size. All the potatoes should be only slightly smaller than a hardball. Most of the peeled potatoes are about the size of a tennis ball, with the exception of Cam's potato. In their haste to win, many of the scouts and especially Cam have removed more than just the potato skin. Only a few scouts have diligently peeled their potatoes to eliminate only the skin.

"What is this?" asks Scouter Weylin, waving Cam's potato for all to see. The potato is the size of a golf ball. "Was no one listening when I explained how to peel a potato?" He holds up a chunk of Cam's potato peel that is about the thickness of a man's hand. "There is far too much waste!"

There is a moment of silence while Scouter Weylin lets his dissatisfaction with their potato-peeling proficiency sink in.

"No patrol has won," declares Scouter Weylin.

Cam's kid-lawyer instincts kick in. He is annoyed! He wants to object to the outcome of the great potato-peel-off race. There was no specific mention about waste in the race rules. It was a race to see which patrol could finish *first*. He decides not to lodge a protest.

"Pack pack pack," commands Scouter Weylin.

The scouts form a parade circle around Scouter Weylin. The flag is taken down and put away. Scouter Weylin closes the meeting with the traditional closing ceremonies. Everyone goes home.

"Aaah! Oh! Tchhh! Oh!" says Ralph talking to the lawn mower. Cam, who is a grade-eight kid, stands waiting and watching, ready to assist if called upon. He holds a flashlight in one hand. Cam was in the wrong place at the wrong time with no place to hide when his father needed somebody to standby, ready in case Ralph needed an extra pair of hands. Ralph is attempting to fix the lawn mower's gas engine. When it comes to gas engines, Ralph is not known for either his patience, which is always in short supply, or his mechanical skills, which are almost nonexistent.

To fix the engine, Ralph must first remove a cap screw from the engine. The screw is difficult to get at because it is partially hidden by other engine components. Ralph crouches by the lawn mower to get a better look at the cap screw. With his left hand, he tilts the heavy lawn mower on its side to a forty-degree angle to get a better look. He can't tilt the lawn mower too far because if he does the gas in the tank will leak out.

"Shine the light there," barks Ralph. The light in the garage is poor.

"Where?" asks Cam.

"There!" says Ralph pointing and glaring at Cam. "Can't you see? Don't they teach you anything at school?" Cam shines the flashlight on the screw. Ralph inspects the screw more closely. The screw will be difficult to remove with a wrench because the neighboring engine components obstruct access to the screw.

"Tchhh!" Can't you keep that light steady where I told you?" Ralph complains. Ralph adjusts the tilt of the lawn mower and shifts his position to get a better look at the screw. Ralph's adjustments make it difficult for Cam to keep the light on the screw. Cam crouches and adjusts his position to light the area of the lawn mower. Ralph lowers the mower. He reaches for a pair of locking pliers, his tool of choice for most things mechanical. The pliers are adjustable, allowing Ralph to adjust how tightly the pliers grip the head of the screw. The tighter the grip, the harder Ralph must squeeze the handles of the pliers to make the pliers close and lock on to the screw. Ralph adjusts the pliers to get a good tight lock. Once he has the grip of death on the screw with the pliers, he can turn the screw to remove it from the engine if the screw isn't too badly seized with rust.

Ralph tilts the lawn mower again. His first attempt to lock the pliers onto the screw fails. "Aaah! Tchhh! If I wanted you to do that, you wouldn't!" snarls Ralph. Cam is not sure whether Ralph is talking to him or the lawn mower. "You son of a..." mutters Ralph at the screw. He is not allowed to swear in front of the kids. Cam decides that Ralph is cursing at the lawn mower and not him. Ralph adjusts the pliers again to make the grip even tighter. Ralph tries again to lock on to the head of the stubborn screw. He squeezes as hard as he can. Slowly the pliers begin to close and lock on the screw. "Come on you..." growls Ralph under his breath. He grits his teeth and squeezes for all he is worth to lock the pliers on the screw. Then 'snap' as the pliers lock on to the screw. Cam watches, waiting for Ralph to turn the screw, but Ralph doesn't move. "Tchhh! Can you not see that?" howls Ralph, snarling, his eyes lashing out at Cam.

Cam looks, but can see nothing. "What?" he asks.

"Tchhh! That! There!" howls Ralph.

"See what?" Cam asks again. He wants to say 'use your words' the way Olivia used to do when he was learning to talk. He knows this would not be the right thing to say.

"Tchhh! That! That! Can't you see!" yelps Ralph jerking his head toward his hand still gripping the pliers. His head seems to be the only thing he can move. The rest of his body is immobilized in the uncomfortable squatting position he earlier assumed. "Unlock it! Unlock it!" Ralph roars again jerking his head at the pliers. Ralph has managed to pinch the flesh of his hand in the pliers when the pliers snapped shut. Ralph can't use his other hand to free himself because he is using it to hold the lawn mower on an angle. If he lowers the lawn mower to free the hand holding the lawn mower, the trapped hand holding the pliers will be forced downward into a more severe angle that will cause even more pain. Cam reaches over and presses the release lever on the pliers, unlocking the pliers and freeing Ralph's hand. Ralph lowers the mower. He looks at his hand. Below the thumb there's a long red pinch mark running across the fleshy part of his hand. Ralph sucks on the angry looking mark, hoping to ease his pain. He retires to the house where he washes and applies a bandage to the wound. There will be no more lawn-mower fixing today.

Cam speculates on an alternate ending to the man-trap-pliers incident. What would have happened had Cam left Ralph trapped by the pliers and returned in a day or so? Would Ralph have gnawed off his hand to free himself from the trap of his own making?

A few days later Cam finds Mike, his brother, holding the flashlight as Ralph growls and snaps while he again tries to remove the screw using the same set of locking pliers.

"Tchhh!"

Cam moves on as fast as he can.

"For pity's sake, why can't you behave like your cousins?" pleads Cam's Mom, Olivia. She says this when Cam, who is a grade-six kid, and his brothers are arguing or fighting and she's had enough and wants them to settle down and stop fighting. Olivia is referring to Cam's cousins who live far away. He rarely sees this set of cousins. According to Olivia, his cousins are angels who never fight, argue, or yell at one another, or anything. At least this is Olivia's story; however Cam rarely has the opportunity to observe his cousins first hand. On those rare occasions when he does see them, they are always on their best behavior. Cam and his brothers are on their best behavior too on these occasions, which is an almost unbearable stretch of time for him and his brothers to maintain. Usually it doesn't take

long for the cracks to show among Cam and his brothers, but
there are plenty of adults around to intervene at the first sign
of trouble. As well, you don't want to let your cousins and
more importantly your aunt and uncle see you for who you
really are, so you try to keep up your side, at least for the
sake of appearances.

Or perhaps his cousins are angels Cam speculates,
wanting to examine the question from all sides. He is
skeptical of this notion. Cousins in a constant state of grace
seems unnatural to him because kids are kids and they fight
and argue most of the time, or at least that's the way it is in
Cam's family. Moreover, Cam and his other set of cousins
who live closer have had their differences many times. So
why should his cousins who live far away be any different?
If they don't fight, why don't they fight? Although, Cam
does notice that his cousins' parents don't seem to argue. He
conjectures that maybe money is the source of his cousins'
apparent happy harmony. Their father has a job that pays
well, so there is more money and less to argue about. Cam
doesn't buy this line of reasoning because kids have
dogfights all the time, as Cam knows well from first-hand
experience.

Over time Cam develops the theory that he probably
has to observe his cousins over a couple of days to see which
cousin will snap first with perhaps a little encouragement
from Cam and his brothers. Sadly, because his angel cousins
usually visit for only a day, there is no chance to observe
their behavior for an extended period of time.

To test his theory about the true nature of his cousins,
Cam has devised a simple test for his so-called angel
cousins. His idea is to lock the three angel cousins in a room.
In the room there is a table. On the table is a single piece of
candy that cannot be divided into smaller pieces. The idea is
to listen and wait to see which one gets the candy and
emerges the victor while the other two lick their wounds.

134

Cam expects there will be a lot of arguing over the candy because candy is a big deal in his family. What kid can resist candy? It's akin to the fruit on the tree of knowledge in the Garden of Eden. Olivia enjoys putting candy in a candy dish and leaving it out for visitors. Cam and his brothers quickly devour the candy, like ravenous wolves scrapping over a kill. Not that they mean to wolf it down all at once in a day. They just can't resist the lure of candy. What's more, if you don't get in there quickly with both paws, another kid will get more than his fair share and there's usually no reward for being the virtuous one that resisted temptation.

Once in a bid to appear virtuous and generous and curry favor with Olivia, Cam put a whole box of chocolates that someone had given him in the refrigerator at Olivia's urging. "They'll keep longer in the fridge," suggested Olivia. "You can have one a week. That way they'll last longer." Olivia was all about making things last longer because she was a kid during the depression when no one had much of anything. You might even share a little with your brothers," she added hoping that Cam might turn angel-cousin virtuous. His kid-lawyer instincts kicked in telling him that if he gave one of the chocolates to each of his brothers and kept the rest for himself he could legitimately claim to have shared his chocolates with his brothers without having given away too many in his precious hoard.

Unfortunately for Cam, after eating a couple of the chocolates during the first week and sharing a token chocolate with each of his brothers, he forgot about his treasure of chocolates in the refrigerator. Several months later when he remembered the chocolates and opened the box, he discovered to his horror that the chocolates had developed a blue, fuzzy mold. He had to throw out the box of chocolates. Olivia had long forgotten about the chocolates tucked away in one of the nether regions of the refrigerator. By this time, she had also forgotten that he had shared.

Olivia was not inclined to keep a running total on how many occasions Cam, or for that matter any of her kids, had acted nobly. Any credit for being magnanimous that he might have gained had long since decayed along with the moldy chocolates.

So Olivia is as apt to blame the virtuous kid, if such a thing exists, along with the others. Even if you are the virtuous one, you probably got away with something else another time Olivia reasons. Therefore, why not blame all the kids? That is, blame all the kids except the angel cousins, who always get a free pass. They could commit murder and Olivia would give them a free pass while blaming all the other kids in the room for the murder.

Olivia complains that she can't leave candy out for even a day before her kids devour all of it. For Cam, if the candy survives a day, that's an incredibly long time. To his way of thinking, his mother's idea of time as it relates to candy seems to be in decades, which to him and his brothers is an eternity.

"Who did this? Who ate all the candy?" Olivia begins as though admonishing a puppy for peeing on the carpet. Olivia hopes for a quick confession from the perpetrator so that she can dispense punishment, which is usually a lecture, and get on with her day. Try for a quick admission of guilt is her usual opening gambit whether the disorder in her world stems from pilfered candy or other nefarious deed too dark to mention here. "I didn't get a piece, not a single piece!" she continues in order to play for sympathy, which she isn't liable to get from hardened kid lawyers.

"You kids should know better." This is another one of Olivia's favorite sayings that she uses regularly. Occasionally the kids should know better. In this case she is right. The kids should know better, which they do. So the only thing that saves them from a worse punishment than a lecture is that Olivia doesn't know which of the kids are most to blame. There is always the possibility that there is a virtuous kid in the pack that Olivia is reluctant to condemn along with the other ne'er-do-wells. Mostly Olivia wants to be fair. So for the kids there is safety in numbers. In reality, all of the kids are equally guilty in this case. And each kid, being a practicing kid lawyer by virtue of his dog-eat-dog existence, already knows how to bend the truth and claim to be the righteous kid in order to try and shift the blame to some other hapless kid. Unable to get a quick confession, she doesn't want to hear in her court the well-polished not-me arguments and legal trickery that her kid lawyers have successfully mastered. She's heard it all before. She knows that she will never get all the stories straight, so she can never get to the truth. The candy incident quickly spirals out of Olivia's control.

Cam wonders, so what does 'for pity's sake' mean?

As a side note, Cam was never able to test the angel cousins with a piece of indivisible candy. As far as Cam is concerned, the jury is still out on the angel status of his cousins.

"Use a horse's twitch," says Ralph staring into the distance, not looking at Cam, who is a grade-five kid. "That's how we did it on the farm when I was a kid. You had to make the horse behave, same way I have to make you kids behave."

When Ralph was a kid and his family lived in the city, he spent his summers on his uncle's farm where horses were still used for ploughing and harvesting crops. If you wanted a horse to behave in a certain way and the horse didn't want to, you put a twitch on its lip. A twitch was a stick with a length of rope attached. The rope had a loop that you put on the horse's lip and then tightened, so that part of the horses lip was caught in the loop. You used the stick as a lever to twist the horse's lip, making the horse *twitch* because it hurt. A horse's lip is very sensitive to this kind of treatment.

137

Cam saw a twitch used once on a TV show. On the show, the horse had this wild look in its eyes, afraid and wanting to escape, but unable to, and so silently enduring. You could make the horse do what you wanted. You made the horse behave. After you were finished, you removed the twitch.

And even though Ralph doesn't really say it with his kids in mind, Cam knows he should pay attention.

Pat, pat, pat, sing Cam's quick grade-nothing feet while he scurries bare foot along the cool hard-packed trail running through the summer forest, enjoying the cool against his bare bum and other bits. Pat, pat, pat, laugh his escaping feet as he follows the animal trail deeper into the cool of the forest, stopping now, watching the quiet, listening to the green, smelling the big. Giggle, giggle, giggle, says his skin wrapped in the forest. "Haa, haa, hee!" he sings to the quiet. "Haa, haa, hee!" sings the silence, sings the green, sings the cool, sings the big. To the sun-bright meadow scampers Cam. "Gubitee, gubitee," he says, smiling at the gubitee. Squats Cam, watching the gubitee on the path. Poop, poop, his bum chuckles. Pat, pat, pat, sing his feet darting down the cool path. "Gubitee, gubitee!" sings Cam.

At 10:37 a.m. the crack of a rifle splits the summer in front of Mrs. Allen's house. It's Wednesday, July 23. The temperature is 79 degrees Fahrenheit. The wind is from the southwest at 5 mph. The prevailing visibility is unlimited.

The sound of the rifle brings grade-four Cam, his brothers and the other neighborhood kids running. A police officer is returning his shotgun to his patrol car parked by the curb when Cam and others arrive at the scene. A motionless porcupine lies on the sidewalk near the car. This is the same porcupine that the kids had watched earlier in the morning while it rested sleepily, high in the crotch of a maple tree out of harm's way in Mrs. Allen's front yard. Mrs. Allen has called the police. She's afraid that the porcupine might injure one of the neighborhood kids. Wearing heavy leather gloves, the officer carefully picks up the porcupine. He drops it with a thud in the trunk of the patrol car and shuts the trunk. He drives off to dispose of the body. There are porcupine quills on the sidewalk. Mrs. Allen produces a broom. She sweeps the quills into the road so that none of the kids will step on a quill in their bare feet. Kids scurry home and quickly return with letter-sized envelopes. They carefully gather a few of the quills on the road and put them in envelopes. Play resumes at 11:22.

That night at the dinner table, Cam and his brothers relate the facts of the porcupine episode to their parents and produce the quills as evidence to show that indeed the event did occur. Everyone has a slightly different perspective, depending on who you were with at the time, what game you were playing, and where you were when you first heard the gun shot. There are slight variations in the observations of the witnesses as the kids corroborate one another's stories.

They are unaware of the door left ajar by their encounter.

8 The Trouble with Normal

Having booked two vacation days, Cam makes the six-hour drive to Wallaceville. He has a job interview with VT, Maple Key Media's main rival. He could have chosen to fly. Instead he decides to turn the trip into a holiday by making the drive.

Along the way, he stops to see the Big Tiger. This is a tourist attraction half way between Bayview and Wallaceville. The original owner constructed a seven-story-high tiger even though tigers are not native to North America. You can see the tiger from the highway when you drive by.

Cam's Dad, Ralph, enjoyed stopping here on their annual vacation when Cam and his brothers were little and the tiger was new. The stop was part of the vacation routine, although you might be forgiven if you thought that the purpose of a vacation was to get away from day-to-day routine. Years later Cam decided that it was Ralph's way of reassuring himself that the world hadn't changed beyond the confines of Bayview. Was it the depression and the war that made him look for certainty, or was it his mathematical mind looking for consistency; a proof is a proof is a proof? Probably he simply didn't know any better, along with most everyone else. Cam hasn't visited the Big Tiger since he was a grade-six kid. Today he decides to stop out of curiosity to see what, if anything, has changed.

At the entrance to the almost empty parking lot there is a big For Sale sign. The Big Tiger has changed ownership several times over the years. The story goes that the original owner was inspired to build the Big Tiger after reading William Blake's poem, *The Tyger*. No one is sure whether this story is true or not. The owner also had plans to build amusement rides and other kinds of family entertainment. This never happened. A small forest of trees in neat rows encloses the Big Tiger. The original owner planted the trees when they were saplings.

The current owner bought the Big Tiger as an investment with the idea of giving his kids summer employment. This was to teach them the value of a dollar and to help them save for their university educations. His kids found better jobs elsewhere. The owner also wanted to fix up the attraction, but this hasn't happened. There is a souvenir shop and a pizza stand in addition to the Big Tiger.

For two dollars you can go inside the tiger through an entrance in one of the tiger's paws and climb the spiral stairs to the top. There is a viewing platform in the tiger's mouth at the top of the stairs where you can see the highway that you recently left.

At the pizza stand you can buy a slice of pizza for two dollars, or more depending on the size of the slice and the number of toppings you want. You can also get cold drinks and milk shakes. The pizza stand is done in a tiger stripe motif that hasn't changed since Cam was last here as a kid. Even the hand-painted menu board above the counter hasn't changed except for the prices. Employees have carefully changed the prices over the years to make the prices look like the board hasn't been altered since it was first installed. In the kitchen, an old-as-the-menu-board fan with plastic strips attached to the face of the fan sits on a shelf. The fan lazily rotates back and forth fanning nothing in particular.

Cam stops and looks at the menu board. Behind the counter is the pizza attendant. He sits hunched on a stool reading a well-worn second-hand copy of *The Sirens of Titan*. He's waiting for Cam to make up his mind. The attendant wears a tiger-striped apron over his regular clothes and tiger-striped paper hat in keeping with the theme of the Big Tiger. A name tag pinned askew on the attendant's apron tells Cam that the attendant's name is George. There are only the two of them at the pizza stand.

Cam clears his throat to get George's attention. George continues reading his book. "Can I have a jumbo slice with three toppings instead of two?" asks Cam. The menu board says that you get two toppings on a jumbo slice.

"No," says George without looking up from his book, "just two toppings, mushroom and pepperoni. No substitutions," adds George pointing up at the menu board without looking up. There in large bold lettering at the bottom of the menu board are the words 'No Substitutions!' with 'Policy of the Management' appended after to give added authority to the no-substitution policy should a would-be customer think about challenging the policy. George turns the page of his book.

"Well," says Cam tentatively, "how big is a jumbo slice?" A moment of silence ensues while George finishes the paragraph he is reading. George has heard this question many times before.

"It's as big as two regular slices," responds George without looking up from his book. "With a jumbo, you also get a can of pop," George volunteers unexpectedly.

"Can I substitute a topping on a jumbo?" asks Cam.

"No substitutions, mushroom and pepperoni," parrots George. He once more points vaguely in the direction of the menu board to reinforce the no-substitutions policy.

"Okay, I'll have a jumbo and a root beer."

"No root beer," responds George while he continues reading.

"How about lemonade?"

"No substitution, a can of pop, no lemonade," answers George, who sounds a little peeved that Cam can't discern the difference between pop and lemonade, which in George's mind are poles apart.

"Well, what do you have?" asks Cam patiently, not wanting to start an argument.

George deliberately sighs just loud enough so that Cam can hear him. He carefully places a bookmark in his book, closes the book, and puts it on a shelf under the counter. He stands up and leans slightly forward over the counter, his hands gripping the edge of the counter as he faces Cam. "Look, I only work here mister. We have regular slices and we have jumbo slices. There are no substitutions with a jumbo or any other combination for that matter. You get a can of pop with the jumbo. We have grape. That's it. Do you want grape with your jumbo?"

"Yes," says Cam. 'Who bit you?' thinks Cam, but doesn't say it.

"Five dollars," replies George. Cam hands him a twenty.

"I don't have change for a twenty," says George, trying not to look annoyed in the interest of customer relations, but looking annoyed all the same. "Do you have anything smaller?"

Cam pulls his change from his pocket and counts the change. "I have four dollars and fifty cents. Will that do?"

"Five dollars," George answers adamantly.

Cam looks again in his wallet. "Oh wait, here's a ten. Will that do?" asks Cam, offering the ten. George takes the ten and gives Cam his change. Then George takes two slices from an already made pizza sitting on a warming tray and transfers the slices to a paper plate printed with tiger stripes. He warms the slices in a microwave oven. Beep, beep, beep, beep says the microwave to tell George that it has completed its assigned task. George places the plate on the counter along with two paper napkins, one for each slice, and a can of grape pop. The straw dispenser on the counter is empty. Cam decides not to ask for a straw. George returns to his stool without waiting to see if there is anything else he can do for Cam. George picks up his book.

Cam finds a nearby picnic table and sits down. The picnic table is painted in tiger stripes. The paint is faded and peeling. Over the years the weather has taken its toll. Cam eats his slices of pizza and drinks his can of grape pop. The pop colors his upper lip purple.

After lunch, Cam decides to wander through the souvenir shop. 'If you break it, then it's sold!' warns an old and tattered sign at the entrance to the shop. The sign is intended to deter kids and adults too from handling the merchandise. The management's policy helps to reduce breakage. Inside the souvenir shop you can buy tiger crap, not crap crap, but tiger related crap: anything from a key chain with a picture of a tiger on it for three dollars to a snow globe with a replica plastic tiger inside. Snow-globe tigers are done in Halloween-orange and black. The snow globes start at ten dollars. For the kids there are stuffed tigers in different shapes and sizes that range in price from five dollars to thirty dollars, not including taxes.

There are also garish plastic replica tigers glued onto half-inch-thick slices of varnished pine wood. Tree bark runs around the edge of each slice of wood to make the wood look even more authentic. Burnt into the wood under the varnish are the words 'Big Tiger'. These items start at ten dollars plus taxes and go up in price from there, depending on the number and size of the tigers on the piece of wood. Several of the pieces have an adult tiger and a couple of tiger cubs to enhance the cuteness. A bunch of the tigers are standing and others are lying down. None of the adult tigers looks too excited about much of anything. The tiger cubs are posed as though engaged in play, or practicing their hunting skills.

Copies of William Blake's poem, *The Tyger*, are available. You can buy a copy for a dollar. If you want a framed copy of the poem, then it will cost you seven dollars plus taxes, but the frame is a piece of crap. The paper that the poem is printed on is brown looking and torn around the

edges to make the paper look old. The font typeface is
Antiqua. The font gives the impression that a fifth-century
monk, who was practiced in the art of calligraphy, has
laboriously sweated over the reproduction of each copy.
Monks, however, would not have considered the poem
sacred text and therefore not worthy of their efforts. And
Blake would not have been keen on monks reproducing his
poem had they done so in the first place. Blake actually
wrote the poem in the late eighteenth century and it was
more than a poem because Blake was an artist who created
an illustration of a tiger to enhance the poem. A modern-day
photograph of a tiger has been plastered on below the poem
to fill up space on the sheet of paper and give the notion that
you're getting your money's worth. The tiger looks like crap
compared to the tiger of Blake's imagination.

Cam doesn't buy anything in the souvenir shop. As he
leaves, he smiles politely at Rose, the sharp-eyed Cerberus
who stands guard at the checkout counter. The ubiquitous
electric fan with plastic strips waves unendingly in the
background behind Rose. She smiles grimly while she gives
Cam the once over, trying to decide if he's slipped a piece of
valuable tiger crap into his pocket. Rose is very good at
identifying customers who prefer a five-finger discount.
Occasionally Rose must confront a light-fingered customer.
Then she has to get George for backup in case things get out
of hand. In her mind, Rose derisively refers to George as *The
Tiger*. He would be no help whatsoever if things turned ugly.
Customers usually deny having taken anything. Then they
get embarrassed and defensive when they realize they've
been caught trying to steal tiger crap.

Cam discovers that the washrooms are not kept as clean
as they once were and smell of piss. On hot, humid summer
days, water condenses and drips from the exposed pipes and
wall tiles in the washrooms. Still with kids in the car, parents
can't always be choosy. For those who can wait, there's a

modern rest stop with a gas station, fast food and clean washrooms about fifteen minutes up the road.

The Big Tiger itself is looking long in the tooth. It lost its tail during a wind storm. After the wind storm, the owner patched the ass end of the tiger to prevent rain damage to the structure. Now the tiger has a bobbed tail, which no one really seems to mind and for a short time more tourists stopped to see the peculiar tiger with the bobbed tail. The tiger's ears are tattered. Old birds' nests lie perched in the ears, resembling the wispy tufts of hair that sprout from old people's ears. The tiger's teeth are chipped where the paint has flaked off. The teeth are worn looking and stained a rust color by the rusting metal frame of the viewing platform in the tiger's mouth. The rain and sun haven't been kind to the tiger. Its coat is faded. Its eyes are faded too. The tiger looks blind or in need of cataract surgery. It needs a coat of paint. However, this is unlikely to happen any time soon because the Big Tiger is not as popular as it once was. Now only a few desperate families stop here because there are washrooms.

Cam pays two dollars. An attendant stamps the back of Cam's hand with the image of a purple tiger, so that the attendant knows that Cam has paid. The stamp is good for the whole day. Cam can climb the Big Tiger as many times as he wants. Each day the attendant uses a different colored ink for the stamp. The color of the ink helps the attendant identify visitors who might return the next day wearing a stamp from their previous visit and attempt to gain access to the Big Tiger without paying a second time. After a couple of days the ink wears off. Most people only climb the tiger once and then leave. They're in a hurry to get back on the road and can't spend too much time here. Cam climbs the stairs to the viewing platform in the tiger's mouth. There is the faint smell of piss on the stairs where little kids have been caught short. The view hasn't changed, except that the trees are taller now. They obstruct slightly the view of the road.

146

Cam returns to his car. He turns on the car radio as he heads for the parking lot exit. He's trying to wash away the memory of his visit to the Big Tiger. Bruce Cockburn is singing about the trouble with normal and how it only gets worse.

Unlocking the door, Cam steps into his motel room at the Peaceful Rest Motel and closes the door. He's standing immediately inside the room. The drawn drapes blot out most of the sunlight of early evening. The quiet hum of the air conditioner whispers sleep. The room is slightly chilled. Without having to look for the light switch, Cam flicks on the lights. He takes one step forward into the room. This is the spot he decides. From here he can see the bathroom and the main room. He begins to relax. Everything in the rooms is present and purposefully placed for ease of use, 'mise en place'. Cam learned this term while watching a cooking show on television. He is fond of applying the term to other situations, such as motel rooms. There are no surprises.

Cam shivers. The soft whirr of the air conditioner calls invitingly. A nap is in order before a late dinner. He turns off the lights and climbs onto the bed. Staring at the ceiling he begins to drift off to sleep. He tries to remember the words to Blake's poem, *The Tyger*. He can only remember snatches of the poem: 'burning in the forests of the night'; 'twist the sinews of the heart'; 'fearful symmetry'. Cam closes his eyes. He gives up trying to remember the words. Instead he tries to remember the impression the poem created when he first encountered it at university. Words such as alive, powerful, compelling, complete, force of nature, and frightening begin to surface. No, not frightening, Cam corrects, terrifying, genius... This is his last thought before falling asleep.

An alarm clock jolts Cam awake at 3:17 a.m. He has overslept and missed dinner. He fumbles in the dark for five

147

minutes before finding the off button. Thrashing in bed, he lurches into sleep. He will be overtired in the morning.

Cam makes his way to the motel breakfast room for the complimentary breakfast that the motel guests are entitled to. Already this morning, he has shined his shoes and had a shave and a shower. His interview is at eleven o'clock. He has time this morning for a leisurely breakfast. He is dressed casually. Later he will put on a suit and tie, which he has laid out on the motel bed in preparation for the interview. Cam is never sure how formally dressed he should be for an interview. He decides to play it safe, choosing to be a little overdressed rather than too casual.

The breakfast room consists of about a half-dozen tables. Guests are helping themselves to the banquet. A room attendant dressed in uniform invisibly cleans the tables and replenishes food supplies. Many guests are seated, eating their food. Others who have finished their breakfasts are milling about, disposing of their mostly plastic eating paraphernalia. Newly arrived guests survey the room to see what food is available and to spy out where they might sit. Most of the people are dressed casually. A few are dressed in business attire.

Luggage scuttles behind a few guests who are looking for a speedy checkout after breakfast. 'Dnp, dnp, dnp,' sputter the little luggage wheels at nothing in particular as they cross the tiled floor of the breakfast room.

Mounted high in a corner of the room is a television. Occasionally a newscaster breaks in between commercials to announce a few news events. The announcer is always careful to present the appropriate facial and vocal cues to show the audience members how they should respond. At the moment the newscaster is talking about a painting by Michelangelo while a picture of the painting is displayed. The announcer wears a serious face. Cam can't quite make out what he is saying about the painting. Then the announcer turns to a news item about a lost cat found in an unbelievable place and that everyone can certainly agree what a miracle it is the cat has survived.

Cam makes a quick scan to see what is available for breakfast. There is the standard cornucopia of breakfast fare. He spoons fruit into a bowl, makes toast, pours a mug of coffee and finds an empty table. Having missed dinner, he is hungry, but doesn't want a big meal because it will make him sleepy during his job interview. He is already feeling tired because his sleep was interrupted. He peels back the foil on a small plastic container of marmalade and spreads the marmalade on his toast. He eats the toast and then his bowl of fruit. While he eats, people come and go, talking about their plans for the day. Finally he turns his attention to his coffee. He adds milk from a small plastic container and then sugar and stirs the coffee with a metal spoon.

'Tink, tink, tink,' the spoon says happily.

Cam wonders if the motel management has consciously kept the metal spoons instead of converting to plastic.

Cam lingers over his coffee, enjoying the solitude. He savors his vacation day by taking a moment to think about his daily routine had he gone to work today. There would be the quick bowl of cereal at the kitchen table while flipping through television channels, trying to catch a glimpse of something useful on the news; then quickly out the door followed by his commute to work; starting his computer and getting a coffee from the lunch room while his computer starts up; inevitably other workers start drifting into work in the normal order in accordance with their routines. Typically by this time of day at work Cam would be on his second cup of coffee. As a rule he limits himself to two cups of coffee a day.

"Is this seat taken?" asks a man smiling. He is standing next to an empty seat at Cam's table. Cam looks up to see who it is. The face is vaguely familiar, but he can't place it. Cam smiles courteously and shakes his head to indicate that the seat is available. "Mind if I sit down?" asks the man, who is dressed in a beige golf shirt with matching casual slacks and shoes. Cam gestures toward the seat inviting the man to sit down, although he is reluctant to share his solitude. The man sits. He folds his hands together, bows his head and closes his eyes. After a moment, he opens his eyes, sits up straight, and begins eating his breakfast. Cam drinks his coffee, trying to remember where he has seen the face before. He is happy for the time being simply to drink his coffee while the mystery man eats. There will be time enough for the inevitable conversation and social pleasantries.

"Hi, I'm Ray. How are you?" says the man after about ten minutes.

"Cam, fine thanks. And you?" Cam responds socially.

"I'm fine," responds Ray with a well-mannered smile. "Are you in town for the game between the Warriors and the Stingers?"

"No," answers Cam, shaking his head. "Job interview. You?"

"Funeral later today."

"Oh," says Cam, never knowing the correct response in these situations, especially when dealing with a stranger. "Family?"

"An old friend."

"I'm sorry," is all that Cam can think to say.

"I was with him toward the end," says Ray wanting to talk. "He had a severe stroke and slipped into a coma for three days. When he came out of it, his speech was badly slurred. No one could understand him. He couldn't move much either. We tried to reassure him and make him comfortable," Ray pauses. "I think he knew his end was near."

"Were you close?"

"We grew up together. Later we went to university together. He studied business. I studied law. We kept in touch after university. He was a successful business man. I never practiced law after university. I went in a different direction. He was the best man at my wedding. When his wife died I helped him get through it. He helped me through difficult times too."

The breakfast room has almost cleared out. The attendant has turned off the television. Cam isn't sure if he should speak, or merely listen. He sips his coffee. He decides to listen.

"I went to the hospital when I heard about his stroke. There wasn't much I could do except provide a little comfort to his family while we waited." Ray gives his coffee a stir. "Then he came out of the coma. He seemed more relaxed than I had seen him in a long time. He had this strange little smile that I hadn't seen since we were kids. I think he was trying to tell us something; I don't know what. He died a little while after from a second massive stroke. I can still see his smile. I miss him," Ray confesses.

Cam is at a loss what to say. He searches for the right words to offer a little comfort. "Maybe what he was trying to say is best said without words," Cam offers. He waits to gage Ray's response before continuing. "Perhaps he did say what he needed to say. He said it with his smile. There was nothing more for him to say." There's a long silence with only Cam, Ray and the big silence in the room. Cam's coffee is cold. Ray is lost in thought.

"Thank you," says Ray after a moment. "Why do you not understand my speech? Even because you cannot hear my word." adds Ray with a small genuine smile.

"Will you be all right?" asks Cam, recognizing that Ray has answered with a biblical reference, but not fully understanding the reference. Ray nods his head. Cam is not sure what else he can say or do. Hesitantly Cam stands up as he prepares to leave, not sure if he's doing the right thing by leaving.

"Thanks. You've been very helpful. I'm sorry. I've monopolized your time. I hope the interview goes well," responds Ray.

Cam returns to his room where he dresses for the interview, unsure of what to make of what transpired a moment ago. Then it occurs to Cam who the man is. He's the Reverend Mortul, the guy who flubbed his lines at the football game. Cam tries to remember what the Reverend said at the game. What did he say? There was something about being blind and being your own worst enemy, or something in that vein. Likely the message got mangled along the way. Cam isn't entirely sure.

9 Gnnnnnnh

The receptionist, Letha, hands Cam a visitor's badge. "You go through those doors." She does a half twist in her chair and gestures at the doors behind her. "Then a left at the second corridor, follow the corridor until you get to the water cooler, then turn right, follow the hallway until you reach the end of the hallway, another right and then the third office on your left. You can't miss it. If you get lost, ask anyone. Tell them you're looking for Spencer Drywell. He's the human resources officer that you're meeting today. Mind the construction. We're renovating. Spencer is expecting you." Letha smiles with a hope-you-got-all-that smile. She turns and looks at Cam to see if indeed he understands. "Good luck," she adds.

Cam isn't sure if she is wishing him good luck in finding the office, or good luck in the interview. He smiles at her with an I-may-look-confident-but-I'm-not-sure-I-got-all-that smile. He gestures with his hand to mimic the sequence of left and right turns. He throws a quizzical look at her to see if he got all the turns right.

Letha nods blankly as though she has already forgotten who he is. She smiles her receptionist smile. "Yes that's right," she says, although she isn't paying attention to his hand gestures. Her mind is juggling a dozen different tasks that she must accomplish in the next half hour. "And remember if you get lost, ask one of the construction workers," she adds, focusing again on sending Cam on his way. "You'll be fine. Don't forget to put on the visitor's badge," she adds pointing to the badge in Cam's hand.

Cam looks at the badge. He clips it to the breast pocket of his suit jacket. The badge dangles awkwardly. He grins uncertainly at Letha before setting out. I'll send up a flare if I get lost, he wants to say.

Cam pushes through the door that Letha pointed at. He is immediately greeted by sheets of construction plastic hung from floor to ceiling, and metal studs where there should be walls. Wraiths wearing bulbous hard hats move behind the construction plastic. The ceiling is skinless; construction workers have stripped away the ceiling tiles. Metal ceiling tile supports, which are the ribs of the ceiling, hang suspended from wires in a lattice pattern. Root-like electrical wiring meanders everywhere, ending in tuberous electrical receptacles that dangle from the ceiling and metal wall studs. Disconnected ventilation ducting worms its way overhead. Above the ducting are the skeletal steel girders that support the floor above and underpin the entire structure of the building. Cam can hear the muffled sound of heavy construction equipment digging far off in the cavernous depths of the building. He has the oddest feeling that he's inside a strange box.

Cam carefully makes his way down the corridor while trying to remember the directions that Letha gave him. After a few twists and turns and not finding the water cooler, which has been moved because of the construction work, he realizes that he is lost.

"Excuse me," says Cam turning to two workers who are installing metal wall studs, "I'm looking for Spencer Drywell's office. Do you know where it is?"

A worker stops what he is doing. He pauses for a moment while he settles on an answer. "You go a couple of hallways over and then left," he says pointing fuzzily with a pair of metal tin snips. "Look for the water cooler."

"Okay thanks," says Cam. He continues his search following the new directions. The water cooler continues to elude him. The muffled sound of construction fades and is replaced by a dampening silence as though Cam is in a sound-proof room. Eventually he finds a row of cramped windowless offices. The offices are untouched by time with their 1950s look when wood panelling was still the predominant office construction material. The office doors are open. All the offices are empty except for one where a man sits behind a desk with his head down, looking at papers on his desk. He is in his early thirties. He is neatly dressed in a shirt and tie. His dim-gray suit jacket hangs from a coat rack in one corner of the room. Cam raps on the open door. The man looks up from his papers.

"Hi, you must be Camden," he says, beaming with a contagious smile. "Come in," he invites with a generous wave of his hand. "Can I call you Cam? I'm Spencer. Call me Spence. I was beginning to wonder where you were. You can get lost in here so easily." Spence coughs as he unsuccessfully tries to clear his throat. "Sorry about the dust," he cheerfully apologizes in his soft voice. He exuberantly shakes Cam's hand.

Cam smiles a broad grin. He's finding Spence infectious. "Yes, I did get a little lost. I sent up a flare. Did you see it?" Cam jokes to show his sense of humor. Immediately he regrets it, concerned that Spence will misinterpret his joke as a criticism. Even his most innocuous jokes are at times misconstrued. "The offices should be nice when finished," Cam adds to end on a positive note. He is on his best behavior. He can't afford a misstep this early in the interview. First impressions can be difficult to overcome. No more jokes. Play it safe.

"Yes, the offices will look nice when they're done. I'm sure," Spence agrees optimistically. "Course they have a lot of work to do before they're finished. Till then, this is my temporary office."

"Have a seat," Spence grins freely, gesturing toward the chair next to the potted plant in the corner. "Are you fond of plants?" asks Spence, nodding in the direction of the plant.

"My wife gave me that one. She insisted that I put it in my office. She said it would add color to the room. I looked up the name of the plant on the Internet. Its Latin name is Podranea alienus. Its common name is Night Sleeper. Don't ask me why. It doesn't require much care. I water it once a week. That reminds me. It needs watering. Would you mind watering it while you're sitting there?"

Before Cam can answer, Spence bends down behind his desk, momentarily disappearing from view. He's holding a small plastic watering can when he pops up again. He hands the can to Cam, who smiles an obligatory smile. Cam twists slightly in his chair and waters the plant. He notices the plant has little seed pods growing on it. He hands the empty watering can to Spence.

"Thank you," Spence cheerfully responds. He vanishes once again behind his desk as he returns the watering can to its former place.

Cam grins. Perhaps this is a test, he thinks, unsure what to make of the request. Did I pass, he wonders as Spence reappears.

"So," says Cam who is eager to start the interview, "I assume you'd like to know about me."

"Yes," interrupts Spence, "but we have to wait for Earle. Part of our interview process you understand," he gleefully adds by way of explanation. "We need a minimum of two people in the room before conducting the interview. Earle is the outgoing manager that you would be replacing. Earle knows the job much better than I do. I'm here to provide a second opinion based on the interview. He's running late. I hope he hasn't forgotten about our interview. Most likely he got lost. Do you think I should organize a search party?" Spence merrily smiles with satisfaction at his own joke. "Let's wait a minute and see if he turns up. I'm sure he will."

"Oh yes, for sure" Cam concurs with a ready-made smile. Now he's got me grinning my face off, he thinks with growing concern. He resists the impulse to bob his head affirmatively.

The two sit, waiting for Earle. A dusty pause covers the room. "How was your trip from Bayview?" Spence finally asks as he casts around for something to talk about while waiting for Earle.

"It was fine," answers Cam with a happy-go-lucky smile, unable to stop himself.

"Did you fly or drive?"

"Drove, stopped at the Big Tiger. I haven't been there since I was a kid," Cam gladly volunteers.

"Is that still around? I thought they demolished it years ago."

"No it's still there. I didn't realize that the Big Tiger is based on a poem by William Blake," adds Cam.

"William Blake?" asks Spence with a happy frown. "I don't recognize the name."

"Yes, you know. 'Tyger tyger, burning bright,'. That William Blake."

"Oh that poem," Spence eagerly responds. "Was that written by, who did you say?"

"William Blake," responds Cam. "Yes."

"Oh is that the guy who wrote the poem? I had no idea. I had to recite it to the entire class when I was in grade three. I never understood it," Spence adds matter-of-factly. "Coincidentally, my son has to recite it in front of his grade-three class. I helped him choose the poem. It has a short and easy rhythm. 'Tyger tyger, burning bright, In the forests of the night;'". Spence blissfully taps a finger on the desk in time with the syllables to demonstrate the rhythm. "Why such a simple poem is so difficult to understand I don't know. It should be child's play." Spence pauses while he ponders. "Anyway, now I'm helping my son memorize it. I know a few memory tricks that my dad taught me when I was learning it. We still have a week before he has to recite it. He should know it well by then," says Spence glowing with satisfaction at the knowledge that he is helping prepare his son for the challenges he'll face in life.

"Blake had this idea about poetic genius," Cam interjects enthusiastically. He sits up a little straighter in his chair now that they have found something in common to talk about.

Spence is befuddled by Cam's comment. Spence smiles noncommittally. There's a cumbersome silence. Spence looks at his watch. "Do you know what the acronym 'VT' stands for?" he asks, casting around for more familiar ground to fill the silence. "Most people don't, you know."

Cam is not sure if he has misheard him. He repeats the question to himself, listening for nuances in the sounds of the letters that would give him a clue about what Spence really said. Cam is at a loss. Perhaps he really did say VD. Possibly there's an underlying moral message that the company espouses, no office fraternizing? From time to time companies promote their own moral message within the company for business reasons, but it seems too early for that. This is only a first interview.

"Did you say 'VD'?" asks Cam.

"No, VT" replies Spence with a shocked look of surprise when he realizes Cam has misheard him.

"E T, extra terrestrial?" Cam asks before Spence can clearly enunciate the letters to resolve the confusion. Perhaps Spence is making a reference to the movie, Cam thinks. In which case he isn't sure where Spence is going with this train of thought. The conversation is not going well.

"No, V as in Victor, T as in Tango," Spence replies with a smiley frown.

"Oh! Victor Tango, VT, the initials of the company! Of course! What was I thinking? Yes, roger, message received. Over," responds Cam. He finds himself once again wearing Spence's infectious smile.

"Yes, that's right!" Spence's jubilant smile returns.

"No, I don't know what it means." answers Cam. He happily shakes his head from side to side, a thrall of Spence's overwhelming Elysian cheerfulness.

"Vision Transmission," answers Spence, trying to get the conversation back on track. "Our founder, Jack Urizen, had a vision when he began the VT broadcasting network, which would ultimately dominate broadcasting across the entire country. This was before satellites and cable TV. Over the years the company has grown and evolved into the company that it is today. Jack died a few years ago, but we carry on in his name. That's a little history about us." Spence decides not to ask anymore unscripted questions.

There is a rap on the door. "I got lost," says Earle rolling his eyes to signal his frustration. "Gnnnnnnh," he adds as though clearing his throat. "You must be Cam. I'm Earle," says Earle in a gargled voice.

Earle is casually dressed. He wears a slate-gray button-down sweater. His gray hair is thinning above the temples and the crown of his head. His hair is arranged in a comb over. Half-frame reading glasses dangle from a white beaded-plastic strap hung around his neck. Earle reminds Cam of employees who have spent their corporate careers flying under the radar of their superiors, popping up only when it is safe to do so.

Cam struggles in the cramped quarters to pull himself to a shaky standing position. He leans on the desk with his left hand for added support. He shakes Earle's hand. "Hi, how are you?" asks Cam with an unintentionally big grin as though he has temporarily forgotten his own self, having voluntarily assumed the irrepressible persona of Spence. Cam is feeling drunk with Spence's insensible cheeriness.

"I'll be better when they finish this construction," responds Earle, "gnnnnnnh. I'll get a chair from one of the other offices and join you." Earle disappears. He returns, rolling a chair into the already cramped office. Cam is pushed further into the corner with the Night Sleeper to allow room for Earle. Cam surreptitiously brushes aside the leaves with his shoulder. The plant is persistent. Earle puts on his reading glasses. He holds a sheet of paper that he has brought with him. He glances at the sheet of paper while ignoring Cam's plight. Cam unsuccessfully continues his fight with the plant. Finally realizing the futility of his struggle, he decides that he can live with the obtrusive plant at least for the moment. He stops brushing at the leaves. He doesn't want to distract Spence and Earle with actions that they might construe as compulsive behavior, a sign of a character flaw.

"What can you tell us about yourself?" asks Earle, looking at Cam over his reading glasses.

"Aaah," interjects Spence before Cam can answer. "Is that the right question?" Spence and Earle look at the sheet of paper that each is holding. Their papers provide a list of approved interview questions.

"Mine is dated today. What's the date on yours?" asks Earle looking at his paper.

"Mine is dated last week. Was there a new approved list of questions released?"

"It hasn't been *officially* released, but will be today," Earle says with a condescending grin. "I was on the revision committee for the interview questions. We made the questions a little more informal in keeping with the best practices used by best-in-class companies."

Spence frowns as best he can. "It hasn't been released yet?" asks Spence. He is unsure if using what is still an unofficial list of the official interview questions is an acceptable practice.

"Yes," answers Earle who, like many managers, loves to think that he is on top of things when others aren't, even when he isn't. In this case, Earle is in the know. "The questions have been through the approval process. We merely need Jeff's signature."

Spence stares uncomprehendingly. Earle looks at Spence expecting a response. The sudden banging of a hammer in the next office surprises the silence. The hammering ends as abruptly as it started. A fine dust falls from the ceiling.

"Jeff?"

"Yes, you know, Jeff," says Earle trying not to roll his eyes at Spence's ignorance. Earle is flabbergasted that Spence doesn't know who Jeff is. "The VP in charge of process improvements," prompts Earle. "He was appointed last month to the position. The questions can be released once Jeff signs off, which is a formality at this point. I spoke to Jeff," Earle reassures.

"Doesn't the CEO have to sign off on this too?" asks Spence.

"No," answers Earle, growing a little irritated while trying not to show it, "not anymore. The sign-off process changed. It changed last week. I helped get the process change through. The CEO's sign off isn't required anymore. It streamlines the process. Gnnnnnnh," adds Earle.

At this juncture, Cam has a minor epiphany when he realizes Earle's throat clearing is Earle's way of saying that no further discussion is required on this topic.

"Okay," says Spence deferring to Earle. "Then let's use your questions." Spence smiles with trepidation, but smile he must.

Earle looks directly at Cam. "What can you tell us about yourself?" asks Earle feeling pleased with himself after winning the discussion.

Cam is relieved. He has prepared an answer in anticipation of the question. "I enjoy the challenges provided by the creative writing process and meeting deadlines. I'm a self-starter; you have to be if you're a writer. I'm a problem solver," says Cam, rapidly spitting out the bullet points of his well-rehearsed answer. "I love overcoming the problems that invariably occur when creating a script whether the

issue is a change to a deadline, competing deadlines, or an
unexpected change in the focus of the script." Cam fires off
his response like a machine gun: A-A-A-A-A-A-A! "I'm
results oriented and organized. Meeting my deadlines is
important to me." He imagines Spence and Earle wearing
plastic army helmets. A-A-A-A-A-A-A! Coooveeeonnng!
Gotcha! His answer lasts several minutes. "Is there anything
I've said that you would like me to go over in more detail?"
he invites when finished answering.

Earle passes the sheet of questions to Spence. There is a
discussion about whether the next question is appropriate
for the interview. The discussion continues for a few minutes
while Spence and Earle debate the merits of the question.

"Gnnnnnnh," adds Earle at the end of their discussion.

"How did you get started as a script writer?" asks
Spence, having skipped the next question on the list.

"There was an ad in a newspaper, the MKM Liberty
Press. My current employer needed a script writer. I had
recently finished university and was looking for work. I
didn't have any definite plans, so I decided to respond to the
ad, thinking I would try script writing to see if I liked it. The
rest is history. I guess you could say that I wandered into the
job," responds Cam. "But I enjoy what I do," he adds
quickly, so as not to give the wrong impression.

The question-and-answer interview continues for about
forty-five minutes. There is the customary discussion
between Spence and Earle about each question before one of
them asks the question, depending on whose turn it is.

"Well," says Spence reading from Earle's paper, "thank
for your time today. We will be making our decision
shortly," says Spence looking at his watch. "Oh look, almost
noon. Would you like lunch in the cafeteria? Earle, can Cam
join you for lunch? I have to run a few errands, so I can't join
you. Otherwise I would." This last part of the interview
about lunch seems an ad-lib on Spence's part. For his part,
Earle looks a little surprised. He didn't think Spence had it in

him to extemporize. Cam decides the invitation to lunch is a good sign.

"Yes, of course," answers Earl, recovering his usual business demeanor. "Gnnnnnnh." He returns the extra chair to the office where it belongs.

"Thank you," says Cam to Spence as they both struggle to stand in the cubicle-sized space. "I hope to hear from you soon," he adds, happy to have escaped the plant.

"Yes, thank you," says Spence with a zealous handshake and smile.

"Are you ready?" asks Earle who has returned. "I'll catch up with you later," says Earle looking at Spence. Earle gives his head a discrete affirmative nod, indicating to Spence that he is pleased with the interview.

"Yes, I'm ready," Cam replies to Earle.

"I know a shortcut," says Earle as he heads off with Cam in tow. After several turns through numerous hallways, they reach the cafeteria. Earle proceeds to a refrigerator provided for the employees. He removes his lunch bag.

"You can get a tray and get whatever you like from the lunch counter," says Earle gesturing toward the wait staff behind the lunch counter. "Today's Thursday, so there are Rueben sandwiches already made, or they'll make a sandwich for you, or you can get a hamburger and fries, or a salad. There are lots of choices. They say the sandwiches are good. I wouldn't know. I bring my lunch." Earle holds up his lunch bag for emphasis. "On Fridays they have fish. The company subsidizes the cafeteria; the prices are reasonable. I'll meet you over there," adds Earle gesturing with a jerk of his head at a table in a corner of the cafeteria.

Cam orders a Rueben sandwich, a drink and fries and pays at the checkout. He joins Earle at his table.

"Are you a Warriors fan?" ask Cam between bites of his sandwich.

"No," says Earle shaking his head while he concentrates on removing the plastic wrap from his tuna fish sandwich. His wife made his lunch the night before. "I'm not much on football. I'm counting the months until retirement."

"How many months?"

"Not many, a couple," Earle answers.

"Are you looking forward to retirement? Any plans after you retire?"

"Oh I don't know, nothing much. Do a little fishing, something like that," replies Earle hazily. Earle works on his sandwich. Occasionally he turns his attention to his carrot sticks.

"You like to fish?" asks Cam between bites of his fries. "Where do you fish?"

"In the lake at the end of the street," Earle says with indifference, "nothing special." Wallaceville is situated next to a large lake.

"Do you have a boat?"

"No, I walk down to the pier, which isn't far. Usually I'll roll up my pants, wade a little into the lake and cast my line," replies Earle, pointing in the direction of the lake.

"Catch anything?" asks Cam having finished his fries.

"Bass, perch or the occasional pike. What I was really hoping was to get a contract to work for VT," Earle volunteers. "You know, help them with their special projects. Sometimes they do that, offer a contract if you're retiring. Course I can't talk about the special projects. They're confidential. Only senior-level management, Kyle and Wade mostly, know about the projects. There are a couple of managers, like myself, who are in the know, and a few of the staff in the lower echelons, not many. Wade made noises about keeping me on with a contract. I don't think that will happen now," Earle adds trying to hide his disappointment. "I'm not after the money so much, but it would keep me busy. Work a few days a week at VT and ease into retirement. My wife thinks I need a hobby. She's afraid I'll be under foot around the house. Gnnnnnnh."

"Who is Wade?"

"Senior VP in the corporation. He's in charge of special projects."

"How do you manage to keep the creative process flowing among the writers?" asks Cam, searching for another topic to keep the conversation going.

"I don't," answers Earle in his usual matter-of-fact way, "there's a process. They follow the process. First the writer finds out what he or she is expected to write about, then writes a draft, then submits the draft for review of accuracy, rewrite, then submits for a peer review, re-write, then submits the draft to..." Earle's explanation stretches on for twenty minutes. Cam loses track of Earle's description after the first thirty seconds. Cam listens with dead ears. He's busy replaying the interview in his head and critiquing his performance. "And then you're done," concludes Earle with a smile of satisfaction. "Well, unless the script requires more changes because marketing isn't satisfied with the direction or tone. The formula is simple," says Earle with the confidence of one who is well practiced in the arcane craft of the VT process. "A science, I mean," says Earle as an afterthought, "we encourage the writers to be creative provided they follow the process."

"It sounds similar to coloring inside the lines, only someone comes along and alters the lines, or changes the picture from a horse to a camel, or jiggles the picture while you're coloring."

"Yes something like that," answers Earle doubtfully. He's not sure that Cam's analogy is quite the one that he would have chosen, but is hesitant to query Cam on his analogy in case he, Earle, has misunderstood. Earle does not want to appear ignorant. "I mean no, but look. Senior management at VT does encourage creativity. There was the list of interview questions that I worked on, for example.

165

There were about ten others on the team from different departments. That requires creativity to craft the questions in exactly the right way, so that everyone is satisfied in the end with the questions. You want a uniform product, in this case the interview questions, across the entire corporation, so that all interviews are the same. That way there's a common base in the corporation, so that everyone who comes to VT for an interview is treated equally. And interviewees can be compared apples to apples, not apples to oranges, if you see what I mean. And of course there are always these process changes that we need to take into account. That can add time and complexity to an existing project when a new process is introduced in the middle of an ongoing project. There are questions about whether or not the new process, or change to an existing process should be applied to an existing project. At times existing projects get grandfathered, or parts of the new process are applied to an existing project. It depends on how far along the project is and how easy it is to introduce the process change. You know. Would the change to the process delay the project unnecessarily, or add too much additional cost? You have to be practical about these things." Earle pauses to catch his breath. "At the end of the day you have to have structure, rules about how things get done in an organization. Otherwise how do people know what to do? Process is simply good business practice. Gnnnnnnh."

"Travel plans perhaps?" asks Cam trying another subject. "I mean after you retire."

"No nothing along that line," answers Earle, finishing the last of his carrot sticks. "Sleep a little later in the morning, that sort of thing. You know."

"Family?" asks Cam.

Earle removes a plastic container from his lunch bag. He removes the lid. In the container are peach slices in heavy syrup. Cam sips his drink and watches Earle while Earle eats the slices with a spoon that he has brought from home. He methodically cuts a peach slice in half with his spoon and then eats each half slice before moving on to the next slice. "My wife and I," answers Earle between bites. He finishes his peaches and then spoons the syrup. Finished, he carefully wipes the container with a paper napkin that he takes from the napkin holder on the table. He re-seals the plastic container. Next he wipes the spoon with a new napkin. Then he places the container and spoon neatly in his lunch bag and zips the bag shut. He leans back in his chair as he has always done after each lunch in a long line of lunches, stretching back to his first day at VT. He smiles contentedly. "Gnnnnnnh," says Earle unaware of his mannerism and pronouncement on all things.

"Usually I go outside for a smoke after lunch. Do you smoke?" asks Earle growing restless. He begins jingling the change in his pant pocket. "There are designated smoking areas outside at the back of the building."

As Cam looks at Earle a sudden and vast sense of emptiness surges up like an artesian well from deep inside as though discovering the overwhelming answer to an unspoken question that he has not dared to ask. The feeling reminds him of one cold winter night in Bayview when he had decided to go for a walk alone. He wasn't paying attention to where he was going and found himself down by the bay. Snow was falling soft and silent. It seemed to deaden everything as it drifted down. The streets were abandoned to the silence. Out of the darkness loomed the high gray walls of the Bayview penitentiary that was built over a hundred and fifty years ago. The meager light from a few streetlights illuminated the lower portions of the walls and the falling snow when it intercepted the light. Above the streetlights, the walls became indistinct gray shapes that reached up into the darkness. The guard towers mounted on turrets on the penitentiary walls were dark and vacant looking. The two massive steel doors that fronted onto the street were shut. The few narrow windows in the penitentiary walls that faced the street were dark and empty. Behind the penitentiary lay the cold blackness of the bay not yet frozen over with ice. The stars were swallowed up in the blackness.

Is this how it ends, Cam asks himself. Is this it: a tuna fish sandwich, a few carrot sticks, peach slices and hoping to stay on at the end of the day? What have I done? Cam fights a rising sense of an empty death: death by a thousand paper cuts.

"Gnnnnnnh," prompts Earle, looking at Cam for an answer.

"No," says Cam, recovering, "I don't smoke."

"Well in that case," says Earle leaning forward confidentially while he continues to jingle the change in his pant pocket, "I shouldn't do this, but do you think you can find your way to Letha's desk by yourself? I'm supposed to escort you out of the building. It's a security thing."

"Yes, I think so," says Cam not sure at all that he can find his way out of the building, but not wanting to admit to his poor sense of direction.

"Okay, then I'll leave you here. Don't forget to hand in the visitor's badge," says Earle. "Well it was nice to meet you. You're sure you can find your way out? You go down the stairs, then a right, a left at the water cooler and then straight. You can't miss it. I'm sure you can find it." Earle anxiously jingles the coins in his pocket. He smiles reassuringly to demonstrate his confidence in Cam's navigational skills.

"Yes, I'll find it," Cam says smiling reluctantly.

Earle leans forward again towards Cam on the other side of the table. "And between you and me," says Earle in a hushed and confidential tone, "I expect you'll be hearing from us. Don't tell anyone I said that. Gnnnnnnh."

Cam smiles a crippled smile. "Thank you."

They shake hands. Earle leaves the cafeteria with his lunch bag in hand. He makes a beeline to the designated smoking area. Cam navigates the stairs. He gets turned around only once where the water cooler should be. Eventually he finds Letha. He turns in his visitor's badge.

10 Wazzlwahzzl

After dinner Cam strolls to the Warriors Coliseum where the Wallaceville Warriors are scheduled to battle the Bayview Stingers. Countless fans have painted their faces in the Warriors colors, purple and gold. Others carry plastic swords that they wave about. They stab and hack away with their swords at stuffed toy bees. A diehard Warriors fan in the crowd bangs away on a bass drum, beating out the syllables Warr-i-ors: boom, boom, BOOM. The fans pick up the chant.

Many fans have donned Warriors regalia for tonight's festivities. A few Warriors fans are dressed like Roman centurions, the mascot of the Wallaceville Warriors. They wear replica centurion helmets that are similar to the kind once worn by Roman legionnaires. The metal helmets are elaborate with embossed detailing and plumed crests made from horse hair. The crests are dyed in Warriors colors. Some fans wear a centurion's cape. Usually these are the fans with the elaborate helmets. Loads of fans wear simpler, brass-looking, plastic helmets with a domed cap and visor. Still other fans have opted for T-shirts with a picture printed on the front of a Roman centurion holding a spear.

Numerous fans are busy kicking the stuffing out of stuffed toy bees tied to sturdy string. With each kick, a bee takes flight and returns for another kick. Kickers, as they are known in Warriors football parlance, like to customize their bees by inserting metal washers in the bee's ass to ensure a fast return flight after each kick. A few kickers have with practice become very proficient at bee kicking in time with the beat of a bass drum. They've turned their kicking into a kind of footbag jig.

Occasionally a 'caper', as they are known in the local vernacular, will attempt to bust a kicker move, but only after tucking the cape into the back of his or her pants to keep the cape out of the way. Many capers look down on this practice because stuffing the cape down the back of your pants is considered undignified.

After a season of kicking, the toy bees look like the bee on Dunc's spreading gut, or worse. When a bee wears out, you can get a replacement from one of the street vendors outside the Warriors Coliseum. Bees start at about five dollars. The more expensive the bee, the longer it will last; quality counts.

A few kickers, mostly from the T-shirt class, have turned professional as street buskers. You have to be really good to turn professional. The Warriors crowd is very critical of their buskers' kicking skills. The crowd rewards only the best with spare change. The criticality of the crowd along with the cost of good-quality stuffed mascots means that you have to be exceptional to make a living as a mascot kicker. Many are called, but few are chosen.

Tonight the buskers are kicking bees. At the next Warriors game it will be the hapless mascot of another rival team. Bees are preferred because their ball shape makes them easy to kick. The shape of many of the other mascots makes them difficult to kick and requires more practice. For example, the trajectory of the horse mascot of the Whissleton Thunders football team is difficult to control when kicked because its legs stick out getting in the way of a good kick.

For the few Stingers fans that are brave enough to show up wearing Stingers paraphernalia, there are taunts of queen bee, Bayview Stinkers, bagless bees, bee barf, BS and other such taunts by the Warriors fans. A few Stingers fans reply in kind with reference to Willies Willnots and Willies Weasels. There are a few heated exchanges, but nothing serious this night because the Wallaceville police move in quickly to break up anything that might get out of hand.

Inside the Coliseum there is the usual pre-game fanfare with trumpets and drums and marching and singing and standing and sitting and pledging and silence at the appropriate moments and head bowing and all the stuff that the fans have learned to expect. The game itself is uneventful. The Warriors win. The Wallaceville fans are happy with the outcome.

Cam joins the exiting fans and begins walking toward the Peaceful Rest Motel. The evening is warm. He's in no hurry as he navigates his way through downtown Wallaceville. The night life is in full swing. Many of the Warriors fans are celebrating their win in the sidewalk cafes and nightclubs. Occasionally music leaks into the night from the open door of a nightclub.

From an alleyway on the edge of the downtown, an unseen door opens. *A Night in Tunisia* pumps out of the doorway, tumbles off the brick walls of the buildings that line the alleyway, and washes over the evening air. The music sounds far off, a little sad and soft, and saying something that Cam has heard before. The music begins to pick up tempo and then suddenly stops when the door shuts.

Cam ventures down the side alley in search of the source of the music. He discovers stairs leading to a basement door where the muffled sound of *A Night in Tunisia* calls enticingly. A small red neon sign over the door announces the 'NotE' nightclub. After the E there's a circle with a dot in the middle and then two lightning bolts. The sign looks like this:

NotE

Most of the patrons call it the Naughty club and smile cautiously because they know that's not the name of the club, at least not in the way that most people see things. Occasionally a few would-be patrons stumble onto the club and mistakenly assume that they've unearthed a strip club. Usually they're disappointed when they discover that the club is not what they expected. A minority stay to listen to the music. The majority leave because they're looking for another kind of entertainment. The club owner, Dylan, won't say what the sign means, insisting instead that you use your imagination. Some patrons think the sign is a reference to the musical note E, which might have special significance for Dylan who is also a musician. When asked if the sign is a reference to the musical note, Dylan simply smiles mysteriously. When pressed, Dylan refers to the nightclub as *The Club*. A few patrons have asked the wait staff the name of the club, but the staff members don't know any more than the patrons. The staff members make up names, like Naughty Moonbeam. A couple of patrons think they know, but won't tell. Others pretend to know even though they don't.

The music pours out when Cam opens the door. He steps into a long narrow room. At the far end is a small cramped stage with musicians, microphones and overhead spot lights that illuminate the stage. The musicians bring the number to an end. They take a break before beginning the next set. Cam makes his way to the bar that lines one wall of the nightclub. The room is filled with dozens of small black-lacquered tables scarcely big enough to hold drinks. There are chairs crowded around each table, making it difficult for Cam to navigate his way to the bar. The place is about half full with patrons. Cam orders a beer at the bar. He moves to an empty table in a corner where he works on his beer while waiting for the next set to start.

It isn't long before the musicians take to the stage. Without introduction they play two numbers with applause by the patrons at the end of each number. The band sounds good. At the end of the second number, the piano player leans forward toward a mike perched over the piano. "Thank you," he says smiling while he plays quietly on the piano. "Thank you very much. That was *How Big Can You Get?* and *The Old Man of the Mountain*," he announces. "Tonight we have Eddie Johnson on alto sax, Big Eddie to his fans." Big Eddie plays a few bars on his sax by way of introduction. "Yeah, you tell 'em Big Eddie," continues the piano player as he resumes playing softly in the background. "On bass we have Keter Brooks." Now the bass player jumps in. Keter plays a few bars while the crowd applauds. "Yeah Keter, sing it. And I'm Jack, The Wave, Peterson," says the piano player smiling. Jack stops playing, stands up, makes a big slow circular wave with his hand at the audience and then launches into a few bars on the piano while standing up. "And we are the Standing Wave Trio," he says and then sits down. Now all three join in and play a few bars of *Half Nelson*.

"Thank you," says Jack after the applause dies down. "And on behalf of *The Club*," says Jack smiling and dropping his voice for special emphasis on The Club to play on the inside joke, "welcome. I hope you enjoy the ride because tonight I hope we can take you to a place where you probably haven't been in a long time," Jack plays a few bars from a tune, "or maybe you have. We'll see. Next we'd love to do a number that's a favorite of the band. I hope you enjoy it. It's called *Sweet Georgia Brown*."

Jack counts the tempo and with that they launch into the number. It starts fast and stays fast with everyone jumping in at the start, then a piano solo, now sax, then bass and then everyone joins in and round and round, and the audience claps at the end of each solo and then more sax, piano, bass and on and on. The momentum is a wild roller coaster that's almost out of control and won't stop, now up, now down, then right, now left, then up, and you don't know where you are and you don't want it to stop, and the whole thing is about to fly apart, and you're getting tossed around, and you're hanging on hard, and then it brakes hard to a stop and the ride is over and the crowd breaks into applause.

"Thank you," says Jack. The applause starts to subside. "Did you enjoy the ride?" The applause wells up again. Jack grins good-naturedly. He plays a few bars from something and waits for the applause to end.

"Next we have a special treat for you," says Jack. "Joining us tonight is John Johnson on vocals. That's right, Big Eddie's little brother. And tonight he's going to make you cry. That's why we call him the Rainmaker." There's a short burst of music while John leaps up from a chair and launches himself onto the stage wearing a happy-to-be-here smile. He reaches for a mike while the crowd applauds. Then he makes a little bow to the audience.

"Thank you," John grins warmly. "Here's a number that Jack wrote that we've been working on. He calls it Wazzlwahzzl. We like it and I hope you will too," John adds. He turns and nods to Jack.

Jack counts out the beat and they're off. There's a fast-paced intro of a couple dozen bars and then John dives into the song. The first time he sings it straight through with lots of improvising by the trio and it sounds great as they spin round and through it. Then they start from the top again. This time John starts to improvise too, adding scat singing to the mix. At first only a little here and there and then more and more until the song is mostly scat.

John is good, not like most singers who sing scat, but don't know what they're singing. They sing scat straight out and it's bent in a bad way because they sing it straight out.

There's no kidness in it. They don't understand. And even if they understood it, they couldn't sing it. They lost their kidness long ago. And probably those listening don't know that the scat singing is bad. It sounds fine to them because they're not listening with their kid ears. And the unkid singers are so focused on singing the song that they forget what scat is all about. It's about kidness and seeing everything big and alive and bigger than big. It's not about a big fake inflatable bee, or a bad half-written detective novel, or the alive stuff squeezed into a formula, or tiger crap, and that kind of shit.

So the unkid singers are pretending in a bad way. But John is pretending in a good way with made-up kid sounds because inside he's still holding on to his kidness. And he's wearing a big kid grin. And perhaps scat singing is simply kids playing, but you can't say that to adults because they don't know how to play and have fun and stuff. And if you told them scat is kid's play, they wouldn't want to play because they've forgotten how to play. And if they haven't forgotten how to play, they wouldn't want to play anyway because that would look childish. And that would be bad because others might say you're being childish. But scat isn't childish. It's kid-like in the best way.

And if a few think scat is only play and fun, they might try to organize it and give adults exercises to do about how to have fun and be a kid again, but it wouldn't be fun because it wouldn't be spontaneous. It would be like trying to laugh when there's nothing to laugh about. And soon the adults would get bored and quit or join an organized sport. Or worse yet, they could make kids join an organized sport so the kids could have fun because it would be about winning or learning a life skill, like cooperation, team building, or other slick Orky shit.

Good scat singing is about hanging on to your kidness like John, who is showing you that you can be a kid too and have fun and be part of the big. Because good scat singing is right up there with *Song of Joy* and *Take the A Train*, or any other great song. You only have to let go and let fly in the right way.

"Yeah, sing it!" yells Cam getting into the song. "Make it roll! Bring it home!"

Now Cam and others in the audience are standing and clapping and cheering and the band is rolling fast and sweet and the end is coming fast and hard and everyone is on their feet and then BANG the number is over and the audience is wild and the applause shoots up like big waves crashing and thrashing and rolling and the fans are yelling for more with waves sweeping over everything.

Cam's voice begins to choke up and a few tears well up because he's in a place he hasn't been in a long time. And his voice too is part of the big wave crashing everywhere on everything.

He stops clapping after a while. The applause and cheering subside. He doesn't know how long he's been clapping and cheering.

The band finishes the set with John singing a couple more numbers. Cam stays for the rest of the sets. By the time the trio ends the last set of the night, there's still a good crowd of patrons, including Cam.

"Thank you for coming out," says Jack wrapping up things while the trio plays quietly, letting things wind down. "I hope you enjoyed yourself and hope you'll come back and see us again sometime. We're here until the end of the week. Thank you and good night."

The stage goes silent. Big Eddie and Keter pack up their instruments. Dylan shuts off the spotlights and turns off the neon sign above the door.

Cam steps into the alley. The hour is late. The air feels fresh and cool against his face. He ambles down the alley to the almost empty street. Relaxed, he walks to his motel.

The next morning Cam showers, eats his continental breakfast without incident and drives home. He decides to bypass the Big Tiger in favor of the new rest stop, Along the Way.

11 The View from Here

Cam prepares the spaghetti and sauce while Anna sets the table in Cam's kitchen.

"Do you want wine with dinner?" asks Anna.

"Yes, good idea, there's a bottle in the cupboard."

"Red or white?"

"Red would go well with the spaghetti. What do you think?"

"Red is fine. Corkscrew?"

"In the drawer with the knives and forks."

"How was the interview?"

"It was fine. The manager that I would be replacing said that I could expect to hear from them. He's about to retire."

"How long before you hear from them?"

"I'm not sure. They didn't say. They don't seem to move very fast at VT."

"Tell me about the interview. How was it?"

"It was odd."

"How so?"

"There's a lot of construction going on in the building where the interview took place. I got lost looking for the interview room. Eventually I found the room where I met the personnel officer, Spence. We tried to kill time while waiting for Earle to show up."

"Who is Earle?"

"He's the retiring manager. The small talk didn't go over very well with Spence; it was a series of miscommunications. Then Earle showed up. He got lost too looking for Spence's office. Then they asked questions from a prepared list of interview questions after discussing who had the most up-to-date list. Turns out the questions are part of their process for interviewing potential employees. Earle would make this peculiar *gnnnnnnh* sound occasionally after he said something. At first I thought he was clearing his throat because the room was dusty with all of the construction going on. Then I realized *gnnnnnnh* is his way of saying that there's nothing more to say on the topic of conversation. The subject is closed. Now move on."

"What about the questions themselves? How did you do with them?"

"Oh they were fine. They both seemed satisfied with my answers."

"Then what happened?"

"I had lunch with Earle in the cafeteria."

"How was lunch?"

"It was a little strange. I tried talking to him, but Earle didn't seem to have much going for himself outside of work. He didn't have any real plans for retirement, just fishing and that seemed to be a way to kill time. He was hoping to stay on at VT under contract after retiring, but that fell through. I felt sorry for him. There didn't seem to be any spark in him only mummy dust."

"That sounds suffocating. It reminds me of being outside on a cold winter's day when the wind's blowing and I can't catch my breath."

"Yes, dry as toast. There's nothing inside. If you opened him up, he'd blow away in the wind," Cam responds. "And if you did open him up, and he started to blow away, I can imagine him watching with indifference and then summing up his life with a 'gnnnnnnh' before disappearing altogether. I don't want to wander down that path and find there's nothing left at the end."

"So what are you going to do?"

"I don't know yet."

180

"What did you think about VT in general?"

"I saw a general-interest piece in the news while I was in Wallaceville," responds Cam, sitting down to dinner. "It was about an engineer. He created this somewhat humanoid-looking mechanical robot mounted on a kind of motorized wheelchair. It had this rubbery latex face. The engineer programmed it so that it could make appropriate facial expressions when talking to somebody. It could smile, frown disapprovingly, look surprised and make other facial expressions." Cam spasms a smile in robot fashion to show Anna. His face jerks taught for a few seconds in a gaping rubbery grin and then snaps back to a deadpan expression. Then he explodes into a frown before jolting back to his deadpan look as though springs in his face suddenly and violently extended and retracted in a quick rendition of an attempted frown. Anna chuckles. "The idea is that the robot can be used to assist in retirement homes to help look after patients because caregivers are in short supply. The robot can move from room to room where it can remind patients to take their medications, or suggest a chess move to a patient."

"So you're a robot?" Anna asks.

"No, not a robot." Cam has a big grin on his face. "Okay, work with me on this one. Do you remember *2001: A Space Odyssey*?"

Anna nods. "The film is a science fiction classic."

"Yes, one of my sci-fi favorites," says Cam warming to the story he is about to tell. "What would have happened if the protagonist, Dr. David Bowman, after disabling the computer, HAL 9000, decided not to investigate the black monolith and so he never discovers the answer to the mystery? What if instead he turns the spaceship around and limps back to earth because the mission is too badly compromised to complete successfully."

"Okay, I'm not sure where you're going with this. Keep going," says Anna smiling.

"Fast forward several decades," says Cam. "Now Dave is old. Things have not gone well for him after the failure of his mission. He finds himself a resident in a warehouse full of old people. The place is a retirement home. Everyone has a cubicle with a bed and a night stand. Each cubicle is sectioned off with faded flimsy curtains the color of dirty dishwater. There are rows and rows of these cubicles. The place smells of old-people smells. The staff is overworked. There's music playing from loud speakers. The music has a tinny quality because the speakers aren't very good. Occasionally the music is interrupted with general announcements, shuffle board starting in area 31 in 15 minutes. Overhead fluorescent lights blink erratically because they're in need of attention. Old Dave has managed to secure a job. He's a kind of caretaker in the warehouse. He earns extra money by doing minor odd jobs around the facility. The money helps pay for his residency in the warehouse. And guess who the robotic assistant is that's there to wrangle the old people?"

"My guess is HAL," answers Anna.

"And you're right," says Cam with a playful grin. "HAL is now obsolete. His space exploring days are over. After a few minor software upgrades to his program and the addition of a humanoid robot body in a wheelchair to make him ambulatory, HAL is now an assistant helping the old people in the warehouse. Can you imagine the conversation between HAL and Dave?"

Anna shakes her head no. "No I can't, but I'm sure you can." She cracks a smile.

"Dave," says Cam in his best HAL voice. "Dave."

"Yes HAL," says Cam in his best old Dave voice and trying to sound a little crotchety. "What is it?"

"I've detected a problem with porto-thunderbox 29," says Cam in his HAL voice. "I predict that it will fail in 24 hours unless it is repaired."

"You smelt it. You dealt it," says Cam in his old Dave voice and trying not to laugh. "Besides, Betty can look after the portable toilets. It's her turn this week," continues Cam in the role of old Dave now sounding more serious. "Go see Betty. One of the inmates has probably put something in it that they shouldn't have. That's usually the case. Betty can fix it."

"Normally I would Dave, but there's a problem."

"Oh, what's that?" says Cam with a reluctant sigh to show that this is a line of questioning that old Dave doesn't want to pursue because it can't lead to a good place.

"Well Dave, you may have noticed that Betty hasn't moved from her chair in the past three days."

"Oh. So what? Don't bother me with this stuff! Talk to Betty."

"Well Dave, you know I would, but Betty is dead, Dave." Cam follows this statement up with a jerky rubbery frown to show the expression that HAL might display with the announcement of Betty's death. Then Cam as old Dave twists slowly halfway around in his chair, as though looking at an imaginary Betty sitting in a chair in the corner of the kitchen. He manages to make the chair squeak on the kitchen floor when he turns it slightly to look at the imaginary dead Betty. Slowly he turns around again to face the table while still pretending to be old Dave. Anna's smile gets bigger.

"Those things are dangerous," says Cam in his old Dave voice. "Remember Frank? He got caught in one of those things when he was trying to fix it. The amber light on the thunderbox was off. They emptied it with Frank inside! The bastards! The amber light was supposed to be on to tell them there was someone inside. What happened?"

"I'm sorry Dave," says Cam in his HAL voice. "There was a malfunction. It won't happen again Dave. I ran a diagnostic. My porto-thunderbox subroutine is fine now. You know I wouldn't do anything to jeopardize the

183

mission." Cam twitches his face into a rubbery and not very reassuring smile the way HAL might.

Anna can stand it no longer. She bursts into laughter and Cam does too. In a little while they stop laughing. Then Cam and Anna look at one another and the laughter starts again and then subsides and then begins again and finally ends. Cam wipes away his tears.

"Stop, stop!" pleads Anna holding her sides. "No more, please!"

"Okay, okay," says Cam, trying to contain himself. "I promise. I'll stop." He jolts into another rubbery HAL smile. Cam and Anna break uncontrollably into laughter again. "Oh that felt good," says Cam when the laughter subsides for the final time. "Was it good for you too?" Anna nods her head yes, barely able to restrain herself.

"So what are you trying to say about VT?" asks Anna after regaining her composure. "VT isn't the company for you. Is it?"

"Yes, that's right," acknowledges Cam. "I don't want to end up like Earle with nothing left inside, always playing it safe, always playing by the rules, not taking a chance, and not believing in yourself because everything since you were born tells you not to believe in yourself."

"So what are you going to do? You could stay where you are, or there's that job with Zanya, or do you have other ideas?"

"I don't know. I'm working on it."

"What would you like to do if you could do anything?" Anna asks.

"What do you remember most about our summer vacation last year?" asks Cam changing the subject. "Is there any one thing that stands out more for you?"

"There was the visit to the old coal mine that they've turned into a historic site," replies Anna. "What was it called? Oh yes, the Atlas Coal Mine. When you suggested that we visit the mine, I didn't think I'd enjoy it, but I did. I

184

liked learning about the miners and their families. They lived hard lives. And it was interesting to hear the guides talk about their encounters with the dead who have stayed on in spirit at the mine site. What did you like best?"

"Remember the hike up Grotto Canyon?"

"Yes, the one with the pictographs, that was good too. What do you remember about the hike?"

"I remember coming back down into the canyon after wandering around in the mountain valley above it. The valley was hot, dry and dusty. When we got back into the canyon, I could feel its coolness. And there was a breeze blowing that made it a nice place to be on a hot day, a kind of garden."

"Yes, I remember that. It was quiet too. There were only a few other people in the canyon. Everyone was being quiet out of respect. And there was that little waterfall immediately off the main canyon. It was like walking into an air conditioned room after the heat of the valley."

"There was a little stream below the falls. The stream followed the gravel bed in the canyon. Do you remember the little pool of water where we stopped and dipped our feet in? There were those two rocks beside the pool that were barely big enough to sit on. The pool was scarcely big enough for our feet."

"The water was cold," says Anna. "It took a little getting used to, but once I was use to it, it was very relaxing."

"And you could watch the stream working its way slowly through the pool, following the stream bed and then disappearing into the gravel. Did you notice the fossilized coral on the rocks by the pool? There we were in a canyon, high in the Rockies and there's fossilized coral that was once a living thing on the sea floor and it was pushed up millions of years ago. It was amazing."

"The canyon was beautiful. I didn't want to leave."

"Yes, it was wonderful. On the way down we found the pictographs that someone had made thousands of years ago.

We missed them on our way up. What were they trying to tell us?" There's a long silence while Cam and Anna ponder the question. "I think it was their way of honoring the sacredness of the place," Cam poses, trying to find the right words.

"And the wonder."

"The beauty."

"Yes," says Anna, "we can only imagine."

"And we're part of it too," says Cam. They sit silently at the kitchen table, thinking about the canyon.

Finally Anna asks, "So back to my original question, if you could do anything you want, what would you do? I'm guessing it has to do with Grotto Canyon."

"Yes, it sounds strange, but I want to be a part of the canyon. I want to be what it is. And I want to try and show other people what the canyon is about," responds Cam struggling for the right words. "Does that make sense?"

"Yes," Anna answers after a short pause. "So how do you get there? How do you turn the canyon into something real that you can show others? You have the imagination and creativity. You're fortunate. Most people don't have your talent, at least not the way you do. I expect your gifts make it harder for you to find your path in life. What about your writing, your detective novel? Is there anything there that might help?"

"I was thinking about my detective novel on the return drive from Wallaceville. I've decided my novel isn't good enough, too formulaic. It doesn't speak about the canyon. Whatever I write needs to speak about the canyon, what the canyon is and what it means to be part of it. My detective novel can never do that. I've decided I'm not going to finish the novel because it doesn't speak to the things that I need to speak about."

"I think you had a vision in the canyon. It was all there to see. You had to connect the dots. It took a little while to make the connections."

"I hadn't thought of it in that way."

"So what's your next step?" Anna asks pleased with her insight.

"I'm trying to work out the beginnings of a new novel. I'm not there yet. I've started to put a few thoughts on paper. There's nothing firm."

"Sounds like a good start. What are your plans in the mean time?"

"Well, VT is out. I'll keep working on scripts at MKM. Oh! Remind me tell you about the jazz trio I found playing in an out-of-the-way jazz club. They were fantastic. I think you'd enjoy them. If I can find where they're playing, we can hear them sometime."

"Are you going to stay in your current job or take the job with Zanya?"

"I'm not sure."

"How about a movie after we finish dinner? I was thinking The Lost View from Here," offers Anna. "The critics are giving it good reviews. Are you interested?"

"Yes, let's do that. Are you up for a walk? The theater isn't far and it's a nice night."

"That sounds good."

"How are things going at school?"

"I'm having a good start to the school year. Establishing a routine in the classroom takes a little while. Many of the kids are eager and they're a joy to work with. Others are in the early stages of grade-eight disease. They're indifferent or openly hostile. Reaching them and possibly turning them around is hard. School is uncool. I may be able to reach a few of them."

"And the ones you can't reach?"

"Other teachers will reach some of them. And some we won't be able to reach," says Anna with a sense of resignation. "A few may turn around in high school. They're in such a hurry to grow up. They think that when they're adults they'll be free and have more control over their lives. I

187

don't blame them wanting more control, considering what some have put up with in their short lives. It seems the more they try to be adults and act big, the less they are. Even after they're grown up, they're still kids only now they're masquerading as adults. And the adults that they're trying to be are really still kids themselves, but not in a good way. Is this making sense?"

"Yes," responds Cam, "they're still kid lawyers only they're grown up now."

"Yes, they're grown-up kid lawyers. That's one way of looking at it. Do you remember when you were a kid and you would meet another kid for the first time. One of you would ask the other what grade he or she was in. It was a way of figuring out where you were in the pecking order. If you were in grade eight and the other kid was in grade six, then you were the more senior and had more authority. The race for adulthood, authority and freedom starts early. Only, the kids seem to be going after the wrong things. By grade eight the battle is on. The parents are no help because they're kid-adults themselves. They know about freedom in a limited sense. But it's the wrong kind of freedom. It's a self-serving freedom. Everything gets turned upside down. The freedom they know about isn't really about freedom at all. Their freedom is an illusion. And I don't mean that the self-less serving of others is freedom either. That's just as bent. I don't mean to be condescending. Teachers are kid-adults too and we struggle like everyone else."

"Yes we're looking in the wrong places. Things get distorted and that gets us in trouble."

"But we have to try. We have to make the effort. Otherwise why are we here?" asks Anna.

Night envelops the bedroom. Anna is almost asleep.

"Tell me a story," says Anna, lying next to Cam in his bed.

"It's your turn to tell a story. I told the story last time."

"You're the storyteller. And you do it so well," Anna encourages.

"We're all storytellers," responds Cam. "Only some are better storytellers than others."

"What do you mean?"

"Well we're all storytellers. Aren't we? Only we don't always call them stories because stories are something that you tell kids, so the word story has this pejorative sense of childishness. Or we ask kids if they've been telling stories when we think they're lying or exaggerating the facts. Adults use stories to convince other adults and kids too to look at things in a certain way. There are good stories and bad stories. The good stories in the vein of a Martin Luther King or a Ghandi can do great things. And the bad stories can get us into a lot of trouble. Look at the millions of lives lost a few wars ago because a big shot told bad stories convincingly and others believed the stories. Only we don't call them stories because the word lacks credibility. We call it a manifesto or a policy or a program or a TV commercial. Now and again we call the stories propaganda, if we're on the side denouncing the story told by somebody else."

"Maybe you should write a story that begins with once upon a war," says Anna with a satisfied smile that Cam can't see in the dark, but can feel.

"That's a good idea."

"Now tell me one of *your* stories. You know the kind. I like to hear your voice."

"Okay, but next time it's definitely your turn to tell a story."

The room goes quiet. Cam thinks for a moment before beginning. "Do you remember the very first hamburger you had? I remember my first hamburger," says Cam without waiting for a reply. "I must have been about four years old. We were sitting at the dining room table. I can remember my feet bumping against the rungs of the chair as my legs flailed away with all that kid energy. Dad brought home some

189

burgers because Mom was in the hospital. She was in labor having a baby; Mike, I think. Dad didn't know how to cook, so he brought home hamburgers."

"Did he ever learn to cook?"

"No."

"How did he survive?"

"He relied on Mom for the cooking. This was before fast food restaurants became popular. Each hamburger came in a wax paper envelope. I can remember opening the envelope, removing the burger and taking my first bite. It was unlike anything I had tasted before, truly special and wonderful. It was the experience of tasting something new for the first time. I can't describe my first hamburger any better than I can describe Grotto Canyon. You have to experience it to understand. And Dad would have made a grunting noise, Nnn," says Cam dropping his voice to make a kind of guttural sound. "That was his way of getting our attention. He would have said: Nnn, do you like that? We silently nodded our heads yes while we ate the hamburgers. Finally he said: You kidlettes eat up. It's good for you." Cam pauses to see if Anna is still listening.

"Kidlettes?" asks Anna.

"Now and again he called us kidlettes."

"I've never heard that one before," murmurs Anna.

"I can see Dad going to the local diner and buying the burgers," Cam continues. "There was a lunch counter that ran the length of the diner and a few booths along the wall opposite the counter. In each booth there was a miniature juke box mounted on the wall. You put money in it and pressed a couple of buttons to make a selection. Then a big juke box in a corner of the diner would start up and play your selection for everyone in the diner to hear."

"I think I know the diner you mean," says Anna beginning to drift off. "Didn't it close down about ten years ago?"

"Yes it did. Anyway, I can imagine Dad sitting down at the counter and saying to the waitress 'gimme three hamburgers to go'," says Cam dropping his voice. "The waitress pulls out her yellow number-two pencil. She writes down the order on one of the small yellow order pads that every waitress used to carry. Then the waitress turns to the short-order cook at the grill and says three burgers to go."

"I'm listening," mumbles Anna.

"Even then the cook must have been a fixture at the diner."

"You knew this guy?"

"Later when I was older, I'd go to the diner and have a milk shake. I used to see him behind the counter. By then he was a little overweight. He wore a white shirt, white pants, white shoes and apron. And he always wore a white wedge cap made of cloth, not a paper wedge cap like the kind that they wear today in fast-food restaurants. By late afternoon his uniform was always a little grimy after a day of cooking."

The dark soaks up the silence.

"Turns out he was a highly decorated war veteran. They did a story on him in the newspaper when he was about to retire after forty-five years at the diner. His war record was a surprise to most. The newspaper quoted him as saying that he was happy to have a family to go home to after putting in his day at the diner." Cam lies in the silence, thinking. "I wonder if that's one of the lessons he learned from his war experience. What do you think?" There's no answer. "Are you awake?"

"Yes," mumbles Anna, fighting to stay awake to hear the end of the story.

Satisfied, Cam continues. "So there's Dad waiting for his order. The cook is standing over the grill cooking the burgers; buttering the buns; adding the condiments; slipping each burger into a wax envelope; putting them in a brown paper bag and handing it to the waitress. She signals with a

191

smile to let Dad know his order is ready. She walks to the cash register. Dad pays the waitress. He takes the bag."

"Where are you going with this?" mutters Anna, who is almost asleep.

"Well, I'm sure they weren't aware of the part they played. They were a part of something, like threads in a story. And because of the thread I have this memory of my first burger. It's a good memory, a part of who I am," says Cam satisfied with the conclusion to his story. "Do you have a memory like that?"

"Mmm," Anna answers.

12 Glystare

"Hi, I'm Terry."

"Hi, I'm Terry."

"We're the two Terries," say the two Terries in unison.

Terry and Terry sit frozen in their chairs. They are trying not to move. A metal rod fastened securely to the floor runs up behind each chair. A small metal u-shaped headrest is fastened to the end of each rod. The two Terries rest their heads firmly against the headrests to keep their heads still and in position at all times. Both Terries wear green stocking bodysuits that run from the neck down, leaving only their heads exposed. Positioned behind them is a large green backdrop. Overhead there is a boom microphone and above this is an array of lights that illuminate the two Terries. Cables spiral in all directions. Two cameras face the Terries.

"And we're here to...," begins one of the Terries.

"Cut. Wait a minute," says a voice emanating from a speaker located off camera. "Terry can you tilt your head slightly to the right?"

"Which Terry?" asks the Terry on the right.

"The one on the left," is the reply.

"My left or your left?" asks the Terry on the left.

"My left."

"So that would be my right?" asks the Terry on the left.

"Yes, let's call you Terry one," says the voice.

"Who is Terry one?" asks the Terry on the left.

"You're Terry one."

"Then I'm Terry two?" says the other Terry.

"Yes, you can be the other Terry," says the voice.

Terry one slants her head.

"No, the other Terry, Terry one your head was fine. Can you tilt it back to where it was?"

Terry one carefully adjusts her head.

"That's good. Now the other Terry, tilt your head a little to the right."

The other Terry angles his head slightly to the right.

"No, your other right; my right, your left," directs the disembodied voice.

The other Terry angles his head in the other direction.

"You need to get bent a little bit more please."

Terry, smiling at the joke, inclines his head a little more.

"Perfect! Now let's try it again."

"Wait," says Terry one, "I think my face needs a touch up."

"Makeup, touch up for the two Terries please."

The makeup artist scurries forward. She makes minor repairs to the makeup of the two Terries.

"Is my head on straight?" grins Terry one.

"Looks fine."

"Is my head bent enough?" asks the other Terry.

"Looks good. Okay, let's try it again when you're ready."

"Hi, I'm Terry," says Terry one with a bright smile.

"Hi, I'm Terry," says the other Terry.

"We're the two Terries. And we're here to tell you all about the great fun coming your way this fall on the Maple Key Network," say the two Terries in unison.

"For you younger kids," continues the other Terry, "all your old favorites are back. There's Orky the Orca, Grazzle Berry Bear, Phoebe the flying pig and, of course, yours truly, Terry and Terry. We'll have games, cartoons, prizes and other cool stuff, so stay tuned. You're in for a wonderful year with all your favorites!"

"And don't forget Uncle Joey will be joining us once again to tell us about the world of Mother Nature," adds Terry one. "He has stories about bears, lions, wolves and whales and other animals. I'm sure you'll enjoy every fun-packed minute as much as Terry."

"And Terry," says the other Terry with an equally luminescent smile. "Oh! And for you older kids don't forget the Freedom Fighters Five! They're back this year with more action and adventure."

"And new this year is Darnel's Raiders," says Terry one. "You're really going to like this one. You'll see specially trained forces that secretly go round the world stopping people who want to destroy our world. Let's watch a short clip from these upcoming shows."

Cam sits on a stool behind the lights and cameras. In his hand is a copy of the script that he wrote for the two Terries. He listens carefully while they deliver their lines. His job is to ensure that the lines are delivered as scripted. A monitor is provided for him so that he can watch the two disembodied Terries. Cam is bathed in a ghostly green light as are the faces of the camera crew, and a few of the studio technicians who are watching monitors.

"Wasn't that fantastic? Wasn't that exciting?" says one of the Terries without waiting for the clip to run. Technicians will insert the clip later.

"So remember to join us this fall for fun and excitement."

"Yes, we hope to see you soon," says a Terry.

"Bye-bye for now," the two Terries say together.

"And cut," says a voice off camera.

"How was that?" asks a Terry.

"Just a minute, we're keying in the special effects to see how it'll look. We need a minute. Don't move. Cam how was that?"

"Good, only one thing," says Cam, "it's Darien's Raiders, not Darnel's Raiders. Otherwise it was fine."

The two Terries sit perfectly still while a technician displays the alternate background on the monitors. The two Terry heads are suspended above an Orky the Orca puppet in a film clip from an upcoming segment of the Orky the Orca show. Orky is in a mining tunnel where he is learning about gold miners working together. Now the scene changes to a graphic artist's rendition of a rainforest where the Terry heads appear embedded in trees. Below them, the cartoon-character Grazzle Berry Bear scampers about on the forest floor, playing with his best friend, Little Sneezy, the orphaned baby elephant. Grazzle Berry Bear smiles his cartoon smile in the way that only bears can. Now the Terry heads float in clouds while Phoebe the flying pig gleefully smiles and zooms around their heads. Then Uncle Joey shows his stuff when the scene switches to the tiger's compound at the Bayview zoo where a tiger paces a well-worn path inside its compound as the voice of Uncle Joey conveys facts about tigers in the wild. The disembodied Terry heads float in midair on each side of the pacing tiger. Next the cartoon Freedom Fighters Five join the fray when the Terry heads are imposed on a city skyscraper as the Freedom Fighters Five demonstrate their powers against one of their recurring foes, Rintrah, who roars like a lion and shoots fire from his fiery mane. Then in the middle of a corn field somewhere in South America, the clean-cut, square-jawed, grim-faced cartoon heroes from Darien's Raiders battle it out against a bunch of grubby and not-so-good-looking guerillas. The two Terry heads are superimposed over the corn stalks as bullets whizz in every direction. Finally all the cartoon role models swirl around the two Terry heads.

"How's it look?" asks Terry one. "Can you digitally insert Darien's Raiders for Darnel's Raiders?"

"The delivery was a little flat," says a voice off camera. "We need more energy, more excitement, more fun and the other Terry needs to smile more. Let's see more teeth. We want smiles as big as Niagara Falls. Try again from the beginning. And remember, it's Darien's Raiders. Okay makeup, check their makeup and then we're ready to go."

"Okay, check head alignment," says the voice after the makeup artist finishes. "Heads look good. Remember lots of energy, lots of over-the-top smiling, and lots of fun. And action."

The two Terries deliver their lines with everything they've got, including lots of big beaming smiles. Terry gets Darien's Raiders correct this time.

"And cut. That was much better. Everyone okay with that take?"

Heads nod approval after several minutes of checking.

"Okay, we're done. Strike the set. Thanks everyone. Thanks, Terry and Terry. Good job. See you upstairs."

A crew member shuts off the overhead lights. The crew begins to strike the set, leaving the two Terries a few moments to themselves. The two Terries slowly stand after sitting for so long. They stretch to get the kinks out as they go to their dressing rooms.

"Hey Terry, you there?" the other Terry says, raising his voice enough to be heard over the dressing room wall that separates the two Terries.

"Yeah, I'm here," answers Terry one.

"I'm glad we're done, another season in the can." He removes his green bodysuit and begins dressing. "We had a good run. How many years has it been?"

"Five, I think."

"We were kids ourselves when we started this show. I'll miss the place, but I'm ready to move on. I wonder who our replacements will be next year. Have you heard anything?"

"No, I'm in the dark too," replies Terry one. She strips away her green bodysuit and starts dressing. "I'll miss the place. It was hard work. I enjoyed it. It was fun working with the kids and watching them grow with the show. I'll miss meeting them at the special events. The annual MKM

Kids' Barbecue was my favorite. Kids have such wonderful imaginations, especially the little ones. Everything is possible for them." Terry one pauses. "We were like that once."

"I'll miss the kids too, but we had to grow up fast. Didn't we? The fact is we lost our naivety, learned about the world. The truth is we had fun using our imaginations. You have to make a living, full stop," the other Terry responds definitively. The other Terry in his short time at MKM has learned to adopt the language of adults.

"I know you shouldn't bite the hand that feeds you. These shows have paid for my education. It's just that sometimes I wonder if we did a disservice to the kids, even though we didn't mean to," she adds, though uncertain of her premise.

"Look, we all have to pay our dues, make sacrifices for the things we want."

"Everything seems the same," Terry one persists. "But something has changed, become the new normal," she says reaching for the right words. "There's something out of kilter." Terry is unhappy with her explanation.

"Nostalgia is nice, but at the end of the day all I know is that my education is paid for thanks to hard work and saving like crazy. What are your plans now that we're finished here?"

"I'm off to university this fall. What about you?"

"Final year of high school for me and university next year," confidently replies the other Terry. "What are you going to study?"

"English lit. What about you?"

"Science, including at least one Physics course. I like Physics. I'm hoping I can get into optometry if my marks are good enough."

"You'll do well," Terry one says reassuringly.

"Yes, and so will you. What do you plan to do with an English degree, teach?"

"I'm ready. Are you? We need to say goodbye to the crew."

"Yep, right behind you. Let's go."

The two Terries return to the set where members of the crew including Cam crowd around and offer their best wishes.

"Congratulations, I've enjoyed working with you," says Cam. "You've been real troopers."

"Thanks," say the two Terries in unison.

"Yes congratulations," says Ed from the back of the crowd. As Ed walks toward the two Terries, the crowd parts like the Red Sea. He hugs Terry one and shakes the other Terry's hand. "Well done. You're about to embark on new adventures, new discoveries. I can remember the first show you two did. You were young and fresh and full of ideas. And now look at the two of you; Terry off to university this year and Terry off to university next year. Wonderful simply wonderful! Remember, you'll always be part of the MKM family. And now if the rest of you don't mind," says Ed glancing at those who are still gathered around, "I need a couple of minutes alone with Terry and Terry. And don't forget the reception upstairs. It starts in fifteen minutes, at seven in the Palazzo room. Oh, and Cam, are you going to the reception now? Can you show Filana the way while I talk to the two Terries? You can get lost too easily around here," says Ed looking towards the back of the shrinking crowd. Cam turns and looks in the same direction where he sees Filana waiting for Ed. She smiles charitably and gives an unobtrusive wave as she walks toward Ed. "Filana wanted to see one of our studios," adds Ed beaming, "and seeing as I wanted to congratulate the two Terries on set, it was an opportunity to kill two birds with one stone."

"Yes," Cam answers, "I can show her."

"Good, meet me at the elevators in the Palazzo. I'll see you in fifteen minutes," says Ed turning his attention to Filana. "Cam can show you the way."

"Don't be too long," replies Filana.

Cam is aware of the eyes that follow Filana as she leaves the studio with him. Her copper-blonde hair is short with side swept bangs. A necklace with a single, fine strand of gold chain loops and drops, ending in a small diamond. She wears a short-halter cocktail dress the color of summer after a late-evening sun shower. Flaring at the waist, her dress reveals and hides.

"So you're Cam," says Filana while they make their way down a hallway. "Ed has told me about you. He tells me you're a good writer. I hear there's the possibility of a new job with Zanya. I hope it works out for you."

"Yes, thanks. I haven't decided yet if I'll take the job. I have a little time yet before I have to decide. I saw your latest picture, The Lost View from Here. I enjoyed it, especially the scene where you turn around and look at the meadow as though seeing it for the first time. That was an incredible piece of film."

"Thanks, the scene seems minor and most people miss its significance. It took quite a few takes to get it right. I enjoyed making the film. My production company is working on another film now. We're in the early stages of development. Can you keep a secret? The working title is The Echoing Green. The script writer came up with the title. I don't know where writers come up with these ideas."

"I'll watch for it. What else are you working on?" Cam directs Filana down another hallway while trying not to get lost as he listens to her.

"I'm working on a new line of women's swimwear for next summer and recently released a new line of cosmetics under the brand name Glystare. I'm the spokesperson. The brand includes a line of perfumes. What do you think?" asks Filana, stopping and holding out a wrist to Cam. "This is called Maginé. You pronounce the name with a French accent. Charming, isn't it? It arouses and conveys a sense of sophistication, mystery and desire."

Cam can feel his feet beginning to wobble. "Yes, a wonderful fragrance."

"And there's our line of jewelry, Angel Wear," Filana continues earnestly. "See? This is an Angel Wear necklace." She raises the necklace that she is wearing so Cam can see it better. "You can't see it, but etched on each diamond is the image of an angel that symbolizes the Angel Wear collection. The angel is trademarked."

Cam stares momentarily. They turn and continue down the hallway. "Very elegant," he states with his voice catching slightly. He clears his throat. They make a turn into another hallway. He wonders if Filana is aware of the affect she has on men.

"Angel Wear is aimed at upper-middle-class women and selling very well. We're moving into other markets segments in Q4 of this year just in time for Christmas. We're launching an advertising campaign too. It's aimed mostly at the middle class for those who are looking for more in their lives. I haven't made an announcement yet. The move into the middle class, I mean. Keep it a secret will you? I'm sure I can count on you."

Cam concentrates on walking while navigating the hallways. He's becoming disoriented. He gestures left. They turn into another hallway, which ends abruptly. They stop.

"We seemed to have reached a dead end. Where does the door go that we just passed?" asks Filana.

"I've zigged when I should have zagged. The door leads to the sub-basement. If we go down there it will save us some time," says Cam. "Otherwise we have a lot of backtracking to do. We'll be late for the reception. Do you mind if we take a shortcut?"

"Yes, let's do that."

Cam swipes his electronic badge, unlocking the door. They descend into a cavernous room where racks of computers extend row upon row in all directions. Neatly labelled electrical and fiber-optic cables run from computer to computer. Cam wonders if any of the wiring runs to the hidden speakers in Yaz's office. Interspersed between the computers are TV monitors that technicians can use to monitor TV signals.

"This is the Broadcast Nexus, the BN," says Cam as the two of them walk toward a set of elevator doors at the far end of the room.

Antennas around the world transmit TV signals in the form of electromagnetic radiation to communication satellites circling above the earth in geosynchronous orbit. Parabolic antennas mounted outside the MKM broadcast building receive and focus TV signals from satellites. Cables thread down through the building to the Broadcast Nexus, where they connect to the computers and monitors that display the TV signals. The electronic equipment swallows all sounds, including the sounds of footsteps. The sound is turned off on all the monitors. The room is warm even though a bank of air conditioners outside the building delivers cool air through overhead ducting to help prevent the computers from overheating. Plastic strands at ducting vents dangle and wave in the breeze. The BN is deserted except for the occasional technician attending to the computers. The overhead lighting is dimmed to reduce the heat and cut the glare on the monitors.

"You shouldn't be down here," challenges one of the technicians that Cam and Filana pass.

"Just passing through," Cam responds with a reassuring smile. "We got lost. We won't be long. We're late for a reception upstairs. This is a shortcut."

"Okay, don't touch anything," the technician cautions with a scowl. "How did you get in here anyway?"

"My badge," says Cam holding up his security badge.

"Well you shouldn't have access," responds the technician who is distrustful of outsiders. "I'll have to get

Security to limit admittance. There are too many people who shouldn't be down here."

"I promise not to touch anything. We'll be careful," adds Cam with a genial smile.

"Someone could easily push the wrong button. Rectifying the problem could take hours. Have a nice evening and enjoy the reception," says the technician, remembering his social etiquette. He reluctantly moves on to another row of computers, not wanting to leave the two unwelcome guests unattended.

Glancing at the monitors along the way, they continue toward the elevator doors. Filana stops in front of one of the monitors stationed a few rows from the elevator. "This is one of my films," she says pointing at the monitor, "the first film my production company made. The title is Under the Pale Moonlight. Adin Huffman played the werewolf. Do you know Adin?" Cam nods his head yes. "Earlier in the film Adin gets into trouble. He seduces a woman. I think her name was Nyree. In the film I mean." Filana continues. "I can't remember who played Nyree. A little later in the film, Adin is attacked by a wolf and becomes a werewolf. Then in this scene Adin in his werewolf form is stalking me. I escape. Later still we make love. Of course he's in human form when we make love and I have no idea that he's a werewolf. Eventually I find out what he really is. At the end of the picture I have to kill Adin, the werewolf that is, to save him. I kill him for his own sake out of pity for him and because if I don't he's going to kill me. It's my big scene, killing him I mean. I don't remember how I killed him in the film."

They watch the scene unfold for a couple of minutes.

"We better get going," says Cam looking a little fretfully at his watch.

"We did okay at the box office, not bad for a first attempt. The scene between Adin and Nyree is very erotic. We had to be careful to be explicit without being too explicit. We leave a little to the audience's imagination, just enough.

203

The wrong film rating would have hurt us at the box office. The script was a little weak. A good script is so important. Of course you know that don't you? Can you turn up the sound? I like this scene."

"We shouldn't touch anything. Remember?"

"It'll be okay. Ed won't mind." Cam hesitates. Filana suddenly reaches forward and pushes a button. The monitor remains silent. On the other side of the room, a monitor displays an error message. A computer adds an entry to a log file. She pushes another button, but the result is the same. The monitor remains silent.

"I wouldn't touch anything. It's not a good idea," Cam cautions.

"Oh well, too bad," says Filana, shrugging at the obstinate monitor. "We better get going. We'll be late." She turns and walks toward the elevator.

Cam follows her. He stops in front of the last monitor before the elevator.

"This is a good film," says Cam pointing at the monitor. He is unable to resist the lure of the film.

Filana has already reached the elevator and doesn't look back. "Which floor?" She steps into the elevator.

Cam looks up from the monitor as the elevator doors begin to close. "Hold the elevator!" he calls with a note of panic. He's too late. "Ten," he shouts seconds before the elevator doors close. Immediately he realizes that he has given her the wrong floor number. He looks at the monitor where Dr. David Bowman is once more beginning his plunge into the black monolith.

A technician appears out of nowhere. He grimaces when he looks at the monitor where Under the Pale Moonlight should be playing, but isn't. He glares at Cam, who smiles feebly.

Cam walks quickly to the elevator doors, hoping to escape the angry glances of the technician. He waits anxiously for the return of the elevator. There's an awkward old-man Johnson moment for Cam while he endures the scowling technician. The elevator doors open. There is no Filana. He steps into the elevator and presses the button that will take him to the Palazzo room. The doors close. The elevator starts its ascent.

"What kept you?" demands Ed when Cam steps out of the elevator and into the vast space of the Palazzo room. "You're late. Where the hell is Filana?" snaps Ed, placing his hands on his hips and looking directly at Cam.

"Isn't she here? We got separated," answers Cam, looking submissively away from Ed's steely glare.

"No, I left her with you," retorts Ed.

The elevator doors open behind Cam before he can say anything more. Jordan and Filana step out of the elevator.

"Look what I found," says Jordan with an obsequious grin, hoping to improve his standing with Ed. "She was on the wrong floor."

Filana hugs Ed. "I'm okay," she says soothingly. "Cam and I got turned around. We got separated trying to take a shortcut."

Cam is relieved, but still a little nervous. He was the one who was supposed to escort Filana. Ed seems satisfied that everything has been restored to its rightful place. He smiles coolly at Cam.

With Filana on his arm, Ed begins his blazing comet passage through the crowd. A retinue of people swirl about him in apogee, perigee or somewhere in between depending on their position in Ed's hierarchy. Jordan remains behind with Cam.

"You can thank me later. You owe me," says Jordan without looking at Cam. Jordan's attention remains focused on Ed's progress through the crowd. "How was the interview?"

"Interview?" asks Cam, wondering if Jordan has heard about Cam's VT interview.

"Yes, your interview with Zanya," says Jordan to make it clear that he knows what's going on. "I saw Yaz in the hallway. He told me that he had arranged your interview with Zanya for lead script writer."

"It was fine, but a little odd," replies Cam with relief.

"Odd?"

"It wasn't the usual sort of interview. We went to an art gallery. Zanya wanted to pick out some artwork for her office. She asked me along to help her decide. I wasn't much help. She found what she was looking for. Then we went to the One-eyed Merchant. We had a couple of drinks and then dinner."

"I hope you don't think that my department is paying for your dinner," asserts Jordan. He continues to watch Ed while Ed proceeds in his prescribed orbit.

"Zanya picked up the bill."

"Good," says Jordan approvingly. "And how was your meeting with Ed?" asks Jordan, assessing the import of Zanya picking up the bill. "Did you talk about the script?"

"He thought the script was fine. Mostly he wanted to talk about what people want and what they're willing to do to get what they want and how our job is to try and give them direction."

"And what is it that most people want?"

"Love, but he doesn't think most people really know what love is."

"Love," scoffs Jordan with a disdainful smirk while thinking how he might use this information. "Love, you're not that green are you? I hope the shareholders don't hear about this. He's running a business, not a website for the lovelorn. Maybe," poses Jordan while he thinks for a moment, "he's launching a social networking website. I wonder if that's what he means, social networking. I've heard rumors."

"He didn't say anything about social networking. He talked about sticking to the script to stay on message. I wouldn't jump to any conclusions." Cam warns, trying to repay Jordan for helping him get out of a difficult situation with Ed.

"Now and then you have to read between the lines to sniff out the truth," answers Jordan knowingly. "The truth is not always what you see or hear. You need to learn to use your imagination, dig deeper. You can be so easily deceived by others. Yes, that must be what he's talking about, a social networking website. I can almost taste it," says Jordan licking his lips with glee and rubbing his hands together as though he has discovered gold or the fountain of youth. "Eureka! Send me an e-mail on Monday about what else happened in the meeting with Ed."

Jordan begins to maneuver himself in front of Ed's current trajectory, in order to intercept Ed as if by happenstance. Cam watches as Jordan casually works his way through the crowd. He reminds Cam of a small clod of clay or a pebble hoping to affix itself to the much larger body of the comet that is Ed. Jordan must try to stick and mold his clay self to the comet's surface, or skip off the comet and through gravitational pull be captured as a satellite of the comet. Achieving orbit around Ed is a tricky business. Jordan has to find precisely the right angle, or he'll go careening off into space. The risk is great, but so are the rewards.

"Hi," says a voice behind Cam. Cam turns around to see Anna, whom he has invited to the reception.

"Hi, you made it," he smiles warmly. "How are you?" They stand for a moment holding hands. "You smell nice."

"Thanks, I'm fine. The perfume is Maginé. How was your day?"

"Fine, I lost Filana."

"What?"

"I'll tell you about it later."

"What's the occasion for the reception?"

"Ed is saying thanks to the two Terries. They were the hosts of a kids' TV show called Kid Power, very popular with younger kids. Ed found the two Terries and breathed life into the program. One of the Terries is off to university and the other is finishing his last year of high school. Ed will have to find new hosts."

"I've never seen Kid Power. I've heard the kids at school talking about it in a derogatory way. You know how older kids are."

"Do you see Jordan over there?" says Cam, looking in Jordan's direction."

"Yes. Why?"

"Just watch. The lip-licking little weasel thinks he's discovered how to measure the volume of an irregularly shaped object, but I don't think so. I think he's missed the mark completely. Watch and see what happens. I'll explain later."

"I don't know what you're talking about."

"Watch this. He's about to speak to Ed. This should be interesting."

Across the room, Jordan has managed to position himself in front of Ed.

"What's he saying? I can't hear them," says Anna.

"I don't know exactly, but watch Jordan's face. I'll fill you in later."

Jordan smiles ambitiously as he engages Ed in conversation.

"Look at Jordan. He's smiling so hard. I wonder if it hurts," Cam comments referring to Jordan's big grin.

Soon Ed ardently shakes his head no and makes short, sharp cutting gestures with his hands to emphasize his point. Ed looks fiercely at Jordan whose smile is sagging under the weight of Ed's glare. Jordan's body language shows that he is taking a beating. Ed continues in his chosen path while the dejected Jordan spins off into space, seeking a quiet corner of the room. Jordan's attempt to join Ed's retinue has failed completely.

"That deflated his grin," Anna observes.

"Good-old one-hand-clapping collides with an object in motion."

"I have no idea what you're talking about," says Anna who after a moment adds, "You really dislike Jordan don't you?"

"Jordan thought that Ed was about to launch a website for social networking. Ed has only this minute told him in language that even Jordan can't misinterpret that there is no such plan. We won't hear from Jordan for a few days while he licks his wounds."

"How do you know all this?" Anna asks.

"I had a short conversation with Jordan before you showed up. Jordan had what he thought was an epiphany. He came to the conclusion that Ed was planning a social networking website. Jordan let his imagination and ambition get the better of him. He tried to join Ed's inner circle, but Ed has scribed a cadre that isn't easy to join. Jordan tried to ingratiate himself with Ed by showing Ed what he thought he knew about Ed's plan for a social networking site. Ed was having none of it. I tried to warn Jordan. He wasn't listening. Jordan will be in the doghouse now. I'll have to stay out of his way for a little while until he gets over this. He'll snarl at me or anyone else who comes near him."

"I didn't think Jordan had that kind of ambition. When I talk to him, he seems rather modest, humble even. In fact the last time I talked to him at one of these gatherings, he denied he had any ambition about moving up the corporate ladder."

"He loves to wear a mask of humility. He'll proclaim to anyone who will listen that he is indeed the humblest man in the universe," Cam laughs at the contradiction. "This way, if his plan to move up the food chain fails, he doesn't lose face."

"What's this about losing Filana?" asks Anna.

"A bedtime story, maybe I'll tell you later," answers Cam raising an eyebrow as he brushes against Anna.

One of the satellites in Ed's miniature solar system changes orbit and intercepts Ed while Cam and Anna talk. A whispered conversation follows between Ed and the satellite. Ed moves to a microphone. "Folks," he announces, "I'm sorry. Something has come up that requires my immediate attention. Please stay and enjoy the entertainment and food." Ed, Filana and some of Ed's inner circle leave by a side door.

A small band in one corner of the colossal room plays a medley of popular songs while images of the two Terries at different times in their careers at MKM are flashed on a giant wall screen. Along another wall, serving staff reveal a banquet of food in honor of the two Terries.

Cam and Anna circulate through the room enjoying the music and food. Occasionally they stop and talk to an MKM associate that Cam knows.

"I'm hungry," says Cam to Anna in a moment when they are by themselves. He raises a mischievous eyebrow.

"But you just ate," she replies, smiling and playing the game.

"I'm hungry," he repeats, brushing gently against her.

"I smell mischief."

"So do I, let's misbehave," he answers playfully.

"This is all in your head."

"Yes, there too, where shall we go?"

"What about a room at the hotel next door? We haven't done that lately."

"Yes." He casts an admiring glance at Anna as they head to the hotel.

Cam is about to turn on the lights in the hotel room when Anna reaches out a hand and stops him.

"Don't turn on the lights. We don't need them. Kiss me here," Anna instructs, closing the door. Cam complies. "Now here," she coaches in the darkness. "Here. You missed a spot and over here too. What about this spot?"

"I missed a spot here," says Cam, kissing her on the nape of the neck.

Anna shudders. "Oh! Yes that was good!" she whispers with a satisfied smile lost in the dark.

Hands explore buttons and fasteners. Clothes rustle and fall away.

"You don't need this," Anna softly persuades.

They shed more clothing.

"Nor you this," Cam gently responds.

Hands caress, explore and linger.

"Do you like this?" murmurs Cam. He explores the soft curves of her warm skin.

"Oh yes," sighs Anna. Their bodies weave together. "More please! There too. Oh, that feels good! What about this?" she whispers kissing new parts of Cam. He moans. They discover new realms in long moments of silence.

Bodies heave and catch and shudder, then quiet. Silence washes through the moment. The heat begins to fade. The scent of Anna's Maginé lingers.

For a time they remain loosely entwined like strands of DNA. They are unwilling to leave the expanse of the moment.

Anna whispers to the darkness, "tell me a story."

The dark remains silent.

"Before I was a boy scout, I was a cub scout," begins the darkness after a moment. "The cub leaders made arrangements with one of the church members to have the cub scouts visit their home and watch home movies of their travels around the world. They were an elderly couple. They must have been in their seventies. At least that's how I remember them. They had money because they travelled to

211

countries that very few could afford to visit in those days. We trooped over to their house, which wasn't far from the church where we held our cub-scout meetings. I don't remember much about their house. They led us to their rec room in the basement where he had set up a film projector and screen. This was just before video cameras became popular. I don't remember the films that they showed us. After I guess about an hour, it was time to go. And this is the important part. I can remember them standing together at the front door when we left. I gave my usual mechanical 'thank you' because that's what I had been taught to say. I knew I'd be quizzed when I got home about whether I had said thank you. The couple smiled and probably said you're welcome and goodbye. I don't remember what they said. And that was the end of it. The cub-scout meeting was over and I went home."

"Why is that the important part?"

"About thirty years later I remembered the incident. There was something about the two of them standing there at the doorway that I can't explain. I have this vague memory of their faces. They both seemed to have this genuine smile. It was modest too. Now when I picture them in my mind, they seem to shine in a quiet way. I don't remember the details of their appearance. Memory is a strange thing.

"What happened to them?"

"I don't know. I only met them that once. We moved to another part of town shortly after. Strange isn't it how you think about these things years later? I did hear that they left their house and land to the church. I don't think they had children. I wonder if the church knew what it was getting."

"What happened to the house and land?"

"The church couldn't afford to keep it. The taxes were more than the church could afford, so they made an arrangement with one of the other local churches. I don't know the details. Much of the land was old growth forest."

The dark quiet fills the room.

"They didn't do anything special while we were in their house. They didn't give us cookies or anything. I guess that in a quiet way they shared themselves and in a way they said see, look here. Do you see? They weren't like politicians or people who try to force their opinion on you, try to control you and make you see things their way. Not like people who try to tell you how the world wags and you better look at it their way and live life the way they tell you because if you don't, there's going to be trouble for you. It wasn't that kind of *look* that says *see* here's how the world works and you better get used to it."

"Well they did have money. That can make things easier."

"I don't think that was it. Lots of people who have money behave badly. But these two behaved well. They were different. They could see something that we couldn't, but we could if we looked hard enough and in the right direction. They could see straight and most everyone else is looking at things crooked. They weren't the same as the rest of us, being afraid and busy chewing off our paws when we get caught doing whatever we're not supposed to be doing, which is most of the time, or being afraid that we'll get caught. So we don't do anything. We're afraid to commit and we feel nervous around the ones who want us to take responsibility for our lives. Only they want us to take responsibility in a way that imposes their view of the world on us. They haven't the imagination or the courage to see the way the world really is."

"There must have been something very honest about the two of them."

"There was gentleness in them, a kindness. There was a kind of communication going on, only not communication in the way that we think about it. They weren't deliberately trying to send a message. They knew something and we didn't and they couldn't really tell us about it directly. You had to *see* it in them. The films they ran that night were really a pretext to see the something in them. Only they didn't plan it that way. To them it was simply letting us see their faraway adventures. I'm sure they didn't know what they showed me that evening. I didn't know. It wasn't until much later that I began to see and then only by finding a lost memory."

Silence falls.

"Something took root that evening," Anna responds, "and then lay dormant waiting for the right moment. Perhaps you had to go through what you have to get to a place where you could appreciate what they showed you."

13 You Can't Get There from Here

Cam extends his arm to signal a right turn. The road heads west, away from Bayview. His bicycle has three gears on the front cluster and eight gears on the rear cluster, giving him lots of range for the road ahead. Each year Cam takes a little longer to leave the houses behind as Bayview expands westward. The city's expansion has slowed to a slouching crawl in recent years as the result of the economic downturn. The houses begin to fall away as the road opens before him. The early morning air is cool against his face. He enjoys the cool air. He can feel the bike's momentum as he works the pedals, picking up speed.

A small clump of cattails sits in the ditch by the side of the road. They bend gently in the wind. The wind is from the east. It pushes Cam from behind, making the ride easier.

In the distance a lane joins the road. If you follow the lane for about a hundred yards, it takes you to a newly constructed church. Cars pass Cam. He listens and watches carefully for the cars as they pass. Many of the cars turn right, into the church lane. He doesn't want a car cutting him off as he passes the lane. His hands rest gently on the brake levers in case he has to stop suddenly. Today he passes the entrance without incident.

The road continues west for about two minutes in bicycle time, and then bends north for three minutes and then west again. Cam begins his climb up the first hill. The hill feels higher this year. Although if you were to measure the hill, you would find that its height hasn't changed. Cam is getting older. He works the shift levers on the handlebar. With each shift of the lever, a derailleur smoothly directs the bike chain to the next gear in the cluster, shift and click, shift and click. He enjoys the sound that the derailleur makes when it shifts. By now the bike is in its lowest gear. Slowly he works his way up the hill, which is a moraine created by a retreating glacier during the last ice age. Reaching the top of the hill, he shifts gears, picking up speed. He coasts down the other side of the hill, catching his breath and resting his legs. He has to pace himself now that the hills are higher. There are more hills ahead of him.

At the bottom of the hill is a T-junction. He must turn either south or north. South takes him up a hill and north takes him down a long steep hill into a valley and then an equally steep climb up the other side. He brakes and quickly checks over his shoulder. He's looking for cars. Cam doesn't always hear them coming. He wonders if the cars have a stealth mode to catch riders unawares. He extends his left arm signalling a left turn. He turns south and begins the climb up the next hill. The climb takes three minutes. He turns west again. There is the promise of several more challenging hills.

The late summer colors of the forest flow by. Cam passes a pond hiding near the edge of the road. The pond is silent now. Earlier in the spring it was alive with the sound of frogs singing. He meets riders who are heading in the opposite direction. With his hands affixed to the handlebar, Cam makes a small wave with his hand to acknowledge the riders. They respond in kind.

Shifting down a few gears, Cam starts climbing the next hill, the steepest hill on his ride. He begins to puff and wheeze, trying to catch his breath while he makes the climb. His over-stretched paper-bag lungs press against his ribs. Even his rickety ribs work to expand, allowing a little extra space in which to suck in a few more molecules of air.

He hears a car approaching from behind. He can hear the car slowing down as it gets closer. Now the car is beside him, matching his speed. He quickly glances sideways at the car. A passenger in the car rolls down the window. Already Cam knows what they want, directions. This has happened many times before. Once he was stopped by a couple who were standing by their car on the side of a road. They were lost. They were looking for a town about an hour's drive by car from where they were. You can't get there from here, Cam wanted to say, but refrained because it wasn't true. The route by car was actually quite easy. He gave them directions and the road map that he was carrying. He didn't need the map anyway. He knew the local roads well enough from his many bicycle trips. They offered to pay him for the map. Cam politely refused.

"Excuse me," shouts the car passenger looking at Cam who is working hard against the physics of the moment. "Do you know the way to Paradise Lake?"

Cam gulps down a bag full of air, trying to pull in enough breath to answer and still continue his climb up the hill. He doesn't want to lose his momentum by stopping. Starting from a stand still on this hill is difficult. If he stops, he will have to walk his bike to the crest of the hill before mounting the bike again. Walking up the hill would not be easy. His cycling shoes are designed for riding, not for walking.

"Yes," Cam pants. "You missed the turn," he gasps, his lungs working hard. "About half a mile back," he gulps for air, "the way you came. The first left," huffs Cam, "you come to."

"Thanks," yells the passenger before rolling up the window. The driver accelerates looking for a place to turn around. A minute later the car returns, going in the opposite direction. By this time, gasping, Cam is at the top of the hill. His lungs are about to explode. The climb has taken him five minutes. He waves while they go by. They wave back and smile appreciatively. Cam glides down the back of the hill, thankful for the chance to rest while he recovers for the next hill.

Somewhat rested, he approaches the next hill where he will pass by a large, metal sign frame secured firmly to the ground next to the road. The sign that the frame once held is gone. Now there is only the empty frame. Cam speculates what sign the frame once held. Perhaps the frame held a realty sign advertising a house for sale, or a sign for a politician seeking voter support. The frame is too well made for either of these possibilities he decides. Probably a commercial sign for a business he concludes. He enjoys looking through the frame. Although the frame appears empty, it is not. At first he sees the forest on the side of the hill that he is approaching. As he gets closer, the scene slowly changes. While he passes beside the sign frame, Cam can look down into the deep valley beside the hill that he is about to ascend. In the foreground when he passes the sign frame, he sees the valley floor below. The tops of the trees that frame the valley are at eye level. In the middle ground, the valley opens into farmland. In the background are hills and forest. The scene is never the same. Cam once saw a deer in the valley. The deer was almost hidden by the forest. It was here, with the aid of the sign frame, that he accidentally discovered the beauty of the rolling countryside for the first time. You can't experience the landscape in the same way from a car. Cars move too fast. They flatten the scene.

Cam climbs two more hills and then passes through a village. The journey to this point has taken about twenty minutes. There's a stop sign at the top of the hill in the village. He stops. He looks for cars. Cautiously he crosses through the intersection and continues west. Cam rides for another ten minutes until he reaches the crossroads. Here the paved road ends and turns into gravel roads in three directions. His bike with its narrow tires is not meant for gravel. He keeps to the paved roads. This is as far as he can go in this direction.

Cam squeezes the brake levers to slow his momentum, stops and dismounts for a short rest before turning back. He checks the display mounted on the handlebar of his bike. The display indicates how far he has travelled and how long it has taken him. He has to reset the display to zero for time and distance before he starts a new ride in order to get an accurate reading for each ride. This time he forgot to zero the settings before starting out. He decides it doesn't matter that he didn't reset the display. He has made the trip enough times to know how far he has travelled and the time it takes.

Cam pulls a blue plastic water bottle from the rack mounted on the bike frame. He opens the spout, squeezes the bottle and drinks.

A small two-seater airplane drones lazily overhead. The sound of the plane fades and is gone.

A small green car kicks up a cloud of dust as it approaches from the north. The car slows and stops for the stop sign at the junction. Inside are four young men. Each wears a baseball cap with the brim turned to the back and the plastic cap adjuster stretched across the forehead. They're grinning and talking and having a good time. One of the passengers nods at Cam who nods back. The car turns east onto the paved road and accelerates away.

In the distance a Mennonite family in a horse-drawn buggy approaches from the south.

From the east, two motorcycles race toward the junction. Both riders are dressed in leather suits to protect them in the event of a fall. The suits match the color of their bikes. One bike is lime green and the other a bright yellow. Their faces are hidden behind the tinted visors of their helmets. They begin to brake and shift into a lower gear: brake, clutch, shift; brake clutch, shift. Smoothly decelerating, they approach the crossroads. They don't want to risk the gravel. Having slowed enough to turn around, they remain seated on their motorcycles. Extending their legs, they awkwardly walk their bikes around until they face east while all the time revving their engines so as not to stall. Picking up speed, they retract their legs and fold them neatly against the body of their bikes like insects taking flight. At the same time to reduce wind resistance, they lay their upper bodies prone over their motorcycle gas tanks to hide behind the small windscreen mounted on the front of each bike. The cowling on the front wraps around their bodies to further reduce wind resistance. Clutch, shift, clutch, shift they change gears and accelerate, their engines whining and fading into the distance as they speed east.

The Mennonite family in their buggy reaches the stop sign at the crossroads. A man and a woman sit on the front wooden seat. The seat is mounted on leaf springs to cushion the ride. Their two young daughters sit on the back seat. The man wears a plain black suit and white shirt. He is not wearing a tie. His hat is black with a flat broad brim to protect his head from the sun and shield his eyes. The woman and two girls are dressed in simple dresses, with bonnets and coats to fend off the chill of the morning. They're dressed in their Sunday best.

Accompanied by the clip clop of the horse's hooves, the carriage wheels clatter across the paved road and again onto the gravel road. The family continues north, passing Cam on the opposite side of the road.

I must look strange to them, Cam thinks to himself standing beside his electric-blue bike with his water bottle in hand. He wears a blue bicycle helmet for protection in case of a fall; sunglasses to shade his eyes and to protect against the ultraviolet rays of the sun; a blue nylon jacket to cut the wind; a long-sleeved purple bicycle shirt with fleece lining to keep him warm; a pair of fingerless, black riding gloves with padding to cushion the palms of his hands on the handlebar; from the waist down, a pair of long, black, spandex tights

220

protect his legs from the cold; and a pair of blue bicycle shoes that clip securely into bicycle pedals.

The man smiles generously and nods at Cam. The man shouts something at Cam about trying to keep up with the two motorcycles. Cam can't quite hear him over the clatter of the buggy wheels and the clopping of the horse's hooves. The man is making a friendly joke. Cam is sure of this. Cam smiles honestly and nods in return. The family continues down the gravel road, heading north, slowly clattering into the distance. Cam watches until they disappear over the crest of a hill.

Near the crest of the hill a lone elm tree stands among the utility poles and fence posts that disappear over the hill. Although it's only late summer, the tree has already lost many of its leaves.

In the field next to the road, a strip of ryegrass hugs the fence line and so remains uncut. The ryegrass whispers as it ripples in the wind.

A song sparrow calls and another answers: call, answer, call, answer and on and on in the way that they have always done. And then quiet and standing still and everything stopped and the coolness of the wind and nothing, and on and on…

In a little while, Cam mounts his bike and heads east along the paved road. He retraces his route towards home. He has to work harder now with the wind against him. His nylon jacket flaps in the wind, heralding his discovery.

For a while, he watches two birds harass a hawk. The hawk drifts unconcerned over the countryside.

He passes a Mennonite farm where families have gathered after church service. The boys in their white shirts and black pants have removed their black blazers. They have laid out a rough baseball diamond in an empty, uneven farm field where they are playing baseball with a bat and ball.

Later, Cam overtakes and passes a man and a woman walking east on the shoulder of the road. The man pulls a child in a wagon. The houses of Bayview steadily grow larger.

14 That's for Little Kids

Dmp dmp, dmp dmp.

Evea sits at Cam's kitchen table eating a salmon sandwich on whole wheat. A glass of milk sits beside her plate. Rhythmically she gently kicks the rungs of the chair, first one foot and then the other and then she repeats the pattern: dmp dmp, dmp dmp.

"Uncle Cam," begins Evea, "did you take geography at school in grade six?"

"Yes, I did back in the *olden* days," answers Cam while he makes a sandwich for himself.

"Did you like it?"

"Yes, what I remember about it. Why do you ask?"

"In geography on Friday, we did an experiment. Our teacher, Miss Penny, talked about the earth rotating around its axis. She likes to do experiments to show us things. She showed us a globe of the earth. Then she closed the window curtains and turned off the lights. She shone a light on the globe and asked us to pretend that the light was the sun. Then she rotated the earth and asked us what we saw. Robert, he's one of the boys in my class, put up his hand and said that half of the globe was in the light and the other half was in the dark. The teacher said this was why the earth had night and day because the earth rotated completely around its axis every twenty-four hours. She said the axis is an imaginary line that goes through the earth between the north and south poles. Did you learn that in school too?"

"Yes. Then what happened?"

"She asked us to sit still and quiet and see if we could feel the earth rotating. And we did."

"Did what?"

"Sit still and quiet."

"And then what?"

"Miss Penny asked those who could feel the earth rotating to put up their hands. Before almost anyone could answer, she said that no one can feel the earth rotating. But I *did* feel something. I felt like I could feel the earth rotating. Only you weren't supposed to feel it. So I didn't put my hand up because I knew that was the wrong answer. One boy, Will, put up his hand, but Miss Penny said that he must be imagining it."

"Maybe you did feel the earth rotating. Some animals are very sensitive to their environment. Last year some seals on the Pacific coast suddenly moved away from where they usually stay. About a week later there was an earthquake along the part of the coast that they had left. I wouldn't be surprised that they could feel it coming weeks before it happened."

There is silence for a few minutes while Evea eats her sandwich. She ponders what Cam has said; dmp dmp, dmp dmp.

"Are we animals?" Evea asks.

"I think so. What do you think?"

"But we have souls. Animals don't have souls."

"Some people believe that everything is alive. What do you think?"

"At Sunday school, they told us that everyone has a soul. The soul is a part of you and inside you. You can't see it. Once I tried looking in the bathroom mirror to see if I could see my soul. I tried looking everywhere in the mirror. I tried turning sideways and looking at the mirror through the corner of my eye. I tried putting my face really close to the mirror. I tried looking at an angle at the sides of the mirror. All I saw were parts of the bathroom that I don't normally

see in the mirror. I tried looking behind the mirror too."
Evea takes a bite of her sandwich.

"Did you see your soul?"

"No I didn't. Uncle Cam have you seen your soul?"

"I'm not sure you can see it. You have to experience it,"
he appends for lack of a better explanation. He frowns.
"Perhaps you have to forget everything and know
everything the way it really is, not the way we've learned to
see." Cam struggles for the right words. "Like trying to make
water flow uphill," he adds, remembering his conversation
with Ed. "Every now and then I think I catch a glimpse of
something bigger." There's a pause.

The dmp sound has stopped as Evea listens intently.

"You have to look in the right places," Cam continues.
"You can't see your soul because you're trying to see it in the
wrong way. There's something really huge in the room and
everywhere and in ways we can't even imagine."

"It sounds a little creepy, but I like your explanation,"
says Evea after a minute, "even though I don't understand."

"You see your soul for the first time even though you've
been looking at it all your life," offers Cam trying again. "In
a way, seeing is like being a little kid again when everything
was possible because you were seeing with little kid's eyes.
Only you're not little anymore. And if you try to tell other
people about what you've seen, they won't see. Sometimes
you can trick people into seeing, even if you don't mean to. I
think music does that, but only for a little while. You catch a
glimpse."

"Uncle Cam," begins Evea, picking up on the little kid
idea, "when you were little, did you say a prayer at night
before going to bed?"

"Yes. I always got the words muddled. I couldn't
remember the words in the right order. I was always asking
God to take my soul before I die. In the prayer you're
supposed to ask God to take your soul *if* you die while
you're sleeping, which sounds creepy to me. My parents,

your grandparents, would get annoyed with me because I couldn't remember the words. I was never very good at memory work."

"What about now," Evea continues, "do you say a prayer at night before you go to bed? You should, you know, because God is listening. They told us that at Sunday school."

"No, I don't."

"But you don't go to church and you don't say grace at the dinner table. How can He hear you? You want God to hear you don't you? You have to say your prayers if you want to go to heaven. Don't you want to go to heaven?"

"I think there are many ways to be heard," Cam responds, "Prayers can be more than words. I don't know that I can explain. Prayers have to come from the heart to be heard. Usually prayers are words and other times they're words with something else and now and again they're something else altogether without any words. I know that sounds vague." Cam pauses while he tries to think of a better explanation. "Prayers are like music. Sometimes there's only singing, and other times there's singing with music, and then there's music without singing. It's all music. And now and then you're inspired and at other times you're not. On occasion we sing and at times we listen."

"But in prayers you can ask for stuff. Only you can't ask for things for yourself; that would be selfish. But you can ask for things for other people."

"Every now and then prayers remind me of a Janis Joplin song," Cam chimes in feeling inspired. "She was a singer. In one of her songs a person prays to the Lord, asking for a Mercedes Benz, a color TV and a night on the town. And if God will buy the next round of drinks, it will prove that the Lord loves the person doing the praying. The song is funny. The person is asking for all these trivial things and for all the wrong reasons. Praying should be about praying for the right things for the right reasons."

226

The dmp sound resumes. "How was your bike ride this morning?" asks Evea looking to change the subject.

"I had a good ride. I'm getting older. I was riding up one of the hills and a rider on a bike passed me as if I was standing still. She was a lot younger than me. She wasn't struggling at all going up the hill. She said hi when she passed me. I gasped out *hi* in return." He feigns an out-of-breath hi to add color to the story.

"Will you take me riding one day?"

"I can when you're a little older. Are we going swimming today?"

"I can't today. I have homework and my parents have guests coming for dinner, so I have to be home early."

"I'm sorry you couldn't come over yesterday."

"There was a sleepover at my friend's house."

For a while now, Cam has realized that Evea is creating a separate and private world in the same way he once did. He wonders how long before she stops coming over all together, only appearing on special occasions, Thanksgiving and such when the families get together. Soon she'll be interested in boys. Perhaps she already is. He wonders who Robert and Will are. Are they simply boys in her class, or is one of them special to Evea? Cam realizes he will probably never know.

"I see there's an Orky the Orca special on TV next weekend," he offers. Immediately he wants to unsay it, realizing she's too old for the show.

The dmp sound stops abruptly. "That's for little kids," Evea answers, a little shocked that her Uncle might think that she still watches the Orky the Orca show. "No one watches that anymore. I liked the show when I was a little kid. Now I watch JHC, Junior High Cafeteria. The show is about kids who go to junior high school. The show takes place in the school's cafeteria. Everyone's watching it." Secretly, Evea still watches Orky the Orca on occasion, but is unwilling to confess her clandestine viewing habits to her Uncle and especially her peers.

"How is your new teacher, Miss Penny? Is she nice?"

"Oh yes. She teaches us lots of things and she makes jokes too. She talks to us like we're not little kids anymore, like she's talking to someone who is more mature, not in grade five anymore," says Evea liking the idea of mature and glad that she has used the word. "She can share things with us because we're older. She'll say things like 'Will, put a sock in it', if Will is talking too much. She doesn't say it in a mean way."

"Yes, I think I know what you mean. I had a teacher like that in grade six. He would say 'go fry ice' but not in a nasty way. It sounded adult, but not quite. Still, he was sharing a part of his world with us instead of treating us like we were little kids. In your teacher's case, she's saying something that she might say to someone more adult."

"Pay attention," Evea adds in her best adult-like voice to further demonstrate her point. She sits up straight. Her hawk eyes focus on an imaginary student sitting in the chair on the opposite side of the kitchen table. "That's what lots of teachers say. They treat you like you're still a kid that needs to be told what to do."

"Yeah," says Cam, "sounds like Miss Penny includes you in her world instead of excluding you."

"Yes, we're not little kids anymore," she emphasizes with satisfaction, happy that her Uncle understands. Evea has finished her sandwich and glass of milk.

"Want to go halvsies on a sandwich?" asks Cam. Evea shakes her head no. He offers her a chocolate-chip cookie, which she accepts.

"Why does Mr. Kenny call you Squib?" Evea asks wanting to know more about the adult world. She is referring to Dunc, whom she has met a few times at Cam's house.

"I think he means scribbler because I'm a writer. Though, if you look up squib in the dictionary, it means a firecracker that fizzes instead of going bang. I'm not sure which way he means squib."

"Mr. Kenny picked the name?"

"Yes, he did."

"What do you call him?"

"Wiff. It has to do with his job. He's a plumber. There are unpleasant smells in his line of work. They're kind of joke names that we use for one another."

"Oh, is it like me calling one of the boys in my class stinky?"

"Probably not, it depends on how you intend it. If the intent is to be hurtful, then stinky is not going to work. You have to know the other person well enough. Nicknames are a way of sharing yourself with someone else. You both have to be comfortable around one another so that neither one is offended."

"What if you wanted somebody to notice you?" queries Evea between bites of cookie.

"Well, I wouldn't recommend calling him stinky. That will get you the wrong kind of attention. Is there a boy in your class that you..."

"Mr. Kenny talks funny," observes Evea before Cam can finish his question. "He'll say things: watch out for the sidehill gouger. What's a sidehill gouger?"

"I don't know. You'd have to ask him. When he was a boy he lived where people talk that way. I like the phrases he uses. I think they're colorful, but then I'm a writer, a storyteller."

"Why do you tell stories? Robert, he's in my class at school, thinks that stories are only made-up stuff. They don't mean anything. Robert's very smart. He's always at the top of the class."

"Stories are my way of making sense of my world, my experiences," responds Cam. "Otherwise everything seems jumbled, mixed up to me. Stories are a way of sharing experiences with others and saying this is who I am. Have you experienced something like this too? What do you make of it?"

"Anna likes your stories. She told me so," says Evea, pleased to share what Anna has shared with her.

Cam smiles with pleasure. "I enjoy telling her stories. She laughs if she thinks the story is funny."

"You should write them down. I like stories too, even if Robert doesn't."

"Which reminds me," begins Cam, "I was in an art gallery a little while ago. You might enjoy some of the art. If you're free, we can go next Saturday."

"I'd like to, but there's a party next Saturday. Another Saturday?" answers Evea sounding a little doubtful.

"Okay, another time," Cam responds a little wistfully. He has resigned himself to the reality that this is likely one of the last times that they will share in this way.

"Are you going deer hunting with Wiff, I mean Mr. Kenny this year?"

"Yes, we always do," Cam answers, between bites of cookie.

"Why do you go hunting?"

"I don't know really. We go hunting every year. I always come back empty handed."

"Cookie," Cam offers not wanting the conversation to end.

"I have to go soon," says Evea reaching for a cookie. "Can you drive me home after I finish my cookie?"

"Sure," Cam replies while hiding his resignation and regret.

15 Jesus Loves Me Stuff

Cam sits in his office cubicle. A few days ago Jordan in his usual way assigned Cam his next project.

"Here," Jordan said tossing a bunch of papers on Cam's desk. "Read this over. Give me an estimate of how much time you need. It shouldn't take more than a week for the first draft."

Cam dutifully submitted his time estimate in the form of a schedule only to learn from Jordan that a deadline for the project had already been established which didn't fit Cam's proposed schedule. After much arm twisting by Jordan, Cam revised his schedule to fit the arbitrary deadline concocted by MKM executives.

Now Cam is having difficulty getting started on the first draft. Finding the right perspective is often difficult. He turns to a replica of an argillite carving that sits on his desk. The original carving was made by an artist from the Pacific Northwest Coast. Cam is fond of holding it in his hand, turning it over and over. He enjoys the tactile sense of the replica. The piece depicts a thunderbird with its talons clasping a tree branch as though resting in a tree. The thunderbird wears a solemn and determined look in its strong eyes and hooked beak. It surveys every detail in its surroundings. Nothing is overlooked. Its strong wings are folded at its sides. You can imagine the thunderbird unfolding its powerful wings and masterfully and naturally taking flight.

On the back and at the bottom of the thunderbird is the upside-down face of a man. In contrast to the bold features of the thunderbird, the man is much less prominent. He is merged into the thunderbird. The man looks solemn and determined. His eyes look straight at you as though looking to see who you are. He wears a head dress that is part of the tail feathers of the thunderbird. His arms, which are the back side of the thunderbird's wings, are against his sides. The backbone of the man and the thunderbird runs up or down, depending on your viewpoint. At the back of the head of the thunderbird, the ear tufts of the thunderbird form the man's legs. The man is part of the thunderbird and not the other way around.

Cam has discovered that he can turn the piece upside down and stand the piece on his desk with the man upright and the thunderbird upside down. In this position the piece is unstable and looks unnatural. It could easily tip over. The man is along for the ride on the back of a much bigger and more powerful being.

Cam wonders at the connection between the thunderbird and the man. He speculates what the man might see about himself if he tried to discover more about his relationship to the thunderbird, in the same way that Evea looks for her soul in the bathroom mirror. He concludes that the man already understands as much as he needs to and there's nothing more to say, or that can be said. There's a power and dignity in the thunderbird and the man is part of this. Enjoy the ride.

An idea about his new project occurs to Cam. He begins typing.

There is a tap tap on his desk. Cam twists around in his chair to see who is there.

"Hi Jordan, how are you?" he says, losing his train of thought.

"Do you have a minute?" ask Jordan. "This won't take long."

Cam crab shuffles his way out of his cubicle. He follows Jordan to an empty office.

"Close the door," Jordan requests. Cam shuts the door and sits down. "I have a new assignment for you, or rather Ed has a special assignment for you," says Jordan coming directly to the point. "Ed wants you to see Zanya. She has a special project for you. They didn't tell me what it is. Any idea what the project might be?"

"It probably has to do with the interview I had with Zanya. Beyond that I don't know."

"Ed wants you for a couple of days for this special project. I'll have to reassign your current project. The difficulty is finding another writer to take over the assignment. They never think about what it takes me to reassign work and still meet my deadlines when they come up with these special projects," complains Jordan rolling his eyes and shaking his head.

Heavy is the head that wears the crown Cam thinks. He tries not to smile a crooked smile. Instead he maintains his poker face not wanting to betray his sentiment.

"They play by the rules as long as it suits them," Jordan grumbles. "And when it doesn't suit them, they have no problem bending the rules to suit their own ends. Well look, don't spend any more time on this *special* project than you absolutely have to, no more than a couple of days. I need you here."

"I'll talk to Zanya and find out what she wants," says Cam not wanting to commit to Jordan's time frame without knowing more about Zanya's project. Cam knows from experience that if Jordan says a couple of days, they probably told him longer for the project, more likely a week.

"When you know more about the project, let me know," Jordan declares. He rises from his chair, appearing to bring the meeting to a close. "Don't send me an e-mail. I never read e-mails. Come and see me in my office," he instructs.

"You'll be the first to know," says Cam. He too rises from his chair, glad that their meeting is over without incident.

"Oh by the way," says Jordan.

Cam can feel his defenses going up. He's seen this scenario before. Jordan enjoys lulling you into a false sense of security to catch you off balance. Cam wonders what old off-balance Jordan has in mind this time.

"The other day," continues Jordan while they stand facing one another across the table, "when you were escorting Filana to the reception, did anything unusual happen?"

"No, not that I remember. Why do you ask?"

"Did you go through the Broadcast Nexus in the sub-basement on the way to the reception?"

"Yes, we did."

"How did you get in?"

"I swiped my badge," Cam responds, knowing there is no point in denying it. There will be a log entry that confirms he swiped his badge. Jordan will have checked with Security for an entry.

"You know you shouldn't go in there?"

"I got turned around. I took a shortcut through the BN to make up time. Ed was waiting upstairs for Filana." Cam invokes the name of Ed in hopes that Jordan's recent encounter with Ed will deter Jordan from pursuing his current line of questioning. His recent wound is just beginning to heal and is still tender to the touch.

"Did you touch anything while you were down there?" Jordan persists.

"No," replies Cam, which is true. He didn't touch anything in the Broadcast Nexus. He also appreciates that telling everything you know isn't always the best policy either.

"Apparently there was a problem with one of the broadcast feeds that night," says Jordan, looking directly at

Cam. "It cost the company tens of thousands in lost advertising revenue. Ed was fuming. He had to leave the reception early. He had to get the problem fixed and explain to the advertisers. There was hell to pay. You know how Ed is when things aren't going his way."

"Yes, I've heard, but I've always managed to avoid that side of him."

There's a pause while Jordan ponders Cam's answer. Jordan decides not to pursue the current line of questioning. "You're fired." Jordan asserts to end the meeting. "Now get back to work," he declares to strengthen the fealty that Jordan believes binds Cam to Jordan as a member of Jordan's staff.

Cam returns to his cubicle.

A short time later, Cam knocks on Zanya's office door. The door is open. Her office assistant is nowhere to be seen.

"Hi Cameron," says Zanya sitting behind her desk. Cam decides not to correct her. "Come in. I've been expecting you. Shut the door."

Cam glances around the office. He notices that the two paintings that Zanya chose at the art gallery are now prominently hung to the viewing advantage of anyone entering her office. The waterfall that Ed provided remains tucked away in one of the far corners of the office. The water is turned off. Cam finds a seat.

"I thought it might be a good idea," begins Zanya, "if we got to know one another a little better. You can see how I work and I can see how you work. We can see if we're a good fit. What do you think?"

"That's a good idea."

"I want you to talk to Preacher Jay tomorrow. Have you heard of him?"

"He's in the old section of the city. Many call him The Rebel."

"He runs a mission called the House of Adam. I want you to conduct a pre-interview with him for one of my shows. Who is he? Is he a rebel as his followers claim? You have a meeting with him tomorrow. I've arranged everything. Talk to my assistant. She can give you the details about when and where. Spend the rest of today finding out what you can about him. There should be information in the news vault. Find out what his angle is. After you talk to him, you have a couple of days to write down your impressions of him. I want you to come up with questions that I can ask him in the interview. It shouldn't be any more than a couple of pages. Let me know what perspective you think I should take in the interview. We can discuss your ideas on Friday. I'll have my assistant set up our follow-up meeting for Friday. Okay?"

"Yes, it sounds fine," replies Cam, glad for the change of pace.

"Good, I'll see you Friday," says Zanya, indicating the meeting is over.

"Okay, Friday," answers Cam standing to leave.

"You can leave the door open," adds Zanya as he leaves the office. "Remember this is a special project. You'll have to keep it quiet. The assignment is on a need-to-know basis."

Early the next morning Cam finds himself in the once-prosperous older section of the city. The address takes him to an old two-storey department store. On the front of the second floor, a neon sign proclaims that 'Jesus saves'. The sign is on at night until 10:30 when an automatic timer turns it off in compliance with the Bayview bylaw regarding commercial signage. Two large window displays front the lower storey of the building. Someone has used store manikins to turn the display areas into dioramas. The previous store owner abandoned the manikins when her business failed.

236

In one window is the depiction of the fall of Adam and Eve. The Eve manikin offers a plastic apple to the Adam manikin. Each manikin stands on a floor base made of heavy sheet metal. A vertical metal rod welded to the base runs up through a hole in the bottom of the manikin's foot to prevent the manikin from toppling over. Adam and Eve stare blankly through their sun-faded manikin eyes. Their pale and faded skin is cracked, similar to the craquelure that you see in old paintings. Several of the fingers on the two manikins are broken off. Someone has re-attached a couple of the fingers with white adhesive tape. A few of the fingers are still missing. Artificial shrubbery strategically placed by the creator of the diorama hides the otherwise exposed breasts and loins of the manikins, although neither manikin has genitals. The previous merchant of the building sold women's clothes. In the background, the creator of the diorama has planted in a plastic bucket a spindly artificial tree that represents the tree of knowledge. A small stuffed toy snake is partially hidden in the tree. The snake is the kind you might win as a first prize in a game of chance at a carnival. The goal of the first small cheap prize is to seduce you into continuing to play in hopes of trading up to a bigger and better prize while spending more money. Everyone who goes to a carnival knows this ploy. Still, many can't resist. Behind the tree, the artist has painted a brick wall and added graffiti to give the setting a contemporary feel. Messages adorn the wall. 'If you can't do the time, don't do the crime' asserts one message.

In the second window display stands a motionless blank-eyed and faded Moses manikin dressed in a robe. The artist has added a moustache and beard to the otherwise feminine looking face. The Moses manikin stands posed, holding over his head a tablet made of extruded polystyrene foam that he is about to smash to the ground. 'You shall not make for yourself an idol' appears on the tablet in large black letters. Another tablet already lies broken on the ground at the feet of the Moses manikin. Instead of a golden calf, there is a derelict motor scooter that the artist has resurrected and painted gold. A second manikin dressed in robes stands beside the scooter. He holds a wrench in his hand as though working on the scooter. Instead of a mountain scene in the background to represent Mount Sinai where God gave Moses the tablets, the creator of the diorama has added a cityscape, representing downtown Bayview, to give the scene a mix of old and contemporary.

A welcome sign is posted on the front door. Cam pushes the door open and enters. The door closes behind him. The room is in semi-darkness except for the light originating from a doorway at the far end of the room and a few flickering overhead fluorescent lights left on for insurance purposes. Cam pauses inside the door while he waits for his eyes to adjust. Folding chairs are arrayed in front of a dais and lectern at the back of the room. Dimly lit pictures of various biblical scenes are painted on the walls. A black motorcycle with chrome trim and twin black leather saddle bags sits to one side, half hidden in the shadows.

"Hello," says Cam raising his voice slightly. There is no answer. He tentatively moves closer to the dais. He stops about half way into the room. "Hello," he says in a louder voice. Still there is no answer. He wonders if this is how it played out for Moses at the burning bush. Cam walks to the dais. "Hello," he shouts.

"Hello," replies a voice emanating from the doorway behind the dais. "Come in. I've been expecting you," says the doorway voice.

Cam walks behind the dais to the door and stands in the doorway. Seated behind an old wooden desk sits a man. He looks to be in his late fifties, but Cam isn't sure. The man's height is indeterminate because he's seated. His head is shaved. An earring with a cross dangles from one ear. He's wearing wire-rim glasses and a faded denim shirt with the shirt sleeves rolled up. A worn black leather jacket hangs on

238

the wide back of his chair. His black leather boots peak out from under the desk.

The room is plainly furnished. There is a bookshelf with a few dusty books carelessly tossed on the shelves. In the corner of the room on a small table sits a coffee maker and coffee supplies. A print of a painting hangs on the wall behind the man. In the foreground of the painting is a well-maintained garden with short, neatly clipped green shrubbery and a pale-blue pond. A path in an off-white color leads from the pond to an empty, simple, white bench in the mid ground of the painting. Immediately behind the bench is the side wall of an old well-maintained building made from off-white fieldstones. To the right of the bench is an unadorned lancet window set in the wall. The window is dark, so you can't see what is happening inside.

An open copy of the Bible, a ball-point pen, and paper with a few notes scrawled in a heavy hand lay scattered on the man's desk. The desk is covered in haphazardly arranged coffee stains where coffee cups and spoons have found temporary resting places.

"You must be Cam. Come in. I'm Jay," says Jay happy to see another face. "I've been working on my Sunday sermon. You're a writer. You can help me. I always have trouble getting started. What do you know about God?" Jay looks at Cam with a critical eye.

"Mostly what I learned at Sunday school," Cam replies. This is true. He did learn most of what he knows in Sunday school, but his God education didn't stop there. When he was a grade-seven kid he attended confirmation classes in the church where his parents, mostly his mother, attended. His father was not a church goer. Once a week after school, Cam and other grade-seven-and-eight kids would make their way to the church basement where the minister would talk about the teachings of Christ. Cam can't recall what the minister said, but at the time he found it interesting.

239

At the end of the series of talks, there was an exam that you had to write. If you passed the exam, you could be confirmed in the church, although now Cam can't remember exactly what it meant to be confirmed in the church.

What he did remember about the confirmation classes were two things. First, there were two girls, one of whom attended the confirmation classes and her friend who belonged to a different religious denomination. She tagged along with her friend because she had eyes for Cam. Cam wasn't sure what to make of this. He hadn't had much experience with girls. The second thing that he remembered about the confirmation classes happened during the confirmation exam. He had studied for the exam, but his friend at the time, Murray, had not. Murray was struggling with the exam questions. "Cam," whispered Murray, who sat at the desk next to Cam when they wrote the exam in the church gymnasium. This was the same gymnasium where the scout meetings were held. Murray was a scout too. "What's the answer to number six?"

A few weeks later at the morning Sunday service, the minister conducted a confirmation ceremony in front of the church members who had congregated along with God to confirm those who had passed the exam. Cam was there and so was Murray, who had barely passed the exam. Cam wondered whether he had done the right thing. Did God care whether or not Murray passed the exam? Did God care that Cam had studied and Murray had not? Did Cam earn extra points with God? What about Moses and the Ten Commandments and the things that Cam's parents had said about such things? Was it enough that Murray had simply tried to buddy up to God by attending the confirmation classes and taking the exam? Was Murray afraid of the unholy wrath of biblical proportions that his parents would have unleashed on him if he had failed the exam?

"Ah! Jesus loves me stuff!" scoffs Jay. "Most of the people who come to my sermons have been kicked in the teeth most of their lives. They've been beaten up pretty badly. They don't want to hear that crap. They've been shit on. They've never had anything and most never will. I try to help them find meaning. Not this free speech junk, or free this or free that, or shit like that. They've never had free anything and most never will. A few of them know they're not free. They know that nothing's free in this world. Everything comes at a price. But they still come through those front doors every Sunday. Others come because they think they're expected to. Some come looking because they're curious about me, or what's inside this place." Jay gestures at his second-hand office. "Curiosity about me is fine because then I can work on them. Curiosity gets them in the door where they can look around. And maybe one of them will say hey there's something here. It's not just some old fart spouting shit. And then there are the ones who come looking for more because they know there's more. God love 'em."

"I noticed the biblical scenes of Adam and Eve, and Moses in the front windows. What's that all about?"

"Yeah, I know. The manikins in the windows look like crap. But it gets people thinking. Who in their right mind would use female manikins for Adam and Moses? What kind of joke is this? These people aren't stupid. They can see. Now and then they see better than the rest of us. Then one or two of them gets curious to see what's going on inside, so they come in. The regulars who come here make jokes about the manikins. Last week one of the women said the Mission got it right even if God didn't. She meant that women would do a better job even if they had to dress like men to get the job done." Jay cracks a big smile.

"What's the theme of your sermon for Sunday?"

"I don't know. I was hoping you could tell me. I'm looking for a little inspiration," says Jay with a grin.

Cam isn't sure what to make of this response.

"They tell me you're a rebel. Are you a rebel?" asks
Cam.

"Hell no, I'm like anyone else. They think I'm a rebel
because I swear once in a while. Well my swearing is
nothing. At times I do it for effect. What's a rebel anyway?
Jesus was a rebel. I'm not. He stood up to those Pharisees
with their 'thou shalt not' crap. All their 'don't heal anyone
on the Sabbath' or we'll beat the snot out of you or worse.
The Pharisees had everyone by the balls and weren't about
to let go. They had a good thing going. The worst part of it
was the Pharisees thought they were doing the right thing.
But they weren't. Today is no different. People think they're
doing good for others, but they're really not helping anyone,
only themselves most of the time even if they don't mean to.
I'm that way too. Course Jesus had bigger fish to fry. Excuse
the pun. He was trying to show everyone that often the rules
don't mean shit. At least that was one of his messages."

"What about the motorcycle out there? Is that yours?"

"Yeah, the motorcycle is mine. The congregation lets me
keep it here. The bike is part of my rebel image. I know a
little about marketing. We all do. It goes with being part of
the Jesus franchise. You can use that if you want for the TV
interview. I mean play up the rebel part. I'm a mechanic by
trade. See," says Jay picking up from his desk a small
handmade trophy that a member of the congregation made.
"The congregation gave me this about ten years ago."

The trophy consists of a wrench secured to a big shiny
bolt on a block of unvarnished pine. The wrench is bent and
twisted. There is a small thin imitation-brass plate with an
inscription written in freehand on the front. The wooden
base is dirty from much handling.

"What does the inscription say?"

"Don't give up your day job," replies Jay without
looking at the plate. He smiles with satisfaction. "I'm not
exactly sure what they were trying to say. Maybe get bent, or
that I'm definitely as bent and twisted as everyone else. A

delegation from the congregation gave it to me one Sunday after a sermon I gave. The sermon was about our life's work here in this world. I suppose that's what the trophy is about, our life's work. At least that's what I like to think. Who knows? I don't. They wouldn't say what the trophy was about. They smiled when they gave it to me. Maybe they didn't know themselves. What do you think they meant by it?"

"I'm guessing they were trying to tell you that you're doing a good job," Cam answers. "What about the other church denominations in Bayview; do you get along with them?"

"Oh yeah, for the most part we get along. A few of them don't take to my Old Testament sermons, Isaiah and those guys. 'And they shall go into the holes of the rocks, and into the caves of the earth, for *fear* of the LORD, and for the *glory* of his majesty, when he ariseth to shake terribly the earth'," says Jay raising his voice. "Isaiah chapter two, verse nineteen. I put extra emphasis on words like fear and glory when I use the quote and put a little body English on it. Then I'll pause for half a minute or so to let their imaginations go to work. Course you always have to give them hope in these types of sermons: 'And I will give children to be their princes and babes shall rule over them'. Isaiah chapter three, verse four. I call these sermons my open-a-can-of-whup-ass sermons. Don't get me wrong. I use the whup-ass sermons only once or twice a year. I prefer the teachings of Christ, not that he didn't pull people up by the short hairs too when he felt they needed it. But now and then you have to shake people up with a little Old Testament stuff too. They get too comfortable, complacent. They start to accept this world without looking at it. You have to ruffle their feathers every so often. I always warn my congregation before I deliver a whup-ass sermon. If they aren't keen on it, they don't have to stay. Mostly they decide to stay, their choice."

"Is that how you refer to it, a whup-ass sermon, when talking to the congregation?" asks Cam.

"Oh sure, I'm not using words they haven't heard before. God's not for the faint of heart. Actually I tell them I'm going to open a can of whup-ass and if they haven't the guts for it, they should leave right now. Course most of them you could roller skate on. They're that tough. Their toughness is a badge of honor in the community and everyone else in the congregation knows it. All of them have seen a lot. So to walk out would be a sign of weakness, a sign that you don't belong. They have a strong sense of community because of the things they've been through."

"So you manipulate them?"

"Oh hell yes," Jay asserts. "Others do it. I try to do it for the right reasons. Others do it to get people riled up. They play on their emotions. Try to put a fire in their belly, get their guts churning and make them afraid. They try to make them see things the wrong way. The same way the Pharisees tried to make them see. Make them blind. People stop using their imaginations. They get trapped in a cliché about freedom and fighting for things that don't mean shit. People get hurt and die when that happens. The people in this community know about suffering. And it happens all the time. They know shit rolls downhill. 'There will be wars and rumors of war'. Hang on a minute," says Jay who interrupts his rant and scribbles a note on a scrap of paper.

"And all the while the ones getting people riled up don't believe what they're saying, or if they do believe, they need a good kick in the ass," Jay continues. "They say it so that they can belong to anything that gives them a little taste of power, or they're scared shitless, or they're the dupes, the chattering class behind somebody higher up the food chain. And these higher ups are the assholes who are the first to run and hide under their beds when things go bad. Haven't the guts to finish what they start. How many chicken-shit Nazis fled to South America at the end of the Second World

War? How many deposed dictators have fled to other countries after raping the people they were supposed to protect? They make me wanna puke!" Jay pauses as he thinks about what he has said. Now Cam writes a note on a piece of paper that he has pulled from his shirt pocket.

"Is there nothing worth fighting for?" Cam asks.

"Oh hell, there's plenty worth fighting for," Jay retorts. "Look at Gandhi. Look at what he did and how he did it. And there are monsters out there that need to be stopped. Look at that little piece of shit, Hitler, and there are lots others too. We need to tell the monsters they're full of shit before they cause trouble and people get hurt and die."

Both Cam and Jay make more notes.

"Look at the war we're in now," says Jay. "Who stood up and said you're full of crap? Go fuck yourself! No one had the balls, not the law makers, not the media, not the judiciary, not the clergy, no one because the ones pushing for the war said if you're against us you're not loyal. You're a traitor to your country. And we can kick the shit out of you if you make trouble for us. They wrapped themselves in the flag. Most didn't want to touch that sacred cow, loyalty. What the hell is loyalty anyway? Loyalty to what? Loyalty to whom? Or if you criticize us, you hurt the military. Our sons and daughters will die and you're the cause of their deaths. You've got the blood of our sons and daughters on your hands because you spoke out against us. That's f'ing rich! They'll die anyway and for what, to keep our country free? What the hell does freedom mean anyway? It's a cliché around here. Most people wouldn't know freedom if it bit 'em on the ass. They'd run from it. They wouldn't know what to do with it. They've twisted free will into monsters, into isms: ism this and ism that. Ah shit!" Jay spits out in disgust.

There's a pause while Cam scribbles additional notes. Jay scowls. He stares at his desktop.

"So, have you got enough information?" Jay asks returning to the thread of their conversation after reflecting on what he has said. "What's the next step?"

"Do you run a soup kitchen, hostel, or anything along those lines?" asks Cam ignoring Jay's question.

"No, we don't do that shit. We can't afford it. The other churches around here look after that. They do a good job too. Even if we could we wouldn't. 'I am the bread of life: he that cometh to me shall never hunger; and he that believeth on me shall never thirst'. Jesus said that, John six verse thirty-five. My mission is about food for the soul. This is about putting a fire in your belly, not food in your belly. And the fire has to be the right kind of fire. Hey, I think I've got my theme for this Sunday, fire in the belly." Jay scrawls another note. "Why don't you come out to this Sunday's sermon? You might enjoy it."

"There were rumors that you kidnapped a kid who was living on the streets," Cam states. "It was in the local newspapers."

"It wasn't kidnapping," Jay shoots back. "I helped a couple of friends get their daughter off the street. She was turning tricks for drug money. It wasn't kidnapping and I was never charged with anything. She and I talked here in this very office. We met once a week for about an hour. It wasn't any of that heavy come to Jesus stuff. I'm not a bully. We talked and nothing else. Talking took a while, but I managed to help get her off the street. She made the choice. She was doing fine last time I saw her. She was free to leave anytime she wanted and on occasion she did leave before we finished a session. At first I had to pay her to attend."

"Well, you can see how people might misinterpret that," Cam interrupts. "You can see how people might look at that."

"I know that looks bad," Jay responds, "I know how people can bend things for their own ends. Some might look at it and say that I was giving her money in exchange for sexual favors. There was nothing sordid or illegal in our meetings. Toward the end she came to the sessions because she wanted to. She chose. Later she tried to give back a little of the money, but I wouldn't take it. It wasn't about the money."

"You can imagine how that might look when a known prostitute with a drug dependency offers you money," Cam interjects, pressing to see how far he can go. "Was there anyone else around during any of the sessions, possibly the janitor for the Mission here? Is there someone who can support what you say?"

"I'm the janitor!" answers Jay becoming annoyed with this continued line of questioning. "There may have been different people come in from time to time while we were talking in my office. I don't remember. Mostly it was only the two of us here talking."

"What did you talk about?" asks Cam.

"We talked about a lot of things," Jay answers. "The process takes time. First I have to gain your trust. I have to find out who you are, what's important to you, where you're going. There are lots of things. Mostly you already know where you should be going. In the end you have to make the decision. You have to want to change. Then you have to take the first step to change. It's up to you, not me. I can't force you. You have to figure out for yourself what you need to do. No one can really help you. And I don't get all churchy and make you pray or crap like that unless you want to pray. You have to find your own door and walk through it."

"You've done this many times before," Cam observes. "Haven't you?"

"Oh yeah, I try to show them a few of the doors in the corners of the room where they haven't looked," answers Jay gesturing around his cramped office. "'For every one who asketh receives; he that seeketh findeth; and to him that knocketh, it shall be opened.' That's Matthew seven, verse eight in the King James Version. The place is bigger than

247

perhaps they've imagined, or been allowed to imagine, or forgotten to imagine. Most are so busy trying to figure out where their next meal is coming from that they've forgotten how big the place really is."

Cam makes a note.

"I can introduce you to several who have changed their lives," Jay offers.

"What about the girl you helped? Can I meet her?"

"Fraid not, she's still healing. You have to respect that. Turning your life around can take years. Letting go of what you've done can take a lifetime. It takes time to get comfortable with who you are becoming and who you were because your past experiences are part of who you are too. It's your life's work, becoming who you are. We're all artists of sorts. We're more than manikins. The canvas is bigger than we can imagine. Hey, I like that idea," says Jay with a grin. Jay jots down a note.

"I'd like to meet some of the others you've helped."

"Okay, I can arrange that," Jay responds, continuing to write. "How about tomorrow?"

"Works for me."

"You know how people's imaginations can get when things get twisted inside," adds Jay. "A few members of the congregation tried to twist the sessions with the girl into something that they weren't. Perhaps they did it out of jealousy or spite or too much time on their hands. I don't know. Then the media got wind of the rumors."

"Thanks, I had to ask. I needed to clear that up, no harm meant."

"No harm done," Jay replies warily. He has grown a little suspicious of Cam's motives.

"So the next step after I meet with these people is talk to Zanya about what I've learned. In a few days an MKM employee will phone and arrange a time and a place for the interview between you and Zanya. The interview might take place in one of our TV studios or here at the Mission. I'm not sure which. They'll work out the details with you when they phone."

"And what have you learned?" asks Jay.

"I've learned," begins Cam searching for the right words, "that you're rough around the edges, but you fit this community. You have a good heart. You're doing your best to look out for others."

"Is that what you're going to tell Zanya," asks Jay, satisfied with Cam's assessment.

"Yes, that's pretty much it, only I'll give her more details."

"Okay, good, thanks for coming. Now if you don't mind, I have to work on my sermon, Creating a Fire in Your Belly," says Jay who is eager to get started on his sermon. "Can you find your way out?"

"Yes, no problem, thanks for your time," replies Cam. He shakes Jay's hand.

"Hope to see you Sunday," replies Jay. He returns to the notes on his desk.

Cam steps onto the street. He turns briefly to look at the manikins in the front windows. Perhaps, he speculates, there is more here than meets the eye.

"How's the special project going?" Jordan asks Cam the next day. Cam is seated in his cubicle.

"Fine, the project is on a need-to-know basis, so I can't talk about it. Those are the rules."

"What's this?" asks Jordan, snatching Cam's notes from his desk.

"They're my background notes from an interview that I did yesterday." Cam holds out his hand for the return of the papers.

"I wish you would learn to write legibly," responds Jordan, attempting to decipher Cam's notes while ignoring his hand. "I can't read this."

"I didn't write them for you," Cam responds firmly while continuing to hold out his hand for the papers. "I don't think Ed would be very happy if he knew that you were reading my notes." Jordan casually places the papers on the desk after suddenly realizing that the scribbled words on the paper could have a career-ending toxicity.

"And how long will this special project take? I have work for you."

"I'll be finished by the end of Friday, after I meet with Zanya."

Jordan rolls his eyes, shakes his head, turns and walks away.

On Friday, Cam knocks on the open door to Zanya's office.

"Hi Cameron, come on in," says Zanya without looking up from the computer monitor on her desk. Cam winces at her continued disregard for his name. His discomfort goes unnoticed. "Let's have a seat on the couch where we can talk," she proposes. "We don't have to be so formal. There's coffee too if you like."

He pours himself a coffee. "Did you get my e-mail about my interview with Jay?"

"Yes, but I haven't read it yet. First I want to hear about the interview in your own words," says Zanya joining Cam. "How did it go with Preacher Jay? What did you learn? Who is he?"

"He has some interesting ideas. His language is rather colorful. You'll have to censor a little of it for TV."

"Yes, but what did he say?" interrupts Zanya who is anxious to hear the details.

"He talked about the people in the community and their rough lives. He talked about freedom and he talked about loyalty. He doesn't think that most people know much about either. He doesn't see himself as a rebel, although he plays to that image to get people into his Mission. He works out of an

250

old store. In the windows of the store front are dioramas. They show biblical scenes. One shows Adam being tempted. The other shows Moses smashing the tablets of the Ten Commandments. Both have a modern backdrop to give the scenes a link to the present. Whoever created the scenes used scrounged female manikins for Adam and Moses. You'll want to get a shot of them."

"That seems strange. Why use female manikins for Adam and Moses? What's he trying to say? Is he questioning their sexuality? Is he mocking the Bible?" Zanya poses looking for an angle for her interview with Jay.

"I don't think it was Jay that created the dioramas. I'm not sure who it was. Possibly it was a member of the congregation. I'm not sure. The issue is money. The Mission doesn't have much. Female mannequins were used because they were the only thing available. Jay doesn't have the resources we have at MKM. And he says the dioramas get people to use their imaginations. It gets them questioning things about today's society. I think it works. I think he's on to something."

"What about the kidnapping? Did he talk about that?"

"I asked him about that." Cam is surprised that Zanya is aware of the allegations before he realizes that she must have other sources of information. "He said it was a misunderstanding. His actions were misconstrued. He was helping to get a girl off the street and was successful. There were a few people who misinterpreted what he was doing. I don't think there's anything in it. No charges were ever laid against him. I interviewed a number of people that he's helped. He's only trying to help the people in his community by helping them to see another way of looking at things. There's nothing sinister in that."

"Where there's smoke, there's fire," Zanya counters. "And the fact that he questions ideas of freedom and loyalty seems disturbing when you think what this country has done for him and others in his community. He sounds dangerous. What if others pick up on his ideas of freedom and begin asking questions about loyalty? Doesn't it strike you as insulting and disloyal to question the ideas that this country is founded on?"

"He's not questioning the ideas. He's questioning the ways in which the ideas are used," Cam answers. "He questions our complacency. He thinks that we're too willing to accept other people's ideas of freedom and that gets us in trouble."

"What kind of trouble?" Zanya asks.

"He used the current war as an example," Cam replies. "He said people were afraid to speak out for fear of reprisal. He's right too. In the lead-up to the war there were lots of headlines in the papers about retaliation against the few who spoke out. Some had their careers ruined and others were threatened with similar consequences."

"Yes, but nothing was ever proven," responds Zanya.

"Well, as you say, where there's smoke there's fire. Although in the case of the allegations of kidnapping and sexual impropriety raised against him, there appears to be only the smoke of overactive imaginations. Maybe somebody was trying to get at him for reasons we'll never know. He doesn't strike me as someone who would abuse his position in the community."

"Well, you never know," says Zanya. "Is he a wolf in sheep's clothing? I've got my assistant, what's her name, doing a little checking."

"He seems sincere to me," says Cam firmly, not liking where this conversation is going.

"You did a good job," Zanya concludes after listening to Cam's report for about half an hour. Smiling, she stands up. "Thanks for the report. I have to get back to other issues. You wouldn't believe what it takes to get a show up and running. There are legal issues and getting the set ready and all kinds of things. My assistant handles most of it. And always there are the ratings to consider."

"There's more than TV ratings," says Cam, standing to leave. "I know ratings are important, but we're part of this community too. I'm concerned where this is going."

"Cameron, relax. It's all good. I'm playing devil's advocate. I want to look at this from all sides. He'll get a fair hearing. I'm not out to ruin him to advance my career if that's what you're thinking. Everything will be fine. I promise not to say anything that isn't true. He's colorful. We can go with that. He'll make a good interview for the show. I'm sure of it. You needn't worry." Zanya smiles mildly. There's an uneasy silence. "You did well. I'm very pleased with your effort," she confidently appends as an afterthought to allay his apprehension.

Cam leaves Zanya's office, uncertain if she is going in the right direction.

16 Ffffffffffft

Shshshshshshshshshshshshshhshshhshshshsh,
squeegee, squeegee.

Shshshshshshshshshshshshshhshshhshshshsh,
squeegee, squeegee.

The car tires shshsh on the wet road, kicking up the
fallen rain that billows and trails behind Dunc's car. Dunc
has pointed his car north to his hunting camp. The road
drifts north occasionally meandering west or east, but
always returning north as the road bends following the lakes
that intermittently emerge out of the forest. Regularly the
wiper blades squeegee the windshield: squeegee, squeegee.

Cam sits in the passenger seat reading a handbook.
With the exception of the tires and the squeegee of the wiper
blades, the car is quiet inside. Dunc has turned off the car
radio. The reception is poor this far north unless you pass
within range of a town that is sufficiently large enough to
warrant a radio station. This far north, there aren't many
places that are adequate in size. Dunc and Cam have been on
the road since crow piss, as Dunc likes to say.

"Hey Squib," says Dunc concentrating on the road
between the drops of rain, "what are ya readin'?"

"Survival guide," Cam answers after finishing a
paragraph. "It explains how to survive in the wilderness if
you get lost or stranded. The guide talks about being
prepared if you get lost in the woods, predicting the
weather, navigating by the stars, finding food, signalling for
rescue, that kind of stuff. A former member of the SAS wrote
it."

"SAS?"

"Special Air Service, a special unit of the British Army."

"Oh, I've heard of them," says Dunc. "Look, I'm tellin' ya, forget the wood-lore crap. If you get lost the only thing you have to remember is to stay put until I find you. Don't go wanderin' off. That's the worst thing you can do. Fire your friggin' rifle three times in the air so I know you're in trouble. I'll find ya."

"For example, the guide talks about using the moon to determine east and west," says Cam ignoring Dunc's advice.

"That book won't do you any good where we're goin' unless you use it to wipe your arse," Dunc retorts.

"The guide is interesting. It might come in handy. You never know."

"Lookit here. If ya paid more attention to why you're here and not worryin' about a bunch of what if stuff, like gettin' lost, you'd be doin' somethin'. You've been comin' to hunt camp for ten friggin' years. And ya still haven't got a deer. Pay attention to what you're doin'. What do ya do in that pop-up wolf-den thing ya call a blind anyway? Your mind wanders like a fart in a hurricane. Stay focused," Dunc instructs. He points to his eyes with a military, two-finger, watch-me gesture while keeping his eyes focused on the road. "Do what I do. That's all there is to it buddy," he grins. "That's all ya need to know," he adds with satisfaction.

The shshsh of the tires continues. 'Squeegee, squeegee,' say the windshield wipers. Cam and Dunc fall into silence while the car eats up the road.

"Did, I tell you about my ancestors when they first came to this country?" Cam asks later. "It was around 1850. They were farmers. The first winter they cooked frozen potatoes and ate any wild game that they caught in the forest. That's all they had to eat the first winter. They had to hunt to survive, not like today."

"Well maybe it should be like it was."

"You'd enjoy building outhouses for a living would you?" Cam retorts. "Outhouses in this country were high tech for a plumber in 1850."

"I'd get by. What would you do Shakespeare? There wasn't much call for script writers in those days."

"I'm not the one that wants to eat frozen potatoes and hunt wild game for dinner makings," says Cam with a teasing smile. "And if you could ask my ancestors if they wanted to keep living that way, they'd laugh at you. They could see that things could be better and they made them better in the same way we do today."

Dunc turns on the car radio. He searches for a radio station. 'Ffffffffft' answers the radio, singing the song of the universe. 'Ffffffffft, ffffffffft'. 'Squeegee, squeegee,' answer the wiper blades. Then, scarcely audible above the fffft of the universe, the radio shifts into song with the car scraping the outer boundary of a weak radio signal from a distant station. 'I'm just a singer in a rock and roll band,' sings the radio. 'Squeegee, squeegee,' answer the wiper blades. 'Ffffffffffft,' says the radio losing the signal.

"Hey! I know that song," says Cam. "It's an old Moody Blues song. Can you get it back?"

"She's gone; can't get her back," Dunc says matter-of-factly.

Dunc continues searching for a radio signal. 'Ffffffft ffffff' says the radio. Dunc gives up on the radio. He turns it off. 'Squeegee squeegee' say the wiper blades.

Cam reads his survival guide.
Shshshshshshshshshshshhshshshshshshshshshshsh shshshshshshshshshhsh.

"Hey Wiff, I'm getting hungry," says Cam after countless car-chewing miles. "What about you?"

"There's a lunch hole 'bout a half hour up the road," answers Dunc concentrating on the crooked road winding through the forest. "We can stop there. I need to get gas too. Gas and eats," he adds with a friendly smirk."

True to Dunc's prediction, a Small Fry restaurant materializes out of the forest. Small Fry is a chain of fast-food restaurants. Their current advertising slogan is 'Nothing tastes like freedom the way it does at Small Fry'. There's even a song created for the slogan urging weary travellers seeking sustenance to experience the Small Fry brand of freedom. The Siren song is about choosing to eat at Small Fry whenever or wherever you want.

Dunc snaps on the turn signal and steers the car into the parking lot.

"I'll get gas later," says Dunc stretching beside the car. "Let's eat. I'm hungry."

The restaurant is a study in Stygian fast-food modernity. Each staff member wears a baggy, ill-fitting uniform with a matching paper wedge cap worn over a hair net. The shirts and pants are done in large checkerboard squares of green and gold. Each attendant wears a clip-on bow tie that is also done in a green-and-gold checkerboard pattern. There is discussion at Small Fry headquarters concerning the elimination of the bow tie. There have been too many incidents where bow ties have accidentally fallen into the potato fryer. The concern is that a Small Fry attendant kid will reach into the hot oil to retrieve their bow tie without thinking.

Two Small Fry attendants stand waiting behind the easy-to-clean stainless steel countertop. A third attendant hovers, constantly cleaning the tables and floor in the oh-so-sparkling-clean dining area. Right now things are quiet, so there isn't much to clean. Above the two counter attendants are three large panels that stretch the length of the counter. The panels announce the menu. In the background behind the counter flit two they-also-serve-who-stand-and-wait attendants who are ready to fly into action the second a customer places an order. Speed is everything. Kid-devouring Cronus is king and foe.

'Beeep, beeep, beeep,' shrieks the fryer; the fries are cooked to perfection in the golden age of fries and one of the attendants better look after them right away. One of the food attendants flies into action to quell the harpy. 'Beeeep, beeeep, beeeep' wails another machine. Its timer has expired. Another attendant navigates a circuitous path through a maze of food-preparation stations in response to the summons by the Minos machine.

"Hi, how may I help you?" says one of the counter attendants through painted wooden eyes. Without looking the attendant automatically places a green and gold plastic tray with a paper place mat on the counter. There's a road map of the immediate area printed in the middle of each place mat. A big red arrow with the words 'You are here' shows you exactly where you are. Advertisements around the border of the map advertise local businesses and attractions, such as the local pioneer museum that pays tribute to the trappers and later the loggers who settled the area. There's also a picture of the big brown beaver monument on the place mat. The monument itself sits next to the turn off to the nearby community of Driftwood. The Big Beaver is a modest one-storey-high affair. Although it is hollow inside, you can't go inside, the way you can the Big Tiger. However, you can have your picture taken while standing beside the monument. The Big Beaver was erected by the local politicians on behalf of the citizens, who are commonly referred to as Driftwooders. The beaver is there to remind you when passing by to visit Driftwood and meet the friendly Driftwooders.

The inhabitants of Gogama, who live about an hour's drive from Driftwood, refer to the citizens of Driftwood as Deadwoodies. There's a friendly rivalry between the two villages.

"I'll have a number four," says Dunc studying the menu without looking at the attendant.

"Would you like the regular sized drink, the tub-o-drink, or the bladder buster?" asks the attendant.

"I'll have the tub-o-drink."

"Regular fries, bucket-o-fries, or the car load?" questions the attendant without looking at Dunc.

"Bucket."

"Number four, tub and bucket," says the attendant into a microphone while pressing buttons on the cash register. "Anything else?" asks the attendant. Immediately the food attendants fly into action to fill the order. They place each ordered item on Dunc's tray as soon as it is ready.

"An apple crisperette."

"We're out of apple crisperettes," replies the attendant in a dull voice, having announced for the Sisyphus time today to numberless Small Fry connoisseurs that there are no apple crisperettes today.

"A blueberry crisperette then," says Dunc after studying the menu for a few more seconds.

"Blueberry," announces the attendant pressing another button on the register. "Anything else?"

"No, that's it."

"That comes to seven dollars and twenty-seven cents please," affirms the attendant.

Dunc pays for his order.

Cam orders a number three with a regular sized drink and a big-o-chunk order of ring-o-onions. Cam and Dunc take their trays and find a vacant table that the cleaning attendant has cleaned for the third time in the past fifteen minutes even though the table wasn't dirty. They remove their burgers from the cardboard envelopes. Immediately they fall to, wolfing down their burgers without exchanging a word.

"Do you remember the first hamburger you ever ate?" asks Cam having finished his meal. He attempts to relax in his chair while he sips his drink through a plastic straw. The plastic chairs are not designed for relaxing. The chairs are designed to get you out of the restaurant as fast as possible to make room for the next customer. The dining area is empty with the exception of Cam, Dunc and the cleaning attendant. Cam toys with the idea of suggesting a new theme for the restaurant chain's next advertising campaign: eat first, taste it later. He eyes the customer suggestion box sitting on the table next to the exit. He decides against it.

"No, but I remember the first time I got laid," Dunc grins. His mouth is stained a blueberry blue from the crisperette as though he's slowly being asphyxiated. "She was a bag of bones. Her name was Sally. I think. Don't remember her last name. It was in high school."

"No, your first hamburger," insists Cam. "Do you remember your first burger, or your first hot dog, or your first anything besides getting laid?"

"Nothin' like that," says Dunc shaking his head no. He sips his tub-o-drink. "Why? Are ya a food fanatic?"

"No, not that. I remember that my first hamburger was special. It was different from this," says Cam gesturing to the restaurant.

"Food is food. It is what it is. Quit your belly achin'. It can't always be a first time. Though I wish she'd had a little more meat on her bones. She was a string bean. I wonder what happened to ol' Sally," says Dunc reaching for a few stray fries that lie scattered on his tray. "She probably got married and had a couple of kids. Women aren't so bad. You gotta make 'em mind. Nothin' to it. Let 'em know who's boss." In the background the Small Fry's freedom song chants quietly from an overhead speaker.

Silence returns to the conversation while they sip their drinks. Dunc contemplates Sally. Cam, who has heard rumors about Dunc and his wife, Emma, searches for a new line of conversation.

260

"And what about you?" asks Dunc before Cam can think of anything to say.

"What, the first time I got laid?" asks Cam.

"No, I know the answer to that one, never. You and Anna, when are ya gettin' hitched? You're gettin' kinda long in the tooth."

"Someday possibly," says Cam noncommittally and not liking the direction that the conversation is taking.

"I should've laid off the tub-o-drink and had a regular instead," Dunc complains. "I have to tap the kidneys. We've still got a few hours before reachin' the cow barn. You 'bout ready?"

"Let me finish my drink first."

"Okay, I have to get gas. I'll meet you outside." Dunc heads for the washroom. Cam sips his drink. He is unable to get comfortable in his chair.

Dunc has fuelled the car and is ready to go by the time Cam emerges from the restaurant having given up on getting comfortable. The rain has stopped. The air has the cold chill of a damp, gray day. Cam shivers against the day.

"Let's go Squib," says Dunc his mouth still stained blueberry blue.

"Lead the way," Cam answers with a grin.

"What's up with you? What are ya grinnin' at?" quizzes Dunc with a grin that makes his blueberry blue mouth stand out even more.

"Oh nothing," says Cam. He fights the urge to laugh. "Let's go."

"Okay, but somethin's up," says Dunc starting the car and pointing it north. "Did anyone ever tell you that you can be about as funny as a fart in an aqualung?"

About two hours later, Dunc turns the car down an old logging road. After a pothole-jarring hour, they come to a small clearing where there's a plain one-room cabin, Dunc's cow barn. Beside the cabin is a shed where Dunc keeps his amphibious ATV.

Dunc turns off the car. "Made it," says Dunc with a big smile.

Dunc shoves open the cabin door. A pot-bellied stove stands in the middle of the cabin. A couple of beds line two of the walls. There is a small table and two wooden chairs at the far end. Above the table, shelves hold basic cooking equipment, eating utensils, an old coffee percolator and a kerosene lamp.

"Put your sleeping bag there," says Dunc pointing to one of the beds. "You bring in the stuff. I'll get a fire started."

Cam and Dunc busy themselves. They say little. Dunc lights the lamp and starts a fire to drive away the cold and damp. While Cam starts dinner, Dunc primes the pump that stands in front of the cabin. He draws water for coffee and washup. Cam puts a pot of beans on the stove. He fries up bacon and eggs in a heavy skillet. When the food is ready, he puts on the coffee percolator. He has brought a small supply of sugar for the coffee. There is a carton of milk and other supplies in an ice cooler that Cam has provided.

"You'll make someone a good wife one of these days," Dunc grins rubbing his itchy scalp. He's satisfied with their progress after the long drive.

Cam divides the food onto two old enamel plates. He hands one plate to Dunc. They eat in silence. The coffee percolates on the stove, filling the cabin with the smell of fresh brewed coffee. After dinner Cam pours a good helping of whiskey into two mugs and leaves the bottle on the table. Then he pours in the strong coffee. He puts one of the mugs on the table in front of Dunc. Dunc doctors his coffee to his liking. Cam does the same. They sit quietly enjoying the warmth of the coffee and the stove.

The dark completely encircles the small cabin. The lamp light peers weakly through the windows into the dark. The cabin light is uneven, leaving shadows in the corners.

Dunc puts a pot of water on the stove. He returns to his coffee while he waits for the water to heat through. When the water is ready, Dunc washes the dishes. He puts more wood in the stove.

"That should keep her goin', eh?" says Dunc. "We have to be up before crow piss. You ready for tomorrow?"

"I'm ready," says Cam. "You?"

"Ready as I'll ever be. If ya see a deer, don't try anythin' fancy. Aim for the lungs. It's your best chance. If ya hit the lungs, the deer might not go down right away, but it won't get far. Watch for a minute and see which way it goes. Don't chase after it right away. That'll only drive it into the bush and make it harder to find."

"Sounds good," says Cam who has heard this same advice every year for the last ten years.

"Why don't ya take the west trail? I'll go east," offers Dunc. "I saw deer tracks near the big tree down by the duck swamp when I was here last. There's bound to be somethin' there."

The big tree is a giant white pine that escaped the logger's axe. The duck swamp, so named by Dunc, is a swamp that only the ducks seem able to navigate. Dunc likes to take the east trail. There's a blind at the end of the trail that he built years ago. He gutted a portable toilet, mounted it on wooden posts and cut a large hole in the side that faces onto a meadow. The blind is a good ten feet above ground, giving it an excellent view. So it is that Dunc always takes the east trail and Cam the west trail. The two fall into silence, each thinking about tomorrow's hunt.

"Do you remember when we were kids and we used to go tobogganin' on that hill down by the creek?" asks Dunc after several minutes.

Fffffffffft

"Yeah, dead-man's hill, I remember," says Cam who is a little taken aback that Dunc has raised this memory or any memory for that matter. Dunc is not one to dwell on the past. Maybe his memory of ol' Sally has stirred other memories. "You had a different name for the hill. What was it, sidehill something or other?"

"Sidehill gouger," Dunc says filling in the blank.

"What's a sidehill gouger anyway?"

"The bogey man," Dunc answers. "The hill had a gouge in the side where we used to run our toboggans."

"Yeah, you'd start down the run," says Cam picking up the thread. "You'd be going all out. Then you'd hit the drop off where the hill is gouged out."

"Yup, over the edge of the hill and drop like a sack of hammers," adds Dunc with a big grin.

"Yeah, you'd float out in space forever, then whump!" says Cam giving the table a light thump with his hand. "You'd hit the hill and finish the run if you managed to hang on. It was great wasn't it?"

"Sure was," adds Dunc. "My ass would be sore for a week, like a lifter from the old man."

"Those were good times," says Cam. "And you were crazy enough to try and take the hill standing up. Did you ever make it to the bottom of the run standing up?"

"Once or twice," answers Dunc. "Mostly I remember bailin' when I hit."

"I'd be dead tired by the time I got home," says Cam because this is how he enjoys remembering their adventures. Cam, after these toboggan adventures, liked to imagine himself as a grizzled, dead-tired war veteran returning home from war. He doesn't mention this aspect to Dunc who has in the past characterized Cam's imaginative wanderings as 'useless as tits on a boar pig'. "Remember that place where we used to stop on the way home for hot chocolate? There was that restaurant out in the middle of nowhere. What was that place called?"

264

"Don't remember," says Dunc.

"The Hofgarten, that was it," says Cam trying to remember the details. "There was never anyone else in the place except the old guy who ran it. He made great hot chocolate. I think he was glad to see customers so he gave us extra."

"The hot chocolate I remember," Dunc responds taking a sip of his coffee. Silence descends. The fire in the stove crackles while they work on their coffees.

"Evea was asking what sidehill gouger means," says Cam interrupting the silence. "She said you used the phrase. I'll tell her next time I see her."

Dunc tilts his chair back, sliding into the shadow until his chair leans against the wall in a corner of the cabin. The lower half of his body is visible. The upper half is hidden in shadow. A feeble light escaping from the air vent on the side of the stove plays sporadically across Dunc's face.

"Evea's a good kid," Dunc offers. "Not like that old woman of mine. She needs a good flapperin' every now and then."

"I'm never sure what you mean by that. I think you twist words so that you can hide behind them."

Dunc moves back into the light. He is about to answer when they hear the howl of a lone wolf. The hair on the back of Cam's neck stands up. The wolf sounds near, how near is difficult to tell. Sound carries in the cold air. Another wolf picks up the howl; 'here I am; where are you?' The sound is from a different direction and sounds fainter. Others pick up the call. Several wolves sound near and others seem far away. The cabin is silent except for the crackle of the fire and the howl of the wolves: call, answer, call, answer. Intermittently they stop howling. A memory disturbed deep in Cam's bones shifts uncomfortably and then goes back to sleep.

"The pack's gatherin'," says Dunc scarcely above a whisper. "They'll howl for awhile and then go quiet. They're

265

gettin' ready for a hunt by the sound of it. They're gray wolves, ghosts of the forest. You won't see 'em. We're okay. They'll stay clear of us." The fire crackles in the silence. They listen to the wolves.

"We better turn in," says Dunc after the wolves have finished their howl. "We can let the fire die down."

"Okay, I need a quick trip to the kybo," says Cam as he stands up.

"Where did you get that name, kybo, anyway?" asks Dunc. "Why can't ya use outhouse, or somethin' that people understand?"

"Hold over from my boy scout days. I say potato. You say potato," replies Cam pronouncing potato differently each time.

"A turd is a turd is a turd," Dunc retorts, throwing in a thunderous fart for good measure. Dunc grins with satisfaction.

"Duncan the brown fighter," says Cam smiling as he pulls open the door, "always taking the highroad."

The light from the cabin floods out silhouetting Cam in the doorway. He steps out onto the cabin doorstep, closing the door behind him. He gives his eyes a moment to adjust. The night sky is clear at the moment. The thin crescent of the moon is beginning to lift above the tops of the trees. It offers little light. Cam steps off into the dark. He stops a few steps from the cabin to enjoy the cold air against his face. He takes a deep breath, taking pleasure in the coolness of the air filling his lungs. He exhales. His breath condenses in the air although he cannot see it in the dark. He looks up at the stars in the clear night sky. He finds Cassiopeia, Orion, and the North Star, which he has learned to identify from his SAS survival guide. There are other stars. They are too numberless to name.

Something deeper than time and all the stars in all the endless galaxies in the universe stirs in Cam.

"My God," Cam whispers, "it's beautiful!" Surprised, he shivers. He stands transfixed as a watcher of the night sky. "Thank you," he answers softly. Thank you, he shouts in an unspoken language before there were words. There is nothing more he can say.

On his return, he opens the cabin door and steps into the warmth of the cabin. Dunc has already turned in. Cam strips down to his camouflaged long underwear, turns out the lamp and climbs into his sleeping bag.

17 Hunting Good Fortune

Dunc and Cam are up and dressed well before crow piss. Dunc revives the fire from the embers in the stove. Cam puts on a pot of coffee. They eat a hurried breakfast of hard boiled eggs, toast and jam. The eggs and jam are compliments of Dunc's wife, Emma.

They speak few words, instead opting to exchange grunts while they eat breakfast and prepare for the hunt.

After a quick washup and a last check of their hunting gear, they head out the door. Each is wearing a hunter-orange parka and hat. Hunter orange is required in the bush at this time of year. You don't want to be mistaken for a deer or other big game. Each of them has a rifle slung over his shoulder. Cam also carries a backpack with additional hunting supplies.

"Did ya see the tracks?" Dunc asks, stopping Cam who is about to set off down the west trail.

"Tracks?" asks Cam keeping his voice low.

Dunc snaps on his flashlight and shines the light at the ground near Cam's feet. Cam crouches down to have a better look.

"Wolf?" asks Cam peering at the paw prints in the sandy soil.

"Too big for coyote."

"Did you hear anything last night?" Cam picks up a twig on the ground.

Dunc shakes his head no. "Just the howlin', must've been after we turned in. You?"

"No." Cam scratches a shape in the sand.

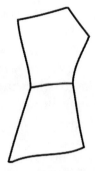

"They don't call 'em the gray ghosts for nothin'," says Dunc with a puzzled look on his face. His voice is barely above a whisper. "I've never seen 'em come this close before." He looks around for other signs of animal tracks. "There must've been somethin' that brought 'em in, the smell of bacon, or a deer; maybe a moose. I don't see any other animal tracks, only wolf. They've headed off down the west trail. I count six of 'em." He snaps off the flashlight.

"Do you think the trail is safe?" asks Cam standing up.

"Oh yeah, they won't bother you," Dunc answers sounding confident. "They're probably long gone anyway. You're not likely to see 'em. I've only seen two in all the time I've been comin' to camp. And they were a long way off. If ya do see one close by, fire off a round in the air. That'll scare 'em off. Got an extra clip? You'll be fine. You better start toenailin' it if you want to get set up before dawn."

The silence of the forest offers no answers. There is only the drip of the rain from the trees after yesterday's rain. Cam reluctantly starts down the trail. He casts a backward glance toward the camp. Dunc turns and takes the east trail, disappearing into the dark.

Dawn is beginning to break behind Cam. He sits in the half dark on his fold-up aluminum camp stool in the cramped quarters of his pop-up blind. He has erected his blind under the big white pine. The blind is a one-man camouflaged tent designed to resemble leaves in the fall. The salesman insisted the blind would blend in well where Cam was going at that time of the year. Cam, however, thinks the blind looks more like a red rock. He wonders if the manufacturer got the leaf pattern wrong, which might explain the discount he got when he bought it.

Plp, ppt, ppt, ppt, plp, ppt, ppt, ppt, ppt, ppt, ppt, plp.

He peers through the mesh flap at the front of the tent. In front of him is a small clearing in the woods. A pair of binoculars hangs around his neck. He has strapped a hunting knife to the belt of his camouflaged pants. He cradles his 30-30 rifle in his lap. His rifle has a silky smooth bolt action. The salesman who sold Cam the rifle told him about the action of the bolt.

"Check this out. It's a beaut'," the tall wiry salesman said, eager to show off the rifle the day Cam ventured into the gun store. "Feel how smooth the action is; smooth as silk, as I like to say." The salesman demonstrated the fluid bolt action of the rifle. "Here, you try. Tell me what you think. Go on, try it. How else will you know?" he said handing the unloaded rifle to Cam.

Cam noticed the salesman had the ten of diamonds tattooed on his forearm. Why the ten of diamonds he wanted to ask the salesman. Why not the queen of diamonds or hearts to represent a loved one? He refrained from asking. He didn't want to lose focus on the business at hand. Later he would look up the meaning on the Internet. The ten of diamonds represents good fortune. What does good fortune mean, questioned Cam. What is fortune anyway? Is it money, a roof over your head and food on the table, good health, or was there more to it? Is it about what you could learn about the world, yourself and your circumstances? Maybe you could see new things that you hadn't seen before and learn about the choices you make based on what you saw. There were so many choices. Which one was the right choice? Which one was the best choice? How did you know if you had chosen well? Cam wondered about these things.

The questions about good fortune and choosing continued to gnaw at him like a song stuck in his head that wouldn't go away.

Cam tried the bolt. "Yup, she's a smooth one," he said, trying to emulate the lingo of the salesman. He wondered how much time the manufacturer spent designing exactly the right sound when you worked the bolt back to eject a spent round and then forward again to load a new round into the chamber: a kind of soft 'clkachik' when you pulled the bolt back and then 'chikaclk' when you pushed it forward. The sound of the bolt exuded dependability and quiet confidence. Cam tries the bolt a couple more times to get the feel. "Yeah, feels good." Cam smiled dubiously, not sure if this was the right answer.

"Smooth as silk," repeated the salesman while giving his head a casual swoop upward to show how happy he was that Cam agreed. "Yep, exactly what I said. Thought you'd agree. Can't go wrong with this one can you?" he added for reinforcement.

The salesman leaned forward, resting his arms on the display case while Cam examined the rifle. In spite of his eagerness, the salesman moved slowly and casually, in a familiar way reminiscent of neighbors talking across a backyard fence. A thick chrome chain looped from the salesman's belt to the wallet in the back pocket of his blue jeans. "Silky smooth," reminded the salesman from behind his black-rimmed glasses. The salesman grinned buoyantly. He pushed his glasses back a little on the bridge of his nose.

Cam had never even held a rifle before let alone fired one, so he didn't really know how silky the bolt action should be.

"Feel how light it is," said the salesman, who was happy to show off the rifle.

Cam dutifully moved the rifle up and down a few times to show that he was getting the heft of it.

"Just seven and a half pounds, not bad. Oh sure, ya can get lighter, but it'll costs a little more," the salesman said, being careful not to overplay the cost of a more expensive rifle in case Cam had deep pockets. "Clip holds four rounds. That's standard these days. You can get a bigger clip. Order it from the manufacturer. Won't take long; a couple of days, tops, guaranteed. Call you when the clip is in," he said smiling enthusiastically. "First rifle, right? Don't want to waste your time, telling you stuff you already know."

Cam nodded his head vaguely. He was a little embarrassed to admit this would be his first rifle. He smiled uneasily, hoping his ignorance wasn't too much in evidence.

"Stock's ergonomically designed." The salesman pointed to the rifle stock. Each time he called Cam's attention to an as yet undiscovered feature of the rifle, the salesman pointed with his finger, or a glance, or a nod of his head in the direction of the feature. "Made of walnut and has a satin finish. Run your hands over that. Nice eh? You bet," he added with a swoop of his head. A little of the salesman's slicked back hair had strayed down over his glasses. He pushed his hair back into place.

Cam ran his hand over the stock of the rifle, enjoying the smooth feel of the stock and the knurled work of the grip.

"Mnnn," Cam answered. His eyes seemed to narrow and focus as though examining a design or manufacturing flaw that has caught his attention. The salesman seemed unconcerned, having encountered many novice would-be gun owners before. Cam raised the rifle to his shoulder to sight down the rifle and to test the ergonomics.

"High-performance recoil pad," added the salesman, nodding toward the rifle butt. "Barrel has a satin finish."

Cam didn't know what high-performance meant and didn't know how many different kinds of finishes a barrel could have or why. Was the finish for an aesthetic reason, or did it have a function, or was it both? He didn't want to ask.

He handed the rifle to the salesman. Unconcerned, the salesman laid it on the counter. Cam regretted not bringing Dunc along. He would know what to do and say.

"Yeah, nice," Cam said noncommittally because he didn't want to appear too eager to buy the first rifle the salesman showed him. "What else ya got?" he asked giving a nod of his head to the bus-long rack of rifles behind the salesman."

The salesman showed Cam several more rifles before Cam settled on the first rifle the salesman had shown him. Cam wasn't sure that he had made a good choice. Later he showed his rifle to Dunc, who, after examining it closely for several minutes, grinned confidently and said, "She's a beauty." Cam felt better about his rifle purchase once it had Dunc's seal of approval.

"What about a scope?" the salesman asked after Cam had chosen a rifle. "You'll want one for accuracy. Here's one," said the salesman seeming to produce a scope magically out of nowhere, like a magician's wand. "Full range of view. Multi-coated optics for maximum light transmission. Waterproof, fog proof and shock proof. Built like a tank. It's simple to adjust. Ya turn these two knobs here. One's horizontal. The other's vertical. See?" the salesman said turning one of the knobs to demonstrate how easy the scope is to adjust. "I can sight it in for you. Course you'll need to fine tune it before hunting. Shouldn't take more than a couple of minutes. Comes with a set of instructions. Tells you exactly what to do. Easy to follow. Can't go wrong."

Cam peered down the rifle scope to see what he could see. At first everything was a blur because he was looking at things in the store that were too close to him. It was only when he aimed the scope out the store window at a weather-beaten leaflet stapled to a pole across the street that things came into focus. The title on the leaflet was 'Call me Ishmael'. Reading a little further, Cam discovered that it was

273

a year-old invitation to a lecture series sponsored by the English department at the university.

"Can set ya up with a camera too," added the salesman, interrupting Cam's reading of the leaflet. "Sits on the scope. One gigabyte flash memory. Up to thirty minutes recording time. Re-live the big moment long after the event. What could be better? A must for any hunter," said the salesman sounding like an advertising brochure. "Mount it yourself, or we can do that for ya, no problem. Whatever floats your boat."

Cam agreed to buy the scope. He bought the camera too when his big-game imagination got the better of him. He wondered if he would ever use the camera.

"Can't get lost with this baby," the salesman continued. So at the urging of the salesman, Cam also bought a GPS device along with other hunting paraphernalia, including a must-have cleaning kit for the rifle, a leather rifle strap, rifle case, camouflaged pants and boots, a hunting knife, deer attractant, and a deer call. Over the years, Cam added more equipment to his pile of hunting equipment. Much of it he had never used, although it seemed a good idea when he bought it.

Strewn on the floor of his blind are matches in a waterproof container, an extra rifle clip loaded with ammunition, extra batteries, a digital camera, lunch in a plastic container, and a thermos of coffee to keep the chill away. He has to keep his feet still so as not to make any noise. Inadvertently kicking a piece of his hunting gear might alert a deer to his presence. His handheld GPS tells him exactly where he is give-or-take about five yards. He wonders what his early farm ancestors would have thought about all his equipment. If they were lucky, they might have had a single-shot breach-loading rifle.

Through the opening in the mesh at the front of his blind, Cam peers out from under his rock. There is no movement in the clearing. He raises his binoculars to search the edge of the clearing. Still there's no sign of activity. Many of the leaves have fallen to the forest floor, creating a carpet of brilliant yellow, red and gold. Fall comes early this far north. A number of leaves cling tenaciously, refusing to give up. Occasionally the wind picks up blowing from west to east, dislodging a few of the remaining leaves. The wind gently shakes the pine tree above him. Drops of water fall from the tree canopy onto his blind with a sporadic ppt, ppt, plp. Intermittently a nearby chickadee softly calls: 'chick a dee dee dee'. A second chickadee pipes in response. He enjoys these moments of solitude.

Cam yawns and shakes off the cold while he waits. He wants to stretch. His arms and legs feel knotted. Perched on his camp stool, he can't get comfortable. The blind, about the size of a chest freezer, confines his movements. He could step out of the blind to stretch, but this would make his presence known and jeopardize his chances for a kill. If his muscles cramp up, he'll have to move. Cam tries to relax.

Ppt, ppt, plp.

'Chick a dee dee dee'.

Cam closes his eyes. He is at his best when not thinking, solely listening and letting the stillness hold him, letting it gather into the 'dee' offered by the chickadee.

Cam opens his eyes with a start, unsure how long he has been away. He raises his binoculars and searches the forest clearing. He lowers his binoculars nervously. At the far end of the clearing near the edge of the forest, stands a white-tailed deer, a buck about four years old by the number of antler points. Cam feels for the rifle resting in his lap without taking his eyes off the deer. Silently he releases the safety. Slowly he raises the rifle. The rifle seems heavier now. He inserts the barrel through a slit in the mesh. He brings the stock of the rifle to rest. He carefully sights the deer through his scope, trying to remember what Dunc said about breathing. The barrel begins to shake, only a little at first, but then more and more. He lowers the rifle. He takes a few deep breaths and manages to stop shaking. He collects himself. Cam looks out the opening in the blind. The deer raises its head. It stands stock still listening warily. Something has caught its attention. Perhaps it heard the release of the safety. Perhaps it smelled Cam's presence. The deer is still within range. Cam slowly and quietly raises the rifle a second time. He is shaking only a little this time. He inhales, then exhales, and then slowly squeezes the trigger the way Dunc showed him. Cam's heart is pounding. The rifle cracks and jerks back. He nervously works the bolt, ejecting the spent shell and ramming a new round into the chamber.

The deer jumps, arching its back. It runs into the bush, away from the sound of the rifle shot. There is no time for a second shot. Cam notes the spot in the clearing where the deer jumped. He watches carefully where the deer goes, but quickly loses sight of it as it runs deeper into the woods. He listens attentively to the sound to determine where it is going: east, then north, then south and then north again. Cam can no longer hear the deer. He must force himself to wait before going after the deer. Any over eagerness now on his part will drive it farther away, reducing his chances of finding it.

His heart is pounding. He notes the time. He opens his thermos and pours a cup of coffee. He raises the cup to drink. His hand is shaking. He tries to steady the cup with both hands. His hands are shaking too violently to drink. He tries to pour the coffee back into the thermos, but can't. He puts the cup down with his trembling hands while trying not to spill. Cam engages the safety on the rifle, listening for the click. To keep himself occupied while he waits, he decides to check the camera on his rifle to take his mind off the waiting. He has forgotten to start the camera. He takes a deep breath and slowly lets it out to try and settle himself. He breathes deeply several more times. Slowly his hands stop shaking. His heart stops racing. Now almost recovered, he leaves his blind. He feels unsteady on his feet. The forest is quiet.

Cam raises his binoculars. He scans the area to see if there is any sign of the deer. He can find nothing. He aims the binoculars at the spot in the clearing where the deer jumped when he fired. From this distance, he can't tell how good his shot was. Cam slings his rifle. Quietly he crosses the clearing. He looks for signs of blood when he reaches the spot where the deer was hit. He can't find any signs in the immediate area. He begins to work his way in the direction that the deer first ran. Soon he finds himself in the thick tangle of the underbrush. He comes across the first signs of blood on a rock. Cam follows the trail looking for more blood and signs that the deer has disturbed the underbrush. That there is only a little blood tells him that he has missed the lungs or some other vital organ. Tracking down the deer will take time.

Cam must watch where he steps. He could easily twist an ankle on the uneven ground. The trail moves east, then north and then east again. He finds himself working deeper into the thick undergrowth of the forest. Deadfall litters the forest floor forcing him to climb over, go under or around. Branches from trees and bushes impede his way. He is constantly raising an arm to protect his eyes and face from tree branches and bushes as he forces his way forward, moving deeper into the forest. He must stay to one side of the deer's trail because he doesn't want to disturb the trail. From time to time he loses the trail. Then he must backtrack and walk a zigzag pattern until he again picks up the trail.

He reaches the top of a steep hill where he stops. He is breathing hard from his exertion. He is beginning to sweat a little. Too much sweat can lead to hypothermia on cold days. He opens his parka a little to cool off. He rests his rifle against a tree. He looks skyward, attempting to gage the time and to get his bearings by the position of the sun. Cloud cover has moved in. The pall of the low overcast hides the sun. He guesses about noon. He has been travelling northeast for about two hours. Recently the trail has turned in the direction of the duck swamp. Cam estimates that he has covered about a mile in the last two hours. His tracking is going slowly. He must be patient.

He searches his parka pockets, wishing that he had not left his lunch and coffee in the blind along with a few of his other supplies, including his handheld GPS and his extra clip of ammunition. He finds a few chocolate-chip cookies in one of his pockets. He looks for more signs of the wounded deer. He eats the cookies, which are soon gone.

After a brief rest, he works his way down the hill following the trail of the deer. Eventually he reaches a stream bed. He looks for signs that the deer crossed the stream and re-entered the woods on the other side. He can see no evidence of deer tracks in the soft earth on the opposite bank.

Cam moves upstream. The stream is overgrown with overhanging bushes and trees that slow his progress. He finds only an empty plastic water bottle that by the look of it was probably discarded years ago. The bottle is snagged in the stream by low hanging branches. Slowly it's making its way downstream toward the duck swamp. He can only guess how it managed to find its way into the middle of nowhere.

Cam backtracks and begins moving downstream having found no upstream evidence of the deer. The stream begins to widen. At each bend in the stream he hopes to catch a glimpse of the deer. Rounding a bend in the stream, he finds a small mud flat that hugs the shoulder of the stream. He scans it carefully for signs of the deer. He is rewarded with deer tracks. The tracks look fresh. He looks carefully for signs of blood. Again he is rewarded with a few drops on leaves lying on the bank.

He follows the muddy bank around another bend in the stream. Cam stops abruptly. His heart begins to pound.

Mixed in with the deer tracks are wolf tracks. He studies these new tracks carefully. They look older than the deer tracks. He can't be certain how much older they are. There are about six of them that crossed to the opposite side of the stream. They appear to be heading toward the duck swamp. Cam speculates if the pack is the same one that visited the camp last night.

He continues downstream. The stream begins to meander and widen. The water is getting deeper as the stream begins to merge with the swamp. He is forced out of the stream bed. He must follow the deer track by hugging the bank. Cam constantly scans for signs of the deer. The trail moves deeper into the swamp. He must be careful where he steps to stay on firm ground. The bottom of the swamp is mostly mud and rotting vegetation. He will quickly sink in the soft muck if he makes a misstep.

By now the stream has disappeared completely. The deer has taken to the sparse higher ground to follow a narrow animal trail through the swamp. Cam follows the trail. There is more blood now, making tracking easier. He surmises from the amount of blood that the deer is losing the battle. It can't be too far away. He hopes that the deer is dead when he finds it and that it is on firm ground and not in the water, which would make retrieval difficult.

Open water intermittently breaks the animal path. Cam can easily jump most of these breaks. A few breaks require a running leap. On one leap he falls short and finds himself in the ice-cold water. He rapidly begins to sink, sucked down by the muck until he is knee deep. He grabs a nearby branch and pulls himself to the other side. His waterproof boots keep his feet dry, but his legs are wet. The tops of his socks are wet too and he doesn't have a change of socks.

During one of his leaps, he misses the weight of his rifle. He realizes that he has left it behind when he stopped to rest. Now he has only his hunting knife. He hopes the deer is dead so that he doesn't have to finish the job with his knife.

Working in close quarters with a wounded animal is dangerous. His unease grows.

Cam works his way deeper into the swamp following the growing trail of blood. He reaches a small island that at its highest is only about a foot above water. The underbrush is especially heavy. The trail of the deer suddenly veers off the trail and plunges into the underbrush. Cam follows the deer. He reaches the massive trunk of a fallen pine tree. The base of the trunk rests on its stump, which partially suspends the trunk above the ground. The trunk is too high to climb over. Cam studies the obstruction for a few moments while he catches his breath. He spies a small opening under the trunk where he can squeeze through. Crouching down on all fours, he slowly claws his way through to the thick brush on the other side. Panting he stands up, realizing only then his danger. Impulsively he jerks back in panic. The tree trunk blocks his retreat. He has little room to maneuver. Instinctively he reaches for his knife. He presses hard against the trunk to gain what little distance he can. His heart is racing. At his feet is the deer. Swiftly he scuttles sideways along the length of the trunk and away from the animal. The dense underbrush impedes his escape. He stops, having gained a little distance between himself and the deer. If it's alive, it could attack, goring him with its antlers. He is breathing hard. There is no movement from the deer. He breaks off a branch and prods the deer. Its dark lifeless eyes stare blankly at Cam. He must be sure the deer is dead. He pokes it again. Still there is no movement. Cautiously he edges closer and gives the deer a quick sharp kick with the toe of his boot. Immediately he retreats. The deer remains motionless. Cam relaxes a little. His breathing begins to slow. The swamp is quiet except for the sound of his breathing. So this is how it ends, alone in the cold and silence, thinks Cam. He shudders.

Recovering himself, he stoops to take a closer look at his prize. He is reminded of a picture in a hunting magazine of the proud hunter crouched down on his knees near the head of the deer that he has killed. The hunter holds up the deer's head by its antlers. He has twisted the head round toward the camera for a good picture. Resting against the body of the deer is the hunter's rifle. The hunter grins widely, pleased with his trophy. Cam feels nothing of the elation from a successful hunt. Instead he feels only emptiness. This is not what he expected. Feelings of doubt and self recrimination begin to rise within him. Why did he let himself get sucked into these hunting trips for all these years? Possibly if Dunc was here there'd be a feeling of excitement. Cam concludes that he is tired. He tries to persuade himself that the excitement will come later. He is not convinced.

Cam stands up. He looks around and notes his location in the swamp. He puts his hunting cap in a prominent spot to make the deer easier to locate. He will need Dunc's help and the ATV to retrieve the deer. He tags the deer and then sets out for the cabin. He must recover his rifle on his way to the cabin.

Cam looks for a shorter way out of the swamp, knowing that he must hurry if he is to recover the deer before dark. Aided by the overcast sky, dark will come early. He can make better time on solid ground. At first he follows the animal trail that winds through the swamp. Then he begins to take small shortcuts. He's making good time. He's pleased with his progress. He leaps without difficulty over the patches of water that form small breaks in his new trail.

In time the shortcuts lead to a larger stretch of water in the swamp. Cam is hesitant to make the jump because of the distance. He is also reluctant to backtrack to the animal trail because this will add more time. He eyes the open stretch of water carefully. He's starting to tire. After various calculations he decides he can make the jump. He will need a good run at it if he is to clear the water. Cam backs up and starts his run. He slips in the mud at the water's edge when he leaps. He reaches firm ground on the far side. He teeters, struggling to regain his balance. He grabs a small bush and pulls himself away from the water's edge. That was close, he sighs.

Cam is almost out of the swamp. The ridge that follows the edge of the swamp is near. If he can make it to the ridge, he can make better time. There is only one last large body of water that he must traverse. He finds a series of five grass-covered tufts of earth protruding just above the water. The tufts lead to the ridge. They are small, allowing room for only one boot, but should provide firm footing. Once he starts to cross, he must move deftly. He won't be able to stop on a tuft. He will have to maintain his forward moment if he is to reach the next tuft in the series and eventually the base of the ridge on the other side of the water.

Cam checks the ground where he will launch himself at the first tuft. The ground looks firm and is free of mud. He has only a short space for a few steps to start his run at the first tuft. Cam backs up. Concentrating, he begins his run. He reaches the water's edge and launches himself. He counts each tuft as he makes contact: one, two, three, four. He teeters on four. Barely holding his balance he leaps to five. Five he counts, teeters and plunges into the water. His arms and legs flail as he desperately fights to get his head above water. He can't find his footing in the soft oozing black muck on the swamp bottom. His heavy boots and wet parka weigh him down. The water turns black and swirls about him as Cam kicks up the black muck. He can see nothing. Finally he breaks the surface. He chokes and gasps for air, inhaling the rotting smell of the methane gas that his thrashing has released from the rotting vegetation on the swamp bottom. He flails the water to gain the short distance to the ridge where he grabs a low-lying tree branch. He pulls himself onto the muddy bank at the base of the ridge. Exhausted he rests on all fours while retching up the black water that he swallowed.

Cold, wet and hungry he struggles to the top of the ridge. He turns briefly to look at the swamp below. He reaches for his binoculars, but they are gone, lost in the swamp. He peers at the small island where he can just make out his hunting cap. He is confident that he can find the deer again when the time comes.

The walking is easier now with firm ground under foot. The ridge runs parallel to the stream that he followed into the swamp. The underbrush along the ridge is light allowing him to make good time. He hikes along the ridge until he intersects his original track that led him down to the stream. He turns away from the ridge and walks in the direction of the spot where he left his rifle. The underbrush grows thicker making the going more difficult. Cam stops to catch his breath. He notes a rock that he passed while tracking the deer. The surroundings begin to look more familiar. His rifle can't be too far now.

Abruptly Cam jerks his head around. He hears something moving in the brush. He can't see what is making the noise. The sound of the movement is barely audible. Cam stands still, holding his breath. He listens carefully. There is more than one, but exactly how many Cam cannot tell. Possibly there are five or six. They are moving too fast and too quietly in this underbrush to be human. Their path is parallel to the track that Cam follows. Cam feels for the knife. It offers little reassurance. He picks up a fallen tree branch that might offer a little protection.

He continues along the track moving quietly. The snapping of twigs and the rustling of leaves announces his presence in spite of his best efforts. Sporadically he stops to listen. He cannot hear his companions, but instinctively knows they are nearby. Reaching the edge of a small meadow, he stops to look before crossing. At the far side of the meadow's edge, Cam sees six shapes move silently in single file through the forest. They are just inside the tree line. The last one in the line of shapes stops at a small opening. This one is completely black. It turns and slightly lowers its head to look directly at Cam who stands frozen. The two briefly examine each other across the meadow. The black form turns and disappears into the forest, following the other shapes.

It is a minute before Cam recovers himself. He moves along the edge of the meadow, not wanting to expose himself by crossing the meadow. He recognizes the stand of trees a short distance ahead on the hill where he stopped to eat. He thrashes clumsily through underbrush and scrambles up the hill, giving up all pretext of moving with the stealth of his near and almost invisible companions. He stops once to catch his breath and listen. Cam senses that his unseen companions are still with him although he cannot hear them. Reaching the stand of trees, he desperately searches for his rifle. Frantically he darts from tree to tree trying to remember where he left it. Cursing himself, he vows never to forget it again. Finally he spots the rifle and rushes to it. He releases the safety and fires a round into the air. The rifle cracks a warning. Trembling, he jerks back the bolt and loads a fresh round into the chamber. He listens. There is only the silence of the forest. Impulsively he fires another round. He loads the last round. He listens again. They're gone. He latches the safety and slings his rifle.

Cam works his way through the brush until he reaches the west trail. When he arrives at the cabin, he pushes the door open. He is greeted by Dunc and the warmth of the stove.

"Where were ya all this time?" Dunc asks with a frown looking at Cam. "What did ya do, take the ditch? You're wet. I was 'bout to come lookin' for ya."

"Got a buck," says Cam stripping off his wet clothes. "I need help getting it out."

"You're lyin'! Where?"

"In the duck swamp, we'll need the ATV," answers Cam putting on dry clothes. "I'll show you where. There's not much time before dark. We need to work fast."

"The duck swamp! You don't mean it." says Dunc incredulously. "What were ya doin' in there?"

"I had to track the deer," says Cam standing by the stove to warm himself. He wolfs down a couple of granola bars. "It didn't die right away. I didn't make a clean shot."

Dunc starts his ATV and backs it out of the shed. Cam jumps in and points Dunc towards the swamp. When they arrive at the deer, they field dress it, load it onto the ATV and head back to the cabin. There's no time for pictures. They stop at Cam's blind and throw his gear onto the ATV. The dark encircles the cabin by the time they return. Cam doesn't mention his encounter with the wolves. He turns in early. He's bone tired after his long day.

The drive back to Bayview the next day is uneventful. Cam knows that this is his last hunting trip.

18 High Windows

Cam raps on the open door to Zanya's office. Shadows are beginning to lengthen in the late afternoon. Soon the sun will begin its daily descent below the horizon.

"Hi Cameron, come on in. I've got something to show you."

"Call me Cam," Cam replies.

Zanya sits on her office couch with her laptop on the coffee table in front of her. She opens a file on the laptop. "I've been busy while you were away," says Zanya enthusiastically. "I have the raw footage from the Preacher Jay interview. You were right. He is colorful. Look at this! It has great potential!"

Cam sits down on the couch next to Zanya. She turns the laptop so that Cam can see the display. She clicks the laptop mouse. There is a brief pause while the computer whirrs away before displaying the first shot of the Mission's store front. There are shots of the store front from different angles. Then there are close ups of the dioramas.

"These are fantastic!" comments Zanya. "They look so," she searches for the right word, "folksy. Yes folksy, wouldn't you say so?"

"Folksy sounds pejorative when used that way. Yes the message is simple enough, but you have to keep the dioramas in context," replies Cam trying to find the right words. "They make you stop and look and ask questions. They're meant to make you look at things differently. Isn't that what art does?"

286

"You're not suggesting this is art, are you? Besides, most of my viewers wouldn't understand it in that framework. Conventional wisdom dictates that you keep it simple for the audience. If you get bogged down in details, your audience loses the thread of the narrative. Common sense, you know that."

"They would understand if you explained it to them."

"The truth is there isn't enough time to explain everything. We're creating a narrative, a story if you want to think of it that way," Zanya offers indifferently. She clicks on another clip and watches along with Cam. "We have to pick and choose what we want to say, or not say." She clicks through more shots with close-ups of the mannequins. "Do you think he set them up deliberately like this, or was it an accident?"

"I'm not sure. Is he the artist? I don't know who set up the dioramas. I didn't ask him."

"*Artist*, you're being generous!" Zanya skips forward in the footage. "Look at this," she says in amazement, as though having stumbled on a lost tribe in the Amazon jungle. The next shots show the inside of the Mission. There are close-ups of the murals with their biblical scenes and modern backdrops in the same style as the dioramas. Then there are shots of Preacher Jay's motorcycle from several angles. "This is great! Who in their wildest imagination could dream this stuff up? I couldn't. This is a gold mine! Look! Look here!" She jumps forward a few shots. A clip shows Preacher Jay silhouetted against his office doorway. Then there's a shot of his office, which is followed by a shot of Jay seated at his desk. "Each time I look at this, I get more excited about its potential. You can't make this stuff up! And who would want to? This is great material."

"Have you actually interviewed him?"

"Oh yes, I brought him into the studio while you were away on your fishing trip. We'll have to censure the language. Sometimes his choice of words is too colorful for

TV. You were right about that. Oh, I hired a writer on contract while you were away. His name is Earle. He's from Wallaceville. He's recently retired, but isn't ready to retire. He wrote the script for the interview. He did a good job. He's only temporary. You can have the final say about whether he stays or goes. He says he knows you. Do you know him?"

"Yes, I've met him," answers Cam, surprised at this news. Perhaps the job isn't secure in spite of what Zanya says, he thinks. "We met..."

"Oh look here!" says Zanya before Cam can explain the connection. She leaps forward to a shot of Preacher Jay in the studio. "Look at that!" says Zanya amazed. "He showed up in his motorcycle gear. What preacher does that? Look at the leather jacket and the pants! I hope they got a shot of the boots too! You couldn't ask for better than this. What imagination! He's a real showman isn't he? What a salesman!"

"Yes, he'll play to the audience to get his message across."

"It must have been hot for him under the lights in his leathers," adds Zanya. "He didn't seem to mind. For the most part, he really seemed to enjoy himself. Listen to this," she volunteers, turning up the volume on the laptop.

"Out of the abundance of the heart the mouth speaks,' Jay can be heard saying. The tinny sound of the laptop speakers makes his voice sound distant.

"What's he talking about?" Cam asks, leaning forward to hear more of what Jay is saying.

"He's talking about the girl he helped."

"Are you sure he's talking about the girl? It doesn't quite fit," interjects Cam, looking at Preacher Jay's body language. "Let's hear more."

"I'm sure he's talking about the girl. I'll explain later. Now listen to this!" Zanya jumps forward in the interview.

"People think they're rebelling against something, but mostly they're not," says Preacher Jay in the interview.

"That sounds treasonous. Doesn't it? He's attacking free speech. Shut up because you don't have anything to say anyway," concludes Zanya. "What do you think?"

Cam is astounded by Zanya's leap in logic. "Not really, I think he's only talking about replacing one bad idea with another idea that's as bad or worse than the first idea, or maybe he's saying that we're protesting about the wrong things. I'd have to hear more."

"My God this is great!" exclaims Zanya seeming to ignore Cam's comment. "This is wonderful! Here's another one. Listen!" says Zanya jumping to another shot.

"If you see the world for what it is, it will immediately be replaced by another," says Preacher Jay with conviction. The strength of his conviction is undercut by the cheap laptop speakers that diminish the strength of his voice, making his voice sound small.

"What kind of flimflam is that? Who in their right mind would believe that the world transforms into something different? What hocus-pocus! Or perhaps he thinks you're transported to another planet in another galaxy. Who knows! I don't. What science fiction! What kind of snake oil is he selling? Who is he trying to fool?"

"He's being a little flamboyant in his choice of words to provoke you into seeing the world in a different way than you normally look at it," Cam responds in earnest while struggling to explain. "He's merely saying that if you see the shortcomings in the way you view the world, who you are, and your place in it, you begin to see it from a different perspective, not that the world physically changes into something different. You can't take him literally. Your viewpoint changes, like an epiphany when you realize there's more to life than this." Cam casually makes a gesture with his hands that is meant to take in Zanya's office as representing the larger world. He frowns, knowing his explanation is inadequate. He tries to think of a better example. He wants to say something about the masturbating-and-going-blind mythology, but he isn't comfortable about what Zanya might conclude from this alternative example.

Zanya frowns. She is astonished that Cam is making disparaging remarks about her office. "What do you mean?" Zanya retorts with a mocking smile as she plays with his sincerity. "I'm sure you're not suggesting that my office isn't tastefully done. I've spent a lot of time decorating this office. Do you mean environmentalism, save the whales and all that?" she suggests, trying to tilt the argument in her favor.

Nuts, Cam thinks to himself. "Well, sort of, but not really." He is unsure how she made the leap to environmentalism. "Jay has more of a spiritual view. Although I'm sure he wouldn't be happy with me compartmentalizing spirituality. It might be that your view of the world changes. For example, you become more environmentally active. I'd have to hear more about what he has to say in the interview."

"Oh and later he talks about opening a can of whup-ass," says Zanya smiling and using her fingers to put quotes around whup-ass. "He's clever. You have to admire him even if he is a little misguided."

"He did talk about his old-testament sermons when I interviewed him. He said it was his way of stirring up people. You know, shaking them out of their complacency. We get too comfortable with who we are and stop looking for something better."

"Oh you mean a better job, or a new car, or house?" says Zanya smiling. "Eureka! This interview is pure gold," She continues without waiting for a response. "I've hit pay dirt! But why are you defending him so? You have such a twisted way of looking at things. I'm not sure if you're too trusting of others, or you choose to play devil's advocate. I can't decide which."

"Can I see more?" Cam interjects, ignoring Zanya's comment. He begins to wonder if the fix is in on Preacher Jay. Has Zanya prejudged him for her own purposes?

"Oh, you will," replies Zanya looking at more footage. "It's getting late. How about an early dinner? I know a restaurant, The Bicycle Clip. It's nearby and the food is good. You'll enjoy it. We can go there and continue this later. I could use your help selecting the some of the excerpts before I go to the Editing department on Monday morning. Have you got time? If we finish tonight, you'll still have the weekend to yourself. I don't want to cut into your weekend. I'll make it up to you. I do appreciate your help."

"Yeah I can help tonight, but I have to make a phone call first," Cam says, remembering his date with Anna, whom he hasn't seen since his departure on the annual hunting trip.

"Good, I'll meet you downstairs in the lobby in about half an hour. Does that suit?"

"That's fine."

Cam returns to his cubicle where he makes a brief phone call to Anna. He meets Zanya in the lobby. They make the short walk to The Bicycle Clip. He follows Zanya into the restaurant. The door shuts with a thud behind him. The maitre d' stands beside a small lectern studying the reservation list and a diagram of the available tables.

"Good evening, Miss Merchant, nice to see you." The maitre d' smiles proficiently. "Would you like a table for two?"

"Yes, table for two," says Zanya adding a nod.

"Your usual table?"

"Yes that would be nice."

They follow the maitre d' into the dining area. The restaurant is a converted church. The owners of the restaurant have converted the nave into the dining area. Lancet windows rising to the base of the arched ceiling add to the ambiance of the room as a place of repose and reflection. Where the holy end used to be a pianist quietly plays *What a Wonderful World* on a baby grand piano. The pianist looks familiar, but Cam can't place where he has seen him before.

The maitre d' directs them to a small booth wrapped into one corner of the former nave. The booth is small with barely enough room for two. The bench seat and back of the booth are lined in rich black leather with leather-covered buttons set in the seat and backrest. The recessed buttons contour the leather as though warping space. It reminds Cam of a graphic artist's two-dimensional depiction of planets warping space on a grid pattern to illustrate Eisenstein's theory of relativity. Usually there are a couple of planets bobbing in close proximity to one another in the artist's rendition. Cam squeezes in beside Zanya. She smiles warmly. Cam reciprocates with a courteous smile. He makes himself as comfortable as he can in the confining space while waiting for the waiter.

A waiter approaches their table. "Good evening, I'm your waiter for this evening. My name is William," he says, gesturing at the name tag pinned to his neatly pressed shirt. "Would you prefer to start with a drink? We have a nice Chardonnay this evening," he suggests presenting the wine list. "Perhaps you'd prefer a few minutes to look it over?"

"No, this shouldn't take long," Zanya answers. They study the wine list while William waits patiently. "I'll have a glass of L'Orbe Noir," Zanya answers after a few minutes. Her pronunciation of L'Orbe Noir is flawless.

"And for you sir?"

"I'd like the Hautes Fenêtres," Cam requests in his best garbled French.

"Very good," says William. "We have several very nice soups tonight. May I suggest the Oriental Duck Consommé, or the Broccoli and Almond to start? And tonight for the main course, we are featuring Chicken Kiev, Shrimp Marinara in a lovely tomato sauce, and stuffed pork tenderloin. I'll get your drinks while you look over the menu." William withdraws.

"How was your fishing trip?" asks Zanya studying the menu.

"It was a hunting trip, not fishing," Cam gently corrects. "We go every year in early fall," he adds pleasantly.

"Then how was your hunting trip? What were you hunting?"

"Deer. I managed to get one for the first time. It was a buck about four years old."

"Congratulations, I wouldn't have taken you for a hunter. You don't seem the type, at least not to me. I mean, you don't look the outdoors type. Have you always been a hunter?"

"No, not really; about ten years ago my friend invited me to go with him on his yearly pilgrimage. I didn't have a good reason to say no. I've been going ever since."

"You don't sound very enthusiastic."

"I think I go for the solitude more than anything. The trip offers a chance to get away. The forest is very peaceful and quiet. Have you ever listened to the wind in the trees, or the patter of rain on leaves? The leaves are brilliant in their fall colors, especially when they're wet."

"What about your friend? Where is he in this picture? I thought you went together."

"We split up for the hunting part. There are two main trails at his hunting camp. He goes one way and I go the other." Cam draws with his fingers on the linen tablecloth two imaginary trails that go in opposite directions.

"Isn't that a long way to go for a little peace and quiet? There are a number of nice health spas in Bayview that can do the same for you. Though your friend isn't the spa type, is he?"

Cam laughs at the idea of Dunc going to a health spa and subjecting himself to colon hydrotherapy, or having his nails done. He is about to respond when William returns with their wine. Zanya and Cam order dinner.

"There's more than peace and quiet," Cam continues after William leaves. "We don't say much, but we enjoy each other's company. There's a comradeship in the experience. And there's the simplicity of sitting in the cabin and enjoying the warmth from the stove on a cold night. You can step outside into the cold air and look at the stars. I enjoy looking up and seeing all the points of light; billions of galaxies with billions of stars all in motion. And the quiet is enormous. I can't do it justice sitting here talking about it. The experience is wonderful." *Pure Imagination* drifts from the piano.

"It sounds a little too rustic for me. Tell me about the deer that you killed. What happened?"

"After I shot it, the deer took a long time to die. I had to track it for quite some time. Eventually I found it on an island in the middle of a swamp."

"Was it dead when you found it?"

"Yes."

"Were you excited?" asks Zanya happily.

"No, it was different, not like in a hunting magazine," says Cam "There was a dark side to the whole thing. The deer was telling me things I didn't want to know. It was an epiphany, but not a happy one. I can't explain it really."

"Well, you certainly have an active imagination," Zanya answers with an insightful smile. "You look at a painting and try to see what the artist is saying. Most of us look, but don't see in the way that you do. We see a deer; a deer is a deer is a deer. You see more. You make connections on a personal level with the things and events that you find. The rest of us make connections too, but not in the way that you do. Maybe you're not happy or satisfied. You're looking for more. And it surprises you when you find it. Now and again it surprises in a good way and every so often it surprises in a bad way. Isn't that so? You look around this room and see

294

things that others don't see. Don't you? You don't mean to be different, but you are." Zanya motions to William who replenishes their wine glasses. "You see more than the rest of us," continues Zanya, "and you make us nervous. You break the rules because you put your own twist on things. Not that you twist things deliberately. You look at things differently. And often you make us afraid. And you can't figure out why we're afraid, can you? You don't mean to make us afraid, but you do. Most of us think we've pretty much got this world figured out. Then you come along and ask have you looked at it from over here. You remember that piece in the art gallery that you were so taken with? To the rest of us it was a novelty. I look at it and say I wouldn't buy that even if I liked it, which I don't, because it wouldn't fit in my apartment or my office. But you didn't care whether it would fit or not. You didn't care about its impracticality. You enjoyed it for what it had to say. You have quite a talent, and you assume that everyone has the same talent. Well here's a newsflash. We don't. And most of us don't want that gift. We don't like being inconvenienced by things we see as impractical. And if nothing else, we are honest-to-God, down-to-earth people. We demand practical solutions."

"You'll make a good TV host. You see things too. You see things about the people around you. We all see in different ways. Perhaps what we see with the heart counts most. Maybe our lives are about what we do with what we see. What did the preacher say in the interview? Out of the abundance of the heart the mouth speaks."

William returns with soup. The pianist plays a medley of songs. *Never Neverland* emanates from the chancel.

"As God is my witness, people want rules," Zanya continues. "They want consistency. They want to know what to expect each and every time. They want order. Otherwise, life would be short, nasty and brutish," she adds, remembering a philosophy lecture from one of her courses during her undergraduate years at university. The course was an elective. The university required that all business students complete one course in the humanities, such as English, Philosophy, Art, History, etc. The intent was to infuse a little of the humanities into the students in hopes that they would take at least a few drops of what they had learned into their careers after graduation. Zanya smiles contentedly. She is pleased that she has remembered. She can't recall the name of the philosopher.

"Sometimes rules get in the way," comments Cam enjoying his soup.

"Then change them. No one said that rules are perfect."

"It's what's behind the rules? The rules are a mask. They hide the truth. The truth can be brutal and sometimes wonderful. It depends on your perspective."

"Are you an anarchist?"

"No not an anarchist, we need structure. The rules tell us who we really are. They tell us about what's in our hearts. The rules paper over what we have chosen in our hearts. In our early years, each of us makes a fundamental choice about who we are. Most of us aren't aware that we've made a choice. The choice is buried too deep inside and it happened too long ago to remember."

"I remember when I chose a career in TV," Zanya offers. "I was sitting in a TV studio audience watching a TV hostess. I remember thinking to myself that is what I want to be. The hostess of the show was in control and seemed to be having a wonderful time talking to exciting guests. And everyone in the audience was genuinely interested in her and her guests. Little did I know how much work it takes to be a TV hostess."

"Well," begins Cam, "TV hostess is *what* you are rather than *who* you are. They're different."

"I confess," replies Zanya, "I always get who and what mixed up."

296

William removes the empty soup dishes. "May I refresh your glasses?" he offers. *Rainbow Connection* drifts through the nave. Zanya nods to William. He dutifully refills the glasses. William returns with their dinners a little while later. He places a covered plate in front of each of them. He uncovers the dishes with a flourish.

"Are you a libertarian?" asks Zanya while they eat. "The kind that believes the fewer rules the better; less government is better government. Everyone has to stand on their own two feet and make their own choices and not be constrained by government rules."

"I don't think it matters whether there are a few rules or a lot of rules when it comes to deciding who you are," Cam answers.

"Well, is it that children need better guidance?" asks Zanya remembering a reference to Socrates in the same philosophy lecture.

"Or can the children guide us?" The *House at Pooh Corner* flows from the chancel. The music rises to a sense of longing and desperation to count the bees in the hive.

"Are you suggesting a theocracy, a Ten Commandments world?"

"No, the Ten Commandments are only another set of rules. I can imagine the conversation that God and Moses must have had on the mountain about the Ten Commandments."

"What's on your mind Moses?" says Cam trying to resemble rolling thunder with a touch of laughter that he imagines to be the voice of God.

"Things are getting a little tense down below," Cam says in an anxious Moses voice. "The people are afraid. They're getting restless. Can you help me out? They need guidance. They don't understand."

"Got their underwear all bunched up again have they? Not too keen on all this wandering in the desert stuff, eh? No, no, come to think of it that comes later doesn't it? If it isn't one thing it's another," says Cam in his deep God voice complaining to Moses, "Are they brain dead? Never mind. I know the answer to that. I bet they're still eating their young aren't they? What a terrible tragedy that is. They've done a lot of pretty crack-brained things since the garden. They're like little kids. You have to keep at them all the time. If only they knew their potential. Not many ever do. What are they afraid of this week anyway? Is it that nonsense about the best-before date?"

"Best-before date?" queries Cam in his Moses voice. "You've lost me."

"Yeah, you know, doomsday," Cam continues using his God voice. "An apocalyptic vision when everyone gets wiped out. Oh come on! You've heard this one, the apocalyptic vision of 2012 when the Mayan calendar ends, or some other catastrophic event? You know, that kind of junk. How annoying! There's even that bit about rebuilding the temple as a precursor to the Apocalypse. They should look in their hearts first, if they want to build a temple."

"Mayan, what's a Mayan?" asks Cam in a confused Moses voice.

"Never mind," Cam continues in his God voice. "It doesn't matter. As I am my witness, there's nothing to be afraid of. Everything is fine. Tell them to have a little faith. Tell you what. I don't usually do this because they'll probably take it the wrong way, but I'll give them ten rules even though handing out rules goes against my better judgement. You know, give them a sense of direction. But remember, they're only rules. And yes, they're carved in stone, but the rules don't matter. What's behind the rules matters most. Am I making sense? Are you getting this? And I don't mean look on the back of the tablets either. Tell them to stop taking everything literally. I know! I'll use both sides of the tablets so that they can't look for more information on the back. That'll fix 'em! That should stop their one-dimensional thinking for a while. Tell them to look at the bigger picture. They can be such pea brains," says Cam trying to sound a little peeved in his God voice. "They're too tied up with this world. They're supposed to be *in* the world not *of* the world. Simple enough isn't it? Geeze! I knew this would happen. I knew it! Nuts!"

"You're rambling. What's a *nuts*?" Cam asks in his Moses voice. "And what does *Geeze* mean?"

"Never mind," commands Cam in his God voice. "The Geeze comes later. Here, take the tablets and go. And when you get down there, try not to get all bent out of shape when you see what they've been up to. You won't like it. Try not to get lost in the rules. There, I've said enough. See you later. Sigh."

"Why are you writing commercials for Ed?" Zanya asks trying not to laugh. "Why aren't you writing novels?"

Later William magically appears and clears away their now-empty plates. "For dessert," begins William, "I can offer you Crêpes Suzette, a specialty of the house; a lovely chocolate mousse, a favorite of the chef; or my personal favorite, crème brûlée.

"No thank you," responds Zanya, "I'll have a coffee."

"We have several coffees. We have Irish Crème Coffee, a nice Italian Coffee, Spanish Coffee, or several different house blends.

"Spanish please," requests Zanya. "What about you Cameron? You should try one of their coffees. They're very good."

"I'll have an Irish Crème," Cam replies, wondering if he's already had too much to drink.

"Don't get me wrong," continues Zanya, while they wait for their coffees, "I think you'll be very useful. I'm happy to have you on board, assuming that MKM will let me make you a formal offer. But why aren't you writing novels?"

"I've never really had much to say. And how you say it matters too. Words are more than simply a way to order a coffee."

Zanya leans closer to Cam. "Do you want to know a secret?" she whispers in his ear. "You have lots to say and you clearly don't know it. You have a strong imagination too. And you're passionate about words and how they're used."

She leans away from Cam. He wobbles. His head twirls. His body begins to slump as though weighed down like a bag of rocks. His body spins uncontrollably in a new orbit. He decides not to tell her about his failed detective novel. After all, he reasons in his twirling brain, you don't have to tell everything you know.

William, smiling indifferently, returns with their coffees.

"Enjoy," says William before leaving their table.

"I'll get a reputation as a bibber," says Cam hoping to impress Zanya with his knowledge of words.

"A what? What's a bibber?"

"A man given to drink."

"Oh relax. You'll be fine," replies Zanya smiling. "Enjoy. We have work to do after dinner."

Cam begins to relax. He sits quietly enjoying his coffee. The pianist is playing a jazz version of *Teddy Bears' Picnic*.

"Did they stop believing?" asks Cam looking around what was once the nave.

"Where did that question come from?" replies Zanya in astonishment. She takes a sip of her coffee. "Oh, I don't know. I expect some of them never believed. You know, saying your prayers at night. You say a prayer, but never really believe it. It doesn't mean anything. You say it because you're expected to, or out of superstition. Mostly out of superstition," Zanya offers offhandedly with a casual toss of her hand. "Why? What does it matter?"

"Some of them must have believed, or it was one great charade for a very long time. I don't think it was a charade."

Cam looks at one of the darkened windows now that the sun has set. "What was going on here?"

"I wouldn't know," says Zanya preoccupied. "We better get going." She signals William for the check. Zanya pays the bill. The door to the restaurant closes with a thud behind them. They find themselves on the street. She hails a cab.

Zanya flips on a few lights in her apartment. The living room is fashionably decorated in a décollage of ideas excavated from an assortment of interior-design magazines.

"Have a seat on the couch." She takes Cam's coat. "I'll get a laptop. How about a brandy or a liqueur? I'm having a liqueur."

"Brandy please."

"Fine, would you mind pouring?" She points to the liquor cabinet.

"Okay, what would you like?" He surveys the well stocked cabinet.

"Oh I don't know. Do you enjoy surprises? I do. Why don't you surprise me," she answers from an office adjacent to the living room.

Cam pours two drinks. Zanya returns with a laptop and sits down beside him on the couch. She places the laptop on the coffee table in front of them. For several hours they review the clips from the interview with each of them making suggestions regarding which ones to use. Occasionally Cam tends bar.

"Were done," says Zanya stretching after a long evening. "It looks good, don't you think? I'm very pleased with the results."

"There're a couple of earlier pieces I'd like to see again." He taps away on Zanya's laptop.

"Okay, while you're doing that I need to change," says Zanya starting towards her bedroom. "I've been in this dress all day. I need to find something more comfortable. Help yourself to a drink."

Cam decides he has had enough to drink.

"What do you think?" says Zanya a short time later. Cam looks up from the laptop. She stands in the hallway entrance leading to her bedroom. She's wearing a strawberry-red, silk robe and matching silk pajamas with open-neck collar. The robe is tide loosely around her waist. "They're silk." She runs her hands over the material. "I love the feel of silk. I found them in Paris. Beautiful aren't they?"

"You look very nice," says Cam trying to hide his surprise.

"I hope you don't mind. It's late and we're both adults." She sits down beside him.

"Here, what do you think of my perfume? She extends her hand in invitation to Cam. "A gift from Filana, she's hoping I'll mention it on my show."

"It smells lovely."

Zanya is pleased with the result. "Now what did you want to show me?"

"This clip would make a good opener." He is distracted by Zanya's perfume. She leans forward slightly to look at the clip. Cam can't help noticing from the corner of his eye the gentle curve of a breast disappearing enticingly beneath her pajama top.

"Yes, a good choice," Zanya says with an approving smile.

"And possibly this one for the closer," Cam tenders. He is feeling disoriented by the brandy, the lateness of the hour and Zanya.

"Yes, an excellent choice." She turns off the computer. "You've done a great job. We've done enough work for one night. What do you think of my slippers? I found them in Paris too."

"Yes, they're very nice," he says looking down at her slippers. He struggles to maintain himself.

"Would you like a drink?" She brushes against Cam as she reaches for the light switch behind him.

"No thanks. I still have a drink."

"I could use one," says Zanya brushing her fingers gently over his thigh. "Would you mind getting me a drink?" Cam returns to the couch with her drink.

"I think I should go," he says with a modicum of conviction. He sits down beside her. "It's after midnight."

"There's nothing to be afraid of. Relax. Enjoy. I love the feel of silk! Do you? It's so sensual, cool and soft. I love the way it glides across my skin. Feel it," she offers, extending her arm to Cam.

"Yes." He touches the end of her sleeve. "It reminds me of a car ride on a summer night when you stick your hand out the car window and move your fingers in the breeze. The air feels light and gentle and soft and cool. Like there's almost nothing there."

"Yes, a good way of putting it. Silk does have that feel doesn't it?" She reaches for a remote and clicks a button. "Music? It helps me relax at the end of a long day." Softly the air fills with *The Girl From Ipanema*. She unties the silk strap of her robe. "How's your drink?" She stands up allowing her robe to slip off. "I'll get you a brandy, or would you prefer a nightcap of some other kind? Why don't you use that prodigious imagination of yours," she proposes. "Or should I draw you a picture?" Without waiting for his response, Zanya walks to the liquor cabinet. "Here's one you might like. It's called Calvados," she says pouring Cam a generous helping. "I picked it up in Basse-Normandie last time I was in France." She returns to the couch where she stands directly in front of Cam, who remains seated. "Here you are," she offers, extending the drink to Cam. Zanya smiles encouragingly.

"I really should go," Cam says indecisively. He reluctantly stands up with Zanya immediately in front of him.

"There's no hurry."

It's late when the taxi driver drops off Cam in front of his house. The house is in darkness. He stumbles in the dark to his bedroom where he flicks on the light.

"Hi."

Cam jumps.

"Did I startle you? I didn't mean to. I missed you," says Anna lying in his bed. "I let myself in with my key. Are you surprised?"

"Yes, you surprised me." He smiles affectionately.

"Why don't you come to bed?" She runs a hand invitingly over the comforter. "I have a surprise for you."

"Oh, what's the surprise?"

Anna throws off the comforter revealing a black satin slip that clings to her body. "What do you think?" she asks smiling seductively. She slips out of bed and kisses Cam.

"You look great. I missed you."

"What's that smell, perfume?"

"Yes, that would be Zanya. We worked late. I need a shower."

"Mind if I join you?" She runs a finger down the front of his shirt. "I missed you."

"I've had a very long day," he replies holding Anna in his arms. "Zanya insisted on working late. I think I only want a shower and sleep."

Disappointed, Anna returns to bed. Cam showers. He climbs into bed snuggling close to Anna. Soon they are asleep.

19 Who?

The late morning sun shines brightly through the window and onto the linoleum floor in Cam's kitchen. Anna, now dressed in pajamas and a bathrobe, sits at the kitchen table. The table along with the matching maple sideboard and hutch are items that Cam's mother, Olivia, purchased soon after Olivia and Ralph moved into the house. The plates and cups in the hutch are souvenirs that Olivia carefully chose on their annual summer vacations when Ralph would pack up the car and tent trailer and point the car in the chosen direction, usually north. On many summer vacations they migrated like birds to the same camping spot. Infrequently they discovered new places, such as the Gaspé or the Rocky Mountains. During each trip Olivia would look for exactly the right plate or cup to bring back as a reminder of the family's summer adventure. One plate depicts Percé Rock enclosed by the waters of the North Atlantic. Another plate shows a painted wooden totem pole and long house with cedar trees in the background. Olivia found it in Banff. Usually there is a matching cup for each plate.

In Olivia's time, the drawers and cupboards of the sideboard accumulated bits of papers and other odds and ends that Olivia didn't know what to do with and wasn't willing to throw away because they might be important one day. After Olivia's death, Cam and his brothers spent the better part of a day helping Ralph go through the contents of the sideboard. There were expired warranty cards for numerous kitchen appliances; old letters with correspondence about the weather from long-dead relatives that Cam and his brothers knew only through passing references made by their parents; photographs of relatives in their Sunday best standing proudly beside their cars, swimming at the beach, pushing a baby carriage, or a picture of a family dog; handwritten recipes for scalloped potatoes or mushroom soup; occasionally tucked away in a recipe book was a ten- or twenty-dollar bill, which Olivia had put there for an indeterminate purpose and then forgotten; yellowed newspaper clippings of war events in which a relative is mentioned in a list of names and other clippings that meant nothing to either Cam or his brothers, but they had to read the entire article in case the piece held a family secret, which it never did.

Sorting through the material was an archaeological dig. What was important? What could be discarded without discarding an important piece of Olivia? Was it the newspaper clippings, or the photographs, the ten- and twenty-dollar bills, or something else? And who was Olivia in all this? Could you know who she was by looking through the bits and pieces?

There was a fading black-and-white photograph of Olivia as a young woman before she married Ralph. It's a bright summer's day. She is seated casually on her parents' lawn. Her head is tilted up slightly as though looking at somebody not in the picture. Wearing a simple print dress with a flower pattern, she leans slightly away from the camera. Her left arm, unseen in the picture, provides support. Her right arm rests languidly on her thigh. Her hand is relaxed. Her legs are half tucked casually and neatly to one side with her dress ending modestly at mid calf in the style of the day. Cam had never seen the picture before. He is struck by how graceful and beautiful she appears, although he had never thought of her as beautiful, but there she is. The photography could not be denied. She had had a life beyond the confines of motherhood that Cam in his kid selfishness had never seen nor appreciated, although Cam had never thought of himself as being selfish toward his mother. What was she thinking when the picture was taken? Perhaps there was a cautious optimism about marriage, a new life with her soon-to-be husband, and raising children. Was she listening to a friend not seen in the picture? Who was she listening to? What was the conversation about? Perhaps they were talking about the upcoming wedding. Was it Cam's father, Ralph, who took the picture? The tone of the picture is casual and relaxed, unlike the regimented and carefully posed pictures that were the hallmark of Ralph's pictures. Perhaps in those days Olivia still had a small amount of power. Cam wondered if the jumble on the sideboard was her way of unconsciously waging guerrilla warfare against the ordered anarchy of Ralph.

Who was Olivia? Her name means extending an olive branch. Was this Olivia too? Cam couldn't remember on how many occasions she had tried to intervene when Ralph was dispensing his signature rough justice. Hitting doesn't help, she would complain with little effect.

And what about Cam's memories of Olivia? Already insatiable time had ripped away many of the memories of his mother. How could you know anyone, Cam thought while helping to sort through the drawers and cupboards of the sideboard? All you could know of anyone were glimpses of who you thought they are or were at a moment in time with each moment quickly stripped away to become a wisp of memory at best. And from time to time old memories would resurface and be retouched because the edges had frayed, or you merely wanted to remember things in a different way than how you thought they had happened in the first place. The mystery that was Olivia was so much bigger than Cam could know or imagine.

During Olivia's time, a stack of dated newspapers always sat on the floor beside the sideboard. Daily she would add to the pile the latest newspaper delivered faithfully by the newspaper boy or girl. If time permitted during her busy day of housekeeping, she would make a cup of tea, take a newspaper, usually from somewhere in the middle of the stack, and read the newspaper while sitting at her kitchen table. The pile of papers never got smaller because she enjoyed reading each paper from start to finish, which meant that it might take her several reading sessions over several days before she could discard the paper. Meanwhile the papers would continue to pile up.

She would become annoyed when one of the kids in the pack interrupted her while she read the newspaper, one of her favorite moments in the day. "I just sat down!" she would quietly complain to whoever wanted her to perform a task that meant temporarily abandoning her moment of rest. "Can't I get a minute to myself?" she would add. And it was true that at the time with four small kids in the house she had little time to herself. It was four against one with each kid ravenously vying for Olivia's attention. If one kid didn't need her assistance, another one did. "Now my tea is cold," she would grumble mostly to herself after she had dealt with the issue of the moment and returned to her newspaper.

The pile of newspapers was always out of sequence, so the newspaper that Olivia was reading on any particular occasion might be yesterday's paper, or it could be a paper that was a month or two old. The age and hence the questionable currency of the information contained in the newspaper didn't seem to matter to her.

Later, when the kids were older, she would comment about an article in the paper to whoever happened to be passing in the kitchen at that moment. Usually she would start the conversation with *they say*, although it was never clear who *they* were that were doing the saying. Often having read a news item about a political scandal or other skulduggery, she would protest against the government of the day if her political party wasn't the government of the day, which it often wasn't. In a number of cases, her information was months out of date and the scandal had since blown over, or new information had come to light that mitigated the severity of the circumstances, or a loyal political soldier of the day had willing or unwilling fallen on his sword for the good of the political party under siege. If Cam pointed out to her that her information was dated, this didn't stop her. She would continue to rail against the government sapping away the independence of the individual. Olivia was proud of her independence. The government was not to be trusted because it gave a free ride to people, who didn't deserve it, at the expense of hard-working tax payers. Trust no one.

In general, Olivia believed that people were greedy and not to be trusted because they were only out for themselves and no one else. Cam often wondered where Olivia had learned to be distrustful of others. Then one day he realized that she had learned it from her parents, who had probably learned it from their parents and so on.

What shocked Cam even more was the day that he realized that his distrust towards others was probably passed down for uncountable generations from a great, great, super-grand coot relative, an old-man Johnson type, who was a soldier in a Roman army or other army in a long-ago conflict, or who had survived a great natural disaster, famine or flood, or a man-made great depression, or been there when Moses delivered the ten commandments the first time and got himself all bent out of shape, or all of the above.

It was during his recent vacation to the Rocky Mountains with Anna that he recognized his distrust the way a fish might react when suddenly realizing that there was this wet stuff all around it that it really hadn't noticed before. Cam had stopped to look at a display of bicycle helmets in a bicycle store in Canmore. While he was looking at the display, a man, who was not a member of the staff, approached Cam and began talking about bicycle helmets.

Who?

"Hi," the man said with a disarming smile, "are you looking for a bicycle helmet too?"

"Hi, yes." Cam smiled reservedly while immediately raising his defenses against this not-to-be-trusted man who was behaving suspiciously. After all, you shouldn't talk to strangers. Cam was sure that he must be up to no good, but what? No one in Bayview was likely to approach another shopper who was a complete stranger and casually start a conversation unless it was to hide their true motives. In his head Cam wondered what shenanigans the stranger was up to. Olivia had often used the word shenanigans. He had never heard his mother use the word in the singular, shenanigan. It was always in the plural because you had to know that strangers were always up to more than one bad thing at any given time.

Cam's imagination ran unchecked while he tried to identify the stranger's motive. "I was thinking of getting a new helmet," Cam replied not wanting to give away too much information, such as where he, Cam, was from; that he was on vacation; that he was here with his girlfriend, Anna; that his name was Cam; that the name of the family dog when Cam was a boy was Robbie; or that he discovered masturbation when he was thirteen and that masturbation was indeed an oh so glorious peak in Darien, which he had since celebrated as many times as there are stars in the sky. "Do you have any suggestions?" Cam asked playing it safe while waiting for the man to reveal his true intentions. Perhaps the man was a fellow biker who only wanted to talk about bicycle helmets, or share bicycle stories, but Cam couldn't be sure and he wasn't about to let his guard down to find out. Let the stranger show his true purpose first. If a stranger offers you candy, don't get in the car Cam thought, which was a lesson that Olivia had taught him early. What candy was this man offering and to what end?

"I like this one," said the man pointing to a bicycle helmet used by off-road bicyclists. "Which one do you like?"

310

"I have a road bike," said Cam hoping he hadn't revealed too much information about himself. "They don't seem to have much of a selection here for road bikes."

"Have you tried Zack's Bicycles? They have a good selection of helmets," offered the man.

"No," replied Cam not wanting to reveal that he didn't know where Zack's Bicycles was because it would mean telling the stranger that he was from out of town.

Withholding information made Cam feel that he was a man of mystery. His man-of-mystery mask gave in Cam's mind an advantage over whomever he was talking to. He had learned about withholding information from his Dad, who had often practiced it on his kids.

"Oh, you didn't know that did you?" Ralph would say after revealing a crucial piece of information at a critical juncture in an animated discussion when he needed an advantage to win the argument.

Usually the information was of a personal nature that served as an example of stoicism and resilience on the part of Ralph. "When I was a kid, we were glad to have potatoes for dinner even if they were bad and had weevils in them. We pushed the weevils to the side of our plates and ate the potatoes because that's all we had and we were glad to have them. And if you knew what was good for you, you didn't say anything at the table," Ralph would add to play on the kids' sympathies when he sprung the trap to make them feel guilty about whatever in his mind was a frivolous desire, such as wanting an ice cream cone, and to warn the kids that carrying on this line of conversation would probably end badly.

Ralph could have easily volunteered the information at anytime in the course of daily events. Instead he chose to deliver it only when it gave him the advantage of control. He always delivered the information as a revelation. And always he implied that it was information that the kids should already know. Of course it was information that they had no way of knowing because Ralph was not one who readily shared.

Heated debates with Ralph were akin to stepping on a land mine and realizing it too late. You didn't want to lift your foot off the land mine because you'd be blown to smithereens. Maybe if you were quick-witted enough you could diffuse the situation if you didn't acknowledge your dire predicament. Usually this was accomplished through an absurd gambit or a joke, much like the Hail Mary ricochet shot advanced by many a desperate kid when he recognized the hopelessness of his plight during a neighborhood game of war. "Mmmm," Cam would say to Ralph while rubbing his stomach, "weevils, protein, yum yum. Don't tell anyone. They'll want some too." Humor, like other weaponry, was honed on the battlefield. And although deployed clumsily at first, with practice humor became an effective weapon in the arsenal of any well-rounded kid.

Usually the gambit failed because Ralph was having none of it, so you got blown to bits anyway. It was a war where you didn't volunteer information to the enemy because the enemy would use it to your detriment. Information was a weapon that was to be revealed for maximum effect only when it gave you the element of surprise and power over your enemy. Ralph didn't realize that he thought of his kids as the enemy.

"I think I'll try Zack's next," Cam responded to the stranger. "Well, I hope you find what you're looking for. I'll see you around," he said automatically when he was about to leave. He knew he would never see the stranger again and was happy to have escaped without having revealed too much about himself that the stranger might have used to his advantage.

"Have a nice day," said the stranger with a grin.

Cam wondered what the grin meant. What did the stranger know that he didn't? He would never know. Years of family trench warfare had left its scars. Charity begins in the home, he suddenly realized.

Cam slowly pushes the eggs around in the fry pan with a wooden spoon. The eggs begin to firm into scrambled eggs. He carefully watches the bacon sizzle in another fry pan to make sure that it doesn't get too crisp. In the toaster, four slices of whole-wheat bread are beginning to brown. The smell of coffee begins to fill the room as the drip-filter coffee machine brews coffee. Two cups of fresh fruit that Cam prepared earlier sit on the kitchen table along with coffee mugs, milk and sugar. Cam plates the eggs, bacon and toast. He slides a plate in front of Anna.

"You haven't told me about the hunting trip," Anna coaxes between bites of bacon. "How was the trip?"

"The trip was fine. I got a deer."

"You don't sound very enthusiastic."

"Have you ever had one of those what-am-I-doing-here moments? After I shot the deer, I had to track it for a few hours before I found it. I had to crawl under a tree trunk. When I stood up, there was the deer lying right at my feet. Its eyes were looking right at me. I was really scared. I thought it was still alive. It must have died only minutes before. It was still warm. I looked at it and I thought why did I kill it? Later I started thinking about why I went hunting every year with Dunc. I realized I did it mostly out of habit. He needed somebody to go hunting with. I didn't have anything better to do at the time, so I went along. And I've been going ever since because it gave me something to do. Then I thought about a few of the major decisions I've made in my life. I appreciated for the first time that I was only going along for the ride. Decisions like becoming a script writer; I fell into the job and I've been doing it ever since because the job is part of my routine more than anything else. I've been drifting along all this time, not paying much attention. And then I thought about you and your love of the kids in your classroom and your dedication

313

as a teacher and how that speaks to who you are. You're a good person inside and that's why I love you." He looks up from his plate at Anna. Both of them have stopped eating.

"You're a good person too, you know? I thought you enjoyed the solitude you find in the woods."

"I could do that anytime. I don't need to go hunting if all I want is a few days of solitude."

"Perhaps you do it out of loyalty to Dunc, out of camaraderie. You enjoy each other's company."

"Yes, there's that, friendship." He pauses. "After I found the deer," Cam continues, wanting Anna to hear the entire story, "I fell into the swamp. I was on my way to get Dunc. I needed his help with the deer. I managed to pull myself out. I was lucky. I almost drowned there alone in the cold and muck." The sunlight on the linoleum inches across the floor.

"There's one more thing about the hunting trip that I haven't told anyone."

"Wasn't a near-death experience enough?" She wants to forbid him from going hunting again, but knows this would be the wrong thing to say.

"I came to a small clearing in the woods on my way back to get Dunc. On the other side of the clearing there was a small pack of wolves moving single file. I could see each one as it slipped through an opening in the woods. They were amazing to watch. They moved so effortlessly and quietly."

"You must have been terrified."

"Yes I was. The last one stopped in the opening. It turned and looked straight at me. I looked pathetic standing there soaked to the skin, my hair wet and matted down, my teeth chattering, and my body shaking with the cold. There wasn't much I could have done had it decided to attack. At that moment I don't know what the wolf was thinking, contempt for a rank amateur in the hunting world. More likely it wasn't thinking so much as just being what it is. The encounter happened so quickly. Then the wolf was gone."

"What about your rifle? You had your rifle."

"I didn't have it! I forgot it by a tree when I was tracking the deer. I had to retrieve it. I found it as fast as I could. The pack was moving in parallel to my course. I don't know; maybe they were sizing me up, or indifferent, or trying to decide if I was a threat. When I found my rifle, I fired two rounds into the air. They disappeared. Then I thought, don't forget what you've learned here today."

"What did you learn?"

"Death kindly stopped for me, to paraphrase Emily Dickinson. I started thinking. What have I accomplished? What have I done with my life? The answer is not much. I write mediocre scripts that are revised to death. I live in my parent's house that I bought from my father's estate. I've played it safe. I've taken the easy road, never daring. I don't want it to end that way. I want my life to mean more than merely getting through it. I don't want to look back at the end of my life and say well I'm glad that's over. I can check that off as done, like a grocery list. I survived," says Cam with a sardonic grin. "I'm tired of hiding under a rock with all the other dead people. I'm tired of living by other people's twisted, dead and clichéd ideas that masquerade as freedom, morality or who knows what. I want to live on my own terms, not someone else's. A wise man once said Orky don't take no shit."

"What do you want to do?" asks Anna trying to help Cam as best she can, but knowing that he must plot his own course.

"I don't know yet. I know I can't go on this way. My life is a hoax, a lie. I can't lie to myself anymore," answers Cam. The clock in the living room begins to chime, filling the silence. "I have to make changes. I don't know what they are yet."

"What about starting a new novel? Write about the things that you've been talking about. Would that help?"

"I'm not ready yet. My life has to mean more than writing novels," Cam responds. "My life is about *who* I am inside. It's about making the who shine out, about being free to express who I am, not this watered down free-speech crap that everyone keeps talking about when they haven't anything to say, or what they have to say isn't worth saying. Life is about not being trapped by someone else's warped ideas that have nothing to do with who I am because they're trapped too and lost like everyone else and what's worse is that they don't know they're trapped. And no compass or GPS can help you find your way because you're looking in the wrong place for the wrong thing. The who inside matters!" says Cam poking his chest adamantly with his finger. "And the who is bigger than anyone can imagine and your imagination can help you get there if you use it in the right way. You have to try. You have to make the who inside of you live. You have to unlearn all this crap that you've learned since you were a kid. You have to let go and start again. Letting go is hard. Everything you know tells you not to let go and most everyone you know tells you not to let go. And many of those who say let go don't really mean let go. They want you to look at the world through their dead eyes. But the reward is beyond anything that you can imagine if you can let go. The reward is wonderful, beautiful! I've seen it. I've touched it. We all have. And it's everywhere and it's beyond everything!" Cam is on the verge of tears. He is surprised by his passion in trying to explain, knowing he can never adequately explain. "I'm tired of being a vegetable. I'm tired of being dead."

Anna reaches her hand across the table and takes his hand. "Keep going. You can do it. You can get there."

"I'm not so sure I can, but I have to try."

20 And So On

Jingle, jingle, jingle.

A floor-to-ceiling reproduction of *The Ancient of Days* hangs against a wall in the Palazzo.

Jingle, jingle, jingle.

Earle stands in front of the reproduction. He is framed by the arms of the compass. A rendition of *My Blue Heaven* plays from the speakers hidden in the ceiling. Neatly arrayed before him in the great hall are over two-hundred round tables draped with white linen table cloths and dinner settings for twelve-hundred people. In front of each dinner setting is the name of a dinner guest on a small white card. Earle's name looks like this:

Earle Puddle

He has found his place at a table near the back of the assembly. At the front of the hall is a dais with a table and place settings for about a dozen MKM senior executives and their dinner guests. Earle sips his Choking Hazard cocktail. He waits for the dinner reception to begin when Ed will introduce the lineup of new TV programs for next year's fall season and several feature-length films currently in production at Maple Key Films.

Jingle, jingle, jingle.

Earle jingles the coins in his right pant pocket. He surveys the room. Jingle, jingle, jingle, jingles Earle in his beige suit with his bone-colored shirt, tawny-and-off-white striped tie and tan suede shoes, which he has carefully

317

brushed for the occasion. Jingle. He pauses his jingling while a thought jingles through his mind. It may be that he is imagining a chance meeting with Ed and how he, Earle, will shine out like a star in the heavenly sky with his brilliant business acumen and thus assure his stellar ascent within the MKM firmament; it may be that he is composing a list of things to say to Zanya, his new boss, to firmly affix his place within her sphere of influence; or it may be that he is trying to remember if he made sure the stove was off before leaving his newly acquired apartment. He has taken an apartment in Bayview as a first step to moving from Wallaceville to Bayview. What his thought actually is, no one will ever know. "Gnnnnnnh," he says.

Jingle, jingle, jingle resumes Earle.

Like Earle, other guests have entered, found their places and now mill about at the back of the hall waiting for dinner to commence. A few guests have taken their seats at their assigned places. The table reserved for special guests at the front of the hall remains empty.

In another area at the back of the Palazzo, Cam and Anna sip their drinks while waiting for the evening's proceedings to begin.

"Hi Cameron," hails a distant voice above the din of the crowd. A bare arm emerges out of the swarm and waves from afar.

"Who is that?" Anna whispers in Cam's ear.

"Zanya."

"Doesn't she know your name?"

"I've tried correcting her several times, but it doesn't seem to sink in." Cam waves at the approaching arm. He smiles cheerily.

"Isn't this exciting?" gleams Zanya emerging from the crowd. "Hi, I'm Zanya. You must be Anna. Cameron told me all about you. Has he told you about the Bicycle Clip? It's a wonderful restaurant. We had dinner there last Friday. Have

318

you been there? You must get Cameron to take you. You'll enjoy it."

"No, I haven't been there and yes Camden and I will have to go." Anna speculates to herself why he has not mentioned The Bicycle Clip.

"I wanted to surprise you," Cam responds in answer to Anna's unspoken speculation.

"I'm sorry for stealing him last Friday," continues Zanya looking at Anna. "It was urgent. I hope I didn't upset your plans. I really needed his help. He did a great job at my apartment," she beams. "He's very good. He has great potential and very creative too. What an imagination he has."

Anna glances at Cam, wondering what happened last Friday. "I didn't know that the two of you were working from your apartment."

"Yes, after dinner. I find working from home can be very productive and relaxing. I enjoy being surrounded by the things I love. Cameron tells me you're a teacher. Do you work from home much, or is most of your time spent in a classroom?"

"I spend a lot of time working from home, marking assignments, preparing lessons, calling parents, organizing field trips, and preparing school assemblies. There's a lot to do. Your tête-à-tête must have been very urgent. Camden was very late getting home on Friday. What were you two working on? Camden won't say. He says the project is a secret. I'm not keen on secrets. Are you?"

"We all have secrets," Zanya notes with a puckish smile. She is unsure what Anna may be implying, but enjoys stirring the water all the same. "Don't we? What fun would there be without secrets?" she adds playfully looking at Cam and making matters worse. "Don't you think? We need a little intrigue in our lives. We crave excitement even if we have to manufacture it. Isn't that what TV and this is all about?" asks Zanya gesturing with her hands. The gesture could refer to Zanya herself, or to the room at large. "In any case, I can tell you the secret now. Ed will announce it tonight, so it won't be a secret much longer. Have you heard of Preacher Jay? He runs a mission in an old run-down section of Bayview. I'm running a piece on him. Cameron did an informal interview with the preacher to get me some background material. I interviewed Jay a few days later. Cameron helped me choose the clips from the interview. I was in a rush. I couldn't wait until Monday for his input. That would have been too late. You know how the TV business works, don't you?" Zanya adds.

Anna smiles uncertainly. "Yes, I know what you mean about rushing," says Anna not wanting to confront the subject directly. "I know what you mean about deadlines. I'm busy trying to get all my marks in for the kids. Of course they've changed the software for entering the marks yet again, so I have to relearn the software before putting the marks in. It creates a lot of additional stress. Every so often you make mistakes with all the stress. Don't you?"

"We're both in the same business, so to speak," remarks Zanya. "We're both trying to educate the masses each in our own way. How do you cope with the stress?"

"I manage. Cam helps. He takes on a few of the chores. He cooks dinner when I have a deadline and a mountain of school work to get through. How do you cope?"

"I enjoy physical exercise when I can make it to the gym. If I can't get to the gym, I work out in my apartment. Often I work out alone or sometimes with a friend. Cameron, can I speak to you in private? Do you mind if I borrow him for a few minutes?"

Anna smiles blandly while Zanya takes Cam by the arm and steers him to a corner of the room. "I've been meaning to talk to you, but I've been so busy with my show. I have bad news. There has been a change of plans. I'm sorry. I can't offer you the lead-writer position. I've found a candidate for the job who has extensive experience in this kind of TV programming. He understands how to get things organized. In the early days at least, my show needs his organizational skills. He can help me implement processes that provide structure to the show for a consistent look and feel. He was a late candidate and until he showed up, you were the primary candidate. I've offered him the job and he has accepted. He says he knows you. His name is Earle. I'm sorry to deliver the news this way, but there wasn't time. My choice has nothing to do with last Friday. You have great ideas. Have I mentioned that you're very creative?" she adds, hoping to soften the blow with a little flattery. "Earle is a better fit for the program at this time. Please don't take it personally. This is business. I'm sure you understand. Don't you?"

Zanya continues to explain while Cam glances around the great hall. Most of the guests, with the exception of those with places reserved at the head table, have seated themselves. They are patiently waiting for the show to begin. A few stragglers are moving to their assigned seats. For a moment, the guests and tables remind him of the merry-go-rounds that he used to ride when he was a kid. The ride could hold about six or seven kids. Each merry-go-round consisted of a metal disk that you could stand or sit on. If you stood, you had to hang on to the metal tubing on top of the disk so as not to get thrown off while it spun round like a neutron star. If you were one of the older kids, you hung onto the tubing and ran for all you were worth along the well-worn path around the merry-go-round. You ran as fast as you could while pushing the merry-go-round to make it turn faster and faster. At the last possible second, you jumped on and hung on against the centripetal force. When it began to slow, you pushed it with one foot, like riding a kid's scooter, to maintain speed and make the ride last longer. When pushing the merry-go-round like a scooter was no longer effective, you had to jump off and push for all you were worth to make it spin faster and then you jumped back on. If you were a little kid, you sat near the center of the disk. If you were a big kid, you stood near the edge to get the full affect of the centripetal force while the merry-go-round spun round. Everyone got dizzy. If you were on the edge, you got dizzy and tired and giddy and you couldn't hang on any longer and let go and fell on the ground, and laughed yourself silly. After you stopped laughing, you got up and stumbled around because you were still dizzy. It was glorious the letting go, the falling down and the laughing for no reason and then standing up and falling down again or stumbling around because you were dizzy and laughing so hard that it made your ribs hurt. It didn't get any better than this.

"I hope you understand and don't take it the wrong way," concludes Zanya looking at Cam who is staring at the seated guests.

"When you were a kid," Cam responds, "did you ever laugh yourself silly for no reason?"

"Is this an old-man Johnson story? I don't think this is the time for another childhood story," she reproaches. "Your nostalgia for childhood has its place, but this is not the place."

"You could call it an old-man Johnson story. Did you ever ride one of those merry-go-rounds that they used to have in playgrounds; the kind you had to push to make them spin around? You'd ride it till you got stupid dizzy and you couldn't hang on any more and then you'd fall off or get off and fall down or stumble around and laugh yourself silly and it was fun. Or you rolled down a hill and you laughed for no reason at all, other than it was unadulterated fun. You did it for the pure joy of it. What happened?" says Cam gesturing at the guests seated at the tables. "Look at those people. They're hanging on to those tables for all they're worth. They've got the grip of death on those tables. They're afraid to let go. They're afraid to play and have fun. They've forgotten who they really are."

322

"You must be disappointed," Zanya observes trying to sound conciliatory. "Why don't you give it a couple of days? Then we can talk more if you prefer."

Cam wonders if he will ever know the true reason for Zanya's choice. Is Earle the better candidate because of his experience? Is her decision the result of the incident in the apartment? Is it something else? Is there a secret undercurrent? In Cam's mind, nothing is ever solely business. There are always the twists and turns of the unspoken. There are so many variables in the equation. He can never know with confidence the true reason behind her choice anymore than you can define pi to its last digit. You can only experience pi by spinning around on a merry-go-round. Cam looks at Zanya and smiles dryly. He knows that after tonight they will never speak again about her decision. It will remain an impenetrable mystery for Cam.

"You know," begins Zanya having misinterpreted his smile, "anything you might say about last Friday would be my word against yours. I can make things difficult if it comes to that. I don't want to. Let's not go there." Zanya smiles courteously, believing that she has trumped his smile.

"I wasn't thinking about that. What happened on Friday is between us, water under the bridge." He is surprised by Zanya's threatening tone. "There's nothing more to say about Friday," he responds with a sense of finality.

"I'm glad to hear you say that," says Zanya smiling. She is not entirely sure that she believes him. "There will be a generous bonus in your next paycheck for your help," she offers with a mollifying smile. "If you decide at any time to apply for another job, let me know if you need a reference. I'd be glad to oblige. You do good work. We should find our seats. They're about to start. Where are you seated? I'm near the front."

"I'm near the back." He is unsure how to take the remark about a reference. Was it a genuine offer, or a threat?

"Remember, if you want to talk more about this later, let me know," says Zanya with a disingenuous smile. She turns and walks away to take her seat.

Cam returns to Anna. They take their seats. The skirl of a bagpipe fills the Palazzo. The other guests at Cam's table have seated themselves. Earle is seated on the far side of the table. He is hidden from Cam by the floral arrangement in the center of the table. The guests rise while a piper in full regalia and playing a regimental march leads Ed to the head table. Ed is accompanied by Filana. Senior MKM executives and their guests trail behind in Ed's wake. As the procession proceeds to the head table, Cam nods to acknowledge Earle, who stands twisted partially around to watch the procession. Earle squints as though not recognizing Cam. Finally Earle simulates surprise. He offers a smile and a bob of his head in recognition.

"Congratulations on the new job," says Cam, raising his voice to be heard above the bagpipe." Earle frowns. He shakes his head and cups his hand to his ear. "We'll talk later," responds Cam with the shake of his head and the discrete wave of his hands to say never mind. Earle repeats the gesture of cupping his ear. 'Later. We'll talk later,' Cam mouths with exaggeration and makes a talking motion with his hands. He smiles benignly. Earle shrugs his shoulders in perplexity. He turns slightly, focusing his attention once again on the procession.

The piper stops playing. The dignitaries, who have reached their assigned places, sit on cue. Guests on the main floor of the great hall wait until the dignitaries are seated and then sit down.

Almost immediately Ed pops up from his chair. He proceeds to the lectern beside the head table. Ed begins reading from a teleprompter. "Good evening. Thank you for coming this evening. I see in the audience tonight many of the luminaries who have helped to make MKM the entertainment giant that it is. What a wonderful group of talented people," comments Ed beaming. "And did you notice the wonderful centerpiece on the tables?" he asks gesturing at the head table. "Filana volunteered to design them especially for this evening. They're beautiful aren't they? Thank you, Filana for your time and creative energy." Filana smiles brightly at the applauding guests. "Now," continues Ed after the applause subsides, "I'm sure you're impatient to hear about our plans for next season. There are a number of exciting surprises! I hope you enjoy tonight's adventure as we look into the future here at MKM. And let's not forget the role that MKM plays in shaping the future of the world beyond this great hall. We have a lot of work to do in the coming year as we get ready for the future. We have a lot to cover here tonight, but before I begin, I know you must be hungry, so let's get started. Bonne appetit!" Ed returns to his place at the head of the table to a round of applause from the audience.

On cue a battalion of servers dressed uniformly in white shirts, and black tie, vests and pants appear in the doorways around the hall. Carrying pre-plated dinners, they scurry about delivering the dinners to the assembled guests, beginning with the guests at the head table. Music from the overhead speakers plays in the background.

"Congratulations Earle," says Cam. He cranes his neck to peer around the large centerpiece in the middle of the table that hides Earle from his view. The centerpiece consists of a piece of ghost-white polystyrene foam carved in the shape of a head that is vaguely reminiscent of Filana, but is indifferent enough to be either female or male. Painted-on eyelashes define closed eyes that hint at a mystery about what may lie behind the closed eyes. A profusion of brilliant red roses and other vegetation emerge from a hollow in the head and cascade down on three sides. Ferns and holly leaves in numerous shades of green abundantly garnish the base.

Earle cranes his head to one side of the centerpiece. He can see only a headless Cam, who has craned his head in the opposite direction. Earle cranes his head to the other side of the centerpiece. With his head almost on the chest of the dinner guest seated next to him, Earle spies Cam.

"Congratulations," Cam repeats. Earle returns a blank look not appearing to understand. "Good luck in your new job," prompts Cam, who is becoming annoyed at Earle's gamesmanship with his feigned ignorance.

"Oh, thanks," Earle finally replies with a look of contrived surprise and false modesty to imply that garnering the job was really nothing.

"Have you met Anna?" asks Cam gesturing toward Anna. "Anna, this is Earle." There are a few back-and-forth contortions by Anna and Earle while they tilt their heads before making eye contact and exchanging pleasantries. "And that's Debbie sitting next to you," gestures Cam to the woman leaning discreetly away from Earle, who has his head resting almost on Debbie's chest. Debbie smiles uncomfortably at Earle, who is genuinely surprised when he realizes his awkward position. He straightens up immediately. "Debbie, this is Anna," adds Cam gesturing to Anna. Debbie waves over the centerpiece in Anna's direction to avoid the discomfort of more neck gyrations.

"I'll wave if you don't mind," says Debbie, her voice seeming to emanate from the centerpiece. "I think there's been enough neck craning for one night, don't you?"

"Yes, I've had enough exercise. I think I have whiplash," quips Anna at the polystyrene foam head. "I'll need a good neck massage after this."

Debbie laughs her queen-of-the-night laugh. "Cam can help you. He gives a great neck massage. He has surprisingly strong fingers. Must be all that typing he does."

"Who is Debbie?" Anna whispers loudly in Cam's ear to be heard above the din of the hall as servers float about and dinner guests attempt to carry on conversations. *I'll Get By* sings Billie Holiday from the speakers in the ceiling.

"She works in the film editing department. We went out a few times. It was a long time ago. By the way, I didn't get the job with Zanya. She gave it to Earle."

Anna reaches over and squeezes his hand. "I'm sorry you didn't get it. Are you disappointed?"

Cam shrugs. "No, if it had happened a few days ago, I would have been upset, but not now."

The remainder of dinner is uneventful. The noise of the hall makes it difficult to carry on a conversation with anyone except the guests seated directly on either side. The Filana head is silent with its eyes closed in sleep. Cam wonders what would happen if the head were suddenly to awaken. Its eyes popping open with surprise and then glancing wildly about in wonder, only able to see the guests immediately in front of it and unable turn its head because it has no body. What would it say? What would the guests do? Some might flee in panic. Others, after the initial alarm, might decide to give it a name. Digby maybe, thinks Cam. He smiles, pleased with his insight. 'Maybe' would make a good last name, Digby Maybe. Guests seated around the table might try to engage Digby in conversation and tell it about the world and Digby's circumstances in the world. At first Digby might be bewildered by the muddle of voices and ideas coming at it from so many different directions. Digby would have to choose someone to trust. Who would it trust? Who would it believe? What would Digby choose to believe?

Cam peers around the centerpiece to see what is happening on the other side of the table. Debbie is trying to engage Earle in conversation. She smiles, occasionally interjecting an innocuous comment or question. Earle jingles along with a jumble of ideas while staring at his plate, not wanting to make eye contact with Debbie. "Gnnnnnnh," says Earle occasionally to his plate. The conversation is one sided. Debbie turns to the guest on her other side in hopes of a better exchange.

After dessert and coffee, Ed approaches the lectern while the servers clear away the last of the dishes as quietly as possible. "Good evening," Ed begins. The audience grows quiet. "Did you enjoy dinner? I did. Are you relaxed? Filana are you relaxed?" Ed asks looking at Filana. Filana grins and nods her head an enthusiastic yes. A large screen descends silently behind the head table. The lights in the hall dim.

Ed continues. "Before we begin, I have a solemn duty. I would like to honor the dedicated workers of the MKM family, who after years of service and a well-deserved retirement have passed away this last year." Solemnly Ed reads the names of the employees. A picture of each worker is momentarily displayed on the giant screen. In the lower-right corner of each image appears a number, indicating the years of service at MKM, and the name of the company division in which the employee served. "Would you please rise and bow your head for a moment of silence," Ed requests after reading the last name. Everyone rises. The hall is quiet.

After a minute of silence, the piper plays *Flowers of the Forest*. The lament starts small in the vast hollow of the dimly lit hall. It grows in strength. Finally it fills every corner with its cry of loss and betrayal as though an immense blankness has swallowed the hall. The lament ends abruptly as it must. The silence lingers. Everyone stands quietly transfixed, not wanting to break the spell. Finally, the guests follow the lead of the dignitaries at the head table and resume their seats. The spell is broken.

"Thank you ladies and gentlemen. And thank you, piper McCall. Well done," says Ed gesturing to the piper who stands beside the stage. The guests warmly applaud the piper who makes a cordial bow to the audience. Ed waits for the applause to subside before he continues.

"Now, let's get down to the main event, the reason why we're here. Who knows why we are here? Please don't say that we're here for a good dinner," Ed jokes. The audience laughs politely and then is silent again except for the occasional cough or the clatter of dishes as the wait staff whisks away the last of the dishes and cutlery. "Does anyone know?" Ed asks rhetorically. "Then let me tell you why we are here tonight. For the past few months, I have been asking members of the staff a question. And that question is," Ed pauses for effect, "can you make water flow uphill?" Ed lets the question linger before continuing. The hall is quiet. "And those of you that I have asked have responded, why of course you can. All you need is a pump and a couple of feet of plastic tubing. Very simple task, there's nothing to it." Ed pauses again to let his audience wonder where he is taking them. "All very true, with a pump and tubing you can make water flow uphill. But can you make water flow uphill without the aid of mechanical devices, or without the aid of any kind of optical device that gives the illusion of water flowing uphill, or without the aid of any other kind of special effect? Before I answer that question, each of you has a pair of 3-D glasses at your place that the servers handed out earlier. Would you please put them on now?"

The sound of rustling, like dry leaves, fills the room while everyone including Ed removes the cellophane wrap from their glasses and puts them on. The audience looks at Ed through their mica-colored lenses. A row of monitors rise up from out of the floor in front of the head table so that the dignitaries can see what is about to transpire without having to twist around in their seats to look at the big screen. Ed waits for the audience to quiet down before revealing how to make water flow uphill.

"Before I tell you, let's watch this," says Ed.

The giant screen jumps to life. An artist's rendition of the Milky Way Galaxy as seen from above swirls into being, filling the entire screen with its rich gold and silver speckled colors. With the aid of the glasses, the galaxy floats in midair as though you could reach out and touch it. The spiral arms revolve slowly about the center. A few members of the wait staff have gathered in the doorways to watch, but without the glasses the image is blurry. There is a small burst of brilliant white light in one of the spiral arms. The disk of light grows in intensity and size until it fills almost the entire screen. The brilliance of the light fades and transforms into the logo of one of the company divisions. The logo includes a golden maple key that represents MKM. The logo fades and is once again replaced by the picture of the Milky Way Galaxy slowly revolving in compressed time in what otherwise would take millions of years. The animation is repeated several times more. Each time a logo of a different MKM division emerges from a different part of the galaxy until all of the divisional logos have appeared. When each logo appears, there is applause from a different sector of the audience. Everyone in the audience is organized into groups according to the company division that they represent.

The picture of the galaxy begins to change. The audience is falling into the galaxy, first into the Orion Arm, then past innumerable star clusters, countless stars, the outer planets of our solar system, then to earth, and falling to earth, first to North America, then into the great rain forest of the northwest, past a enormous waterfall with its thunder filling the hall, then to the forest floor, and then to a single small brook of clear, glacial melt water tumbling over and around a small rock. With the exception of the sound of the brook, a blanket of silence fills the hall.

"What if I told you that you can suspend the laws of physics," says the disembodied voice of Ed to the darkened hall. "How? I'll tell you how." The sound of the brook stops. There is silence. The brook continues spilling over and around the rock. "Beautiful picture, isn't it?" Ed asks. There is no response from the audience, only the occasional dry muffled cough, as though an errant wind has found its way into the hall. The brook begins to recede, first to the waterfall, then the forest, the continent, the earth and so on until the Milky Way Galaxy once again fills the screen.

"Now, if I may with your indulgence," says Ed directing his attention to the audience. All of the audience members appear transfixed as though pinned to their seats, resembling a museum display of butterflies mounted on pins with each butterfly having its own small neatly printed hand-written label to identify the species and subspecies of butterfly. The Milky Way Galaxy recedes. First, neighboring galaxies appear and then more distant galaxies. Galaxies of different shapes and sizes and at various angles lie suspended in front of the audience.

As Ed is about to explain, a small mushroom-colored spot forms in the center of the screen. At first it is ignored by the audience as a small technical glitch. But the spot grows, floating in front of the audience until it fills half the screen and is too big for anyone to ignore. "Edward," says a voice that fills the darkened hall. The spot grows bigger still and begins to spin. "Edward," says the voice, sounding like somebody who has a bone caught in his throat. There's a smattering of applause from various members of the audience who recognize the well-known voice. The spot begins to spin faster and faster. It grows in size until it blots out all the galaxies.

"Yes," says Ed, who is well rehearsed in what is about to happen. "Who's there?" says Ed looking up at the ceiling as though looking for the source of the voice.

The shape begins to spin into a recognizable shape. It stops spinning with a jolt. The apparition floats upside down in front of the audience. It is the face of a man who is wearing 3-D glasses. He has a taupe complexion, skin the texture of pine bark, and a shock of neatly coiffed off-white hair. The phantom seems as ancient as petrified wood. He is older than the Orky the Orca show, older than cable TV,

331

older than TV, older than radio, film, and everything. The audience, recognizing the face, ruptures into applause.

"Well! Hello Adin!" exclaims Ed pretending surprise. "Ladies and gentlemen, Adin Huffman," says Ed by way of introduction. The audience applauds again. Ed waits for the applause to die down. "Adin, you realize you're upside down, don't you?"

"Am I?" Adin replies. "Are you sure I'm the one who is upside down? Perhaps you are upside down. Oh well, never mind. Just a minute," says Adin. The vision slowly rotates until it is right-side up. "There, how's that? Whoa!" says Adin with a jolt of surprise. The apparition appears to take in the audience through its 3-D glasses for the first time. "Nice audience. They almost look three dimensional. Isn't this delicious?" says the spectre pretending to see the audience. "They look good enough to eat. Oh, look at that one in the scrumptious lemon-chiffon dress! Oh, and what about that one over there in the salmon pink! What's her name?"

"Adin, behave! Remember where you are," Ed admonishes. "Dinner is over."

"Well at least get her name for me will you?" Adin pleads. "There could be a second dessert later. What do you think Edward?"

Adin was a popular talk-show host who had an afternoon talk show on MKM TV for many years. His show is almost as old as the Orky the Orca show. Adin got his start in film, before the advent of TV. Next to his major film role when he appeared as the wolf man in Under the Pale Moonlight, his biggest role in film was that of a wolf man in a series of half-hour episodes. Each week a new episode in the series played in a theater near you before the main film attraction. With the use of trick photography by the film crew and the magic of makeup artists, Adin spent much of his time in front of cameras changing back and forth between his human character and the wolf man in the weekly serial. When he wasn't busy changing between his two characters, he spent his time in front of the camera growling at the other characters in the series, or snapping and snarling at nothing at all because the script called for a bunch of snapping and snarling. It was a low-budget serial. The story was set in a forest constructed of cardboard trees and other similar props where Adin lurked about while waiting for his next prey. Usually he didn't have to wait very long for a victim.

Adin's favorite scenes were the ones when, as his tortured human self, he got to show remorse for his terrible deeds as the wolf man while knowing that he would continue down the path of destruction he had chosen, but couldn't help himself. He was unable to change his dark ways. He was fond of these scenes because he got to show that he could be more than a wolf man. Inwardly at such moments, he seemed to rise to his higher self, seeing for a moment the truth of it all, or at least glimpsing the truth about himself. He might have been a greater actor had he managed to hang on to that truth.

Unfortunately, Adin was easily distracted for the wrong reasons by his acting career or his 'climb to the stars' as he enjoyed calling it. He reasoned that a big name in the film industry would one day recognize his acting ability and give his career the boost that he believed he richly deserved after years of sacrifice. He might have at least stopped being a wolf man had he paid attention to his glimpse of the truth. Poor Adin, not everyone glimpses the truth and fewer still hang on to it.

The wolf-man series was hard work. Eventually the series was killed by a silver bullet when TV grew in popularity. After the series ended, Adin created a new level of hell for himself. He auditioned for the role of a wolf man for a late-afternoon kid's TV show on MKM TV, which was just getting started. The name of the TV show was The Wuffman. It was Adin's previous wolf-man experience that got him the job. Adin's job in his new wolf-man role was to entertain kids and pass along advice about behaving like adults.

His new job was even harder than before. Adin had to be at the TV station at four o'clock every morning because it took hours to apply the wolf-man makeup. He found the makeup and costume 'itchy as hell', to use Adin's words. The costume was especially uncomfortable when he was trapped under the hot lights of the TV studio. This made him irritable. Being irritable was bad because the show aired live in front of a studio audience full of kids. The work was exhausting. Adin put in long days. Occasionally he would snap at the kids. At which time he would growl things in the vein of 'grow up kid' or 'get lost kid'. In terror a bunch of the kids would pee their pants, which wasn't good for Adin who didn't really understand kids anyway.

For a time, he was also required by contract to make additional appearances in the role of The Wuffman during intermissions at afternoon matinees in theaters when theaters still had intermissions. Adin's appearances didn't work out so well. There were a lot of grade-nothing kids who cried at the site of The Wuffman and peed their pants when Adin leapt and prowled about the stage while snapping and growling at the kids in the audience. Adin was very convincing as The Wuffman. There was a lot of pant peeing in those days. The parents complained about The Wuffman. The MKM Theater managers complained because of the smell of pee left on the theater seats and the cost of cleaning. Quietly MKM discontinued Adin's appearances in theaters.

After three years of playing The Wuffman, Adin got his big break at MKM when he auditioned for the role of a talk-show host. His distinctive voice, which he had cultivated during his wolf-man years, proved to be the deciding factor in his favor. His show, Busy Buzz about Town, which was later changed to The Adin Huffman Show, became very successful. Adin became a well-known celebrity across North American when more and more TV stations and later cable networks picked up his show.

Adin felt better about things too. He no longer felt trapped under the hot lights in front of a bunch of dopey kids and having to wear an itchy-as-hell costume that smelled of sweat. Adin had a long and successful run playing the TV host because he learned exactly what to say, when to say it and how to say it without actually saying anything.

Now having seen too many seasons, he is an old TV relic telling an ancient story that goes way back even before the invention of counting. There appeared to be no going back for Adin Huffman.

"What brings you here?" asks Ed.

There is a slight pause before Adin responds because Adin's part is prerecorded. "I've come to help you," replies Adin. "The audience must have the patience of Job to put up with your mumbo jumbo," Adin chuckles. A muted chuckle rises from the audience. Many in the audience are old enough to remember Adin's voice when he played The Wuffman. A few of the audience members can remember peeing their pants, a memory they would like to forget if they could. "Why don't you have a seat and I'll show you how to lead this parade. Give Edward a drink. Make it a Grateful Dead. That should keep him happy."

"Okay, you win," Ed smiles his best showman smile. He sits down to enjoy the show.

"Forget that stuff about water flowing uphill because it isn't going to happen. It doesn't matter," begins Adin addressing the audience. "Now watch this," commands Adin, "while the old master takes you on a journey of discovery. Hang onto your glasses!" The face of Adin shrinks and disappears as though sucked inward from a point between his eyes. The galaxies wink into being once again. "Are you still with me?" whispers Adin in his distinctive voice, speaking to each guest about the unspoken secret that lies in each of them. Adin's voice hints at possibilities in undiscovered realms where galaxies and the universe and all that we are and know or can ever know are by comparison only dust. The audience is attentive. The audience is quiet and still.

"Something's happening. Look!" orders Adin. One of the galaxies grows brighter and explodes, shooting brilliant, white droplets across the screen. "Ladies and gentlemen please welcome a promising new TV program, At the Crossroads," declares Adin. The droplets suddenly coalesce into the words 'At the Crossroads' that blaze across the screen, resembling a flag flying proudly in the wind while *Amazing Grace* plays proud and strong. "Hosted by Reverend Mortul," adds Adin, "whom I'm sure many of you know, or will know soon."

The scene immediately snaps to a smiling Reverend Mortul who is standing with his arms outstretched at his sides in the form of a cross. The camera angle changes to look down slightly from above. It pans completely around the Reverend. You can see a small bald spot on the crown of his head while the camera pans. *Amazing Grace* ends abruptly. The scene transitions to Reverend Mortul seated in a wing-back chair. In the background are several bookshelves crammed with imposing books. Opposite Reverend Mortul sits an up-and-coming singer and entertainer, Logan Whitewood. The Reverend appears relaxed as he talks to the entertainer.

Adin explains that the Reverend will interview famous people from different professions about their spirituality in half-hour interviews. Adin names a few of the people that the Reverend will interview including famous politicians, lawyers, business men, professional sports stars and entertainers of all kinds. There's a short clip from the interview with Logan.

"Tell me about the religious influences in your life when you were a boy growing up," prompts the Reverend, who spent hours preparing the questions for the interview.

"Well," replies Logan, "my earliest memories are of Sunday school, when I was about four. We'd sing songs. Then there would be a lesson from the Bible, things like that. Later there was the boys' choir. They were always looking for new choir members, so Mom signed me up. That's where I got my first real taste for singing. I guess my singing career started with those old hymns."

"And what about now?" asks the Reverend leaning forward slightly, listening attentively to hear or see the answer to an unspoken question about the quiet struggle within, not the overconfident, TV-preacher answer regurgitated by many. Is the struggle there? Is there a sign in the eyes, voice or body language of the entertainer?

"Well," begins Logan enthusiastically to convey a veneer of energy and life, "I still go to church if that's what you mean. Mom always insisted."

Disappointed, the Reverend leans back while the entertainer continues. The Reverend has reservations about the quality of the guests that MKM has lined up for his show. He worries that the show is little more than a promotional spot by MKM for the guests in order to advance the careers of the guests, or to advance the causes that they represent as causes worthy of the public's support. The Reverend is willing to go along in hopes of having more influence in guest selection in later episodes. The entertainer's answer fades.

The song, *What is the Soul of a Man*, builds. The Reverend insisted on this song for the closing theme as emphatically as he insisted on the title for the show, At the Crossroads. The producer insisted upon *Amazing Grace* for the opening to the show. The Reverend, who is fond of the song, thinks it is over used and in danger of losing its power. The interview shrinks to the size of the head of a pin in the center of the screen and disappears. The galaxies bloom once again.

"Masterful! Thrilling!" the disembodied voice of Adin says in a way that makes you want to believe. "Oh look over there. What's happening in that galaxy? Let's watch and see."

Another galaxy expands and explodes. The show is called Amazing. Contestants in teams of two run through a maze searching for treasure in one-hour episodes. The prizes range from vacation trips to faraway places, to luxury cars, to bags of money. The walls of the maze are movable and can change during the course of an episode. There are traps, snares and gins operated by the Maze Minions who are there to thwart the contestants. The Maze Minions are also known as the Maze Monkeys, and the Worker Bees. Each week there is a different theme location, Rome, Athens, New York, a zoo, outer space, Poop Land, Hell, Olympus, etc. Of course nothing is what it seems. Several of the theme locations appear idyllic, an English countryside for example. These idyllic settings are often the worst ones with lots of manure traps and so on. Contestants and Maze Minions are attired appropriately to suit the theme. The show has a host whose job it is to run the contestants through the maze. For protection every contestant must wear a bulbous helmet the size of a watermelon, and a mouth guard that makes talking difficult. The contestants are bumped, thumped, pinched, pulled, pushed, hit, hosed, hammered, dropped, slammed, beaned, bopped, shoved, tripped, trapped, snared, roped, spun, twanged, thwapped, slapped, flicked, tackled, clipped, rolled, etc. by the Maze Minions using devices that are too numerous to mention. The Maze Minions grin and laugh a lot. They enjoy their work as does the host, and the producer of the show.

The show is set up in such a way that only one team can win the prize offered each week. There are no secondary prizes. Winning is everything to the contestants. The possibility of winning makes the contestants feel that they are free and empowered in this ever-changing maze where the promise of victory always seems possible. The contestants believe that the only thing that stands between them and triumph is their willingness to persevere against adversity, which is the intended message of the show. Do they have the strength and the guts to go the distance?

Lots of people apply to be contestants on the show. The contestants are not allowed to choose their partner. This is left to the producer of the show, who insists on paring disparate contestants with conflicting views to add to the excitement. For example, a pro-abortionist is paired with a right-to-life contestant, or a right-wing conservative paired with a left-wing liberal. Some contestants have been known to try and circumvent the pairing process by claiming beliefs that are abhorrent to their true beliefs in hopes of a pairing with someone who shares their real beliefs. Often this ploy fails when other disingenuous contestants holding opposite beliefs espouse views that are also repugnant to their actual beliefs. The pairing process seems haphazard, but in the end works most of the time. The show is billed as a comedy.

On the big screen there's a brief montage of contestants being pummelled in various ways by the Maze Minions. The TV audience will be encouraged to pick a team and root for that team, as in professional sports. If your team wins, you share vicariously in the glory. If your team loses, there's always next week when you can pick a new team.

The producer expects that a number of TV audience members will choose to root for the Maze Minions, who are encouraged to develop their own TV personas. To help the audience identify with the Maze Minion characters, the writers of the show gave much thought to the name assigned to each character. The first writer thought that their names should be variations on biblical names: Mose, Nebbie and Issie. However, the producer thought that certain audience members might be offended. The second writer thought they should be named after construction tools: Jack Hammer, Dozer, and Back Hoe. The producer thought many of the female members of the audience would have difficulty identifying with characters having such names and Back Hoe had a questionable ring to it. The third writer wanted to name them after bodily fluids such as Phlegm, Pus, Belch and Pizzle, even though Belch was a gas and not a fluid and Pizzle wasn't a real word, but was highly suggestive. The producer quickly rejected these types of names. The fourth writer wanted to use the names of Shakespearean characters, such as Caesar, Cleo, Ariel and Caliban, but no one thought the audience members would understand these references.

Finally, it was left to the marketing department to decide the names. After due diligence that included analysis of names using propriety marketing surveys from companies that specialize in researching names, and through audience focus groups, and in consultation with the legal department, the naming department, the advertising department and several other departments, the vice president of marketing announced in a meeting with the writers the types of names that the writers could use.

"The Maze Minions must have names like Bing, Bang, Boo, Muffin, T-biscuit, etcetera," said the marketing guy. "If you want to use names other than these, check first with the MKM Naming department, MKMN. You know the drill."

The writers liked these names because they reminded them of *Waiting for Godot*. There was only a small hitch when the writers wanted to use etcetera as one of the character names. MKMN insisted that the writers use And So On because MKMN's Naming Guide, which is used throughout MKM, states that etcetera cannot be used. MKMN reasoned that etcetera is difficult to dub into other languages. This was an important consideration because the show might be picked up in countries where the native language isn't English. Writers must instead use And So On, which the writers did. They decided that And So On was a good name too.

The producer randomly gave each of the Maze Minions a T-shirt with a name on it that each minion had to wear when on camera. The T-shirts helped the members of the audience identify the individual Maze Minion characters. Occasionally the producer would instruct the Maze Minion characters to switch T-shirts. The test audiences didn't seem to notice the switch. In spite of the T-shirt switching or because of the switching, And So On would become one of the most popular characters. All of the Maze Minion members in the cast took a turn at being And So On.

The audience in the great hall laughs at the appropriate moments during the montage from the Amazing show. The 3-D imagery adds to the enjoyment because it provides depth of field to the contest even though the 3-D technology makes the contestants appear flat. The montage ends and is sucked into a black hole. The galaxies reappear.

"Wow! Edward, you've got a winner on your hands! I can see a Hardaun in your future!" exclaims Adin. A Hardaun is an award given to reality TV shows by the National Organization of Broadcasters, NOB. The award is named for Quinlan Hardaun whose TV production company, One Hand Flapping, pioneered reality TV shows. "I hear rumors of a two-hour opening episode. Is this true, Edward? I can hardly wait!"

"Now let's look at what's happening in Movie land!" exclaims Adin before Ed can reply. "Mr. 3-D technician, show us the future! Another galaxy blasts apart, shooting brilliant, white droplets that coalesce to announce a new movie, Dead Men Tell No Tales. This is a spy story. One of the stars of the film is Logan Whitewood, who is making his first appearance in film as an actor. There's a short clip from the film. It's Logan's big scene. Logan's character plays dead in order to live to tell the tale to his spy-master boss. Later, when Logan is interviewed by a TV host who specializes in interviewing celebrities, Logan emphasizes that the key to his big scene was controlling his breathing in order to appear dead.

There are rumors that the renowned School of Shadow Arts may nominate Logan for the prestigious Ophelia award, which recognizes the outstanding work of an actor in the portrayal of a dead person. The award is named after Ophelia Waterdown (her stage name) who was known for her outstanding on-screen portrayal of dead people. Unfortunately, Ophelia became type cast for her portrayal of dead people and wasn't able to find work in other acting roles. For a time she had her own school, the School of Laudanum, SoL. She was feeling bitter about the type casting when she named the school and thought the name a good joke. At the school she instructed actors how to survive in the acting business by playing dead for a living. The school didn't do well, possibly because of its name, or possibly because few aspiring actors could understand the difficulty in playing dead convincingly. It seemed to come naturally to most actors. Playing dead was a no-brainer it seemed to them. Eventually the school closed, which made her feel even more resentful. Ophelia became troubled and drowned herself in her bath tub. The truth was covered up to protect her good name and her outstanding body of work for her convincing portrayals of the dead.

After her death, her portrayal of the dead developed a small cult following. For a little while there was talk of a film festival celebrating her work and the work of other actors who had followed in her footsteps by playing dead. The idea of a film festival died because no one could figure out how to make a festival of this kind generate a profit.

Adin's voice returns to fill the void while galaxies once again pop up like popcorn on the screen. "Is Logan here tonight? Logan, stand up. Good job!" Logan stands. He smiles ecstatically and bows. The audience breaks into applause. Logan is thrilled to death by the attention. "All right, that's enough bowing. Logan, you can sit down now. Don't milk it to death. There's plenty of time for that later," chimes Adin. The crowd laughs when Logan obediently sits down.

Next Adin introduces the film Never Let the Truth. The film is based on a novel by a well-known and highly respected novelist. There is a brief scene from the movie.

Adin introduces several more motion pictures and TV shows, including Zanya's, that are currently in production. After the last galaxy bursts and a black hole devours the last film clip, Adin returns the proceedings to Ed and then disappears.

"Thank you Adin," begins Ed looking again ceiling ward as though speaking to a godly being. "Wasn't that a great job ladies and gentlemen?" The audience breaks into applause. "Adin, are you there?" asks Ed as the applause dies down. There is no response from the darkness. "He must be gone. So...," continues Ed.

"Edward," interrupts Adin, whose face abruptly reappears on the screen. He is still wearing his 3-D glasses.

"Oh! You are still there," responds Ed, looking at the screen. "Yes Adin, what is it?"

"About my fee...," Adin alludes. Members of the audience begin to chuckle. Adin is notorious throughout the entertainment industry for hounding any company that doesn't promptly pay his appearance fee.

"No need to worry," Ed responds reassuringly. "You should have it very soon. I sent it by special courier. Everything is alright."

Adin beams. "Okay, thanks Edward. Have a good evening," says Adin. Adin's face begins to spin, twist and rotate as it is sucked into a black hole. This is followed by another round of applause by the audience. The big screen ascends. The TV monitors in front of the head table descend. Members of the audience remove their 3-D glasses. The lights come up in the hall.

"Is he gone?" asks Ed. The hall is quiet. "I think he must be gone. So, what do you think of your future?" Ed starts again. Once more the audience erupts into applause. "You have a lot of work to do to make all this happen," Ed cautions. "Are you ready?" There is a round of thunderous applause. "All right!" beams Ed who has forgotten to remove his 3-D glasses. "Well, I see by the clock that we're out of time. I'm afraid I'll have to save the explanation on how to make water flow uphill for another occasion." There are puzzled looks on the faces of many in the audience. No one is certain why Ed wants to pursue this line of thought in the first place. "Meanwhile, think of an answer," adds Ed. "Drive safely and thank you for coming. Good night."

The audience stands. Piper McCall emerges from behind a partition beside the head table. He pipes the head-table luminaries out of the hall. Members of the audience follow.

21 You Don't Say

The next morning Cam showers, dresses, and so on as he prepares for the day ahead. He eats a bowl of Liberty Puff cereal and then rinses the bowl. Today will be his last full day at MKM.

He steers his car along the twisting road, up the valley, and away from the bay. His drive to work is uneventful. He hardly notices anymore the abandoned houses that are the result of the recent and severe economic downturn. Derelict houses are easy to spot. They're the ones with plywood nailed over the windows and doorways. In many cases, vandals have ripped away the plywood, kicked in doors, and smashed windows. These houses have a look of surprise about them. Cam feels threatened by the decay when he chooses to think about it.

He parks his car in an MKM parking lot beside the Bayview museum, which sits on the opposite side of the street to MKM headquarters. On the front of the museum wall stretches a huge banner that spans the entire length of the block-long building. The banner announces an exhibit on Roman emperors, their imperial powers, their triumphs and their failures. Regardless of whether an emperor won or failed in an endeavor, especially war, the emperor always presented the outcome as a triumph, 'missionis effactus sum' (mission accomplished). Even the worst defeat could be turned into a triumph with a little imagination. Failure was not an option.

Most wars were fought for economic gain. Emperors would try to hide this fact from the citizens that wars were fought for control over a resource, a trade route, or a geographical region of financial interest. Instead an emperor would make up farcical stories that would appeal to the citizens about righting a wrong or restoring freedom to an oppressed people, or Roman glory and honor, or noble shit like that. Critics of an emperor were silenced. Speaking out was often fatal.

Cam learned this and more about emperors when he and Anna took the guided tour of the exhibit. He didn't think it was any different than today.

At the end of the tour, the guide warned that we are doomed to repeat the mistakes of the past unless we learn the lessons from the past. Cam didn't think this was true. He figured that we can't help ourselves because we're kid adults fighting over a bowl of Liberty Puff cereal, or a piece of seemingly indivisible candy, or anything imaginable. Cam has lost count of the number of wars his country has fought in his lifetime. He wonders how many more he will see.

His tour of the exhibit reminded him of the monkey trap he heard about once on TV. The trap was a hollowed out coconut tethered to a stake. There was a small opening in the coconut that was only big enough for a monkey to reach inside with its paw. It was a tight fit. Inside the coconut was a nut or a piece of fruit that was tempting to monkeys. A monkey would reach in and grab the treat, making a fist when it grasped the delicacy. When the monkey tried to remove the goody, its fist was too big for the hole. The monkey was trapped and in its panic didn't know enough to let go. It was caught and became somebody's dinner, or was sold as a pet.

As he approaches the MKM complex of sky-scraping buildings, Cam notices that there are the usual groups of protestors in the plaza. The plaza is gargantuan and could easily hold a handful of football stadiums. It dwarfs anyone who steps onto it. Ed insisted on the enormous space. He said it was to give people who used it a sense of openness, freedom and their place in the grand scheme of things. MKM allows protesters to use the space provided they behave themselves, don't bother anyone else, and don't try to enter MKM headquarters. Protestors who break the unwritten rules are escorted from the premises by MKM Security, MKMS.

In the plaza, a few sighted people are protesting on behalf of blind people about a film that will soon air on an MKM cable channel. The movie takes place on a remote island where everyone is blind. Almost everyone on the island is behaving badly. The protestors see the movie as an attack on blind people, which it is in a way but not in the way that the protestors see it, or don't see it depending on your point of view.

There are the usual religious fundamentalists who through dogged determination over the years have established a kind of squatter's rights in one corner of the plaza. Today they are protesting a movie, The Exasperation of Jesus. They don't appreciate the way Jesus is depicted. In the movie, Jesus spends his time being annoyed while he tries to convey his message. There's a scene in which Jesus is trying to explain about houses. "No, no!" says the exasperated Jesus talking to his would-be followers. "When I say a house divided, I don't mean a real house. Not a house, house," Jesus adds. "I mean each of you. You are a house! You mustn't be divided within yourself. You can have only one master!" says Jesus looking for understanding among the blank expressions of the listeners.

"Then why didn't you say that?" asks one in the crowd. "I am my own master in my own house. I serve no one," the would-be follower says with confidence.

"Yes," says another in the crowd, "my house has only one room."

"I have influence with the king," proudly announces another. "I can ask the king to pass a law that a house can be only one room. The king could include a grandfather clause in the law to exempt multi-roomed houses that already exist. There could be a renovation clause that says two-room dwellings must be converted into one-room dwellings within five years. That would give the carpenters like your dad and other trades people lots of work. Of course there might have to be exemptions for bigger houses, like mine. The law could state that if the dwelling has three rooms or more, one wall has to be knocked down, making two rooms one in a symbolic gesture. It can be done," added the follower cheerfully, feeling satisfied with his can-do attitude.

"Sounds good to me, I don't see a problem," adds another follower.

"No, no, you don't get it!" responds Jesus pleading for understanding. "That's not what I mean! I don't mean knocking down walls in the house where you live. I'm talking about knocking down walls inside of you where you *really* live," entreats Jesus. "Don't you get it? Don't you *see?*" pleads Jesus becoming ever more frustrated at the way his words have become warped by the members of the crowd.

"No, I can see quite well," confidently answers one of the members of the crowd. Others nod their agreement.

"You'll have to be clearer in what you mean, Jesus, if you want us to follow you," adds another. "Speak plainly!" he adds growing more frustrated with Jesus' convoluted way of speaking.

The scene continues on for another two minutes or so before Jesus throws up his hands in exasperation. "I give up. You're clueless!" Jesus heads to the nearest olive grove.

A follower calls after Jesus. "Wait, where are you going? Show us another miracle so that we may believe."

"No!" retorts Christ over his shoulder, walking away. "You've seen enough. What do you take me for, a street-corner magician?"

The members of the crowd are confused. There's a discussion in the crowd.

"What's got into him?" one asks. There's a collective shrug.

"We were trying to help you," shouts another at the departing Jesus.

"Well if he's going to be that way, there are plenty of others that we can follow," adds a third. "He doesn't have the market cornered on religion."

"Come on, let's go," adds another voice.

Jesus prays to God. He asks for patience and that God go easy on the dunderheads.

The fundamentalist have managed to get the film banned from a number of the Bayview movie theaters. The Exasperation of Jesus is based on a novel, Voices of Children. Another religious fundamentalist group that frequents the plaza is working on the book angle. There is talk of a book burning.

Cam starts across the plaza. He watches as a lone man wanders more or less in a circle that encompasses the entire plaza. The journey takes him about an hour. The man is a regular fixture in the plaza. He is carrying a placard that states: 'One will be taken and the other left'. In the corner of the placard are the words Matthew 24:40. On the other side of the placard is the picture of a man whose body is disintegrating into dust while his soul emerges and ascends upward. The man in the plaza is handing out leaflets while he makes his circuit around the plaza.

One windy day on his way to work, Cam found one of these leaflets blowing around. Cam picked it up and read it. The leaflet stated that one day soon, maybe today because you never know, the bodies of the chosen will disintegrate where they stand and their souls ascend to heaven. And that's too bad for you, and others like you who are left behind because you're about to get the ass whupping of your sorry little life for your shit-bad behavior. However, there might still be time to become one of the chosen, so come on out to the next meeting of the Church of the Whup-Ass.

The man with the placard is a former member of Preacher Jay's congregation. The man enjoyed most of all Jay's twice-annual whup-ass sermons. He left Jay's congregation and founded his own church, the Church of the Whup-Ass, because there weren't enough whup-ass sermons for the man's keen sense of right and wrong. The name of the church was considered a marketing coup because it was edgy enough to attract a few initial followers who then roped in more new followers.

It turns out that there are a lot of people who feel that other people need their asses whupped when they get out of line, which is most of the time as far as the followers of the Church of the Whup-Ass are concerned. In the new congregation, there is enough whupping of asses to satisfy everyone. Now the church is doing well with many new members every week. The church's popularity is proving a drain on other church denominations in Bayview. There is talk of establishing a second Church of the Whup-Ass in Wallaceville. People in Wallaceville need their asses whupped too and maybe even more than the people of Bayview, reason the church elders who often refer to Wallaceville as Gomorrah.

There is even discussion of establishing a private school with classes for kindergarten through grade eight. There is no way the parents want their kids to be the unprepared bridesmaids when Jesus comes knocking.

A lot of parents feel that the name of the school would have to change. 'School for the Church of the Whup-Ass' doesn't seem appropriate. Parents think that their children might be bullied by kids from other schools. 'Hey kid, come here. I'll give your ass a good whupping so you can go to heaven sooner', parents imagine kids from other schools saying and then doing. The parents reason that if there is any kid ass whupping that needs to be done, it should be the sole prerogative of the parents. The 'School for the Enlightenment of Children' has been bandied about by the church elders as an alternative name. Other parents believe it should be the 'School for the Church of the Whup-Ass'. They reason that it is the kids' cross to bear for Jesus and will toughen up the kids for the harsh reality they will face as crusaders for Jesus. The kids must be prepared to make sacrifices in the name of Jesus.

A large faction of the congregation have even suggested a military theme for the school with berets and marching to give the kids the discipline they will need in the name of Jesus. The proponents of the paramilitary faction affectionately refer to the kids as the Tough Nuts for Jesus, TNJ. The TNJ kids are envisioned as hard nuts, like the hard outer shell of a hazel nut. The advocates are convinced that one day the sacrifice of the TNJ kids in the name of God will serve God well in the coming battle of Armageddon during the end times, which are expected almost any day now, give or take a few decades or so. Parents can hardly wait for the TNJ kids and Jesus too for that matter to kick ass in the name of God. They reason there is a lot of ass kicking that must be done and the parishioners want to make sure the TNJ kids are ready, willing, and able to get their fair share of the ass-kicking action. The parishioners are very proud of the education that they plan to give their little soldiers in the name of Jesus. A final decision on the name of the school is expected soon.

As Cam approaches the entrance to the main tower in the MKM complex, a woman appears out of nowhere and offers Cam a leaflet printed on a half-sheet of paper. Without thinking, Cam takes the leaflet and continues into the building.

Normally Cam declines proffered leaflets. Once he accepted a leaflet from a stranger who, after making successful contact with Cam, approached Cam every time he saw Cam in the plaza. The stranger tried to engage Cam in conversation about the rightness of his cause, Smoking for Freedom. The stranger, who assumed that Cam was a smoker too, argued that his country had fought many wars on behalf of all smokers so that smokers could smoke cigarettes anywhere they chose. Restricting where they could smoke was an infringement on smokers' freedom everywhere, and a betrayal of everything that his country stood for. Cam felt akin to the monkey that had fallen victim to the coconut trap. He had made a serious lapse in vigilance regarding the acceptance of leaflets from strangers. There was no way to return the leaflet and end the relationship. For the longest time, there seemed no escape from Smokey as Cam referred to him. Smokey was constantly smoking and reeked of cigarette smoke. Cam could smell Smokey before he saw him. One day Cam dropped his politeness and told Smokey to buzz off, which is the only phrase that came to mind at the time. That was the last time Cam saw him.

Sitting at his desk in his cubicle, Cam is stunned when he reads the leaflet that he accepted from the woman.

Preacher Jay is innocent!

Stop Maple Key Media!

Rally noon today

Maple Key Media Plaza

Later, while Cam stands in the plaza waiting for the rally to begin, he notices that MKM has dispatched a news team to cover the rally. The news department plans to air a clip about the rally on the six o'clock news tonight. This is expected to boost the ratings for Zanya's show, You Don't Say. Her interview with Jay airs tonight after the news. The timing of the rally couldn't be better.

News teams from the small, independent media outlets in Bayview are also in attendance. MKM allows them on MKM turf. Their presence portrays MKM in a generous light and promotes to the TV audience the idea of independence and freedom of expression. Provided these independent outlets aren't cutting too deeply into the MKM revenue stream of advertising dollars, they are tolerated. In fact MKM sometimes invites the independents to attend events if the independents' participation will result in free advertising for MKM.

A few protestors carrying placards in support of Preacher Jay mill about while they wait for the rally to begin. Cam notices that there are more media representatives than rally participants. Protestors from other plaza groups have scurried over to hear what the speaker has to say. Cam looks up towards Ed's office at the top of the main tower in the MKM complex. He wonders if Ed is watching. There's a discussion among the protest leaders about how to proceed.

A member of MKMS is in attendance in case things get out of hand. There's a speaker mike clipped to the epaulette on the security guard's shirt so that he is in constant contact with the MKMS central office. MKMS can quickly dispatch more security guards if necessary.

"If you want to make the six o'clock news, you need to get moving," shouts the MKM reporter at the rally leaders. "We're running out of time. I have a deadline." The TV cameras are running. A camera man pans the crowd and the plaza for an establishing shot.

After a few more minutes of discussion among the rally leaders, a woman, Eleanor, steps forward to act as spokesperson. She is wearing an out-of-fashion brown tweed jacket and matching skirt. She's thin and wiry looking, having endured a lot in her life. One of the protestors has brought a step stool that Eleanor steps onto. Another of the rally organizers hands her a megaphone. Eleanor is nervous. She's not used to speaking in front of an audience. She begins to speak, but no one except those standing next to her can hear her.

"We can't hear you," shouts the MKM reporter. "The megaphone is off. Turn it on."

Flustered, Eleanor looks at the megaphone. With help from a supporter, she finds the switch and turns it on. "Is that better?" she asks, holding the megaphone to her mouth. Rally members nod yes. "Thanks for coming out today. I'll get right to the point."

"Who are you?" interrupts the MKM reporter.

"My name is Eleanor. I'm a member of Preacher Jay's congregation," answers Eleanor. There's a toughness and matter-of-factness to Eleanor that belies her nervousness. She is plain spoken and used to getting directly to the point. She's had to fight for everything that she has. "You may know Preacher Jay. He runs a store-front mission called the House of Adam in the old south-end of the city," Eleanor takes a breath. "A couple of weeks ago he did an interview for a show called You Don't Say. It's an MKM show. The interview features Jay and his work at the Mission. The interview airs in tonight's episode of You Don't Say. Yesterday we learned that You Don't Say plans to attack the good name and good works of Preacher Jay. They've dug up some dirt about him that You Don't Say will also include in the episode, along with the interview featuring Preacher Jay." Eleanor pauses while she lets this sink in. The wind blows. Discarded leaflets from an assortment of protest campaigns scuttle across the plaza.

"What are the allegations?" asks the MKM reporter.

"They're going to say that he had sex with a young woman. She's a member of the congregation. They're going to say that he had sex with her when he was supposed to be counseling her. That he took advantage of her when she was vulnerable. That he broke his bond of trust. Absolutely none of this is true, lies, all of it."

"What proof does You Don't Say have?"

"You Don't Say met with the woman making the allegations. They interviewed her for the show. They weren't supposed to interview her, but they did. We've seen the clip from the show," answers Eleanor. "If you hold your questions to the end, I'll be glad to answer them at that time."

"How do you know what they're going to say?" interrupts the MKM reporter.

"A concerned MKM employee gave us a clip from tonight's show. The clip shows the woman making the allegations," answers Eleanor."

"Who is your source at MKM?" asks the MKM reporter.

"I can't tell you the name. The person would be fired," responds Eleanor."

"How do you know the allegations are false?"

"Jay has ministered to his congregation for close to fifteen years. We know him. He's helped many people. He wouldn't do that. That kind of garbage isn't in him," answers Eleanor firmly. "Would you please hold your questions until I'm finished?"

"Have you talked to anyone at You Don't Say?"

"We've called a representative several times. They're not returning our calls."

"What do you want?"

"Don't run tonight's episode," Eleanor answers. "Give us time to work with MKM. We want to make sure the truth gets out. All we're asking for is a little time and a chance to talk to the You Don't Say people in order to set the record straight. Work with us. All we want is the truth to come out. We're not trying to hide anything. We have nothing to hide. We believe in the integrity of Preacher Jay. We know he is innocent."

"Have there been other allegations of sexual impropriety against him?"

"No."

"Has he been accused of abusing his office of trust before?"

"No, he's a good man. I've known him for the past fifteen years. So have many of the people in his congregation who are here today. You can ask them yourselves after I've said what I have to say. They'll vouch for him."

"What's the name of the women who he is alleged to have had sex with?"

"I can't tell you her name. It needs to be kept confidential to protect her."

"Won't we find out when the show is aired?"

"No, they've disguised her voice and hidden her face to protect her anonymity."

"Has she brought formal charges against Preacher Jay?"

"No, and she doesn't plan to either," Eleanor responds.

"Then where do these allegations stem from?"

"The woman was vulnerable. She was going through a rough patch. We've all seen bad times at different points in our lives. I'm sure you can understand that. She said things that weren't true. She knows they were wrong. She's sorry for what she said. She'd take it back if she could, but she can't; it's all recorded. The You Don't Say people aren't interested in her retraction."

"Have you spoken with her?"

"Yes, I have and so have others here today. We've spoken to her parents too. They're upset. They know what she did was wrong."

"How old was she when this was alleged to have occurred?"

"At the time she was 22."

"When is this alleged to have happened?"

"About a year ago," replies Eleanor.

"Is it alleged that this happened more than once?"

"Yes, three times, but the allegations are not true!"

"Why isn't she here? Wouldn't her presence here today answer a lot of questions?"

"She's undergoing treatment for drug abuse in a rehab program. Asking her to be here today would only hurt her chances for recovery. She's ashamed of what she said. The House of Adam is not a wealthy Mission," adds Eleanor. "This kind of publicity could hurt the Mission, close it down."

"Are you doing this to protect the Mission?"

"No, we're doing this because Preacher Jay has done nothing wrong," Eleanor responds adamantly.

"Have you anything you want to add?"

"The allegations raised against Preacher Jay are false! I'm asking MKM not to air the show tonight. Work with us to present the truth. Don't ruin the reputation of Preacher Jay. Talk to us after I'm finished here. We can tell you more about Jay and his good works in the community. Are there any other questions?" There's a pause while Eleanor waits for a response from the reporters. The MKM reporter makes a cutting motion with his hand. The MKM camera operator turns off the camera. The reporters begin to disperse. "If there are no other questions, then thank you for coming. If you need my phone number, come and see me."

A few of the independent reporters approach the members of the congregation to ask more questions. Cam stands on the edge of the crowd, listening to the parishioners defend Jay to the reporters. He learns nothing more. He returns to MKM headquarters.

Cam knocks on the open door to Zanya's office.

"Hi Cameron, come in," Zanya says coolly. "I thought I might see you today. What did you think of the theater in the plaza?"

"You knew about it?"

"Of course I did. Who do you think orchestrated it?"

"You set that up?"

"Well, not exactly."

"What do you mean?"

357

"I didn't arrange the time and place. I authorized my assistant, what's her name, Vanessa, to make the clip of the woman and her allegations available to certain members of Jay's congregation. The rest was up to them. Their timing couldn't have been better what with the show airing tonight. Their rally will make the evening news. It will boost my ratings."

"How did you find her?"

"Oh, that was easy. People like to talk. It didn't take long to find someone from the Mission who was willing to give me the woman's name."

"What about the claim that the allegations aren't true?"

"What is the truth? The truth is what you make it. All I can do is present the evidence as I see it and let my audience decide. Do you want to see the clip in question?" Zanya swivels around the computer monitor so that Cam can see. She runs the clip in which the woman accuses Preacher Jay of sexual impropriety. Cam watches in disbelief.

"I don't believe it."

"Seeing is believing, isn't it? It didn't take much either to get an interview with the woman."

"What does that mean?"

"I told her I would see what I could do about getting her into a drug rehab program in exchange for the interview."

"You made promises to her?"

"No not really. I didn't make any promises. I only said that I would *see* what I could do about getting her into a rehab program. And I did my part. My assistant found a public rehab program that would accept her. I've done my good deed. And besides, she was free to say whatever she wanted in the interview. I asked open-ended questions about her relationship with Jay and let her talk. She chose what she wanted to say. You can see the result."

"But you must have known that she would bend the facts if she thought it would help get her into a rehab program. She must have been desperate."

"The fact is she was free to say whatever she wanted. I didn't force her."

"Have you talked to any members of the congregation about this?"

"No, and I don't intend to. The story goes as is. Including her interview in tonight's show is in everyone's interest. Honest to God, I don't know why you're sticking up for this preacher! Why you continue to support him is beyond me."

"I just want to make sure he gets a fair hearing, nothing more."

"He will get a fair hearing. We'll let the public decide. Now I have to get on with other things. Reverend Mortul is interviewing me in an hour for his show. Do you know the Reverend Mortul? Thanks for dropping by. I'm very busy," adds Zanya not waiting for Cam to respond to her question. He stands up to leave. "Cameron," adds Zanya as he is leaving, "I don't think you need to come back here again. I've been patient. Now you need to move on."

"I'll take this to Ed."

"You're welcome to take it to Ed or anyone else you like. I have no objections. You needn't threaten me. I think you'll find that Ed will back me on this. He's given me carte blanche to develop the show the way I see best without interference beyond the usual mission goals and legal gibberish. I've broken no laws. And if you're thinking of going to the Legal department, I'll save you the trouble. They've already given me their blessing on this interview."

"Does Legal know about the rehab program?"

"Yes. Goodbye Cameron. Will you shut the door on your way out? Thanks," says Zanya with an understated smile of satisfaction.

Cam waits in Ed's outer office most of the afternoon. The walls are silent. An employee has found the switch that turns off the music. Cam finally gets to see Ed late in the afternoon.

"Hi Cam," says Ed who stands looking out his office window at the plaza below. "I've had a busy day. What's on your mind?"

"The issue is Zanya's show, You Don't Say. The episode she's airing tonight is about one of the local preachers, Preacher Jay. The show is very damning. I doubt very much that the claims are true. They're a distortion. I'm asking that you delay the airing of the show until the facts are verified."

"You're asking a lot. You know I won't interfere provided the show hasn't strayed from its mandate. You know, follows the script. What does Legal say?"

"Legal approved the episode. Have you seen the clip?"

"No I haven't. I don't have time to review all of the shows before they air. That's why I have the Bowdlerization department. I'm sure the Bowdlerization people would have redacted anything that was inappropriate. And Legal is there to make sure the people in front of the camera don't say anything that will get me in hot water and lead to a lawsuit. If Bowdlerization and Legal have approved it, I'm good with it. I don't want to interfere with a show's freedom to pursue its mission. You should know that. I set the mission goals. They follow them. It's really quite simple. Here look," says Ed without waiting for a response from Cam. "The news team is airing the item about today's rally now." Ed turns up the sound for the local MKM news channel.

"In local news today," begins the newscaster, "members of the House of Adam rallied in the Maple Key Media plaza to protest the airing of tonight's episode of You Don't Say, a new MKM investigative show. The members of the Mission are protesting the treatment of their leader, Preacher Jay, regarding alleged sexual impropriety with a female member of the House of Adam." While the newscaster continues, the newscast runs a clip of the rally. The clip begins with an establishing shot of those in attendance at the rally in the plaza.

"Is that you? What were you doing at the rally?" asks Ed, growing suspicious.

"Yes, I was there. I wanted to hear what they had to say. I did the initial interview with Jay."

"Okay, let's hear the rest of this," says Ed. "Quiet."

The clip continues. The camera angle hides Eleanor's face behind the megaphone. 'They're going to say that he had sex with a young woman,' says Eleanor. 'She's a member of the congregation. They're going to say that he had sex with her when he was supposed to be counseling her. That he took advantage of her when she was vulnerable. That he broke his bond of trust.' The clip cuts to the MKM reporter asking why the woman isn't at the rally. Then the news clip returns to the newscaster in the TV studio without Eleanor's answer to the question. "This episode of You Don't Say airs tonight on this local MKM channel, immediately after this newscast. Check your local TV listings for more information," adds the newscaster.

"I don't see a problem. We'll run the show." Ed wears a look of incredulity. "Why are you bothering me with this?" asks Ed, throwing up his hands. "I'm sure Zanya's checked her facts. If we need to issue an apology later, we will. It won't be the first time I've had to apologize for a screw up that's aired on an MKM show."

"But even the news item is distorted," counters Cam. "The clip doesn't show the speaker at the rally denying the claims against Preacher Jay. It only shows the speaker stating what the allegations are. And it doesn't show the explanation on why the woman making the claims isn't at the rally. The reporter asks the question why she isn't there, and then the news clip leaves it to the TV audience to answer the question. That clip is little more than gossip to inflame the audience's appetite for scandal. The clip is designed to get the audience worked up into a state of righteous anger. It manipulates the audience's sense of injustice done to a woman by someone in a position of trust. The item appeals to their sense of equality because it's about a preacher abusing his position of trust and responsibility in a society where everyone is believed to be equal. The news clip is a cheap advertisement for You Don't Say. Can't you at least delay the show until the true facts are established?"

"Look. It is what it is. We've already aired the news clip. We'll go ahead with the episode," says Ed firmly. "If there's any fall out, I'll deal with it when the time comes."

"You could ruin this man and his work," says Cam trying to remain calm.

"The fact is, we don't live in a perfect world, but I trust that Zanya and the others at MKM have done their due diligence on this story. Thanks for raising the concern, but next time...," warns Ed letting his sentence trail off. "Now I have other business. You know the way out." Ed adds brusquely.

Cam swipes his electronic badge to unlock the door to the sub-basement. MKMS hasn't yet updated security to limit access to the Broadcast Nexus. It takes him a little while to find what he is looking for in the racks of computers while avoiding the technicians that hover about monitoring computers. A monitor beside the computer shows that the opening introduction to the first installment of You Don't Say started a minute ago. Cam randomly pushes a couple of buttons. He kills the broadcast feed. The monitor goes blank. The computer shuts down. All over Bayview, across the country and in other countries people stare at blank TV screens. Cam can imagine the yowl of anguish and then anger emanating from Zanya's office.

By the time the technician has restored the feed, there is insufficient time to run You Don't Say in its assigned time slot. The technician decides to run a short cartoon in the time remaining. It's an Orky the Orca cartoon where Orky defends his adopted country and all that it stands for. Orky is originally from the ocean where borders are less discernible than the land-locked country that he now calls home. Aliens from the ocean deep are intent on convincing Orky that he can fly. Fortunately Orky's friends point out the absurdity of a flying Orca. After that, it's all over but the crying as Orky unleashes his mighty flippers and flukes to drive the aliens into the deepest part of the Mariana Trench where they came from in the first place. Later, Orky feels sorry for the aliens. He vows to one day free the aliens from their ludicrous flying idea so that they can be strong and free like Orky in his chosen country.

An MKMS officer escorts Cam from the premises while Orky is busy defeating the aliens. This is the penultimate time that Cam will set foot on MKM property.

22 End of Days

"In local news," begins the MKM TV anchor for the morning newscast, "last night the airing of the MKM program, You Don't Say, was unexpectedly and deliberately terminated by a rogue MKM employee."

Cam listens while he eats breakfast. He had expected to feel nervous and unable to eat, but he finds the opposite is true. He has even taken the time to prepare a breakfast of pancakes with strawberries, sausages and coffee, forgoing his usual workday breakfast of Liberty Puff cereal. A condemned man's last breakfast, he wonders. Funny, he doesn't feel condemned. He's mildly surprised and pleased by his sense of calm. He doesn't feel trapped. He should feel nervous. This morning will be difficult, but he's not bothered by this. Instead he has a sense of release. He should have left MKM long ago, he decides. Why he didn't let go sooner, he now finds hard to understand. What held him back? What changed? Was it Anna's influence? Was it the hunting trip? Maybe it was all of these things and things he didn't even realize.

His thoughts turn to Jordan who will feel betrayed. He will have questions for Cam that center on Jordan's role in this debacle. Jordan's superiors will want to know how and why this fiasco was allowed to happen on his watch. His inability to control the situation won't look good. Jordan will look to build a defense that distances himself from Cam. He will paint a picture of a strained relationship between himself and Cam and that Cam has changed since his interview with Preacher Jay. Then Jordan will talk about his heavy workload and that he can't be expected to keep on top of all his employees' activities. He'll imply that all the special projects make it difficult to control all aspects of his department.

No doubt Jordan will bump opportunely into Zanya in a hallway, if he hasn't already done so. There will be an exchange of information. Jordan will dig like a badger to discover her role in the matter. Then they'll decide that neither one of them is to blame. The conversation will conclude when Jordan shrugs his shoulders to indicate that there was nothing that either one of them could have done to stop Cam, who was more warped than either one of them had realized. They'll walk away from their meeting having gleaned a few facts that they'll use to fortify their defensive positions in the impending skirmish with upper management.

Security might have questions too. Their questions might be difficult. Certainly Security will not allow him to enter the MKM building unescorted.

"The employee is thought to have direct links with the church group known as the House of Adam," continues the newscaster. "The act of sabotage was allegedly carried out by Cameron Draw." They could at least get the name right, thinks Cam. "He is believed to be a radical supporter of the House of Adam."

Cam wonders who wrote the news copy. He knows most of the writers at MKM. Pejorative phrases such as 'radical supporter' are certainly intended to create a twisted view of his character. He tries to imagine himself in the role of a wild-eyed right-wing Christian fundamentalist carrying a placard and making a circuit of the MKM plaza. His placard admonishes, 'The End of Days is NOW! Sucks to be you!' With a half smile he decides the image of a radical doesn't fit. He's relieved that his association with MKM is almost over even though his future after MKM is uncertain.

"Here he is shown attending yesterday's protest rally held by members of the House of Adam." A film clip shows Cam attending the rally. A special-effects technician has added a circle around Cam's face to identify him clearly to the TV viewers. "The rally was held to protest the airing of an episode of You Don't Say."

There is another short clip from the rally in which Eleanor describes the accusations against Preacher Jay. The newscaster continues after the clip. "In the episode of You Don't Say, questions of sexual impropriety are raised about the leader of the sect, Preacher Jay. The allegations stem from Preacher Jay's relationship with a young woman." There's a short clip in which Zanya is seen interviewing the young woman.

"A spokesperson for the House of Adam denies any links with the MKM employee. Charges against the alleged perpetrator, Cameron Draw, may be pending. A spokesperson for You Don't Say stands by the interview. You can see the complete You Don't Say interview tonight at eight p.m. during prime time on this station."

The phone rings. Cam turns off the TV. A news reporter from the rival network, Vision Transmission, is calling. The reporter asks for an interview. Cam answers the reporter's questions as best he can and then hangs up the phone. He wonders if the reporter will get his name right.

Cam is relaxed as he drives to work. The drive is uneventful. He has brought along a cardboard box to clear out his desk. An MKMS officer is waiting for him when he enters the MKM building. His MKM security badge no longer works at the security gate. The officer lets Cam in and escorts him to his desk. The officer remains with him while he gathers his personal belongings. Employees who are usually at their desks at this hour are absent. After he gathers his belongings, the officer escorts him to a small windowless meeting room where he is asked to wait. The guard remains in the hallway outside the office.

Jordan arrives soon after. He closes the door behind him and sits down. Without saying a word, Jordan presses a few buttons on a computer keyboard on the table. Clickety-click. His hands betray his nervousness as he taps on the keyboard. He doesn't look at Cam. A large flat-screen monitor on one of the walls comes to life. Clickety-click taps Jordan typing a password. A computer whirrs into action. 'Password incorrect', the computer responds in big letters on the monitor. 'Please try again', the computer adds helpfully. Jordan pulls a small card from the breast pocket of his shirt. With his hand shaking, he squints at the card for a moment as he studies the password written on the card. He grasps the card with both hands to steady it. He puts the card down on the table. Clickety-click types Jordan attempting the password again. The result is the same. Jordan sighs. His irritation begins to show.

"Do you want me to try?" offers Cam.

Jordan glances behind to make sure the door is closed. "Don't tell anyone, okay?" The defeated Jordan slides the card across the table. "I shouldn't be doing this," Jordan adds sheepishly. "You're breaching security protocol. I'll have to change the password later."

Cam studies the password, then clickety-click. He slides the card back to Jordan who returns it to his pocket.

A clip taken by a security camera in the Broadcast Nexus begins to play on the monitor. The clip shows Cam at the monitor that he used to end the broadcast of You Don't Say. The short clip ends.

For a moment there is silence while Jordan lets the import of what Cam has seen sink in. "Well?" coughs Jordan as though he has nonchalantly tossed a grenade. Jordan's eyes grow larger while with the twitch of a hand he proffers the question for added emphasis and to relieve his nervousness. His voice is calm in spite of his edginess. "Anything to say?" asks Jordan waiting for the bang.

There is silence for a minute while Cam decides how to
respond. What do you tell somebody like Jordan who
doesn't appreciate the sound of one hand clapping? Could
any explanation that you provide satisfy him? It seems
unlikely. How do you tell Jordan in a way that he will
understand?

Jordan runs the clip again to relieve his jumpiness and
in case the revelation of the clip that he has lobbed at Cam
has stunned him too badly to respond.

"Well?" poses Jordan after the clip finishes for the
second time. "I can understand that you're disappointed
about not getting the job with Zanya. Is that what this is
about?" Silence hangs in the air. "I spoke to Zanya this
morning. She said you came to see her yesterday. That you
had a concern about her piece on Preacher Jay, but nothing
serious," Jordan appends, trying to maintain a calm exterior.
"This isn't the first time either is it that you've done this?
There was that werewolf movie the night you escorted
Filana. Was that a test run for pulling the plug on Zanya's
show if you didn't get the job?"

Cam realizes how little Jordan knows him even though
they have worked together for many years. Do we know so
little about one another, Cam wonders. Jordan must be
panicked that this incident will make him look bad. Possibly
Jordan's next salary raise or his job is on the line.

"How long have you been planning to sabotage Zanya's
show?"

Sabotage, there was a word that Cam didn't expect, the
language of a terrorist disconnected from reality. He didn't
feel he was a terrorist. 'And the just man rages in the wilds',
comes to Cam.

"We didn't have security cameras in the Broadcast
Nexus the first time you pulled this," Jordan reveals, hoping
that this bomb will ignite Cam into making a rash statement
that Jordan can use to his advantage. "They were installed
last week. You didn't know about the cameras did you? Did

you think you could get away with it again?" jabs Jordan who is doing his best to present a calm exterior in the face of Cam's silence. "I'm giving you a chance to explain. Why did you do it?" demands Jordan. For a moment a light seems to flicker in Jordan's eyes as though there's something almost unfamiliar buried deep in him that really does want to know. "You had a good career here. In another fifteen years or so you could have retired with a good retirement package," he adds. His eyes narrow to slits as he attempts to assess the damage he has inflicted with this last incendiary. "You would have been set for the rest of your life," says Jordan extinguishing any pretext of light. "I've got another five years and I'm out. Did you not get along with Zanya?" he adds as an afterthought.

"Zanya's piece about Preacher Jay lacked balance," begins Cam. He is remarkably cool as he tries to explain. His coolness surprises even himself. "She was out to score points for herself and maybe ruin Jay's work at the Mission. He deserved a fair hearing and she wasn't going to give it to him. I tried to stop her. I went to Zanya, but she wouldn't budge. I even went to Ed." Jordan's head jerks back, betraying his shock at this news. His edginess grows. "In the end I decided that there was only one thing I could do and that was to stop the broadcast feed. I ran out of options. I knew it would be the end of my career here."

"You had a choice. Why didn't you ignore Zanya's sensationalism if that's what you thought it was? So she has a flair for infotainment! So what?" questions Jordan thumping his hand on the table to show his growing frustration. "Who is this Preacher Jay anyway? What's he to you? You didn't really think you could stop the broadcast did you?" Jordan lobs another grenade, hoping to provoke Cam. "The interview airs tonight."

Cam makes no response. There is nothing more that he can say that would help Jordan understand. Jordan grows impatient. He has heard enough.

The office door opens as if on cue. An officer from Employee Opportunities, EO, enters the room. The officer introduces himself. Jordan pulls a sheet of paper from his shirt pocket. Slowly and deliberately Jordan unfolds the paper. He places the paper on the table. He reads the words on the paper without looking at Cam. The paper is a job aid created by EO that states exactly what to say to an employee when terminating with cause. Jordan has only to insert Cam's name in the appropriate place as he reads from the job aid. His voice is tense as he reads the words. Jordan announces in unequivocal terms in the presence of a witness, the EO officer, that Cam's employment is terminated at MKM, and that there is no possibility of reinstatement of employment at any time in the future. It takes Jordan about twenty seconds to read the statement. After Jordan finishes, he folds the paper, puts it in his shirt pocket. As directed by the job aid, he leaves the office without speaking or looking at Cam. There must be no opportunity for fruitless debate according to the job aid. Jordan closes the door behind him.

The rest is a ritual. The EO officer runs through the checklist of things that must be said and done when terminating an employee.

The security officer escorts Cam from the building after the formalities. He finds himself in the MKM plaza with his cardboard box of belongings. There are the usual rallies and protests that are either being organized, or are already in progress. He looks up towards Ed's office. He wonders if Ed is watching. Cam decides that it doesn't matter. He walks with a surprisingly light step across the plaza to his car.

23 Tyger Tyger

Cam stands in the parking lot of the Big Tiger. When not working on the new restaurant, he has labored to apply a primer coat of all-weather white paint to the outer shell of the Big Tiger. He has managed to obliterate the harlequin that the tiger had become. The patch work layers of paint were a legacy of the many owners who sanitized the tiger's appearance to suit the public. There was a period in the late 1960s when the tiger was briefly a vivid blue, purple and green to satisfy the public's desire for all things psychedelic. In his mind's eye he can see the completed work on the blank canvas that stands before him. Recently he has painted the tiger's head with a palette of rich tiger browns, whites, blacks, and oranges. He draws his inspiration from William Blake's *The Tyger*.

Today Cam has applied shades of saffron, burnt saffron, chickadee white and Gothic black to seize the fire that must burn in the tiger's eyes. He gazes with a critical eye. He assesses his work, looking for the awful mystery in the tiger's eyes. Cam is pleased with his progress. He smiles. The last of the day's light fades on this late-spring evening as he admires his work. Two and a half years have passed since his departure from MKM.

A car pulls into the far end of the parking lot. Cam has closed the park for renovations. The car's lights shine on him, making it hard to see the occupant. He is about to wave off the car when he recognizes it. He grins exuberantly and makes a big wave with his arm. The car pulls up beside him.

"I'm too late," Anna says disappointedly as she gets out her car. "I was hoping to see the tiger before dark."

"Just a minute, I can fix that." Cam walks over to a small utility shed. After a little fumbling, he throws a switch. Immediately the tiger leaps to life when spotlights around it burst into light. "So what do you think?" he asks returning to Anna's side.

"I love it! You've made a great start. The eyes are wonderful. There's something about the eyes as if they're looking directly into you. The tiger is sizing you up. There's something threatening in the eyes, menacing and defiant too. You've done a fantastic job. Oh, you fixed the tail too! That looks much better. A tiger with a bobbed tail is definitely lame. I can't wait to see it finished! This is exciting! Buying this place after it went bankrupt was a fantastic idea."

"I was hoping you'd notice the eyes. Do you think others will see? I spent a lot of time on them. They need more work to get them right, but they're almost there. I hired a couple of art students from the university. They helped paint the head. And they've had several great suggestions about the eyes. You should meet them. You'd like them." responds Cam smiling. "The tail wasn't easy. My welding skills aren't what they should be. I hope it holds." He casts a weather eye at the trees as gusts of wind blowing off the lake begin to pick up. The wind buffets the trees more violently with each gust. Cam gestures at the trees. "I've thinned the trees a little around the tiger to make it little more visible, but still provide cover. The trees give it a sense of menace as if the tiger is stalking you. You know it's there, but still partially hidden, wild and dangerous, powerful and alive. You're attracted to it and you're scared by it at the same time. In spite of the risk, you're pulled in. The spotlights will need adjusting, but that can be done later when the tiger is finished."

"Hey Cam," calls a voice from the direction of what once was the souvenir shop, and soon-to-be restaurant.

"Hey George, how's it going?" yells Cam.

"I'm finished for the day. I'll be back tomorrow."

"Okay, see you Saturday."

"Hi George," says Anna waving at him.

"Hi Anna, I'll see you tomorrow. I have to go now. I need sleep."

"Shut the gate on your way out, will you?" Cam shouts.

"Okay." George starts his car and is gone.

"How's George doing?"

"He's doing very well. Did you know he used to be the pizza kid here in the summer? He has a degree in food management services now. I gave him a budget. We talked about the vision for the restaurant, nothing tawdry and it has to be in keeping with the tiger. He came up with a lot of brilliant ideas for the restaurant. I had some plans drawn up. I want people to come, enjoy the food and see the tiger. Maybe a visitor will see the tiger for what it is even though it isn't a work of art. Maybe someone will see it for what it's meant to be. What do you think?"

"Perhaps they'll see," Anna ponders. "You can never tell with art. Art is a living thing. You put it out there and hope others will see what you see. You never know who it might surprise. But for most people a tiger is a tiger is a tiger. And for the record, I think your tiger is a work of art, or will be when you're finished."

A strong gust of wind shakes the trees. The wind grows stronger. A storm front is moving in. Cam watches the tail nervously hoping it will hold. A particularly strong gust hits. The tiger's tail wavers slightly, swaying with the gust.

"Is the tail supposed to move like that?"

"Nope, that's not good," he tenses his body, trying to hold the tail steady. Another gust hits. It is more than the tail can endure. A few of the welds break. With the tail now affixed half on and half off, the tail slowly falls limp, twisting slightly as the tip of the tail descends to rest on the ground. "Nuts," says Cam, his body relaxing after his failed effort to save the tail. "Well, the arse is out of her," he adds with a grin.

"Yep, the arse is out of her," Anna offers, laughing at Cam's choice of words. "Is that a Duncism?"

"Yeah, that's a Dunc phrase alright."

"A work in progress," Anna tenders. "You'll get the tiger right. I can help you fix the tail tomorrow if you like." Anna shivers. "I'm getting cold. Can we go inside?"

Cam turns off the lights. Wrapped in the silence of the darkness they admire the stars while they walk to Cam's temporary residence, a trailer that he has set up in the parking lot.

"Dunc was here the other day," says Cam seated at the table as they eat dinner. "He's going to do the plumbing and help with the coordination of the construction work for the restaurant. Dunc knows a lot about construction. He says he can help us with the technical aspects of the renovation."

"How's Dunc doing?"

"He's good. His dragon tattoo is finished. He showed it to me. I took a picture so he can see it. I'll show you later."

"How does his dragon look?"

"Fine if you're into that kind of thing. Dunc's big on his dragon. He said it *took* well, but said his back felt like grillades."

"What are grillades?"

"Strips of salt pork fried until crisp, according to Dunc. He spent most of his time trying not to scratch while he was here. He said his back would be fine in about a week. He started talking about the annual deer hunting trip."

"Are you going?"

"No, I don't think so. He's managed to talk one of his church buddies into going."

"There was an interview with Preacher Jay the other night on the Vision Transmission channel," Anna starts. "He had to close the House of Adam after the MKM interview. Too many of the Mission's members wandered away."

"I don't think the House of Adam ever had much money," offers Cam. "The loss of membership must have been more than the Mission could take."

"They showed a clip of the front of the Mission," continues Anna. "The mannequins are still there. They look a little worse for wear and even more faded if that's possible. The building is still vacant. VT interviewed Jay at the garage where he still works as a mechanic. The VT piece claims that MKM deliberately undermined the Mission for MKM's own ends. And get this! Zanya is no longer the host of You Don't Say! MKM quietly replaced her. There were hints of questionable tactics to boost the show's ratings. They replaced her with that guy. You know the one. He's been around for ages. Oh, what's his name?" asks Anna, searching for a name. "Adin Huffman, he's the one."

"I'm not surprised she's gone."

Lightning jolts the sky, lighting up the parking lot. Thunder booms, rattling the trailer windows.

"That was close."

"You enjoy thunderstorms. Don't you?"

Cam smiles happily. "Yes, it cleans things out." He is rewarded with another flash of lightning and a crack of thunder.

A small portable radio perched on a window ledge for better reception crackles with static from the passing thunderstorm. Radio reception is poor at the best of times. Between the crackle of the static, Bruce Cockburn sings quietly in the background about the burden of the angel/beast. Cam reaches for the radio and turns it off as the song concludes. The wind pushes hard against the trailer. They listen to the storm until it moves off.

"I went into Bayview a couple of weeks ago," Cam begins again. "I needed primer paint for the tiger. I decided to see Jay while I was there. I found him hunched over a car engine. I wasn't sure what kind of reception I would get."

"When did you last see him?"

"At the pre-interview I did for Zanya. I wasn't sure that he would remember me, but he did. I offered to buy him a coffee. He was a little reluctant at first. Eventually he decided in favor. We talked. He understood what I did to stop the broadcast. He said it wasn't necessary. He said he missed the House of Adam. Then he said he forgave the people at MKM who had done this. He said they didn't know any better. I don't know if he was including me with the MKM people that he was forgiving. I felt better after talking to him. He had to get back to work. He was on his coffee break. We didn't talk very long."

"Sounds like you left on good terms."

"I think so. I almost forgot. The sale of the house was finalized this week."

"After all these years you did it! Well done. How does it feel giving up the house? You spent a lot of years in that house."

"I gave most of the contents of the house to my brothers; things they wanted. I got rid of the rest. I kept the picture that hung in the living room and a few other things. I put them in storage. We divided up the old family photographs. I don't miss the place. It was time for me to move on. I should have done it years ago. There are lots of memories, some of them good."

"You're living in exile out here," Anna observes, "but you don't see it that way, do you? You're happy here aren't you?"

"I can afford to live the way I want, at least for a little while. This place is coming along. And I like being out here. I love the quiet at night. And I can see the stars. I have time to think without too many distractions. I started writing a new novel this week. Between the novel, fixing up this place, and the occasional freelance writing contract that I pick up,

I'm busier than I've ever been. And I'm enjoying my new life. The only thing I miss is you," says Cam looking at Anna and squeezing her hand."

"I miss you too."

"Oh, and VT wants to send a camera crew out here to profile the remaking of the Big Tiger. That'll be fun."

"Wow, great, free publicity!" Anna smiles enthusiastically. "That'll help get this place going again. I thought of something else that will interest you. Do you remember the night that Ed took a strip out of Jordan because Jordan talked to Ed about an MKM social networking website? There was an MKM press release this week. They announced the launch of MKM's new social networking website. They've named it TatterTalk. Apparently the website has been in the works for a couple of years." Anna shakes her head in disbelief. "I'm glad you're out of MKM politics, but I worry you'll turn into a recluse out here."

"This is the right place for me now. I'm happy here. Would you like to hear the first chapter of my novel? It's a draft."

"Yes," answers Anna, pleased that he is willing to share his draft with her.

He rummages through the papers on a small writing desk where he has set up his computer. After searching, he finds a printed copy of the first chapter. He begins reading aloud. "The booming grows louder like exploding artillery shells fired in volleys from a distant battery of howitzers: boom, boom, boom. The sound of the bursting shells closes in on Adam, who remains indifferent to the booming." Cam reads the entire chapter. He returns the copy to the writing desk. In the silence there are only the unpredictable gusts of wind slamming against the trailer. Another storm is moving in.

"What do you think?"

"Your first chapter is a very good beginning. I can't wait to hear more."

Later that night as they lie in bed in the dark, "tell me a story," Anna requests.

A new thunderstorm has moved in with flashes of lighting and the accompanying peals of thunder. There is silence for a moment from the other side of the bed. A bright flash of lightning tears the dark, followed immediately by an explosion of thunder that shakes the trailer.

"Did I ever tell you about string theory?"

"You mean string theory as in physics?"

"Not that kind of string theory. I mean real string theory, kid string theory."

"What is kid sting theory?"

"Do you remember when you were a kid and you started losing your baby teeth? Here, let me see," says Cam in his Dad voice that Anna recognizes immediately. "Open your mouth. Let me see you wiggle it." Then Cam continues in his normal voice while he explains. "Whoever had a loose tooth would wiggle his tooth back and forth with his tongue while standing in front of Dad to show him how loose the tooth really was. Dad would inspect your efforts. He was the arbiter of whether a tooth was ready to come out or not. There was an incentive to convince him because each tooth garnered twenty-five cents from the tooth fairy. For a kid, this was big money. Then he would say, okay, it's ready," says Cam switching to his Dad voice. "Now you could move onto the next stage in the process, which was extracting the tooth. This is where string theory comes into the picture."

"I was wondering when you'd get around to explaining string theory."

"Mom kept this ball of string in a kitchen drawer. The ball was made up of bits of string that she had collected and wound into a ball in case she needed a piece to tie up a parcel or something."

"Now I see where you're going. Olivia was a saver I take it?"

"Yes. You would get this ball of string and find a piece that you thought was the right length. The string was usually a little dirty depending on its origin, but you didn't care as long as it would do the job. The string couldn't be too short or too long because then it wouldn't work right. Sometimes you had to tie a couple of pieces of string together with a good, strong, dependable granny knot in order to get the right length. The next step was to tie the string to the wiggly tooth. This took practice. First you had to tie a slip knot on one end of the string. Of course there was lots of encouragement from Dad. Here, don't you know nothing?" says Cam assuming his authoritative Dad voice regarding all things related to slip knots. "Here, let me show you. Here's how you tie a slip knot. Then you had to put the slip knot on the tooth and carefully pull the knot taught around the tooth," says Cam slipping back into his regular voice. "Usually there were several failed attempts, but eventually you would secure the string to the tooth. From time to time you needed help from an older sibling, who would reach his dirty paw into your mouth to tie the string to the tooth. So there you were with this dirty piece of string dangling from your mouth and the other end dragging on the floor."

"Where was Olivia in all this?"

"Usually she was sitting on the couch, watching that no one got hurt. Tooth extraction occurred at night. She would have us in our pajamas ready for bed."

"That was smart of her to stay out of it."

"Now you needed a door. You'd look for the heaviest door in the house so that it had lots of inertia when you swung it. Usually you'd give the door a couple of swings to test that it had the right momentum when the time came for you to swing it. It took a critical eye and steady hand to assess the door. You had to take into account the resistance created by the air when you swung the door. There was a little physics involved. Next you tied the loose end of the string to the doorknob. You had to stand still at precisely the right distance from the door so that the string would pull taught and yank out the tooth before the door shut and lost its momentum. When you were ready, you'd give the door a push. If you were trusting, you could ask a sibling to push the door shut, but this was rare. You didn't want to put your life in the hands of a sibling."

"And your tooth came out?"

"Well, yes, but more often no because you tended to stand too close. The door would close shut before the string was taught. It took nerves of steel to stand at exactly the right distance and swing the door."

"What happened next after the first failed attempt?"

"You had two choices. You could adjust your distance relative to the door and try again, or you could, if dissatisfied with the door, look for another door that you thought more suitable even though all the doors in the house were the same."

"What did you do?"

"I'd adjust my distance after a first attempt and try again. We were persistent. Money was involved. Mom expected us to save the money. Of course we would spend it on candy at the first opportunity. At times you'd get the distance right, only to have the slip knot fail for reasons unknown and the string come off the tooth as the string pulled taught. So then you'd have to retie the string to the tooth and try again. If the door failed a second time because you had the wrong distance, you'd look for another door. Pulling a tooth was an engineering feat."

"Were you successful?"

"Eventually you'd step on the sting that was dragging on the floor and pull out the tooth."

"So you were successful?" Anna asks after she stops laughing.

"Yes eventually. Although you might not notice right away that the tooth was gone. You'd be so busy concentrating on removing the tooth that you didn't notice. Usually somebody else would notice first and point out that the string wasn't dangling anymore from your mouth. Then you'd have to launch into a search to find the tooth that was somewhere on the floor."

"Did you find it?"

"Yes after a little searching. The string lying on the floor was a big clue as to where to look."

"So that's kid string theory?"

"Yes, it's a special and largely unexplored realm of true physics."

Outside the wind howls. The trailer shakes. Lightning leaps across the black sky. The thunder roars. The tiger burns bright in the forests of the night.

Epilogue

Cam and Anna now reside in Gogama, which sits near the divide between two great watersheds. Cam's first novel proved successful beyond his wildest dreams. Anna continues to teach. The Big Tiger and the restaurant are doing well. Cam sold the attraction to George, who has plans for expansion. Cam is currently working on his next novel.

Oh Yeah, One More Thing

If you're looking for the Pass the String video clip on the Internet, the clip doesn't exist. I made that up. Use your imagination. Make your own video clip and post it to a web page if you choose. Everything else in the book is true, well sort of anyway.